WHEN IT'S
REAL

erin watt
WHEN IT'S
REAL

HARLEQUIN®TEEN

Recycling programs
for this product may
not exist in your area.

ISBN-13: 978-1-335-14416-4

When It's Real

Printed in U.S.A.

To Margo.

We loved you before you bought this book, and we love you even more after you helped us polish this manuscript into the gem it is. Thank you for being our editor, our cheerleader, our friend.

1

HIM

"Please tell me every girl in there is of legal age."

"Every girl in there is of legal age," I dutifully repeat to my manager, Jim Tolson.

Truth is, I have no clue if everyone's legal. When I came home last night from the studio, the party was already raging. I didn't take the time to card anyone before grabbing a beer and chatting up some eager girls who proclaimed that they were so in love with my music that they sang it in their sleep. It sounded vaguely like an invitation, but I wasn't interested. My buddy Luke took them off my hands and then I wandered around trying to figure out if I knew even a quarter of the people in my house.

I ended up counting seven, tops, that I actually recognized.

Jim presses his already thin lips together before taking a seat in the lounger across from me. There's a girl passed out on it, so he's forced to perch on the end. Jim once told me that the biggest hazard of working with a young rock star is the age of his groupies. Sitting this close to a bikini-clad teenager makes him visibly edgy.

"Keep that line in mind in case TMI asks you about it on the street today," Jim warns.

"Noted." Also noted? Avoid any celeb hot spots today. I have zero desire to be papped.

"How was the studio last night?"

I roll my eyes. As if Jim didn't have the studio tech on the phone immediately after I left, replaying the track. "You know exactly how it was. Crappy. Worse than crappy. I think a barking Chihuahua could lay down better vocals than me right now."

I lean back and stroke my throat. Nothing's wrong with my vocal cords. Jim and I got that checked out with a doctor a few months ago. But the notes that were coming out yesterday lacked…something. All my music seems flat these days.

I haven't recorded anything decent since my last album. I can't pinpoint the problem. It could be the lyrics or the rhythm or the melody. It's everything and nothing, and no amount of tweaking has helped me.

I run my fingers over the six strings of my Gibson, knowing my frustration must show on my face.

"Come on, let's walk a little." Jim dips his head toward the girl. She looks passed out, but she could be faking it.

With a sigh, I set the guitar on the cushion and rise to my feet.

"Didn't know you liked walks on the beach, Jim. Should we start quoting poetry to each other before you propose?" I joke. But he's probably right about putting some distance between us and the groupie. We don't need some yappy fan talking about my music block to the tabloids. I give them enough to talk about already.

"Did you see the latest social media numbers?" He holds his phone up.

"Is that an actual question?"

We stop at the railing on my wraparound deck. I wish we could walk down to the beach, but it's public, and the last time I tried setting foot on the sand in the back of my house, I came away with my swim trunks torn off and a bloody nose. That was three years ago. The tabloids turned it into a story about me getting into a fight with my ex and terrorizing young children.

"You're losing followers at a rate of a thousand a week."

"Sounds dire." Sounds awesome, actually. Maybe I'll finally be able take advantage of my beachfront property.

His perfectly unlined face, courtesy of some of the best Swiss knives money can buy, is marred by irritation. "This is serious, Oakley."

"So what? Who cares if I lose followers?"

"Do you want to be taken seriously as an artist?"

This lecture again? I've heard it from Jim a million frickin' times since he signed me when I was fourteen. "You know I do."

"Then you have to shape up," he huffs.

"Why?" What does *shaping up* have to do with making great music? If anything, maybe I need to be wilder, really stretch the limits of everything in life.

But...haven't I done that already? I feel like I've drunk, smoked, ingested and experienced nearly everything the world has to offer in the past five years. Am I already the washed-up pop star before I hit my twenties?

A tinge of fear scrapes down my spine at the thought.

"Because your label is on the verge of dropping you," Jim warns.

I practically clap like a child at this news. We've been at odds for months. "So let them."

"How do you think you're going to have your next album made? The studio's already rejected your last two attempts.

You want to experiment with your sound? Use poetry as lyrics? Write about things other than heartache and pretty girls who don't love you back?"

I stare sullenly at the water.

He grabs my arm. "Pay attention, Oak."

I give him a *what the hell are you doing* look, and he lets go of my arm. We both know I don't like being touched.

"They aren't going to let you cut the record you want if you keep alienating your audience."

"Exactly," I say smugly. "So why do I care if the label drops me?"

"Because labels exist to make money, and they won't produce your next album unless it's one they can actually market. If you want to win another Grammy, if you want to be taken seriously by your peers, then your only chance is to rehabilitate your image. You haven't had a record out since you were seventeen. That was two years ago. It's like a decade in the music business."

"Adele released at nineteen and twenty-five."

"You aren't fuckin' Adele."

"I'm bigger," I say, and it's not a boast. We both know it's true.

Since I released my first album at fourteen, I've had unreal success. Every album has gone double platinum, with my self-titled *Ford* reaching the rare Diamond. That year I did thirty international tour stops, all stadium tours, all sellouts. There are fewer than ten artists in the world who do stadium tours. Everyone else is relegated to arenas, auditoriums, halls and clubs.

"*Were* bigger," Jim says bluntly. "In fact, you're on the verge of being a has-been at nineteen."

I tense up as he voices my earlier fear.

"Congratulations, kid. Twenty years from now, you'll be

sitting in a chair on *Hollywood Squares* and some kid will ask their mother, 'who's Oakley Ford?' and the mom will say—"

"I get it," I say tightly.

"No. You don't get it. Your existence will have been so fleeting that even that parent will turn to her kid and say, 'I have no idea who that is.'" Jim's tone turns pleading. "Look, Oak, I want you to be successful with the music you want to make, but you have to work with me. The industry is run by a bunch of old white men who are high on coke and power. They love knocking you artists around. They get off on it. Don't give them any more reason to decide that you're the fall guy. You're better than that. I believe in you, but you gotta start believing in yourself, too."

"I do believe in myself."

Does it sound as fake to Jim's ears as it does to mine?

"Then act like it."

Translation? Grow up.

I reach over and take the phone from his hand. The social media number beside my name is still in the eight digits. Millions of people follow me and eat up all the ridiculous things my PR team posts daily. My shoes. My hands. Man, the hands post got over a million likes and launched an equal number of fictional stories. Those girls have very vivid imaginations. Vivid, *dirty* imaginations.

"So what's your suggestion?" I mutter.

Jim sighs with relief. "I have a plan. I want you to date someone."

"No way. We already tried the girlfriend thing."

During the launch of *Ford*, management hooked me up with April Showers. Yup, that's her real name—I saw it on her driver's license. April was an up-and-coming reality television star and we all thought she'd know the score. A fake relationship to keep both our names on magazine covers and headlining every gossip site on the web. Yes, there'd be hate from certain corners, but the nonstop media attention and speculation would drive our visibility through the roof. Our names would be on everyone's lips from here to China and back again.

The press strategy worked like a charm. We couldn't sneeze without someone taking our picture. We dominated celebrity gossip for six months, and the *Ford* tour was a smashing success. April sat in the front row of more fashion shows than I knew actually existed and went on to sign a huge two-year modeling contract with a major agency.

Everything was great until the end of the tour. What everyone, including me, had failed to recognize was that if they threw two teenagers together and told them to act like they were in love, stuff was going to happen. Stuff did happen. The only problem? April thought stuff would continue to happen after the tour was over. When I told her it wouldn't, she wasn't happy—and she had a big enough platform to tell the world *exactly* how unhappy she was.

"This won't be another April thing," Jim assures me. "We want to appeal to all the girls out there who dream of walking down the red carpet but think it's out of reach. We don't want a model or a star. We want your fans to think you're attainable."

Against my better judgment, I ask, "And how do we do that?"

"We conjure up a normal. She starts posting to you on your social media accounts. Flirting with you online. People see you interact. Then you invite her to a concert. You meet, fall in love and *boom*. Serious heartthrob status again."

"My fans hated April," I remind him.

"Some did, but millions loved her. Millions more will love

you if you fall for an ordinary girl, because each and every one of those girls is going to think that she's their stand-in."

I clench my teeth. "No."

If Jim was trying to think up a way to torture me, this is absolutely it, because I hate social media. I grew up having my baby steps photographed and sold to the highest bidder. For charity, my mom later claimed. The public gets a ton of me. I want to keep some parts of my life private, which is why I pay a couple of people a fortune so I don't have to touch that stuff.

"If you do this…" Jim pauses enticingly. "King will produce your album."

My head swivels around so fast that Jim jumps back in surprise. "You serious?"

Donovan King is the best producer in the country. He's worked on everything from rap to country to rock albums, turning artists into legends. I once read an interview where he said he'd never work with a pop star and their soulless commercial music, no matter how much anyone paid him. Working with King is a dream of mine, but he's turned down every overture I've ever made.

If he wasn't interested in producing *Ford*, then why this latest album? Why now?

Jim grins. Well, as much as his plastic face allows him to smile. "Yes. He said if you were serious, then he'd be interested, but he needs a show of faith."

"And a girlfriend is that show of faith?" I ask incredulously.

"Not a girlfriend. It's what dating a nonfamous, ordinary girl signifies. That you're down-to-earth, making music for the sake of music, not for the sake of money and fame."

"I *am* down-to-earth," I protest.

Jim responds with a snort. He jerks his thumb at the French

doors behind us. "Tell me something—what's the name of that girl who's passed out in there?"

I try not to cringe. "I...don't know," I mumble.

"That's what I thought." He frowns now. "Do you want to know what Nicky Novak was photographed doing last night?"

My head is starting to spin. "What the hell does Novak have to do with anything?" Nicky Novak is a sixteen-year-old pop star I've never even met. His boy band just released their debut album, and apparently it's topping the charts. The group is giving 1D a run for their money.

"Ask me what Novak was doing," Jim prompts.

"Fine. Whatever. What was Novak doing?"

"Bowling." My manager crosses his arms over his chest. "He got papped on a bowling date with his girlfriend—some girl he's been dating since middle school."

"Well, good for him." I give another eye roll. "You want me to go bowling, is that it? You think *that* will convince King to work with me? Seeing me roll some gutter balls?" It's hard to keep the sarcasm out of my voice.

"I just told you what I want," Jim grumbles. "If you want King to produce your album, you need to show him you're serious, that you're ready to stop partying with girls whose names you don't know and settle down with someone who will ground you."

"I can tell him that."

"He needs proof."

My gaze shifts back to the ocean, and I stand there for a moment, watching the surf crash against the beach. This album I've been working on these past two years—no, the one I'm *trying* to work on and failing—suddenly feels as if it's actually within my reach. A producer like King could help me move past this creative block and make the kind of music I've always wanted.

And all I have to do in return is date a normal? I guess I can do that. I mean, every artist has to make sacrifices for his art at one point in his life.

Right?

2

HER

"No."

"You haven't even heard what I want," my sister objects.

"I don't need to. You have that look in your eye." I pull the bacon out of the microwave and dump four slices on each plate.

"What look?" Paisley checks her reflection on the back of the spoon I used to stir the eggs.

"The one that says I'm not going to like what you have to say." I pause as I dish up the rest of the twins' breakfast. "Or that I'm too young to understand."

"Ha. Everyone knows you're more together than most adults. I wish you were more impulsive, actually. It'd make this easier."

"Breakfast is ready!" I shout.

The clatter of shoes on the staircase makes Paisley sigh. Our little brothers are incredibly loud, eat an incredible amount of food and are getting incredibly expensive. All I can say is, thank goodness for Paisley's new job. We're barely keeping our heads above water, even though Paisley has performed miracles with what little insurance money our parents left us. I'm adding to the family account with my waitressing job at Sharkey's, but we don't have much extra left over. Spencer and Shane insist that we don't need to worry about college tuition for them because they plan on full-ride athletic scholarships. But unless it's for competitive eating, I'm not going to count on it.

As the twins practically fall face-first into their breakfast, Paisley pours their milk and shoves a paper towel next to their plates. Hopefully they'll use it instead of the kitchen towel. Again, I'm not holding my breath.

I drink my coffee-infused milk, watching my twelve-year-old brothers inhale the first of what will likely be their six meals of the day. As they grumble about the shortness of Christmas break, I think about how glorious it is that I haven't had one class this year, unlike them.

"Vaughn," Paisley says urgently. "I still need to talk to you."

"I already told you no."

"I'm serious."

"Oh, fine. Talk."

"Outside." She jerks her head toward the back door.

"We're not listening," says Spencer.

Shane nods in agreement because that's their shtick. Spencer talks and Shane backs up everything his brother says, even if he disagrees.

"Outside." Paisley's head jerk looks painful this time, so I take pity on her.

"Lead the way."

The screen door slams shut behind us. I take another sip of my rapidly cooling drink as I watch Paisley search for words, which is worrisome because Paisley is never at a loss for words.

"Okay, so I want you to hear me out. Don't say anything until the very end."

"Did you drink one too many Red Bulls this morning?" I ask. We both know Paisley kind of has a caffeine addiction.

"Vaughn!"

"Okay. Okay." I zip my lips shut. "Not another word."

She rolls her eyes. "You do the lip-zipping after the last word, not before."

"Details, shmetails. Now talk. I promise not to interrupt."

She takes a deep breath. "Okay, so you know how they finally gave me my own cubicle, so I don't have to share with that other assistant anymore?"

I nod. "They" are her bosses at Diamond Talent Management. Paisley's official job title is Brand Coverage Assistant, but technically she's a glorified gofer—she goes on coffee runs, makes a zillion photocopies and spends an insane amount of time scheduling meetings. I swear, the people she works for hold more meetings than the UN.

"Well, my cube has this little bulletin board on the wall. I'm allowed to put up pictures, so yesterday I brought in a few photos. You know, like the one of Mom and Dad that we love, where they're kissing on the boardwalk? And one of the twins at baseball camp. And then I put up the one I took of you at the beach bonfire we had for your birthday last month."

I have to fight the urge not to make a waving motion with my hand to tell her to speed up. Paisley takes *forever* to get to the point.

"Anyway, so get this! Jim Tolson is walking by my cube—"

"Who's Jim Tolson?" I ask, breaking my vow of silence.

"He's my boss's brother. He manages some of the biggest musicians in the world." Paisley is so excited her cheeks are flushed. "So he's walking by, and he sees the picture of you on my bulletin board and asks if he could borrow it for a minute—"

"Ew! I do *not* like where this story is going."

She shoots me a dirty look. "I'm not done. You promised to be quiet until I was done."

I swallow a sigh. "Sorry."

"So I'm, like, sure, go ahead, but just make sure to bring it back because that's my favorite picture of my little sister. So he takes the photo and disappears into his brother's office for a while. He's got all these assistants in there and they're all talking about your picture—"

Okay, now I *really* don't like where this is heading.

"Something major is going down at the agency," Paisley adds. "I have no idea what, because I'm a lowly assistant, but Mr. Tolson has been in and out, arguing with his brother all week, and they keep having these secret meetings in the conference room."

I swear, if she doesn't get to the point soon, I'm going to lose my mind.

"So at the end of the day, my boss—Leo—calls me into Jim's office and they start asking me all these questions about you." She must see my worried look, because she's quick to reassure me. "Nothing too personal. Jim wanted to know how old you are, what your interests are, if you've ever been in trouble with the law—"

"Um, *what*?"

Paisley huffs in annoyance. "He just wants to make sure you're not a criminal."

Forget this vow of silence. I'm too confused to stick to it. "Why does this agent—"

"Manager," she corrects.

"Manager..." I roll my eyes. "Why does this manager care so much about me? And you said he manages musicians—is he trying to sign me as a client or something? You told him I can't carry a tune, right?"

"Oh, totally. That was one of his questions, if you had any

'musical aspirations.'" She air-quotes that. "He was pretty happy when I told him you're (a) not musical and (b) interested in becoming a teacher."

"Is it a matchmaking thing then? Because, gross. How old is this dude?" I ask skeptically.

She waves a hand. "In his thirties, I think. And that's not it."

"Is there an *it*? Because I'm beginning to wonder."

Paisley pauses for a beat. Then she blurts out her next words in one breath. "They want you to pretend to be Oakley Ford's girlfriend this year."

I spray the concrete steps with lukewarm coffee mixed with spit. "What?"

"I promise you it isn't as bad as it sounds."

She runs a hand through her ordinarily perfectly styled black bob, and I notice for the first time that her hair is sticking up on the sides. Paisley's usually so polished, from the top of her shiny head to the tips of the flats that she buffs every night.

"Mr. Tolson thinks you're perfect for the job," she tells me. "He said you're pretty but not in an over-the-top way. More like a natural, girl-next-door type. I described you as down-to-earth, and he thinks that will complement Oakley, because Oakley can be really intense sometimes—"

"Okay, let's back up," I cut in. "Are you talking about Oakley Ford, pop icon? Oakley Ford, the guy with so many girls' names tattooed on his body he's like a phone directory of former Victoria's Secret models? Oakley Ford, who tried to depants a monk in Angkor Wat and nearly caused an international incident? That Oakley Ford?"

"Yeah, him." She scrunches up her nose. "And he's only got one tattoo of a woman's name and it's his mom's."

I raise an eyebrow. "Did he tell you that or did you make a personal inspection?"

Oakley's nineteen and Paisley's twenty-three, so I guess

it *could* happen, but that's kinda disgusting. Not because he's younger, but because Paisley's too awesome to be some celebrejerk's castoff.

"Ew, Vaughn."

"Look, if you're serious, the answer is still no. In fact, there are so many reasons for me to say no that I don't know if we have time for me to list them all. But here's one—I don't even like Oakley Ford."

"You played his album on repeat for, like, three months."

"When I was *fifteen*!" Oakley Ford was a phase. Like BFF necklaces and Hannah Montana. Plus, his antics got really unappealing. After the tenth or so picture of him making out with some random girl at a club, he got kind of slimy in my eyes.

Paisley runs her hand through her hair again. "I know this is your year off. And I want you to have that, I swear. But this thing isn't going to take up very much of your time. An hour or two maybe every other day. A couple nights. A couple weekends. It's the same as if you were waiting tables at Sharkey's."

"Um, aren't you forgetting something?"

She blinks. "What?"

"I have a boyfriend!"

"W?"

"Yes, W." For some reason, Paisley hates W. She says his name is stupid and that he's stupid, but I love him anyway. William Wilkerson isn't the greatest name to be saddled with, but that's not his fault. It's also why we call him W. "There have to be dozens of girls who want to pretend-date Oakley Ford. And why does he need a fake girlfriend anyway? He could probably walk down to the Four Seasons on Wilshire, point to the first girl that drove by and have her in a hotel room in five seconds flat."

"That's the whole problem." She throws up her arms. "They tried the whole fake girlfriend thing with him before, but she fell for him and he broke her heart. I think half of the bad publicity the guy gets is because of her."

"Are you talking about April Showers?" I gasp. "That was *fake*? Oh, man, I believed in ShOak. My childhood dreams are crushed." I'm only half-kidding. Fifteen was a tough year for me, and not just because it was the year my parents died.

Paisley punches me in the shoulder. "You just said you didn't like him."

"Well, not after he cheated on April with that Brazilian swimsuit model." I chew on the corner of my lip. "Fake, really?"

"Really."

Hmmm. I might have to rethink my opinion of Oakley. Still, doesn't mean I want to be the next fake girlfriend to be fake dumped and fake cheated on.

"So you'll do it?"

I stare at her. "I make a couple hundred a night at Sharkey's. You said before Christmas we were doing fine." I narrow my eyes. "Is there something you're not telling me?"

Last year I found Paisley crying at the dinner table at two in the morning. She admitted that Mom and Dad didn't leave us in the greatest financial position. The insurance money kept us afloat at the beginning, but last summer she'd had to get a second mortgage to cover all the bills, and she was thinking of leaving college to get a job. Appalled, I sat down and made her go over everything with me, because she was a year away from graduating. I got my diploma early by taking summer courses, online ones to supplement my high school studies, and special permission from the school to take advanced classes. And then I found a job. Serving steak and iceberg lettuce wedges isn't fancy, but it pays the bills.

Or so I thought.

"No. We're fine. I mean…" She trails off.

"Then my answer is no." I've never been interested in the other side of LA. It seems so artificial, and I do enough pretending as it is.

I have my hand on the screen door when Paisley drops her next bomb. "They'll pay you twenty thousand a month."

I spin around slowly, my mouth hanging open. "Are you effing kidding me?"

"Don't swear," she says automatically, but her eyes are bright with excitement. "And that's for a full year of commitment."

"That would…"

"Put the boys through college? Pay off both our mortgages? Make everything easier for us? Yes."

I blow my overgrown bangs out of my face. This proposition is *insane*. I mean, who pays such an obscene amount of money to some random girl to pretend to be a pop star's girlfriend for a year? Maybe that's normal in the entertainment industry, but I grew up with parents who were elementary school teachers.

I suddenly wonder what Mom and Dad would say if they were alive to hear this crazy offer. Would they encourage me to do it, or tell me to run, run for my life? I honestly don't know. They were all about exploring new opportunities, taking the road less traveled. It was one of my favorite things about them, and I miss my fun-loving, impulsive parents. I miss them a lot.

That said, their love of spontaneity is part of the reason why we're hurting for money.

"An opportunity like this doesn't come along every day, but you don't have to say yes," Paisley assures me. Her words say one thing; her strained tone says another.

"How long do I have to think about it?"

"Jim Tolson wants an answer tomorrow morning. And if it's a yes, he wants you to come to the agency to meet with him and Oakley."

Oakley. Oakley frickin' Ford.

This is...nuts.

"Fine, I'll think about it." I let out a breath. "You'll have my answer in the morning."

Twenty thousand dollars a month, *Vaughn...*

Yeah. I'm pretty sure we both know what my answer is going to be.

3

HER

I said yes.

Because (1) It's a lot of money. And (2) *It's a lot of money.*

Guess that makes me a kinda sorta gold digger? I'm not sure if my situation fits the exact definition, but I can't deny I feel like one as I follow Paisley into the elevator the next morning.

Diamond Talent Management is an entire building. Not just a couple of floors, but an entire glass-covered, needs-an-elevator-and-a-security-team building. The scowly but hot guards with the earpieces give me the willies, but Paisley walks by them with a wave. I copy the motion. I kind of wish I hadn't had that second cup of coffee this morning. It's sloshing around in my stomach like a tidal wave.

The elevators are a shiny brass, and there's a guy in a suit whose only job appears to be spraying them constantly with cleaner and wiping them down. He's got a jaw that would look good on the side of a mountain and a butt tight enough to rival any football player's.

Paisley gets off on the sixth floor, which is emblazoned with Music Division in big gold letters on a dark wood backdrop.

The receptionist is more beautiful than half the actresses on the tabloid covers. I try not to gawk at her perfectly outlined lips and wicked winged eyeliner.

"You're staring," Paisley mumbles under her breath as we pass the reception desk.

"I can't help it. Does Diamond only hire people who could star in their own movies?"

"Looks aren't everything," she says airily, but I don't believe her because clearly Diamond requires photo applications. Gotta be beautiful to work in show biz, I guess, even if you're behind the scenes.

We're ushered into a huge conference room, where I stop in my tracks. It's full of people. At least ten of them.

I quickly scan the table, but I don't recognize anyone, and the one person I *would* recognize—and who this meeting is about—isn't even there.

A tall man with dark hair and plastic skin stands up from the head of the table. "Good morning, Vaughn. I'm Jim Tolson, Oakley's manager. It's a pleasure to meet you."

I awkwardly shake the hand he extends. "Nice to meet you, too, Mr. Tolson."

"Please, call me Jim. Have a seat. You, too, Paisley."

As my sister and I settle in the chairs closest to his, he goes around and makes a bunch of introductions I can hardly keep up with.

"This is Claudia Hamilton, Oakley's publicist, and her team." He gestures to a redhead with huge boobs, then at the three people—two men and a woman—flanking her. Next, his hand moves toward three stone-faced men on the other side of the table. "Nigel Bahri and his associates. Oakley's lawyers."

Lawyers? I cast a panicky look at Paisley, who squeezes my hand under the table.

"And finally, this is my assistant Nina—" he nods at the petite blonde to his right "—and her assistants. Greg—" a nod to the African-American guy to his left "—and Max." A nod to the slightly overweight guy next to Greg.

Jeez. His assistant has assistants?

Once the introductions are out of the way, Jim wastes no time getting down to business. "So, your sister has already provided you with some details about this arrangement, but before I tell you more, I have some questions for you."

"Um. Okay. Hit me." My voice sounds unusually loud in this massive conference room. The echo feels endless.

"Why don't you start by telling us a little about yourself?" he suggests.

I'm not sure what he wants me to say. Does he expect me to recite my life story? *Well, I was born in California. I live in El Segundo. My parents died in a car accident when I was fifteen.*

Or maybe he wants trivia-type stuff? *My favorite color is green. I'm scared of butterflies. I hate cats.*

My confusion must show on my face, because Jim gives me a few prompts. "What are your interests? What do you aspire to do after high school?"

"Oh, I'm done with high school already," I admit.

"Are you in college?" Claudia, the publicist, twists and frowns at Paisley. "She may need to miss classes. How old are you again?"

"Seventeen."

"Age of consent in California is eighteen." This reminder comes from the end of the table, where the lawyers, plural, are sitting.

Claudia waves her hand dismissively. "They're dating. Nothing more. Besides, Oakley's audience is mostly young girls. Anyone older and it won't have the same impact." She turns to me. "What are you currently doing?"

"I'm working. I took the year off to work to help our family." I've said it so many times, but even the passing mention of Mom and Dad being gone still makes my heart clench.

"Paisley and Vaughn's parents died a couple of years ago," Jim explains.

Paisley and I cringe as the entire table gives us pitying looks, except for Claudia, who beams. "Wonderful. An intelligent, plucky orphan," she says, and her voice is so high and squeaky it hurts my ears. "This backstory gets better and better. She's just what we're looking for."

We? I'm even more confused. I thought this was about me pretending to be Oakley Ford's girlfriend, so why am I in a conference room filled with strangers? Shouldn't my soon-to-be fake boyfriend be here, too?

"Do you plan on attending college?" Jim asks.

I nod. "I got into USC and Cal State, but I deferred until next fall." I wipe my sweaty palms against my jeans as I trot out my practiced speech about wanting to have real life experience before school but how I eventually plan to go into teaching.

From the corner of my eye, I notice Claudia's "team" taking diligent notes. My confession that I like to draw triggers several interested looks from the PR section.

"Are you good?" Claudia asks bluntly.

I shrug. "I'm okay, I guess. I mostly do pencil sketches. Usually just faces."

"She's being modest," Paisley speaks up, her voice firm. "Vaughn's drawings are amazing."

Claudia's blue eyes shine with excitement as she turns to her team, and then four voices chime out, "Fan art!"

"I'm sorry...what?" I say in bewilderment.

"That's how we'll make first contact. We've been brainstorming various online meet-cutes, but they all felt *so* contrived. But this has potential. Picture this—you Tweet a gorgeous sketch you drew of Oakley, and he's so blown away he *Tweets you back*!" Oakley's high-voiced publicist begins to make rapid hand gestures as she gets more and more excited by the picture she's painting. "And his followers will take notice, because he so rarely replies to Tweets. Oakley tells you how your piece *touched* him. It brought tears to his eyes. You Tweet back and forth a few times, and then…" She pauses for effect. *"He follows you."*

This prompts simultaneous gasps from her three assistants.

"Yes," one of them says with a vigorous nod of her head.

"But," another speaks up hesitantly, "we need to address the sister issue."

"Right," Claudia agrees. "Hmmm. Yes."

Paisley and I exchange flabbergasted looks. It's like these people are speaking a different language.

Jim sees our faces and quickly clarifies. "The fact that Paisley works for this agency will no doubt come out. Once the press digs that up, they'll start concocting wild theories about how the relationship is a scam arranged by Oakley's manager—"

I can't help but snort.

Jim doesn't seem to be as amused by the truth as I am. "—who just so happens to be related to the head of this agency. So we need to provide a plausible reason why a Diamond employee's sister is suddenly involved with one of the agency's clients."

"We'll blame it on coincidence," Claudia says with total confidence. "One of Vaughn's Tweets to Oakley will be this—" She moves her fingers through the air like she's conveying a headline "'Oh-em-gee! I just realized my big sis works at the same agency that reps you! How cool is that!'"

I try not to roll my eyes.

"That could work," Jim says thoughtfully. "And then we'll

get Paisley—" he glances at my sister "—to give a short interview about her role in the relationship."

"My role?" Paisley sounds uncertain.

Claudia can obviously read Jim's mind, because she starts nodding again. I'm surprised her head is still attached to her neck at this rate. "Yes, you'll give a statement about how you could *not* believe it when Oakley's manager called you into his brother's office and told you that Oakley wanted your sister's phone number."

Paisley starts nodding, too, and I almost reach over to smack her. Why is she feeding into these people's craziness?

"I have a few more questions for Vaughn," Jim says. "Your sister said you were dating someone?"

I don't miss the way Paisley's lips curl slightly at the reminder of W. Ugh. One of these days she's going to have to suck it up and accept that I'm in love with the guy.

"Yeah, I have a boyfriend," I reply awkwardly. "And actually, my Twitter and Instagram have lots of pictures of the two of us."

Jim turns to Claudia, who falls silent. I can see the wheels in her bouncy head turning and turning.

"You'll announce a breakup on your social media," she decides. "We'll spend two—no, three, weeks focusing on the split. First will be your despondent post announcing the end of the relationship, then we'll document your grieving process, how you're so upset and—"

"Listening to Oakley Ford's albums on repeat," one of the assistants finishes animatedly.

Claudia's eyes light up. "Yes!" She claps her hands together. "Oakley's music pulls you from the dark abyss of heartache."

I almost gag.

"And that's what inspires you to draw his face, which leads

to our social media meet-cute." She glances at Jim. "It still works."

He looks pleased. "All right. What about Vaughn's appearance? How do we feel about that?"

Everyone at the table swings their heads toward me. Their gazes pierce me, assessing me like I'm a specimen under a microscope. My cheeks heat up, and Paisley squeezes my hand again.

All of a sudden, the critiques start pouring in.

"The bangs are too long," Claudia chirps. "We'll trim them."

"Hair itself needs a trim, too. And that shade of brown looks too fake."

"It's my real hair color!" I protest, but nobody's listening to me.

"The honey-brown eyes are nice. I like the gold flecks. We'll forgo colored contacts."

"Shirt's a little too baggy. Are your shirts always this baggy, Vaughn?"

"Isn't normal what we are going for?" someone disagrees. "If we make her pretty, then the fans won't be able to relate."

I have never been more humiliated in my life.

"Oh, one last thing," Claudia says suddenly. "Are you a virgin?"

Scratch that—it's possible to be more embarrassed. There are a few coughs from other people at the table. Jim pretends the traffic in the hallway outside the room is fascinating, while the lawyers all stare stone-faced down the length of the table.

"Do I have to answer that?" I cast a dark look at my sister, who shakes her head.

"That can't be important," Paisley says to the man who's more or less her boss.

Jim ignores her. Clearly this question is one he wants the answer to, as well.

I want to hug her for standing up for me. I'm pretty sure my cheeks are officially as red as Claudia's hair.

"If you're worried there's some sort of sex scandal in Vaughn's past, don't be," my sister assures the table. "Vaughn is the definition of *good girl*."

I don't know why, but Paisley's view of me kind of stings. I mean, I know I'm not Miss Badass, but I'm not a Goody Two-shoes, either.

Claudia shrugs. "We'll do a thorough background check, nonetheless."

Background check? My sex status shows up in someone's report? I'm about to burst in outrage when Jim steps in.

"All right, I think we can all agree that this arrangement shows promise." He clasps both hands together and glances at the lawyer section of the table. "Nigel, why don't you and the boys draft a rough contract and jot down any negotiation points you anticipate? Oakley will be here in an hour, so we can get into the finer details then."

I frown. We're all just supposed to wait around for an hour until His Majesty gets here? And now that I think about it, do *I* need a lawyer? I whisper the question to Paisley, who voices the question to her boss.

"The contract will be very straightforward," Jim assures us. "Basically, it will state that you've agreed to enter into a service contract and that should you, at any time, no longer be able to perform your duties, the contract can be terminated. Any goods or monies received up to that time are yours to keep."

I bite my lip. This is starting to feel exceptionally complicated. But I guess when twenty thousand dollars—a month!—is involved, I should have expected complicated.

"How about this?" Jim suggests. "Why don't we sit down

with Oakley and go over the contract details? Then you can read the agreement Nigel's firm drafts, and *then* you can decide where we go from there."

"Okay," I answer, because that sounds very reasonable despite the ridiculousness of the situation.

Next to me, Paisley winks and gives me a not-very-subtle thumbs-up of encouragement. I shoot her a wan smile in return.

If I just remember why I'm doing this—so my brothers can go to college, so Paisley can stop worrying about how we're going to pay the bills… If I can just keep focusing on all that, then maybe I'll stop feeling like I'm going to throw up.

4

HER

I'm hungry and my stomach's been announcing that fact for the last thirty minutes. Still, no one suggests we take a break for lunch, even though it's close to noon and Oakley Ford still hasn't appeared. It's been two hours. Jim and the lawyers have left the room, but everyone else is glued to their chairs.

"Here's a granola bar. And a Coke." Paisley sets the snacks on the table in front of me.

"No wonder you like working here," I joke. "The free lunches are so fancy."

But since I'm starving, I shove half the bar in my mouth—at the exact same moment that Oakley Ford throws open the door.

Two burly guys with arms like tree trunks follow him inside. One plants himself next to the entrance while the other trails behind the singer. I barely notice Jim and the lawyers entering and closing the door, because I'm too busy staring at Oakley.

He's taller than I thought he'd be. Everyone in Hollywood is short. Zac Efron is barely taller than my five-six. Same with

Daniel Radcliffe. At six-four, Ansel Elgort is a veritable giant. Oakley looks to be Elgort-size, but with way more muscles.

He's even hotter in person. It's not the sandy-blond hair spiked up in the front and cut short in the back. Or his moss-green eyes. Or his chiseled jaw. He actually has an aura. You hear of things like that, but until you've experienced it in person, you don't believe it exists.

But he has it.

Everyone in the room is responding. People are sitting up and straightening their clothes. I dimly register Paisley smoothing her perfect hair into place.

And I can't look away.

Oakley's jeans are low enough that the brand of underwear he's wearing is visible as he reaches across the sideboard to grab a bottle of water. His arm muscles are defined enough to be noticeable, and I watch in fascination as the right biceps flexes when he twists the bottle cap off. Those muscles remind me of the shirtless spread he did for *Vogue* a couple of months ago. It was all over the web because the editorial spread had one shot of him in underwear only, and the size of his crotch got everyone speculating whether he stuffed a sock down his shorts.

I forget I'm eating my granola bar. I forget that I'm sitting at a table with a bunch of lawyers. I forget my own name.

"Sorry. Traffic," he says before settling in the seat at the very end of the table. The bodyguard stands at his shoulder.

I find myself nodding, because LA does have horrible traffic. Of course this beautiful god wouldn't make us mere mortals wait for him because he was doing something—is his hair wet? Did he just *shower*? Is it getting hot in the conference room?

This is Oakley Ford and I *did* listen to his album on repeat when I was fifteen. And fine, I might have harbored a teeny-tiny crush on him, which was why I was so upset when he cheated on his girlfriend. His fake girlfriend.

Which I'm going to be.

Fake.

I don't like fake, but I'm good at it. Faking things, that is.

Paisley nudges me.

"What?" Then I realize I still have the stupid granola bar hanging out of my mouth.

A quick scan of the room reveals that everyone has noticed this. Claudia wears a worried expression. Jim is resigned. I don't want to look at Oakley, but I do anyway. His face shows a cross between horror and fascination. The glance he throws his manager definitely says *You've got to be kidding*.

The only thing to do is act like I don't care. I bite off the bar and start chewing. The health bar, never an appealing item to begin with, tastes like cardboard. Everyone watches me, and I chew even slower. Then I take a big swallow of Coke before wiping my mouth with the napkin that Paisley miraculously produces. I'm certain I'm redder than the receptionist's lipstick, but I pretend that it's no big deal. See how good I am at acting like everything is perfect?

"So this is her?" Oakley waves a hand in my general direction. I've heard him speak in interviews before, but his voice sounds even better in person. Deep and raspy and hypnotizing.

Jim hesitates and then looks down at his phone. Whatever he sees there stiffens his resolve. He sets the phone down. "Oakley Ford, this is Vaughn Bennett. Vaughn, Oakley."

I start to rise and hold out my hand, but stop halfway out of my seat when Oakley leans back and clasps his hands behind his head.

Okay then.

Suddenly all my nervousness and embarrassment drain away.

Relief settles in their place. I take another sip of my Coke. Surprise, surprise—Mr. Famous is a total jerk.

For a moment there, I felt like I was in danger of being sucked in by his magnetism. That I'd forget W, the money, April Showers, Brazilian supermodels and become caught up in his force field. But a guy who mocks me because I had the nerve to eat a granola bar while we all waited on his late ass? Who doesn't have the courtesy to shake my hand?

There's no way I'd ever fall for a guy like that.

I sneak a look at Paisley, who's smiling slightly. She must have had the same concerns.

"So are we going to talk about terms? Like, what are my work hours?" I ask coolly, cradling the pop can between my hands.

"Work hours?" Claudia echoes, a tiny furrow appearing on her forehead.

"Yeah, since this is my job."

She titters. "Not a job, more like a…"

"Role?" one of her assistants offers.

"Yes. A role in a long, romantic movie. And you're the two leads."

I feel actual bile rise up in my throat.

Oakley grumbles with impatience. "Let's get on with it."

Quickly, Claudia outlines our meet-cute with the drawing and the Twitter stuff. When she's finished, Oakley yawns.

"Sure. Whatever. You're going to handle it, right?"

"Well, not me, but Amy here will." Claudia tips her head to the raven-haired woman on her right.

Amy holds up her phone in acknowledgment.

"Great." He slaps his hands down on the table. "Then we're done?"

Seriously? I waited over two hours and got only a granola bar and an extra serving of humiliation for this five-minute demonstration of how Oakley Ford isn't even going to participate in this charade? Instead, I'll be fake flirting with the assistant of one of his media people.

I turn to Paisley, who gives me a small, rueful shrug.

"No. We're not done," Jim barks from the other end of the table. The two of them exchange glares, but whatever power Jim holds over Oakley, it's enough to get the young star to resettle into his chair.

"Let's hear the rest of it." He makes a tired gesture toward Claudia.

She picks up her notepad. "We'll need the first date. We don't think you should have any physical contact until after the third—" she looks at her assistants and then at Jim "—fourth date? I mean, we're trying to sell this as a wholesome romance."

Everyone starts throwing ideas out about when and *how* the touching will happen. Someone says he should kiss me on the forehead. Another suggests a hand on the small of my back. There's another vote for hand-holding.

I'm still struggling with the concept of *any* touching when Paisley, the traitor, asks, "When did you and W start holding hands?"

Before I can answer, Oakley jumps in, snickering softly. "You dated a guy named W?"

"So what?" Wow. His first words to me are to make fun of my boyfriend's name? It's like Oakley's *trying* to get me to dislike him.

"Sounds like a pretentious asshat." He leans back in his leather chair and folds his arms across his chest. The action makes his biceps flex again.

I drag my eyes away. "Okay, Mr. I-Name-All-My-Albums-After-Me Ford."

Someone at the end of the table gasps at my audacity, but

Oakley's unfazed by my insult. "Even Madonna has a full collection of letters in her name."

"W is not pretentious."

"If you say so." He smirks.

"I do. He's awesome. And sweet."

"So why'd you break up with him?"

"I didn't," I say indignantly.

His brow creases. "So he broke up with you?" He sounds... confused. Like that doesn't make sense to him.

"He hasn't!"

Oakley shifts to Claudia. "So my down-to-earth, wholesome, normal girlfriend is a cheater?" He raises his eyebrows. "That's gonna go over well."

"Oh, you mean the *fake* breakup," I say. For a minute there, I'd forgotten.

He looks like he wants to roll his eyes, but refrains.

"He'll break up with her tomorrow. The sooner, the better. We'll give it approximately two weeks after the breakup, and then she'll Tweet you the drawing. Then there'll be a series of dates, but no touching." Claudia turns to me. "When did you have your first kiss?"

"Ever?" I realize it's a stupid question, but my mind is stuck on the breaking up with W bit. I haven't thought this whole thing through. I've been so focused on the money and how we'd be able to pay off the mortgage, pay for the twins' college, allow Paisley to sleep better at night, that I hadn't given any thought to the actual details of how this whole thing was going to work.

"Yeah, ever," Oakley says, and this time he *does* roll his eyes.

These personal questions suck. "When was yours?" I counter, still focused on the W issue. Lately, he's been pulling away. He says it's my fault that I don't act like an adult about our relationship because I'm still refusing to have sex with him.

"With tongue? I think I was eleven. It was with Donna Foster, the daughter of my dad's side chick."

My eyes grow wide. He French-kissed at eleven? I still thought boys had cooties at that age. Oakley would probably pee with laughter if he knew I was a virgin.

"You?" he prompts.

"Um…" Jeez, now I'm even more embarrassed, but for another reason. "Sixteen," I mumble.

"How sweet. Just like the saying."

I curl my fingers into fists. If Claudia's team wasn't sitting between the two of us, I might've reached over and smacked his smug smile off his smug face.

Paisley grips my hand, an unspoken gesture for me to get it together.

Even Claudia must sense that my patience is coming to an end. Hurriedly, she says, "Let's do hand-holding on the third date and then a kiss on the fourth date. We'll keep the first couple of dates under wraps, but leak the later ones to the paps."

"Hold up, we're going to kiss? I have a boyfriend," I remind the room. "No one said there'd be kissing."

"We're gonna have a year-long relationship and we don't kiss? Why don't we just announce that it's fake from the beginning?" Oakley mocks.

"But…but…" Yeah, I *definitely* didn't think this through. I quickly turn to Paisley for help.

She grimaces. "They're right. No one is going to believe that you and Oakley haven't kissed. Not if you're serious." Her tone is apologetic, but her words don't provide me any relief.

"You don't expect me to…" I trail off, not able to bring myself to say the words out loud.

"Of course not," Jim interjects briskly. "We're not *that* kind of agency."

He tries to play it off as a joke, but, um, they kind of *are*. They're hiring this guy a girlfriend and they expect us to kiss.

How am I going to explain this to W? *Sorry, babe, not willing to have sex with you yet, but I'm going to kiss another guy. In public.*

That will go over well.

Claudia leans forward. "This is no different than if you were acting on a television show. Remember, you're playing a part in a big love story."

Her assurance doesn't help, either. I may not know what I want in life. I may just be telling everyone I want to be a teacher because that's easier than admitting I'm clueless about my future and that I'd rather hide as a waitress for the next five years. But I do know that the entertainment industry doesn't interest me.

Paisley squeezes my hand again, probably to remind me why I'm doing this. By playing the role of a girlfriend, I get to lift the burden off my big sister's shoulders and provide for my brothers. It's not like I'm signing my entire life over. It's just one year.

"What do I need to do?" I ask, feeling resigned.

"Just a few kisses, some hand-holding. It's nothing, really." Claudia waves her hand airily. "And it doesn't need to be in the contract other than some general terms about physical contact when necessary."

"Does any of this need to be in the contract?" Oakley sounds annoyed.

"I agree. If this ever got out, it would be terrible for Oak's image," Jim points out.

"The terms need to be specific so that the girl can be held to them," one of the suits replies. Then he and Jim engage in some furious whispering until the lawyer presses his lips together in unhappy surrender. "Fine, it can be general, then. A general contract of employment."

Once that's decided, Claudia returns to her list. I wonder how long it is. I glance at the big white clock on the wall. It's going on three hours and I'm exhausted.

"Let's talk about her look again."

"I'm not changing my look," I mutter. "I like my look."

I like my comfy skinny jeans, assortment of colorful T-shirts and the Vans that W and I doodled on during morning advisory last spring. The sneakers are filled with details marking our favorite dates. There's a wizard's wand along the left sole because we're both Harry Potter fans. Then there's the light post to signify the Urban Light display on Wilshire, where W kissed me for the first time. Where there was definitely tongue. His initials are on the back of one shoe and mine are on the other. He has a pair of them, too, but he doesn't wear his. He says he doesn't want to ruin them.

"You have a look?" Oakley raises his eyebrows.

"Yeah, and it's better than yours," I retort, tired of his attitude. "Would it kill you to wear pants that actually fit around your waist? No one wants to see your underwear."

"Baby, everyone wants to see my underwear. I get paid a hundred grand per pap pic."

"Baby?" I scoff.

He leans forward, threading his surprisingly elegant fingers together. "Don't like that one? Pick another, then. You're my *girlfriend*," he reminds me mockingly.

"So you're into infants?"

"What?" He rears back. "No. Fine. How about—" he pretends to think and then snaps his fingers "—old lady?"

"Great." I give him my fakest smile. "I'll call you...dick cheese."

"Vaughn, gross," my sister interjects.

Oakley covers his mouth. I swear I see a smile. I wait for

his response and I'm not disappointed. "I have no problem with that, crabby patty."

"All right, that's enough of that. None of this needs to be in the contract." Oakley's lawyer rattles his papers in agitation.

I turn back to Claudia. I've given in on the kissing. On the dates. On this made-for-the-media breakup with my boyfriend, but no way am I going to let them change my look. I've got to fight for *something*. "I thought you wanted a normal girl. I'm a normal girl. This is what some normal girls wear."

When Claudia and Jim exchange a glance, I know I've won this one. They agree to keep my look…for now.

"But when we take pictures, at least let us do your makeup. You'll want us to," Claudia promises.

Um. That doesn't sound ominous or anything.

The negotiation goes on. When will our first official picture be released? Where will the dates take place? Will I go to an awards show with him? How about fashion week in New York? How often should I be seen with him? Every day? Every other day?

Oh, and I would not get Oakley's phone number. Like I care.

But I still find it weird, because what nineteen-year-old isn't allowed to give his number to his own girlfriend? And how does he communicate with his friends? Wait—does he even have friends? Or are they all fake like me?

I peer at him from underneath my lashes and feel a pang of sympathy. Oh, brother. Am I actually starting to feel sorry for him? I think I might be.

But then my stomach growls and reminds me that we're still mad. And unfed.

"You'll text Amy or me if you want to get ahold of Oakley," Claudia says.

"I feel like I need my own people. My people can text your people," I joke.

No one laughs. Instead, Claudia looks like she's seriously considering it, but then decides against it. "No, I think two nonteens Tweeting each other and commenting on Instagram would appear too contrived. And your voice, we want to preserve that. Whereas Amy has been running Oak's page for a couple of years now."

I have a voice?

"Whatever." I'm exhausted and hungry. One granola bar wasn't enough, and my stomach rumbles again to alert everyone to that fact.

"Is the granola bar all you've had today?" Oakley asks.

A burst of surprise jolts me. Out of all the people in this room, Oakley's the one to ask? "I had breakfast, but I like to eat like a normal person."

A faint smile touches his lips. "Jim, we need to eat."

"Oh, sure." Jim turns to Paisley. "Run and get us one of everything from the café across the street."

I see a chance for fresh air and an escape. "I'll go, too." Not to mention that I don't want to be here without Paisley.

"Oh, no, we'll need you here," Jim objects.

"I'm sorry," I murmur to my sister. She doesn't need to wait on me.

Paisley laughs. "It's my job, silly. I'll be right back."

She trots out like she's glad to be out of there, while I watch her exit and wish I could go with her.

On the other side of the table, Oakley leans back, crosses his arms again and looks smug, like he cured world hunger. "Well?" he prompts.

"Well, what?"

"Aren't you going to thank me?"

"Why? Paisley's the one getting the food."

"You wouldn't be having lunch without me."

I point to the clock. "I've been sitting in this conference room for five hours. Prisoners in maximum security receive better treatment. If it weren't for you, I'd be lying on the beach rereading *The Handmaid's Tale* and I would have eaten something. But sure, thank you for alerting your manager to send my sister to get me food."

He doesn't like my smart-ass response. "It's too cold for the beach."

"I never said I was going to swim." I speak in the same tone I use when I tell my little brothers they're acting like immature idiots.

"Why are you at the beach, then?"

I gape at him. "Why does anyone go to the beach? Because it's awesome."

"If you say so," he responds, but the smugness he's previously displayed is dialed down a watt as if my reasons for liking the beach are important…or even interesting. Or he might be confused about why I'd choose to go there rather than sit five feet away from his holy presence.

But I'm not going to tell him.

Instead, I drain the rest of my Coke, slam it on the table with more force than necessary and then sit back and refuse to say another word.

Is it childish?

Oh, yeah.

But it feels really, really good.

5

HIM

Jim drags me into his office before I can make a run for the elevator bank. My bodyguards, Big D and Tyrese, remain outside the door, but they have a perfect view of us because the office is a big glass cube. I don't know how he gets any work done with the whole floor being able to see him at all times.

My entire life is a big glass cube. I can't even remember a time when I had actual privacy.

"Do not run her off," is the first thing Jim snaps at me.

"Who?"

"Vaughn Bennett. She's the perfect candidate to play your fake girlfriend. We need her."

"Yeah, in the way I need an enema. Did you see the mouth on that chick?"

"Oakley. I'm warning you."

"About what?" I roll my eyes and flop into the huge leather chair behind the massive desk.

He doesn't say a word about me sitting in his chair. He can't, because I'm Oakley fuckin' Ford.

"Number one," Jim begins, "don't flirt with her—"

"Isn't that kind of the point? We're supposed to be dating."

"The point is to rehab your image. Vaughn's going to play a pivotal role in that, which brings me to number two—don't antagonize her."

She started it, I almost say, but that would just make me sound like a five-year-old. It's true, though. Vaughn Bennett was the one acting all rude and giving me lip. All *I* did was point out that her boyfriend sounds like a pretentious douche. Not my fault some people can't handle a helpful truth bomb.

"Couldn't you have hired someone who's a little less... bitchy?" I grumble.

"You mean someone who's a little more adoring?" Jim replies, and his knowing smile grates on my nerves.

Fine, so maybe I'm pissed about Vaughn's total lack of... respect, I guess? I don't expect every girl I meet to throw herself at my feet and declare her undying love for me, but come on, she could've at least said she liked my music or something. Or congratulated me on my last Grammy.

Where does this chick get off, acting like she's doing me a favor just by sitting in the same conference room as me? I'm *Oakley Ford*.

"You've changed your mind about working with King, then?" Jim asks.

I glare at him. "There's got to be another way. Let's call him up again."

"Sure." Jim pulls out his phone and tosses it down the desk. It slides to a halt halfway between us. "Call him. He's number ten on my favorites."

This feels like a dare. I grab the phone and start to press Dial when I realize I'm looking at Jim's recent call list. About every fifth call is to King. My eyes flick up to meet Jim's, and what I see in his gaze doesn't sit well in my gut. It's a mix of regret and resignation.

He dips his head. "I've tried to call him. He won't take my calls about you. He's not interested, not until you show him you're not a spoiled little jerk who'd rather party at nightclubs than make good music. So if you have a better idea, I'm all ears, but short of taking him to a cabin and going all *Misery* on his ass, he's not going to work with you."

I can't maintain eye contact anymore, because I don't have a different idea. I rub my throat and wonder how I lost my mojo.

If pretending to date a girl I don't know, who doesn't like me, gets it back, then I'll be the best boyfriend that this chick has ever had.

Which can't be hard considering her current one is named *W.*

I get home an hour later to find a half-dressed couple making out on my bed.

I stand there in the doorway for a second, trying to figure out what the hell is going on, but the skinny blonde on my California king mattress notices me and unleashes an ear-piercing shriek.

"Oh! My! God! You're Oakley Ford!"

Then, wearing nothing but a short skirt and skimpy bra, she flies off the bed and launches herself at me.

My man Tyrese appears out of nowhere and steps in her path.

Anger and annoyance swirl in my gut as I peer at the guy on the bed. I vaguely recognize him—I think it's one of Luke's friends. But why is he in my bedroom?

He zips up his pants and scrambles off the bed. He's either drunk or high or both as he slurs, "Oak, bro. You're home early. Luke said you wouldna be back for a couple hours."

As if that makes it okay that he's fooling around on my bed?

I'm so disgusted I can't even answer. I just jerk my head at

Tyrese, who clamps one meaty hand on the girl's arm and his other meaty hand around the guy's shoulder.

"Time to go," my bodyguard announces in his baritone voice.

"No, wait!" the blonde whines. "I just wanna get a picture with Oakley! Oakley, I'm your biggest fan! I love you! Can I please get—"

Her pleas fade away as Tyrese drags the couple down the sweeping marble staircase.

I hear a door click and turn to find a member of my cleaning staff stepping out of one of the guest rooms. "Is everything all right, Mr. Ford?" she asks with a timid expression.

"Everything's fine." I hook my thumb at my bedroom. "Burn those sheets," I say curtly, and then I stalk past her toward the east wing, where Luke has been crashing for the past few days.

I throw his door open without knocking. "Get out," I snap.

Luke was sprawled on the bed watching TV, but now he bolts to his feet, his panicky gaze finding mine. "Oak," he says weakly. "You're back early."

"Yeah, I am," I bite out. "And now it's time for you to go."

"But…" He's visibly gulping. "Come on, man, I already told you, I've got nowhere else to stay while my place is being fumigated."

"Not my problem anymore."

"Oak—"

"Why the hell are there strangers in my room, Luke? We had an agreement. I give you a place to crash, you don't invite people over without running it by me first."

"I know, I'm sorry. It was a stupid thing to do, bro. But Charlie's girl is, like, obsessed with you, and it's her birthday, and Charlie just wanted to show her your room. You know," he says feebly, "like a birthday present."

I gape at him. Does he expect me to buy that?

"How much and how many times?" I ask in a flat voice.

Luke gulps again. "Wh-what?"

"How much do you charge 'em for the experience of screwing in Oakley Ford's bedroom, and how many times have you done it?"

When the tips of his ears turn red, I know I'm right. And now all the disgust I feel is directed at myself. I should've known Luke would screw me over eventually. They always do.

I met him a couple years ago at the studio. I was rehearsing with the house band, he was playing bass guitar, and we hit it off instantly. We liked the same music, same video games, same everything. The two of us ran wild in the LA club scene for a while there. I invited him to go on tour with me. But these last few months, Luke's turned into a leech. Borrowing money from me, getting me to sign stuff he can sell online.

And now this? Yeah. I think this "friendship" has run its course.

"Forget it, don't answer that," I mutter. "Just get your stuff and go."

"Don't be like that, bro."

My patience is nonexistent. "D," I call over my shoulder.

Big D appears behind me. He crosses his enormous arms over his enormous chest then proceeds to glare daggers at Luke until the bassist sighs in defeat and starts gathering up his belongings.

With my bodyguard handling the sitch, I march off and take the stairs two at a time. This day just keeps getting worse and worse, starting with the meeting with my new fake girlfriend, a chick with a smart mouth and a chip on her shoulder, and ending with yet another person I considered a friend showing his true colors.

I'm seething as I burst into the media room on the main

floor and grab a beer from the fridge. Yeah, I'm underage, but there's been booze, drugs and girls at my disposal for as long as I can remember.

I twist open the cap and heave myself onto the leather sectional. It's only five o'clock and I'm legit ready to call it a day.

Tyrese pokes his shiny shaved head into the room and grunts, "All taken care of, Oak."

"Thanks, Ty." I take a swig of beer and click the remote.

"D's heading out," he tells me.

I nod. Both my bodyguards stick to me like glue during the day, but only Ty sticks around on the nights I go out or have people over. Big D actually has a wife and kid. Ty's single.

"Lemme know if you need anything."

"Thanks."

After he disappears, I turn up the volume and do some channel surfing, but nothing holds my interest for very long. I watch ten minutes of a documentary about komodo dragons. Five minutes of some crappy sitcom. A few minutes of sports highlights. A few seconds of the five o'clock news, which is just long enough to bum me out, so I quickly change channels again.

I'm about to turn off the TV altogether when a familiar face catches my eye. The channel I'm on is playing TMI, a mindless show where two asshats watch paparazzi footage and offer color commentary on it. The screen shows a tall, willowy blonde in skintight jeans and a flowy blue top leaving LAX airport.

That blonde is my mother.

"—and not too concerned about her son's latest scandal," the male host is saying.

Wait, I have a latest scandal? I scan my brain trying to think of what I've done lately, but I come up blank.

A melodic giggle pours out of the surround sound. I know that giggle well.

"Oh, pshaw! My son is a healthy, red-blooded nineteen-year-old. If making out with a pretty and *legal-age* girl outside a nightclub is a crime—"

Right. *That* scandal.

"—then go ahead and lock up half the teenage boys in this town," my mother finishes. Then she pops her oversize sunglasses over her eyes and slides into the waiting limo in the airport pickup area.

"Maybe Oakley is just following his mommy's example," remarks the female host with spiky pink hair. "Because obviously Katrina Ford herself has no problems canoodling outside nightclubs. This pic was taken in London last night."

A picture of my mom locking lips with some silver fox flashes on the screen. I turn off the TV before the commentary kicks in. I'm less concerned about Mom's London shenanigans and more concerned about the fact that she's back in LA.

And she didn't even bother calling me.

Crap, or maybe she did, I realize a second later when I check my phone to discover a missed call from Mom's LA number. I forgot I put my phone on silent during the conference at Diamond.

I hit the button to return the call then sit through at least ten rings before my mother's voice chirps in my ear.

"Hi, baby!"

"Hey, Mom. When'd you get back in town?"

"This morning." There's a flurry of noise in the background, what sounds like loud hammering and the whir of power tools. "Hold on a second, sweetheart. I'm going upstairs because I can barely hear you. I'm having renovations done on the main floor."

Again? I swear, that woman renovates her Malibu beach house every other month.

"Okay, I can hear you now. Anyway, I called to make sure you're still planning to make an appearance at the charity benefit that the studio is hosting this weekend."

My jaw stiffens. I guess it's too much to hope that she called to actually *talk* to her only son.

"What's the charity again?" I ask woodenly.

"Hmmm, I don't remember. Cruelty against animals, maybe? No, I think it's for cancer research." Mom pauses. "No, that's not right, either. It definitely has something to do with animals."

I'm not gonna lie—my mother is an airhead.

She's not dumb or anything. She can memorize a hundred-page script in less than a day. And when she's passionate about something, she throws her whole heart and soul into it. Except the thing is...she's passionate about the dumbest shit. Shoes. Redecorating the multimillion-dollar house she got in the divorce. Whatever new fad diet is making the rounds.

Katrina Ford was the queen of rom coms, vivacious and drop-dead gorgeous, but truth is, she doesn't have much substance. She's not winning any Mother of the Year awards, either, but I'm used to living in the background of her self-absorbed bubble.

It's not like my dad is any better. Mom at least remembers to call me. Sometimes. Dustin Ford is too busy being an Academy Award–winning actor to remember he has a son.

"And sweetheart, please don't bring a date," Mom is saying. "If you show up with some girl on your arm, all the focus will be on that and not the charity we're trying to raise money for."

The charity whose name and purpose she doesn't even know.

"I'll get Bitsy to text you the details. I expect at least an hour of your time."

"Sure, whatever you want, Mom."

"That's my boy." She pauses again. "Have you spoken to your father lately?"

"Not for a few months," I admit. "Last I heard, he was in Hawaii with Chloe."

"Which one is Chloe again? The one with the boob job or the one with the botched Botox?"

"I honestly don't remember." Ever since my parents' divorce two years ago, my father's love life has been a revolving door of surgically enhanced women. Hell, that was his life even before the divorce.

Hence the divorce.

"Well, when you do speak to him, tell him there's a box of his stuff that's been sitting in the foyer closet for almost a year, and if he or one of his people doesn't pick it up soon, I'm going to burn it in the fire pit out back."

"Why don't you tell him yourself?" I grumble.

"Oh, baby, you know your father and I only speak through our lawyers—and mine is out of town at the moment. So be a good boy, Oak, and pass along that message to Dusty." Her voice goes muffled for a second. "Absolutely not!" she calls to someone who isn't me. "That paneling *must* be preserved!" Mom's voice gets clearer again. "Oakley, baby, I have to go. These contractors are trying to *destroy* my house! I'll see you this weekend."

She hangs up without saying goodbye.

The silence in the house makes my skin itch. Without Luke and his merry band of leeches, the place feels like a museum. I flick on the television again and crank up the sound.

Great. Now I'm pretending I'm not alone by turning the TV volume up. Mindlessly, I watch a bunch of shows about jacking up cars until I can't stand the stupid manufactured drama. Hits too close to home, I guess. I grab my phone, and my finger hovers over the screen. I could ask Tyrese to call one of those girls who just want to touch Oakley Ford. That'd be good for an hour or two. I could light up a joint. Drink myself into a stupor. Or I could just go to bed. Because if I'm trying to turn over a new leaf, like I promised Jim, none of those other options fit with the plan.

I turn the television off. In the front room, Tyrese is sitting in an oversize armchair, flipping through something on his phone.

"I'm going to bed."

"You are?" He looks up in surprise. It's barely ten. "Alone?"

"Yeah. I'm supposed to be a good boy now. Can't be having honeys over when I'm preparing to romance another girl, right?"

Tyrese shrugs. "I guess not. But Big D's the family man, not me."

And we both know where Big D is right now. Not out at the club picking up a random chick. "I'll see you tomorrow."

"Night, brother."

"Night."

6

HER

I'm up at dawn the next morning despite getting almost no sleep. In the kitchen, Paisley is in her usual zombie-like pre-caffeinated state with a buttered bagel on the table and a half-filled coffeepot in her hand. I grab the pot from her before she crashes it into the side of the refrigerator. My sister can't function without her caffeine fix.

After our parents died, I started drinking the foul stuff with her. It's part of my routine now, but I always dilute it with milk. Paisley calls my coffee half and half. Half coffee, half milk.

"I heard you get up at three," she mumbles as she takes a seat at the glass-topped breakfast table. "You okay?"

"Couldn't sleep." I dump out the tap water and pull a pitcher of water from the fridge. "You seriously think this is the right thing to do?" I ask as I pour the water into the coffeemaker's reservoir and scoop out fresh grounds into the filter. "I kept obsessing about it last night, and it's not the fake-dating thing that gets me—" I'm a champion at pretending "—it's the length of time. An entire year, Paisley?"

I take a seat next to her and rip off a piece of her bagel.

"I know it seems like a long time, but unless it's a serious relationship, there's no point in even doing this charade." She sounds tired, too. "You don't have to do it if you don't want to. We'll be fine without the money."

Guilt rushes through me when I hear the note of defeat in her voice. Paisley's held our family together with sheer will and grit. When social services wanted to split us up and send the twins into foster care, Paisley was having none of it. She hustled her way through school, taking more classes than I thought you were allowed to cram into one year, and graduated in three years instead of four. She worked two jobs until she landed this one at Diamond. Meanwhile, I ran the household—cooking, cleaning and making sure the twins' lives remained as stable as possible.

Despite all our efforts, I know we're barely treading water.

One year is nothing compared to what Paisley has sacrificed.

"I'm doing it," I say firmly. "That's why I got up at three. To sign the papers." And to sweat about how I'm going to sell this idea to W. I turn to watch the coffee drip into the pot. "I mean, it's not like I have to eat bugs or poop or something gross. There are way worse things to do for money than fake-date Oakley Ford, right?"

"Right." She smiles with relief. "And he's not a bad guy. He can be charming when he wants to, and you'll get to do so many fun things. I'll make sure your dates are full of stuff you like to do."

"Great." I try to summon up some enthusiasm for Paisley's sake. It's obvious that the prospect of all that cash is lifting a huge burden from her shoulders, and I would be a terrible, selfish sister to not want that for her. Still, I can't stop thinking about how much my life is going to change.

"Something is still bothering you," she says, breaking off another piece of bagel for me.

I stick it in my mouth and chew for a moment before admitting, "It's W. I don't know how I'm going to sell this to him."

Paisley shakes her head. "You can't tell him all the details. The nondisclosure agreement wouldn't allow it."

"I know." I rub a nonexistent spot on the table. "How strict are those things?"

"The NDA? Very strict," Paisley says, her eyes wide with alarm. "Do you remember Sarah Hopkins?"

"The nanny who banged Mark Lattimer and broke up his marriage?"

Mark Lattimer is the front man for the rock band Flight. He went through an ugly divorce last year. It was in every online gossip column and every grocery store tabloid for about three months. The scrutiny didn't die down until the next scandal came along.

"Didn't she have a drug problem and was turning tricks to pay for it?" I ask.

"Yup, and you know how all the gossip rags got that information?"

I didn't know before, but I think I do now.

"She signed an NDA, but then decided that she was tired of taking the fall for Mark and Lana's failed marriage. Everyone inside the circle knew they had an open relationship. She was fine with the nanny until the two of them got caught in public. Afterward, Sarah was paid off but she wouldn't go quietly. So Jim released all that information to the tabloids. He pretty much ruined her life."

"So if I break it, Jim will drop a bomb on our house."

"Our lives," Paisley corrects grimly. "Oakley Ford is worth millions to Jim. His last tour grossed two hundred and fifty million dollars."

I gape at her. I didn't know numbers went up that high in real life. "So what you're saying is, either I do this one hundred percent, or not at all."

"That's exactly what I'm saying. You can only tell W what the agreement says you can tell him. Anything more than that, and Jim will crush us like a bug."

Us. Not me, but my whole family.

Paisley drives the twins to school, and I clean the house, prep for dinner and try to force some lunch down before taking the bus to USC to see W. His last class of the day is at 2:00 p.m.

Jim Tolson sent a courier over with another NDA—this one for W's signature. It's like he has a million of them on his laptop, ready to spring on the unsuspecting.

With only a week into the new college semester, no one in the dorms seems interested in studying. Several of the doors are open when I arrive, and all sorts of different music and sounds are streaming into the hallway.

Part of me regrets not enrolling this year. W wanted me to, but after watching Paisley bust her ass to make sure all our bills were paid, I wanted to do my part. Taking a year off and making some real money made the most sense. Still...every time I walk into W's dorm and see all the pretty girls wandering the halls, I'm gripped with a sudden case of nerves.

"Knock, knock," I announce at the open door.

W and his roommates are lounging on their hand-me-down sofa, playing Madden. Two girls I don't know are curled up on a love seat in the corner. They always have girls in here. As with everything, I pretend it doesn't bother me, because the last thing I want to do is look like the jealous, immature girlfriend from high school.

W jumps up immediately. "V, I didn't know you were coming."

"I texted you."

He grimaces. "We were playing. Guys, I'm out. My girl's here."

"Put a sock on the doorknob," Mark yells as W slams the door to the bedroom. Mark's a kid from upstate who's always asking me how good W is in bed—as if he knows that we've never done it and enjoys needling me about it.

W grins at me, hands at his hips. "Do I need to put the sock on?"

"There are people out there," I remind him.

He laughs and tackles me onto the bed. "So? There's no one but you and me in here."

I shiver when his hand tunnels under my T-shirt.

W makes me feel good, but I'm not ready to take that next step yet. And especially not when his roommates are outside the room playing a video game, and two strange girls I don't know are sitting there.

I push at his hand. "I'm not having my first time with an audience."

We've had this discussion before. He resists at first but then pulls his hand out from under my shirt to rest it on my jean-clad hip. Part of his brown hair falls across his forehead as he rolls onto his side. I push it away so I can see his chocolate-brown eyes. He looks gorgeous, as always. More gorgeous than Oakley Ford, that's for sure.

Really, scoffs my internal voice. *You've got to be kidding.*

Okay, W isn't better-looking than Oakley, but he's nicer and sweeter and I love him and that counts for everything.

"All right." He smiles, crinkles forming beside his beautiful eyes. "Did the twins look up that skate park I texted you about?"

"The one over in Boyle Heights? That's, like, in a different country." Anything that requires someone from LA to get on the freeway is considered a low-scale crime given the congestion. A trip to Boyle Heights might not require a passport, but it would require a huge effort. While I love my brothers, I don't love them *that* much.

"Yeah, but if you bring them over here, we can hang out. That'd be nice, hmmm?" His mouth dips down to kiss the side of my neck.

We both know the twins won't go, but it's sweet that W's trying to get us all together. "Actually, yes. I see the wisdom of your plan." I curl into his embrace and meet his wandering lips with my own.

"The benefits of dating a college guy," he teases.

We kiss some more, and when we break apart for air, the reason why I've come today pokes me in the spine.

"Hey, I need to ask you a favor."

"The answer is yes." He tickles my belly.

I practiced a little speech on the bus, but it didn't sound right. I give it anyway. "So you know how I took the year off to help Paisley?"

"Uh-huh." His lips find my ear.

"I have an opportunity to make some huge money this year. It would set us up for a long time."

"Sounds good." He moves from my ear to my neck and then tugs my loose-fitting T-shirt over the curve of my shoulder.

Allowing him to kiss me when I'm about to break the news that I need to fake-date a pop star makes me feel too guilty to enjoy his attention. So I slide off the bed to go stand by the window.

"I need you to not be mad and to understand."

W frowns and swings his legs over the edge of the bed. He leans back on his elbows, his long, lanky frame looking familiar and wonderful, and I question my decision all over again. "This is beginning to sound like the kind of speech Danny Jones gave Karen because he was going to NYU and didn't want to have a long-distance relationship."

"No, it's nothing like that." I rub my forehead. "It's…this job requires me to do something you're not going to like."

"Are you starring in a porno?" His eyebrows are all the way to his hairline.

"No, W, God."

"Just spit it out, V."

I release a frustrated breath. "I can't say more until you sign this." I hand him the one-page contract that states W can be told some but not all of the particulars.

He pushes the paper to the side. "I'm not signing anything. What the hell, Vaughn?"

"Don't swear," I say automatically.

"Don't channel your sister," he grouses. He and Paisley aren't fans of each other. She thinks he pressures me, and he thinks she's too uptight.

"I know this sounds crazy, but if you don't sign it, I can't tell you any details and it sounds worse without the details, trust me."

"Then trust *me*." W grabs the paper and tosses it on the bed behind him. "You can tell me anything. You know I'm a vault."

It's not that I don't trust W, but this is my entire family's future on the line.

"If it was just me, then yeah, I'd tell you, but I already promised the agency I wouldn't say anything unless you sign this."

His eyes narrow. "What agency?"

"Where Paisley works. Diamond Tal—"

"Diamond Talent Management?" he exclaims. "They're the

ones giving you this job? Why didn't you say that in the first place? Of course I'll sign it. Where do you need my signature?"

I watch as W rushes to his desk to grab a pen. He's practically buzzing with excitement.

He doesn't look up as he scrawls his name across all the lines, even the ones I think Jim is supposed to sign on behalf of Oakley. He dots the last *i* in his last name with a flourish. "All right. Lay it on me."

I get up and drag W back to the bed so I can sit beside him and hold his hand while I explain this bit of insanity to him. "Okay, this is all I can say—I'm doing something for the agency, sort of like a social media campaign." It sounds ridiculous when I say it out loud, but that's all the NDA allows me to reveal. "They know that you and I are dating, and—"

"They know about me?" His eyes are shiny and eager. "Did Paisley tell them about the show? I thought she hated it! Which episode did they like? The one where we rated the end zone celebrations? Or the one where we dressed up and pretended to be the dogs playing poker picture? We got so many hits for that one even though it's not on brand."

I wrinkle my forehead. "Uh, no, it's not about the show."

"It's not? But you mentioned it, right?"

"Not exactly." I wince. It hadn't occurred to me that W's first thought would go to his show, and now I feel bad I hadn't brought it up to Jim Tolson.

"Why not?"

There's a note of betrayal in his tone. W and his roommates started up a YouTube channel back in September, where they post videos of themselves talking about sports highlights. Their show is called the Bro Hards, and it's...argh, okay, it's kind of dumb.

But because I'm a supportive girlfriend, I diligently watch

every video and make sure to leave an encouraging comment even though I don't find it at all entertaining.

"I don't know. It didn't come up," I answer, suddenly wishing I'd bargained for that.

After all, it would've been easy enough and it would go a long way toward making W more comfortable with my deal with Oakley. I make a mental note to talk to Jim the next time I see him.

"Anyway, our relationship is a bit of a problem for the agency. It interferes with some of my...duties. I can't have a boyfriend that people know about, so they want us to break up publicly—" when he frowns, I hurry on "—but not for real. For real, we'll still date. Except..." I grimace. "We can't be seen together in public."

W stares at me blankly. "You want me to break up with you but not really?"

"Yes." Oh, gosh. It sounds monumentally stupid.

"Is this you wanting to break up with me, V? Because I didn't even know we were having problems. If you don't want to go out anymore, just tell me." He says it so matter-of-factly, like breaking up wouldn't kill him.

It would kill me, though. "Do you want to break up with me?" I blurt out, frantic with worry.

W's my anchor. We started dating before my parents died, and through that grief-stricken summer, he'd stood by me the whole time, despite my tendency to burst out in tears at random moments. Like when we were at the mall and I saw the Father's Day advertisement in the Hallmark store window. I'd gone home that night and resolved to be the fun girlfriend again, and I haven't cried in front of him since.

I was so worried he'd break up with me once he started college without me, but he didn't. He told me he loved me and that he was going to stick with me, even if it meant dialing back some of the plans he'd made for both of us.

"Of course not." He pulls me down on his lap, another frown creasing his face. "But how's this supposed to work?" His hands run up under my shirt. "We're supposed to be having fun together this year."

"I know," I say miserably. "But it's a lot of money."

W frowns. "You and Paisley are doing fine. Didn't you say she earns enough now not to have to work two jobs?"

"Yes, but—"

"And didn't you delay coming to school this year because you had to work?"

"Yes, but—"

"Then you don't need this one," he says with the confidence of someone who's never worried about a bill in his life.

W's family has money. They even sprang for him to have a dorm room at De Neve Plaza, where he has a two-room suite and a private bathroom he shares with only three other guys. When I looked up how much this suite costs each semester, I nearly swallowed my gum.

"I do, W. I need this job. My family needs it." I take his hands, the ones he's using to try to take my shirt off, and press them between mine.

"Is this Paisley's idea? Because you know she hates me."

"She doesn't hate you."

W grunts in disbelief. His fingers brush the top of the waistband of my jeans and I force myself not to flinch away. This is W. I *love* W. Therefore I should love his touch, not tense up when I see it moving toward me.

My sister hasn't ever flat-out said I shouldn't have sex with W, but I know she thinks I'm too young. Part of her reluctance comes from her own first time, which she willingly—and vocally—says was terrible. After our parents' funeral, Paisley was lonely, depressed and worried about how she was going to take care of us. So she ended up sleeping with someone she didn't know very well because she needed some comfort. And it was so horrible, I found her crying the next day. I'm not saying that scarred me, but I definitely didn't want to rush into things with W after that.

"Fine, let's pretend I go along with it," W says slowly. "Who would be doing the breaking up?"

His complete one-eighty startles me. I guess I should be relieved that W is agreeable to this, but instead, his casual attitude rubs me the wrong way. One of the great things about W is that he's so easygoing. He never hassles me about my lack of ambition or the fact that I have zero clue what I'm supposed to be doing with my life. If I can't make a date because I want to be with my family or I'm working extra shifts, he never complains. I tell myself that's healthy and good. In the months after my parents' deaths, his laid-back attitude was just what I needed.

And since I need him to be cool with this, it shouldn't irritate me that he's asking about how our fake breakup is going to shake down as casually as if he's checking on the weather.

"How do you want it to happen?" I counter.

He shrugs. "I should probably do it, but I don't want any of your friends accusing me of cheating. We'll just say that it wasn't working out anymore."

Cheating? Do I tell him now or later that I'm supposed to kiss Oakley Ford? Not that either option is available to me, because I'm forbidden from telling W that Oakley is involved. Obviously he'll find out soon enough, but the agreement I signed forbids me from saying Oakley's name.

This is all so screwed up.

"I'll make sure everyone knows that you didn't do anything wrong," I promise, all the while fighting my growing unease.

"Good." He pauses. "And...we can still see each other in secret?"

I get the feeling that's not the question he wanted to ask—he hesitated too long before voicing it. But I nod anyway. "It'll have to be at my house, though. And we're not allowed to text at all during the breakup. We can talk on the phone, but there can't be any paper trails. So no texts, Snapchats, Instagram comments, all that stuff."

"That's like some real James Bond shit right there." He wiggles his eyebrows. "So I'll be having a secret affair with my girlfriend? That's kinda hot."

I swallow my relief. This is good. He's joking about it already, and for some reason, that tells me we're going to be okay.

"Sneaking around will totally be hot," I say enticingly.

That gets me a devilish grin in response. "What else?"

Crap. This is the hard part. "I might be photographed with certain celebrities—"

His eyes light up. "Like who?"

"I don't know yet," I lie. "But if you do see any pictures of me on the internet, you need to know they're not real." I throw in another lie. "Most of them will probably be Photoshopped. Seriously, anything I do this year will *not* be real. It'll all be staged, like...think of it as a reality TV show that Diamond is producing."

He nods. "Speaking of television shows..."

My uneasiness grows as I wait for him to continue.

"If I give you, like, a clip reel of my show, can you pass it along to one of the agents?" he asks hopefully. "I never asked Paisley because we both know she won't do it, but now her contacts are your contacts, too, right?"

The request rubs me the wrong way, even though I'd already made up my mind to mention it to Jim. I force myself to swallow my annoyance.

"I mean, you're going to be spending a lot of time with all these Hollywood types, industry people, and you know how hard the boys and I work on this show." There's something defiant in his eyes now. "This is a chance for us to get our foot in the door. And you said so yourself—you could totally see us getting our own TV show."

I rue the day I ever wrote that YouTube comment. "Don't you want to concentrate on getting your communications degree?" I point out, hoping the reminder will derail him.

But W waves his hand dismissively. "The only reason I'm a comm major is to get into broadcasting. I want to be a sportscaster. You know that. So if I can fast-track that goal, why not?" When I don't answer, he flattens his lips unhappily. "Are you saying you don't want to do this for me?"

"That's not what—"

"I don't think it's asking for too much," he interrupts. "Because if I'm going to be without my girlfriend for a few months—"

"A year," I whisper.

His jaw falls open. "A year? This fake breakup is going to last a year?" He throws up his hands in astonishment. "See? This is a huge sacrifice on my part! It'll be way easier to deal with all this if I at least get a career opportunity out of it."

And knowing you'd be helping me support my family isn't enough?

I bite my tongue before the angry words can escape. I see his point, I guess. A year is a long time, and I'm pretty sure we'll both get tired of sneaking around sooner rather than later. Besides, it's not like Diamond is going to sign him, so maybe if he receives some constructive criticism from an actual authority, he'll finally realize that this YouTube thing is a total waste of time.

"You're right," I agree. "We can't pass up any career opportunities."

His expression brightens.

"Email me whatever you want and I'll give it to the right people."

"Fuck yeah, baby! You're the best!" He tugs me into his arms and kisses me until I'm breathless, and we're both laughing when we finally pull apart.

Well, *he's* laughing, and I'm faking it. Story of my life, I guess.

7

HER

On Friday night, forty-eight hours after my trip to USC, W and I "break up." Before I left his dorm that day, he kissed me, said he loved me, and promised to send me his clip reel as soon as possible. While I don't feel entirely comfortable vouching for W's stupid show to Jim Tolson, I'm worried that if I don't, W won't be on board with this Oakley job anymore and will break up with me for real. And I'm desperate for him to support me on this.

Since we don't go on Facebook very often, our breakup is fed to the masses in two ways.

1) W removes my Twitter and Instagram handle from his bios. Both used to say "Madly in love with @VeryVaughn." Now they say nothing.

2) I Tweet thirty-one characters of pure misery:

Vaughn Bennett @VeryVaughn
Breakups SUCK #heartbroken #fml

Within minutes, Tweets and Instagram DMs come pouring in from our friends. I sit on my bed with a carton of chocolate chip ice cream in my lap and a spoon sticking out the corner of my mouth, fighting back tears as I stare at my laptop screen.

@MandiHunt343 OMG, W! What happened to ur bio?? Did u and V break up??

@CarrieCarebearDawes YOU AND W BROKE UP?

@KikiSimpson omg vaughn. when did this happen?

@Tracyloves1D if that asshole W cheated on you, I am gonna KICK HIS ASSSSSS!

Carrie, Kiki and Tracy are friends of mine from high school. I'm closest with Carrie, so I shoot her a return message confirming that yes, W and I broke up. She instantly responds and offers to come over with some ice cream. I tell her I'm already good on the ice cream front and we agree to meet up for lunch on Sunday.

Since Oakley's publicist told me I have to respond to any Tweets regarding the breakup, I force myself to answer Kiki and Tracy, but I don't offer any details. W was adamant that he didn't want to look (a) weak or (b) like a bad guy. Thus, the breakup was his idea and I'm not allowed to accuse him of any wrongdoing.

Our official story is that he dumped me because he didn't want to be in a long-term relationship now that he's in college. I make sure to tell Tracy there was no cheating involved. Then I shove another spoonful of chocolaty goodness in my mouth and force myself not to cry.

It's not a real breakup, I remind myself, but it doesn't ease the huge ball of pain in my stomach. I want so badly to text W. No, I want to call him and hear his voice assuring me that all these Tweets are just honest responses to a phony situation.

But I can't. Claudia forbade any contact between the two of us for at least a week—"to give the breakup time to settle"— so I can't pick up the phone and call him for reassurance. She claimed she was monitoring us closely. I don't know what that means, but I'm a little afraid of her and Jim, so I don't call him even though I'm dying to.

"Vaughn?" My sister knocks softly on my bedroom door.

"Yeah?" I call out in a shaky voice. The fake breakup feels all too real.

"Can I come in?"

"Yeah, whatever."

Paisley walks inside, takes one look at the ice cream and my teary expression and joins me on the bed. Her brown eyes peer at the computer screen then fill with sympathy.

"I'm so sorry. I know this must be awful for you." She bites her lip. "It's not too late to back out."

"Yeah, it is." I can't stop thinking about the money. "But the year will go by fast, right?"

Paisley nods.

I swallow another mouthful of ice cream. "You know what the worst part is? Well, the second worst part, because not being able to talk to W is the first one. But Oakley Ford is such a jerk. He wouldn't even shake my hand at the meeting. How's he going to bring himself to touch me in public?"

"He noticed you were hungry and got you food. That's something. Plus, he's pretty to look at," Paisley points out.

Yeah, at least there's that.

My sister slides off the bed. "I'm taking the twins to see a movie tonight. You wanna come?"

I shake my head. "Nah, I'm just going to stay home and

wallow in my misery. I plan on gaining at least five pounds of ice cream weight."

"Don't gain too much," she teases. "Otherwise Oakley Ford might change his mind about dating you."

That doesn't sound too bad, actually. Maybe I should open another carton of Ben & Jerry's.

Paisley leans down to kiss my cheek. "You're doing a good thing here. Seriously. This is going to help us more than you know."

I do know. But that doesn't mean I have to pretend to be happy about it. I miss W already, and it's only been two days since I spoke to him.

After Paisley leaves I give myself over to ice cream therapy. I eat it slowly. So slowly that it's sort of a soupy mess by the time I reach the bottom. I swirl the remains around as I re-think this Oakley plan for the hundredth time.

Did Paisley come to me because she knows, deep down, that I'm unprepared to face the real world? That I have no plans for myself? That unlike every other kid I went to school with, I'm hopelessly lost about my future and that playing make-believe with some random celebrity is right up my plastic existence?

The melted ice cream holds no answers. Sighing, I close all my web browsers and open my music library. I can either keep wallowing or I can follow this stupid course I've set for myself. I guess the latter is more productive, so I scroll until I find the album I'm looking for, click on the first track and then place the laptop beside me on the bed.

As I rummage through the bottom drawer of my desk for a sketchbook, the intro to one of Oakley Ford's most popular singles, "Hold On," wafts out of the computer speakers. The moment it comes on, I'm suddenly transported back to my sophomore year of high school. I was *obsessed* with this album. Weirdly enough, it doesn't remind me of Oakley, but of W.

W and I started going out around the time *Ford* was released. He used to make fun of me for liking it, but then I heard him humming one of the songs once and got him to admit he liked it, too. Then I doodled two hands clasped together on my Vans to capture the moment.

I find a sketchbook and a set of drawing pencils, but I don't start sketching yet. First I go online again and look up pictures of Oakley, because I'm not sure I can draw him from memory.

Okay, I'll admit it. This guy is hot. Like ridiculously hot. That mussed-up blond hair, and those piercing green eyes, and his toned, muscular body always covered in ripped jeans and tight T-shirts. Goodness.

I click through picture after picture of him. Live shots from his concerts. Paparazzi shots of him around LA. Shots of him and his mom at her movie premieres. Shots of him on the set of one of his dad's films.

Oakley Ford lives on a different planet, as far as I'm concerned. He's a celebrity with a capital *C*. The only son of Katrina and Dustin Ford, a Hollywood power couple, or at least they used to be before their divorce. He's won Grammys and People's Choice Awards and he got green slime dumped on him after he performed at the Nickelodeon awards show when he was fourteen. He's been on the covers of a zillion magazines, including that super sexy *Vogue* shoot I'm now looking at.

I decide to pick a photo from that spread, the one where he's sitting against a black backdrop, just staring at the camera. His gaze is so intense it actually gives me shivers.

I start sketching to the sound of his beautiful, raspy voice singing to me in my bedroom.

A week after the fake breakup W comes over and we hang out in my bedroom. We fool around on my bed for hours before he reluctantly says he needs to leave.

"It's late. I should get back," he announces around ten.

I want to protest that it's not late at all, but I'm not the one who has class in the morning. "'Kay."

My reluctance must show because he kisses me gently on the forehead. "At least we're allowed to see each other, right? This isn't so bad."

Not bad? This week without contact has been torture. I hung out with Kiki and Carrie a few times, and, in true BFF fashion, they spent the whole time assuring me that W is a jackass and I'm better off without him. I played along even though trashing the boy I'm still in love with was pure agony. But, again, I don't want to be the clingy, childish girlfriend so I just smile and nod.

"I hate this," he mutters as we head downstairs.

Relief wells up inside me. He's feeling it, too, thank goodness. "Me, too."

We stand in the front hall and just hug for several moments, his forehead resting against mine, his arms around my waist. I think about all the hugs we've exchanged over these past two years. All the inside jokes and the random texts and the fact that I've never once gone to bed without W calling me to say goodnight.

"Mark and I decided which episodes we think are the best," he says, his warm breath tickling my nose. "He's going to edit it all together this week and then I'll email you the file."

I stiffen slightly, and hope he doesn't notice.

"I can't wait to hear what that agent thinks about the show."

"Me, too," I say with forced cheerfulness. Then I try to distract myself by breathing in the familiar scent of his lemony aftershave.

After one last kiss, I watch with bleak eyes as he walks out to his car. It's the same older-model SUV he drove in high school, and as he drives away, I think longingly of all the heart-pounding make-out sessions we had in that car.

Upstairs, I flop onto my bed and Tweet about my heartache again.

Vaughn Bennett @VeryVaughn
Listening to Ford on repeat = best cure for a broken heart.

I'm lying on both counts, because I'm not listening to *Ford*, and there isn't a cure for a broken heart. Even a fake one.

"You need to post the drawing tonight," Claudia announces when I take the phone from Paisley.

Claudia isn't calling my number…yet. I'm sure that will change once my relationship with Oakley is front-page news.

It's been two weeks since my "breakup," so I've been expecting this request since the first deposit hit Paisley's account, but that doesn't mean I've been looking forward to it.

Since I'm not allowed to quit my job yet, I worked four shifts waiting tables at Sharkey's and looking suitably depressed about the breakup in front of my coworkers. That's not a chore at all. Neither is depositing the twenty thousand dollar check—the first of many. It was decided that the checks would be made out to my sister just in case, because if it somehow leaked that Diamond Talent Management was writing me checks, the vultures would immediately start circling. If it's under Paisley's name, the agency can claim the payments are part of her salary.

The lies they're building seem complicated and unnecessary, but I haven't ever done this before, whereas I get the sense that this is business as usual for Claudia.

"Why tonight?" I grumble, mostly for the sake of being contrary. Since she's technically my boss, I probably shouldn't be grumbling at her, but this is the weirdest work relationship ever. A part of me is hoping I'll get fired.

"Because we need to move this along. Post the drawing. Oak will see it in a couple of hours. After he favorites the Tweet, be prepared for a barrage of messages. Respond only to a few of them."

"Maybe you should tell me which ones to respond to," I murmur sarcastically.

"Oh, no. This should all be organic," Claudia objects, choosing to ignore my snappishness. "But you're going to be getting so many, you won't be able to answer them all. By tomorrow morning, you'll be a social media star! Just remember that not everyone will love you. The fans are possessive of Oak, so ignore the mean ones and focus on the ones that are encouraging. Don't forget that they all wish they were you, no matter what they post!"

After giving that questionable piece of encouragement, she hangs up. I pull out the drawing I finally got around to finishing a couple of days ago. I wonder what Oakley will think of it. It's not bad, but I'm not in love with it, and not simply because his face isn't exactly how I wanted it to be. I worked on his eyes for a long time, but it was hard to capture their liveliness in black-and-white. He has good eyes, I think as I trace my finger over them.

No, it's not my technical mistakes, but something else that's missing. Something about Oakley Ford that I can't put on the page.

I wiggle my lips back and forth in indecision. I don't like that a piece of my art is going up on social media for millions of people to gawk at and criticize. But this is what I signed up for.

I pick up my phone, snap a quick pic, and then Tweet it out.

Vaughn Bennett @VeryVaughn

Breakups are a little easier when you're imagining this face next to yours.

It takes only three hours from the time Oakley faves the drawing before the first response shows up in my stream. Less than a minute later, I get a text from Carrie.

Did u see Oakley Ford faved your pic?!

I play dumb and text back He did??

Yes! Get on Twitter. Your timeline is blowing up! U should get his snap!

I'm not getting his snap bc he liked a pic.

Never know! Slide into his DMs like a pro, girl!

And then I can't respond to her anymore, because every second—or maybe it's every millisecond—I get a new notification.

@pledo5514 @1doodlebug1 @caryneo @paulyn_N just followed @VeryVaughn

Did @OakleyFord just fave some girl's pic @VeryVaughn

@OakleyFord follow me back. Pls. I luv u. @VeryVaughn

@luv_oakley_hands @VeryVaughn This pic is sooooo amazing. Need 1 in my locker.

@VeryVaughn God, basic pic or what? Go back to art school, btch

@OakleyFord_stanNo1 @VeryVaughn Preach. Looked at her history. Not even a fan let alone a stan. Get out.

@VeryVaughn your not even cute. @OakleyFord ur hot af

@selleuni5 @OakFordHeart @unicornio @wammalamma @ magg1e_han50n and 244 more just followed @VeryVaughn

Oh, wow. I racked up more than two hundred new followers in the span of ten seconds. That's *nuts*.

Paisley pokes her head in my room. "Claudia called. She thinks you should start replying. Apparently you're getting hundreds of responses."

"I know." I hold up my phone, a tad dazed. "They're pretty much about how basic and not cute I am and how he can do so much better than me."

My sister gives me a wry grin. "It's the internet. People say stupid stuff all the time on the internet. Want some help with that?"

I shake my head. I signed a contract and it's time to do my part, so I spend the next hour answering random Tweets with the appropriate OMGs and !!!!! while ignoring the "your so ugly" comments. The insulters have one thing in common. They're not good with homophones and that provides me with the tiniest bit of pleasure.

The last text I get before I go to bed is from W.

What the fuck V! Call me.

8

HIM

"Why didn't I see this picture before it went out?" I ask Jim.

It's past ten, the house is dead again and I'm staring at a pencil sketch of my face on Ty's phone. He's in the front room trying to hide his laughter from me.

"You don't like it?" Jim says, his surprise echoing through the line. "I think it's good. Actually, it's better than I thought it was going to be. Your fans are loving it."

I zoom in on my mouth. Is that how she sees me? Pouty and sullen? I look like a little boy who got his favorite toy taken away. But I'll sound even more childish complaining about it to Jim, so I latch on to a different excuse.

"Have you seen all the shit that other girls are sending? Doesn't Twitter have some kind of rules?" I don't know why I'm shocked. I'm used to getting private naked pics all the time, but some of these girls look…young. Way too young for even me.

When Jim signed me up for Snapchat, I got about a thousand nudes before I uploaded my first snap. I accidentally responded to one of them, which led to a weird stalker experience. Having four fourteen-year-old girls follow you around on their bicycles is scary.

"Ignore them," Jim advises. "In fact, you can ignore all of this. Claudia will handle your responses."

Tired of looking at myself, I toss Tyrese's phone onto the marble kitchen counter. "What's our timeline on King?" I demand, because getting my music made is the only reason I'm going through with this crap.

"Nothing's going to happen with him for a while. Put it out of your mind. Why don't you use this time to write new music? Maybe your new girlfriend will give you some inspiration."

"Hardeeharhar." Since Vaughn doesn't like me much, all my songs would be about irrational girls and their incorrect snap judgments.

And what did I ever do to her, anyway? Traffic in LA *is* bad, and Jim knows better than to schedule a meeting before noon. I'm a night owl.

"I hope you don't think I'm going to stay in my house this entire year," I mutter.

"No, I realize a bored Oak is a dangerous one. Frankly, I don't care what you do all year, other than keep your nose clean. King will come around. You let me worry about that. Now I'm going home to my pretty wife."

"I can't tell if you're mocking me or scolding me."

"It's both, kid," Jim says cheerfully before he hangs up.

The picture on Ty's phone keeps taunting me. I want to write something back to Vaughn, but I have no idea how to log in to my own Twitter account. Social media is a total time suck. When I first went on, I was shocked by the number of people who sent messages that they'd never have the balls to say to me in person. I argued with a few of them.

That's when Claudia stepped in and took over my account—

all of them. And after the gang of four, as I like to refer to them, I was happy enough to let her take the wheel.

I pick up Ty's phone when it buzzes. Some girl just snapped him a dirty message. I swipe it away.

"Ty, why do you have a Twitter account?"

"Football, brother." He wanders into the kitchen, apparently done with his laughing fit. "Lots of pros on Twitter."

"Yeah?"

"Yeah, see here." He pulls the phone out of my hand and taps on something before setting it back in front of me. "I've got my fantasy follows and then a bunch of athletes."

I read his timeline. It's full of stats, links to football videos and articles. "No wonder you kick my ass in fantasy football."

"You need a secret Twitter account."

"Yeah, that'd go over well with Claudia." I hop off the bar stool and rummage around in the fridge for something to eat. I pass over the veggies, cheese, health drinks, and grab a beer. "Wanna play some FIFA?"

"Sure. You ready for an ass-kicking?"

"Bring it on."

I toss him a beer and we make our way to the living room. Ty slips on the headset with the mic while I don my headphones. I'm not allowed to have a mic attached to mine. One time I was bellowing out curses and someone figured out that I sounded a helluvalot like Oakley Ford. They recorded me, put the sound bite up on the internet and I got a bunch of people mad because I cursed too much at the age of sixteen.

Hell, do any of these parents even listen to their kids? I swear, ninety-nine percent of the *I'm going to bang your mother* insults are delivered by preteens.

Ty and I play for a couple of hours, and he does proceed to kick my ass. I soothe my ego by playing some random on the internet and finally log a win.

Once we're done playing, my eyes stray to his phone again. "Can you log in?" I ask.

"To your account?"

"Yeah."

"No. I don't know your deets. I can call Claudia, though."

I toss Ty's phone back and forth between my hands. As far as I can tell, Vaughn hasn't responded to "my" fave'ing of her picture. She couldn't be less interested in my attention. She reminds me of my parents.

I scowl. "No."

I end up going to bed early again.

When I wake up, it's morning. I walk over to the floor-to-ceiling windows and flip the switch that turns the glass from opaque to see-through. Outside there are birds chirping and I see a couple of people running on the beach. One of these days I'm going back to that private island Jim booked after the *Ford* tour. I could leave the house there without a security detail.

I shove away from the windows. Big D isn't scheduled to arrive until noon, because that's normally about the time I roll out of bed. It's been two weeks since I've had anyone in this place except me, the housekeeper and my bodyguards.

I kind of miss that asshole Luke. He wasn't *that* bad. After all, maybe if I was in his shoes, I'd be doing the same thing... trying to leverage my friend's success into something more for me.

I've never had to do that. I didn't have to play a thousand gigs on the road before getting some A/R guy to notice me. Mom sent a phone video to her friend, who shared it with a friend, and I was signed to a label at thirteen. My first album was released with a huge marketing push before I turned fifteen. I churned out three more successful albums before I hit my current block.

I wasn't ever in Luke's position—or, hell, Vaughn's—where I had to cozy up to someone in exchange for money.

Gotta admit, my attitude toward Vaughn when we met was kinda shitty. In my defense, I wasn't exactly open-minded going into that meeting, because I'd already had one made-for-the-media relationship and that was a complete disaster. Only a star-fucker would agree to this nonsense, especially when she already has a boyfriend.

But Vaughn hadn't come off as stuck-up or fame-obsessed in any way. She was hot, but she wore almost no makeup. She didn't dress up, and she'd argued hard that she didn't want a new look. She had a confidence about her appearance that my last fake girlfriend never had.

And she didn't try to impress me. There were no hair flips, lip bites or eye flutters in my direction. The picture she drew is good, but it looks like it was drawn by someone who thought I was an April Showers—ego-driven and assholic.

Yeah, Vaughn definitely wasn't impressed with me at the meeting. And while I hate admitting this, her attitude bothers me. I mean, I don't expect everyone I meet to like me. It's just that she was so…openly hostile.

I pick up my phone and download the Twitter app. I want to see what she said in reply. Only…crap. I can't log in without a username and password.

I don't want to, but I end up calling Jim.

"Have you seen the news?" he crows when he answers.

Our world's a little sick when what I fave on Twitter is considered news. A mass killing in Africa doesn't get as many eyeballs as me liking some random girl's art. "I need to log in to my Twitter account."

"Why? Are you unhappy with how it's going? Claudia and I talked this morning. Everyone's excited. You're getting the best press you've had in months. Hold on, I'll read some to you."

I can hear street noise. "Are you texting and driving?"

"Yes. How do you think I get anything done in this town?"

"Forget it. I'll look it up myself."

I hang up before he can kill himself trying to read the gossip column headlines.

I hit the most famous celeb site I know and immediately see a smarmy picture of me side-eying a camera.

Oakley Ford's Tweet Makes a Fan's Dream Come True!

Ford fangirls take notice!

Last night global superstar Oakley Ford set his saplings on fire when he favorited a fan's drawing of him. According to the girl's Twitter account, seventeen-year-old Vaughn just broke up with a longtime boyfriend and she's been consoling herself by playing Ford's self-titled release on repeat.

Ford's been notoriously quiet on Twitter except for the occasional shout-out to a fellow artist, so this activity was definitely out of character! We weren't the only ones who noticed. Fans jumped all over his fave by Retweeting the picture. The artist's own account grew from 89 followers to 8000. Her account exploded after Oakley Ford Tweeted her back.

Is this a new romance for Oakley? He hasn't been linked to anyone—for more than a night—since April Showers. Gossip Central caught up with April outside Nice Guy in LA. April appeared blindsided by the news that Oakley is finally moving on, telling us, "You know more about Oakley's life than I do." Ford's people haven't commented.

The fan interaction has spurred #Fordfangoals to trend on Twitter. It's been two years since we've had any new Oakley Ford music. Maybe Vaughn will serve as new inspiration!

Christ. I follow the link to the Twitter page to read about my so-called interaction with Vaughn.

Oakley Ford ✅ **Verified** @VeryVaughn Thanks for sketching my left side. It's my best.

I scroll through what seems like a thousand Tweets before I get to her response.

Vaughn Bennett @OakleyFord Haha! U don't have a bad side.

Oakley Ford ✅ **Verified** @VeryVaughn Do you have a red pencil? I'm blushing.

Excuse me while I vomit. *I'm blushing?* What a lame-ass response. I'm Oakley Ford. I don't blush. What do I have to be embarrassed about?

@jelly_bean1984 @ OakleyFord Please Oak I luv u. Please fave my tweet!!!!!

@cassandra.vega.5 @ OakleyFord ur soooooo bbbbeeutiful. I ♥ ♥♥ u so much! Ur my bae!

@OakleyFord_stanNo1 @ OakleyFord Love you Oakley. Can't wait for another album.

This is frickin' impossible. I tap on Vaughn's stream and breathe a sigh of relief. It's so much easier to read.

Vaughn Bennett @OakleyFord I don't believe u blush. But I do have a red pencil.

She Tweeted another picture of just a cheek and some lightly shaded red on the upper curve. Nice. Even though it's not an accurate representation, I can't deny her talent.

I swipe past dozens of people replying to her, and find mine.

Oakley Ford ✓ **Verified** @VeryVaughn So you're taking requests. I'd like to see a self-portrait.

Vaughn Bennett @OakleyFord Like this?

I eagerly scroll. Shit, did she send me a—it's a sketch of her phone.

Oakley Ford ✓ **Verified** @VeryVaughn Modern and sleek. I like it.

These responses are terrible. If I were replying, I'd have said something like—

I dial Jim again. "I want access to my Twitter account. If I'm dating this chick, I should be able to respond to her directly."

"What? Why would you want to do that?"

"Because I do. So do I get access or do I make up a different account?"

"Hold on." He sighs then barks to some assistant. "Get Claudia on the phone and find out how to get Oak on Twitter."

9

HER

"Are you supposed to be dating Oakley Ford?!"

W's loud, angry voice hurts my eardrums, but I don't ask him to calm down. This is the first opportunity we've had to talk on the phone since my online conversation with Oakley began. My boyfriend has clearly saved up his frustration from these past twenty-four hours and it all comes pouring out now.

"I can't confirm or deny that," I answer with a sigh.

"Bull! You don't know how many of our friends called and texted to tell me you're flirting online with Oakley Ford!"

My guard snaps up. "I hope you didn't say anything about my job. You signed an NDA, W. If you break it, Diamond will—"

"Ruin my life," he finishes sourly. "Yeah, I know."

Ugh, this is not about W's life, but I know from past experience that I'm going to have to listen to him bitch and moan until he gets it out of his system. "So what did you tell everyone?"

"That we're both upset about our breakup and that flirting with some celebredouche is your way of trying to get over me."

I wince at his word choice, but only say, "Thank you."

There's a long pause.

"What exactly are you doing with Ford?" W mutters.

"Not much." I hesitate. "We're just going to be hanging out—for the cameras—a few times. And there *might* be a kiss. No, a peck. And none of it is real, remember?"

"It better not be." My heart flips a little over his jealousy, only to die a quick death at his next words. "I'm not happy looking like a loser here."

A whiny voice sounds from my bedroom doorway. "Vaughn! We need our phone back!"

I hold up one finger to silence Shane. "I promise, it's all a show," I assure my boyfriend. "Just like reality TV."

"We need to call Kenny!" Spencer shouts, coming up to stand beside his twin. They both glare at me, the gold in their hazel eyes sparking angrily. At twelve, the two are already taller than my five feet six inches and could easily wrestle the phone away.

I sigh. "I have to go. The twins need their phone. I'll see you this weekend, okay?"

"Okay." He hesitates again. "I love you."

"Love you, too," I answer, and the twins release simultaneous groans and then proceed to make gagging noises, their light brown hair flopping all over the place.

I hang up and toss the phone to Spencer. "Here, you brats. Go call your precious Kenny."

After they dart off, I collapse on the bed and curse the day I let Paisley convince me to meet with Jim Tolson and his entourage.

Claudia believes that someone could pull our phone records, so for two months I can't call W on my own phone or my sister's, which means I'm at the mercy of two twelve-year-old boys.

And I actually had to ask Claudia's permission before I could make the call. And then *she* had to hold a stupid brainstorming session with her PR team to determine if it makes sense for W to keep in touch with his ex-girlfriend's little brothers. I reminded her that W was a part of my family for two years, so of course he would be close with my brothers.

"Phone," my sister's voice says, jolting me out of my thoughts. Paisley walks into my room and holds out her iPhone. "Claudia."

A silent scream goes off inside me. Oh, my God. I *cannot* deal with another one of Claudia's dumb requests right now.

"You're going to make your account private today," Claudia says instead of *hello*.

"Why? Because of all my new followers?" I woke up this morning to discover I have twenty-five thousand new followers on Twitter. I almost died from shock.

"Because we want to fuel the fire even more. If you suddenly go private, Oakley's fangirls won't be able to follow you and it will drive them crazy. They'll start gossiping on their own feeds and speculating about why you're private, and the ones who are already following you will start screen-shotting your Tweets and turn you into an even hotter commodity."

I don't bother to argue. I've given up on trying to figure out the logic of a publicist.

"Fine," I say. "Anything else?"

"Yes. Amy's emailing you an archive of your Twitter account. Start deleting all the pictures with your ex-boyfriend."

I'm outraged. "How did you get an archive of my account? And how did you get my email address?"

"From Jim. Don't ask how he got it. He'll never tell," Claudia chirps. "Anyway, we'd like all traces of your ex-boyfriend gone from your account by tomorrow. You did it, of course, to erase him from your life."

Bitterness climbs up my throat. "If you have access to my archive, why don't *you* delete them?"

"Oh, of course. We'd be happy to do it for you. We just thought you might like to do it yourself. Getting over an ex is a difficult process for a teenage girl."

I imagine some stranger going through my pictures of W and clicking the little trash can button, and I realize she has a point. "Forget it. I'll do it. And he's not my ex, Claudia!"

"He is in the eyes of the world." She's starting to sound annoyed with me. "One last thing. We need you to go out to dinner with your family tonight."

I wrinkle my brow. "Why?"

"Lord, Vaughn, is that your favorite word—'*why*'? Careful, sweetie, or I'm going to start answering with 'because I said so.'"

I clench my teeth so hard my jaw twitches. "Why do I need to go out for dinner, Claudia?"

"Because it's family night. As of right now, you and your siblings go out once a week for family night."

I respond with her favorite word. "Why?"

"Because that's what wholesome people do!" There's a loud, frustrated huff in my ear, and then her voice softens. "Is your Instagram linked to your Twitter?"

"Yeah. Wh—" I halt before the rest of the question slips out. She's already pissed off at me as it is.

"Good. At dinner tonight, post a picture of you and your family. It doesn't matter if the brothers are in it. But your sister has to be."

"I assume you know what I'm going to ask."

She heaves out an exasperated sigh. "It'll be an organic way to reveal that your sister works at Diamond. Oakley will comment on the picture, and then that bit of information will come out."

"Fine. I'll post something tonight."

I hang up without saying goodbye then holler at the door, "Paisley, get in here."

She appears within seconds. "What's up?"

"Tell the twins to put on some nice clothes," I say as I toss her cell phone over. "We're going out to dinner."

"Why?"

"It's family night."

My sister arches a brow. "Why?"

Oh, wow. That word really *is* annoying. "Because that's what wholesome people do!" I shout, and then I march to my closet to find something to wear.

10

HIM

#squadgoals #dinnertime #whyisthewaitsolong

I stare at the picture of Vaughn's family on Instagram. They're all squeezed together as they wait to be seated at some random restaurant I don't think I've ever heard of before. I can't remember the last time I ate with my mom and dad. Hmmm. The last time I sat down at the same table with Mom and had a fork in my hand was...the Golden Globe Awards last year?

Holy shit. I almost laugh at the sad absurdity of the situation. Dad, on the other hand, I haven't eaten with in years. Old man can hold a grudge like nobody's business.

I feel a strange tightness in my chest. That isn't...nah...it isn't envy. I flick the app closed and stare out the windows. What I need to do is get out of the damn house. I've been stuck inside these walls and the studio—where nothing but garbage is getting recorded—for too long.

Purposefully, I stride to the kitchen where I find Tyrese. "Let's get some grub."

He tucks away his phone. "What do you have in mind?"

"I don't know. How about—" A wicked idea pops into my head.

"Uh-uh." Ty rocks back on his heels. "I'm not liking the look of that smile on your face. It says we're about to get into trouble."

"How about fondue?" I reply innocently.

I need to figure out what to wear. A hat and sunglasses aren't going to be enough.

"Sure. There's a place over on La Cienega Boulevard," he says.

Ty's a foodie. Man knows all of the good places, but I don't want to go to Restaurant Row.

"I was thinking about Fondue Heaven over on—" I open the app, and sure enough, Vaughn has her Instagram geolocation on. "El Segundo. It's on Main Street."

Ty looks offended and faintly disgusted as he trails after me into my room. "A chain, brother? In El Segundo? That's an hour away."

I ignore him as I rifle through my walk-in closet. I should wear my lowest slung pants. The ones that hover around my ass crack. I wonder if I got rid of those? I dig around in the back of the closet.

"Those folks are gonna be gone before you get there," Ty says from behind me. He's not slow.

"Not if we take a chopper. That's fifteen minutes. The apps are probably being served at that time." I find the pair of ratty jeans that I hate in a pile under an old pair of sneaks. I lift the denim to my nose. They smell clean. Musty but clean.

Ty raises a judgmental eyebrow. "Really?"

"My jeans or the chopper?" I ask, stripping out of my sweats and pulling on the pants. I haven't worn them for a couple years so it's a tight fit. I've bulked up since my Slim Jim, sixteen-year-old days.

"Both."

I slip a dark hoodie over my T-shirt and rub my hands to-gether. "Ready?"

"You have me on record that I think this is a bad idea, right?" Ty asks as he turns into the parking lot.

"I heard you the first three times." I adjust my hat using the visor mirror in the car we're renting. It's not a full disguise, but I'm banking on the fact that no one's going to expect to see Oakley Ford in El Segundo at a fondue chain restaurant.

"Jim's a scary man and I've got family," Ty reminds me.

"What family? You have kids I don't know about?"

"Sisters."

Right. I've met Ty's sisters. If anyone should be afraid, it's Jim, because those chicks put the *F* in *fierce*. Highly protec-tive of their "baby" brother and with no filter, they tell it like it is. "Honey—" that's what they call me. I'm not sure they even know my name anymore "—Honey, you gotta pull those pants up before you start a riot."

At fifteen and dumber than a box of rocks, I told Shanora, Ty's oldest sister, this was the style. "Honey, that's no style. I didn't see wannabe hoodrat on the shelves last time I was in Macy's," she replied. "What you have is a lack of imagination."

Because of her advice, I'd ditched the saggy jeans, back-ward cap and wife-beater, and tried to find a style that hit somewhere between rock god and Abercrombie douche. Not sure I've found it yet.

"Jim knows that this is my idea. He's not going to blame you." I flip up the visor. "He's never blamed you in the past."

Ty only grunts as he pulls into a parking space. While the lot itself is busy, there aren't a ton of people around, and the few restaurant goers outside are taking zero notice of me. A couple walks right by me and doesn't stop. I give Ty a surreptitious thumbs-up behind their backs.

He shakes his head.

Excitement courses through me. I feel like I'm breaking the law, getting away with something I definitely shouldn't by having dinner at this subpar chain restaurant. I can see my next interview. *"What's the most exciting thing you've done since the Ford tour?"*

"Well, I went to eat fondue and no one noticed me. That was the highlight of year nineteen of my life."

"You let me do the talking with people," Ty says as he opens the door. "Your voice is too recognizable. Let's at least get some food in our system before we have to make a run for it."

"Sounds like a plan." My voice does have a distinctive rasp. A writer from *Billboard* once asked if I smoked a lot of cigarettes as a kid. She was only half-joking. But nope, just how I was born.

Inside the restaurant there's a crowd of folks waiting to be seated. Ty muscles his way to the front while I hang back and scan the interior. Near the kitchen, a table of four catches my eye.

"The wait's going to be about twenty minutes," the harried hostess informs Ty.

"No problem," I say. "We're meeting someone." I point to Vaughn's table.

The hostess looks surprised. "They didn't tell me."

"No worries." Then I start walking before the lady can ruin my surprise.

"So much for letting me do the talking," Ty mutters in my ear.

I ignore him and drop down next to Vaughn, pushing her over closer to her sister. "What're we having?"

She turns, her mouth open to deliver some kind of rebuke, then proceeds to stare at me for a good long moment.

I stare back, finding myself drawn to her wide mouth. She's

not wearing lipstick, or even a hint of any other makeup. Her dark hair is pulled up in a messy ponytail, with her bangs falling into her eyes and framing the sides of her face.

My new girlfriend is kind of a scrub, but she's a hot scrub. Her thin see-through sweater and skinny jeans reveal enough curves to make my pants feel even more uncomfortable.

"I'd tell you to take a picture because it lasts longer," I remark, "but you've already drawn me."

I snatch her long two-pronged stick right out of her hand, stab a piece of bread and drop it into the cheese.

She finally recovers enough to ask, "What are you doing here?"

"Eating, hopefully. Should we order more food?"

Across from me, Ty settles in next to Vaughn's brothers, who watch him with wide eyes and half-open mouths. He's an impressive figure—just a couple inches below my six-two. But he has an air of menace around him that I assume he acquired in the military, where he served ten years before he left to join the bodyguard service. Ty uses it to scare away overzealous groupies and lure the ladies into his bed.

One glance toward Vaughn's older sister reveals that she's not immune. She's pink in the cheeks and keeps sneaking peeks at him while she thinks he doesn't notice. He notices. But he's not going to tap anyone on Jim's payroll because of the whole not-shitting-where-you-eat thing.

"Is this our first date?" Vaughn whispers uncertainly. "I didn't get any instructions from Claudia."

I barely manage to keep from rolling my eyes. "Since we're the ones seeing each other, I think we can make these decisions."

She nibbles on her lip. Not because she wants me to bite it—which is sorta what I'm thinking about at the moment because her mouth is definitely her best feature—but because she's worried she's pissed Claudia off. I don't mean to be an egotistical ass here, but shouldn't *I* be the one she's worried about pissing off?

A waitress bumps into my side before I can point that out. "Oh, I'm sorry. I didn't realize you were expecting more people. Do you need a different table?"

We all look around at the full restaurant.

"No." Vaughn sighs as if she's being asked to negotiate a peace treaty between the Koreans. "I'll move."

She scoots over, and I get both cheeks onto the vinyl bench. The waitress sets down new silverware and two glasses of water. I keep my head down. Beside me, Vaughn tenses up.

"I don't like this," she protests under her breath as soon as the waitress moves on. "What if someone recognizes you?"

"The waitress didn't," I point out.

"You were looking at your feet. Do you plan to eat that way the entire time?"

"Stop worrying." Vaughn is worse than Jim, I decide. "How do I know when my food is done?"

"It was done five minutes ago," one of the twins informs me. The other one is taking turns staring at Ty and then me. I'm not sure which one of us is more intriguing to him. I bet it's Ty. My demographic doesn't usually include preteen boys.

They look identical, except one's wearing a plain white T-shirt and the other one is wearing a skate brand. I was paid about a million bucks to roll around on one of their boards a couple of years ago. I still have a half dozen in my garage.

"You like SkateBoiz?" I ask the kid.

He nods and then exchanges a look with his brother. The two have an entire conversation with their eyes before the talky twin turns back. "Yeah. It's a cool board."

"I've got a stack of them at my house. They need wheels, but you interested?"

His eyes light up. "Yeah, that'd be—" He jerks back, shooting a frown in Vaughn's direction.

I tilt my head so I can see her better. "Did you just kick your brother?"

"Maybe. So what?" she replies huffily.

"I can't give my shit away?"

"Don't say *shit*," Paisley interjects.

This time my eye-roll is unpreventable. "How old are they?" I look to the twins. "Twelve? Thirteen?"

"Twelve," the one in the white shirt says. He nearly vibrates with excitement.

"So, twelve. That means they know more curse words than I can say in one sentence."

"Maybe, but we don't use them," Paisley says.

The boys cover their mouths, and even Vaughn's mouth takes on a reluctant smile.

"Paisley has a thing about cursing. She's not a fan," Vaughn explains. "We have a swear jar and I don't think Paisley's had to drop one quarter in it—ever."

"Whereas you're losing your shirt to the jar," Paisley retorts.

"Vaughn has a potty mouth," one of the twins says.

"I do not," she protests. "I haven't had to put anything in the jar for a couple of weeks."

"A new record for you," Paisley teases.

"The jar is for a good cause." Vaughn's cute nose tips upward. "The twins' college fund."

I glance at Ty, who's stretched a long arm along the back of the booth. He's wearing a faint grin, the gentle ribbing between the siblings probably reminding him of his own family.

"So back to the skateboard decks," I say. "I've got a bunch of 'em from an old endorsement deal. They're collecting dust and aren't even usable because I have no wheels on them. I can give them away to some strangers or…" I spread my hands innocently, leaving the twins to fill in the blanks.

They take the bait. "Yeah, Vaughn. Why can't he give them to us? They aren't doing him any good."

"Fine. What else do you have lying around the house? We could use a new TV. Maybe a car. We only have the one. How many extras do you have?" Vaughn snaps.

"Five, but I don't think I'll give you a car until our third or fourth date."

"You gotta put out for that," the white-shirt kid says.

"Spencer!" both girls admonish.

They look ready to lay into their brother, but I place a hand in the middle of the table to get everyone's attention. A scolding from his sisters in front of me? This kid will die.

"Nah. A gift is a gift." I lean over the table and pin the pipsqueak with a serious stare. "I'm not making you do anything for those skateboards, am I?"

Spencer shrinks back in his chair. "No, sir."

This kid is trying to show off for me. I get this a lot. Luke does it all the time—trying to appear as bro as bro can be in an effort to make up for whatever he perceives as his own inadequacies. No different than me wearing these stupid-ass pants, I realize in an uncomfortable moment of clarity.

"It doesn't matter how big the gift is," I tell Spencer. "No one does anything to deserve presents. You just give them because you want to make the other person feel good."

I pluck the forgotten bread out of the cheese pot and stick it into my mouth. Like the other twin said, it was done five minutes ago. I eat it, as terrible as it tastes, and then skewer another piece because I'm hungry and the food's here and I'm not going anywhere.

11

HER

"So if you're Spencer, what's your name?" Oakley asks Shane, and I feel bad when I realize I haven't even introduced them.

"It's Shane." Paisley jumps in before I can. "And Shane, Spence, this is Ty and—" She falters and then lowers her voice to a whisper. "Oakley Ford."

My brothers don't even blink. "The singer guy?" Spencer asks.

Oakley grins. "Yeah. The singer guy."

The twins exchange a look and then shrug, completely indifferent. I don't think either one of them has ever listened to an Oakley Ford album in their short lives. They're both into heavy metal, which is probably a good thing because if they were huge Ford fans, they might've caused a scene.

"But you can call me Oak," he says cheerfully, popping some of the bread into his mouth without even dipping it into the cheese pot.

"We're going to need more food," I whisper to Paisley.

"I know," she answers. "I think he might eat as much as both the twins."

"And what about Ty?" I point out.

She blushes. "Oh, yeah, him, too."

Oh, my God! Paisley has a crush on Oakley Ford's bodyguard. I can't wait to tease her about this tonight. I'm not sure I blame her, though—the guy is hot. He's a bit too muscular for me, but his face is Hollywood-pretty with cheekbones like cut glass and dark brown eyes that remind me of melted chocolate.

The waitress shows up, delivering our pots of heated oil and the fresh meats. Ty smiles at her. "Can we have two more platters of those things?"

She nods. "Sure. For you and...?" She turns to Oakley, who's suddenly taken a deep interest in my phone.

"Yeah, both of us," Ty says.

Oakley ducks his head again and somehow scoots closer to me. His jean-clad leg brushes up against mine, and my sweater feels too thin with his arm so close to mine. I swear we're almost sitting on top of each other. I can feel his muscles flex and bunch as he reaches for more food.

"Can you move over?" I wiggle my butt to show him how uncomfortable I am. I need some distance.

"No. I barely have one ass cheek on the bench."

The twins giggle.

"Oh, shit, how much was that?" Oakley grins.

"Now you're just doing it on purpose," I accuse.

"I'm just making a contribution to the twins' college fund," he says with a wink at the boys.

They grin back. And then Shane, who never talks to anyone but Spencer, starts grilling Oakley about the types of decks he has. Are they short or longboards? Midsize cruisers? Does he have a favorite wheel?

It's the most interest I've seen the twins show a stranger in the last couple of years. They used to be reckless and crazy, doing wild stunts on their bikes and boards, but Mom and Dad's deaths made them feel vulnerable and unsafe. They still ride and skate, but not as often and not very far from the house, which is why W's suggestion to drive to Boyle Heights was a nonstarter.

"Nah, I haven't boarded in a couple of years," Oakley admits. "I tried, but the public places are hard for me to keep a low profile at, and if I rent out the park that means kids don't get to use it during that time. I kind of gave it up when I went on tour."

Shane nods, but I don't think he gets it, how limiting Oakley's life must be. I feel a smidge of sympathy for my fake boyfriend.

"Are you going to have to crawl under the table and hide?" I ask.

"Hope not." As he stretches past me to dip a loaded skewer into the cooking pot, his arm brushes against my boob.

My body reacts, and somehow, even through his hoodie, he can tell.

He turns to me.

I freeze.

That's when the flash goes off.

"Time to go, boys and girls," murmurs Tyrese.

I have never, *ever* in my life seen anyone move so fast. One second I'm squished in the booth next to Oakley; the next, he and Tyrese are ushering me and my siblings toward the door.

"I swear that's Oakley Ford's bodyguard!" a girl squeals from the booth next to the one we were just sitting at. "I recognize him from that concert documentary MTV aired last year—"

I don't get to hear the rest of that sentence because we're already on the other side of the room. Tyrese halts only to toss two hundred-dollar bills at the hostess, tells her that "should cover us," and then pushes everyone out the door.

Oakley, meanwhile, is laughing his ass off. "You!" he sputters to his bodyguard. "They recognized *you*."

Tyrese doesn't even crack a smile. He shoves Oakley toward the passenger side of a sleek silver Mercedes. "Get in," he barks then glances at the rest of us. "Claudia's gonna want to have a chat about this. Text me your address and we'll meet you there."

Wait. They're coming to my house? *Why?*

Tyrese doesn't give me a chance to protest—he's already sliding behind the wheel of the Benz and starting the engine.

I turn to my sister, dumbfounded. "What the heck just happened?"

She sighs. "Welcome to the wonderful world of Oakley Ford."

@1doodlebug1 Someone saw Oakley Ford and his bodyguard at Fondue Heaven w some family! Check out this snap!

Tyrese wasn't kidding. Not only did Claudia want to have a chat, apparently it was so important she couldn't even do it over the phone. Oakley's entire publicity team gets on a *helicopter* and flies to El Segundo. Then they take a fleet of Escalades to our modest split-level house and park the three huge vehicles at the curb. As if *that's* not going to draw attention.

Now we're all gathered around my living room, which is way too small to accommodate this many people. Tyrese is standing in the doorway. Paisley and the twins sit on one side of the sectional. Oakley and I sit on the other. And Oakley's PR team looms over us as Claudia rips into her client for his reckless behavior.

"What the hell were you thinking?" she yells in that Mickey Mouse voice of hers. "You are *not* allowed to make these kinds of decisions without consulting me first!"

Oakley crosses his arms and looks bored.

"Vaughn, get on Twitter!" Claudia snaps, and when I open

my mouth to question her, she holds up one hand in warning. "I swear to God, if you ask *why*, I am going to *lose my mind*!" Her face is redder than a tomato.

"Pretty sure you already have," Oakley murmurs under his breath.

I fight hard not to snicker, and rummage around in my canvas bag for my phone. I pull up Twitter and dutifully wait for Claudia's next command.

"Compose a Tweet to Oak about your sister working at his agency," she orders before turning to glare at Oakley. "Are you happy with yourself, Oak? You totally screwed up our timeline! The sister Tweet was supposed to happen *before* the first date!"

One of the assistants—Amy, I think—speaks up soothingly. "It can still work, Claudia. We'll just spin it to say that Vaughn DM'd Oakley her phone number, they went out and *that's* when they realized her sister works at Diamond. Easy fix."

"It'd better be," Claudia mutters, and she looks so upset I feel a bit sorry for her.

I quickly send the Tweet before her cheeks can get any redder.

Vaughn Bennett @OakleyFord OMG! Can't believe my sis works at your agency! #smallworld

One of the phones in Amy's hand buzzes. She hands her stuff to another of Claudia's assistants and types something in the phone.

A second later mine beeps. I read her reply and roll my eyes.

Oakley Ford ✔ **Verified** @VeryVaughn Small world...or maybe it's fate.

Claudia glances at her own phone and releases a long breath. "All right. Good. The two of you need to keep Tweeting for a while so it doesn't look like you were only on there to establish the Paisley connection."

"But my account is private now," I remind her. "Why do we have to keep talking online?"

"Because you still have followers and those people will sell these Tweets to the tabloids."

"No, they won't."

Claudia looks at me like I'm dumb. And she doesn't even bother trying to correct me.

Reality slaps me across the face. Oakley and I are not partners in crime. We're not sharing a moment of anything here. He doesn't Tweet me. He never liked my drawing. I don't even know if he's seen it. It's Amy who is behind all those Tweets and likes and favorites.

I scoot over a little so that my leg isn't so close to his.

He raises his eyebrow and, without looking away from me, holds out his hand. Amy shoots panicked eyes toward Claudia, who purses her lips into a tight frown.

But Oakley wins this round because Amy drops the phone in his hand seconds later.

Mine beeps again, and this time I gasp.

Oakley Ford ✅ **Verified** @VeryVaughn BTW—you looked smoking hot 2nite.

"Really?" I demand, gaping at Oakley.

Claudia reads his latest Tweet and groans. "For Pete's sake, Oakley!"

He blinks innocently. "What? I can't tell my girl she looks hot?"

My heart rate speeds up. Ugh. All the adrenaline from fleeing the restaurant must finally be catching up to me. That's the only explanation for why hearing his raspy voice call me "hot" would turn my heart into a stupid dolphin.

"It's inappropriate," Claudia says in exasperation. "We want lighthearted flirting, not…" She searches for the right word.

"Perviness," Amy supplies.

Claudia nods in agreement. "Keep it PG," she orders.

"How about triple X?" he counters.

"Oakley."

"Just one X?"

"*Oakley.*"

"Fine, I'll stick to R-rated."

I bite my lip to stop from laughing. This guy is incorrigible.

"All right, what now…" Claudia muses. "Well. Obviously you're going to have to go out tomorrow night."

"Two nights in a row?" I balk.

She nods firmly. "Yes, because young love means you can't wait to see each other. You want to spend every minute together."

Um, no thanks. I might be entertained by Oakley's antics right now, but that doesn't mean I want to see him again so soon.

Claudia notices my unhappy expression and flicks up one eyebrow. "If you wanted space, you shouldn't have had your first date in public."

I'm quick to protest. "I was out with my family. *He's* the one who decided to crash our dinner."

Every pair of eyes in the room shifts toward Oakley, who's flipping through a *Cosmo* magazine he grabbed off the coffee table.

He looks up and shrugs. "I was hungry."

12

HIM

BeeBee_OF @OakleyFord_stanNo1 Please take screenshot of her account. It's private.

OakleyFord_stanNo1 @BeeBee_OF Here u go.

BeeBee_OF @OakleyFord_stanNo1 She's not even that cute.

OakleyFord_stanNo1 @BeeBee_OF I kno but we gotta respect Oakley's choices. At least it's not April Umbrella

BeeBee_OF @OakleyFord_stanNo1 true, but I hate her. Why can't it be me?

BeeBee_OF @OakleyFord Pls follow me bae!

Vaughn shows up at my beachfront home around seven. She's wearing jeans with a hole in the knee, a striped tank top and a big scowl.

"I cannot believe you sent a car for me!" she fumes as she enters the huge foyer.

"Hello to you, too," I crack.

"It took us two hours to get here! I could've just taken the bus. It would've been way faster, and then your poor driver wouldn't have had to sit in LA traffic there and back."

She's worried about the driver? That's a first. The last time I sent a Towncar to pick up a date, the chick complained that it wasn't a limo.

"It's Marco's job," I tell Vaughn. "Trust me, he gets paid a fortune to sit in traffic."

She doesn't look appeased, and she barely even glances at her surroundings. Most people oooh and ahhh over the white marble floor, the high ceiling and the sparkling crystal chandelier, but Vaughn couldn't care less.

Tyrese closes the front doors behind her and shoots me a wry grin over her head. *Good luck with this one*, he seems to be saying.

Awesome. We're already off to a great start. "C'mon, let's go to the living room," I say with a sigh.

Vaughn follows me down the wide marble hallway, clutching her oversize canvas purse at her side like she's afraid I'll try to snatch it from her. I lead her into the enormous media room and gesture to the sectional.

"Sit down. You want something to drink?" I drift over to the bar area and open the stainless-steel fridge. "I've got beer, Coke, OJ, water—"

"Water, please."

I grab a bottle of water and a beer for me then join her on the couch.

"You hungry?"

"I ate before I came." She's huddled over her phone, engrossed by whatever's on the screen, but when she hears Ty's footsteps edging toward the door, her head snaps up. "Where are you going?" she asks him, sounding nervous.

"Leaving you two alone." His lips twitch. "Seeing as how you're on a date and all."

"Oh, no, please, stay," she blurts out. "You can hang with us. Let's play Monopoly or something. Please."

My jaw hardens. Seriously? She's literally *begging* Ty not to go. And she wants to play a board game? On a frickin' date? I've never been more insulted in my life.

"Uh…sounds fun, but…nah." Looking like he's choking down laughter, Ty ducks out of the room and shuts the door.

I twist off the bottle cap and glare at my date. "Monopoly? Really?"

Her brown eyes flicker with resignation. "It's fine. We don't have to play. I brought a book."

To punctuate that, she sticks her hand in her monster purse and legit pulls out a paperback. I can't see the title. I don't care what the title is. Because this is fucking unacceptable.

"You realize there are millions of girls out there who would kill to be sitting beside me right now?" I say tightly.

She flips the book open, not even looking at me. "Yeah? Then why are you paying me to do it?"

I bristle at the reminder, but choose to ignore it. "Put the damn book away," I order.

"Why? It's not like this is a real date."

"You just said so yourself—I'm paying you to be here. And I'm not spending my hard-earned money on sitting here and watching you read." I scowl at her. "I decide what we're gonna do."

Her eyes flash for a moment, but she manages to rein in the comeback she clearly wants to hurl my way. Very methodically, she closes the book and puts it back in her bag. Then she primly clasps her hands in her lap. "Fine. What would you like to do, *Oakley*?"

"Call me Oak," I say automatically.

"Pass." She smirks. "I repeat—what would you like to do?"

I smirk back. "Make out."

Vaughn squeaks in horror. "Ew. No."

Ew?

I grit my teeth. "Don't act like you don't think I'm hot. I see the way you check me out."

A blush blooms on her cheeks. "I have *never* checked you out."

"Yeah, right. Yesterday at the fondue place, you couldn't quit staring at my arms." A cocky grin stretches my lips as I lift one arm and flex for her. "You like the gun show, huh?"

Her face turns even redder. "Stop being a jerk."

"Stop pretending I'm not hot."

Vaughn stares at me for a minute, her expression going from embarrassed to outraged to disbelieving. "You're the most conceited person I've ever met."

I shrug.

"And PS? Even if I did think you were hot, I still wouldn't make out with you. I have a boyfriend, remember?"

"Right. Z."

"W," she growls.

I knew that, but I kinda like making her eyes blaze with anger like that. If she's angry at me, then that means she's not ignoring me. I don't like being ignored.

"You're gonna have to make out with me eventually. It's part of the deal," I remind her.

"I have to kiss you. Not make out with you. There's a dif-ference."

I laugh. Is that what she tells herself? "Really? Because our lips will be pressed together. My hands will be somewhere on your body. Maybe your ass. In your hair. My tongue's gonna be in your mouth."

Her eyes flash again and this time the heat in them isn't entirely because she's pissed off. Then again, I could be imagining things.

"I'm good with my tongue, Vaughn." I smile at her. "You're gonna find that out soon enough."

"There will be no tongue," she sputters. "No one said there would be tongue!"

I can't help myself. "You never swap spit with ol' Xylophone? You sure this kid isn't using you as a beard?"

"Oh, my God. It's W, which you know, and what I do with W is none of your damned business." She folds her arms across her chest and stares straight at the blank television screen.

My retort stalls in my throat because her action pushes her tits together in a pretty fantastic way. I wonder if I should tell her that I can now see the white lace of her bra cups peeking over the top of her tank. Nah, what she doesn't know can't hurt her.

Besides, if she's going to be a complete asshole, I should get the pleasure of looking at her rack. I leisurely inspect her as I tip the bottle back. Vaughn is about as far from my type as possible. I like them leggy, with big boobs and a lot of hair. She's got the hair, but she's kind of on the short side—I'd peg her around five and a half feet—and she doesn't have a ton going on upstairs, but what she does have is nice to look at.

"What do you want to watch?" she asks.

I almost say *you* but catch myself in time. She looks like a girl who slaps. Hard. "Movie?"

"Sure."

I pick up the remote and turn the TV on. A few more flicks and I'm at the movie listings. "Pick one."

She picks the first one on the list, which tells me she doesn't care what we're watching. Unfortunately, she's chosen my dad's latest Oscar bait flick, but I don't mention that. It's a World War II epic with long battle scenes. Dad is particularly proud that he survived a Navy SEAL's two-week-long training period to prep for this movie, and he'll tell anyone who'll listen about how he coulda been a SEAL if it wasn't for his whole passion for acting.

The man can't drink tap water, for Christ's sake.

I don't think what movie she picked registers with Vaughn. She doesn't watch the opening credits, but instead spends the entire time with her nose pressed to her phone.

"What're you doing?" I'm annoyed that she's not watching the movie even though I can't stand my dad.

"Checking my boyfriend's Instagram," she says wistfully.

Jesus. Again with the guy. I narrow my eyes. "You're not supposed to have contact with him." I sound jealous, but I'm really not. I just don't want to break in another chick for this pretend gig. It's hard enough with Vaughn. Who knows what kind of female I'd get next? With my luck, it'd be a stage-five clinger who thinks we're going to get married. AKA April Showers but on emotional steroids.

"*Public* contact." She juts her chin toward me defiantly. "No one said I'm not allowed to look at his Instagram. I do everything else Claudia demands, including quitting my job."

"You have a job?" I'm paying the girl a fortune and she has another job?

"I did. I was a waitress at Sharkey's." She crosses her arms again.

Forcibly, I move my eyes to the coffee table. "Never heard of it."

"It's a chain. They serve steak."

I roll my eyes. "Sounds like you loved it."

"I made good money there."

"Did Alphabet love it?"

She scowls. "No, why?"

I pluck her phone from her hand and scan the feed. W is attending college and his feed consists of his "crew," a bunch of backward-hat-wearing bro dudes who are surgically attached to red Solo cups and too much plaid. "He looks like a douche."

She grabs the phone back. "He's not a douche. He's great."

"Okay, tell me what's so great about him," I challenge.

"He's kind...he's funny..." She trails off. "He's kind."

Kind? Man, if any girl ever describes me as *kind* in the same lukewarm tone, I hope someone takes me out back and shoots me. "You said that already."

Her jaw snaps shut and she stares at the television.

That's no fun. "Besides the fact that he's *kind,*" I say sarcastically, "why him out of all the guys you could have?"

She casts me a dirty glance. "You make it sound like there's a buffet of guys and I can just pick out anyone I want. It doesn't work that way in the real world. The person you like has to like you back."

"Are you saying you like W because he was your only choice?" I ask incredulously. I can't believe that. This girl? She's got to have a few of the high school guys after her. I never went to an actual high school, but Vaughn's a babe in her own way. I'd totally want to tap that ass between classes.

"He wasn't my only choice. I like him. I don't have to justify my feelings to you."

"How'd you meet?"

"Why do you want to know?"

Because I'd rather shave my legs than watch my dad act. "I figure the two of us should get to know each other, seeing as we have to spend an entire year together. Sitting in complete silence during all our dates doesn't sound like a boatload of fun. Not to mention you may want to consider being a little nicer, considering that I'm paying you a fucking fortune for this gig."

Her brown eyes widen and her plump lips fall open, forming a little circle—one that has me conjuring up some dirty ideas.

Then she scoffs. "Oh, come on, like you're actually the one paying."

"Who the hell else would it be? The tooth fairy?"

"I thought it was Jim."

"Who do you think writes checks to Jim?" I scrunch my eyebrows. Is she that clueless?

"Oh."

I guess so. "Yeah, *oh*."

"What is it that you want to know?"

The question comes out as a sigh, as if it's such a burden to talk to me, and suddenly I'm done. There are worse things than watching a film starring my dad, and one of them is trying to drag out boring details from an ordinary girl who has to be paid to sit and watch a movie with me.

"Whatever. Let's just watch the movie," I mutter irritably.

We both stare at the screen again, but I don't think we're watching the same film. Instead of seeing Dad point a gun at a Nazi deserter, my eyes conjure up the sight of him spotting my Double Platinum record on the mantel next to his Oscar. *What the hell is this trash doing here?* Mom titters. *Honey, Oak's second album sold another million copies.* Dad sneers. *He sings songs that preteens buy for ninety-nine cents.* He pulls it off the mantel and shoves it at Mom. *Find somewhere else for that shit.* The scene flips from the living room to the deck, where I come home early from the studio to find him screwing his latest assistant over the edge of Mom's balcony. No wonder she gets the place redecorated all the time. There's a fade cut and a new action shot of Dad standing at the end of Jim's conference table, telling me that I'm a dumbass if I sign the contract for three more records.

And I'd have killed myself if I stayed in that house one more minute with him, so I signed the contract. It takes money to fund a legal emancipation, after all.

"This movie's kinda boring," Vaughn remarks, breaking into the lame drama that's replaying itself in my head. She tugs on her messy ponytail.

I stretch my arm across the back of the sofa until the ends of her rich dark brown hair brush the back of my hand. "I'll make sure to pass that critique along to my dad."

She pinks up immediately. "Oh. Oh, my God. I forgot Dustin Ford was your dad. Is your dad, I mean. That must be awesome."

Unbelievable. The first sign of enthusiasm from her and it's toward my asshole old man? "Yup. The one and only Dustin Ford." Do I sound bitter? I clamp my mouth shut.

"Oh," she says for the third time tonight. But her embarrassment lasts only a beat, because she rallies to add, "Well, I'm not going to pretend I like it just because he's your father."

I don't tell her that it's the one nice thing she's said to me tonight. Instead, I reach for the remote and turn the movie off.

She picks up her bottle of water and rolls it between her hands. "Should we try the get-to-know-you thing again?"

"Sure." I flip my hand over and rub a few errant strands of hair between my fingers. Her hair does seem unreal. It's a deep mahogany and there are a dozen shades of red and brown in it. It's probably from a bottle. Nothing out here is natural.

"Okay, me first. Why wouldn't you shake my hand?"

"I'm not a fan of being touched." Ironic given that I'm surreptitiously fondling her hair. I continue to do it anyway. "I'm constantly being grabbed when I go out, even though I have Big D and Tyrese at my side. When I'm in private, I prefer to be the one to initiate contact. It's nothing personal. And now it's my turn. Why are you doing this?"

"Money." She looks at me under her lashes. "My parents were kinda irresponsible and left us with a lot of debt. Paisley's held our family together and it'd be incredibly selfish of me to *not* step up when I had the opportunity."

I rub my forehead as the implication hits me. I'm being mean to an orphan. A family of orphans. And it doesn't escape me that we're both kind of in the same situation—two teenagers without any parents in the picture. My folks aren't dead, but they might as well be, considering how often I see them.

"My turn again," she says. She turns toward me, pulling a knee up onto the sofa and tucking her foot under a jean-clad thigh.

"Why are you doing this? Out of all the people in the world, I would think that you'd have the least amount of trouble finding someone to go out with—even a 'normal' person." She air quotes the word *normal*.

It's hard to hide that I'm fondling her hair when she's staring at me, so I pull my arm away on the pretense of reaching for my beer, which tastes like warm piss.

"Everyone in LA says they want someone normal, whatever that is, but in the end they don't because creative types are made differently, live differently. I'm crazy, and everybody else I run with is slightly crazy. You have to be to want to live in a fishbowl and have no privacy. Where ninety-nine percent of your relationships—whether they're friendships or fuck buddies—are set up for publicity purposes."

I throw back the rest of the warm-ass beer before continuing. "That's a long way of answering your question, but the short answer is no normal girl can handle me." Vaughn opens her mouth to object, but I barrel on. "I'm not saying it's because I'm great, even though I am—"

She snickers.

"But it's because she won't be patient enough to understand there are times that I get so lost in the music I can't remember to eat, drink or take a shit. All I want to do is sing and play my guitar until my fingers bleed and my voice is sore." I can't count the times that April would pound on my home studio door and whine that she was bored. "No normal girl is gonna be able to handle it when I go on tour and find a naked groupie in my hotel suite who got my room number from the bellhop she blew in the stairwell. No normal girl is gonna be able to stand the long concert tours unless she wants to come with, and I promise you by the third tour stop, she'll be begging to be left behind because she's tired of the long hours of doing jack shit followed by listening to the same damn set list followed by an endless amount of glad-handing with the tour promoters followed by another flight, bus ride, radio, print and television interview where the people ask the same damn question a million times. So that's why you're here and not someone else."

She's silent for a long time, and when she does open her mouth, she says something completely unexpected. "That was actually two long answers. Not a short one and a long one."

"Does it answer your question?" I mutter.

Vaughn bites her bottom lip. "Yeah. It does."

13

HER

1doodlebug1 @OakleyFord_stanNo1 They were out together again? Any pics?

OakleyFord_stanNo1 @1doodlebug1 No! just the tweet from @OakleyFord.

1doodlebug1 @OakleyFord_stanNo1 is it serious? R they going out together? Why no pics?

OakleyFord_stanNo1 @1doodlebug1 Ugh. I kno.

Notification of date number three doesn't come from Claudia or Oakley. Instead, it's a khaki-clad delivery guy who sticks a white box with a big black ribbon in my hands and orders me to *sign here*.

I barely scrawl the tip of my finger across the screen before he's down the steps and climbing into his white delivery van.

"Thanks," I call after him, but it's a wasted effort.

Gingerly, I carry the box into the kitchen where I've been answering Tweets for the last two hours. Claudia sent me a message this morning ordering me to respond to my fans—the ones that made the cut before the account went private.

I have no fans. I have…girls who went crazy after Oakley Tweeted from his account that *next time he'd remember to feed me.*

If I could tell those girls the truth—that Oakley is a condescending jerk who thinks that normal girls can't handle a guy like him because we'd be too jealous or impatient or unsympathetic—they'd move on to crushing on someone else.

One of them is already calling W hot. I had to force myself to delete a response that told the girl to keep her grubby mitts off my boyfriend. Because I'm not supposed to have a boyfriend.

I settled for Tweeting back responses like "I don't know what's happening, either," and "This is all new to me."

Paisley called at noon to tell me how happy Claudia was with my *performance*. That put me in a bad mood, which this fancy box with its set of interlocking embossed GGs on the top only worsens.

I'm kind of scared to open it. The most designer thing I own is one of my mom's Coach purses. Until a few days ago, I was a waitress at Sharkey's, serving steaks in borrowed polyester black pants that are too tight and a white button-down shirt that's too big.

I flip the lid over the card again to make sure it's got my name on it. It does. The envelope is addressed to *Vaughn* in beautiful calligraphy. The card says, "Wear this tonight."

The bow comes undone with one tug and I lift the top of the box off. Inside, under a layer of tissue paper is…it's a shirt…I guess. I hold it up and can pretty much see through the lace fabric to the back door. Underneath it is a short black skirt and sky-high pumps.

My stomach sinks. So our third date must be in public.

Since I'm not allowed to have direct contact with Claudia, I text my sister.

Where am I going tonight?

There's no response. She must be in a meeting.

I carry the items upstairs and lay the two pieces of clothing on the bed. I slip the shoes on and they're weirdly too big and too small at the same time. My toes are squished into the pointy toes, but there's a gap between my heel and the back of the shoe. Plus, they're so high I feel like I'm tipping forward. The only thing keeping them on my feet is the wide cuff around the ankle.

I try to maneuver around the bedroom, but my ankles feel unstable and strange. I look about as sexy as a horse.

I try on the rest of the outfit—what little of it there is. The shirt is just as sheer as I'd feared, with lace flowers placed around a few strategic places in front. The rest is a see-through mesh. I hate it. It's probably the most expensive thing that's ever touched my skin, but I hate it.

I pull on the skirt and then look at myself in the mirror hanging on the back of my door. I look like…an awkward reject from a Nutcracker casting call.

If I'm going to have my picture taken tonight—which I assume is the purpose of this public date and my specially couriered outfit—then I need some help. Carrie might be my closest friend, but Kiki is the one who does everyone's hair and makeup at sleepovers.

Kiki, when you're done with class, can u come over?

She texts back immediately.

Will Oakley Ford be there?

No. I'm supposed to see him tonight. He sent me this.

I take a picture of myself, arm across my boobs because the appliqued flowers are not big enough.

OMG! Is that Gucci?

Yeah, but u can c my boobs thru the shirt. I can't go out like this.

Oakley Ford sent u a sxy outfit from Gucci?

Can u come ovr or not?

YYYYYYY!

Kiki must break several traffic laws, because she shows up thirty minutes after school lets out.

"Hey, girl," she squeals when I open the door. "Is he here?"

"No."

"Oh, okay," she says with obvious disappointment, but she rallies immediately, lifting her backpack. "I brought my stuff. How much time do we have?"

I pull her inside. "The twins won't be home for another forty-five. Paisley doesn't come home until six. Sometimes seven or eight, depending on what kind of work they have for her. Why? Do you need to be someplace?"

Kiki laughs and trots up the stairs. "Not until your fam gets home, Vaughn. When are you going out?"

"I don't know," I admit.

Her eyes widen. Not in dismay, but excitement. "This is so amazing! It's a mystery date. He sends you clothes and then picks you up and whisks you off to someplace wild. God, I wish Justin could be more spontaneous. His idea of a date these days is to drive me over to Colin's house so the two of them can go over their fantasy lineup for the weekend. And the last thing he bought me was a grande mocha at Starbucks."

I bite my lip because I want to tell her that that's a hundred times better than my fake date with Oakley last night. I settle for, "Justin's not so bad."

She snorts. "He's no Oakley Ford, that's for sure."

We reach my room, where Kiki inspects the clothes Claudia sent.

"I don't think I can wear these," I admit.

"Why not?" She studies the shirt and then the skirt. The shoes with the ankle cuff and buckle get the most attention. I think I see a spot of drool on the side of her mouth.

"It's see-through and I'm not comfortable with a bunch of fancy famous people looking at my nips."

"How about a black tank?"

The only thing Kiki and I manage to find that's remotely acceptable is an American Eagle bralette. All my tanks are the athletic kind and even I can tell that's not going to work under the mesh and delicate embroidery.

Kiki makes me put the bra and shirt on and then sets out to put my hair in curlers.

"Do you have a look you want me to copy or should I just do what I think is best?"

"Just do whatever."

"Goodie. I'm going to go with big loose curls, a smoky eye and then a mauve lip. How do you feel about fake eyelashes?"

"I tried to wear them to prom last year and found them on W's shoulder at the after-party."

She laughs. "We're gonna skip those."

"Good call."

I watch as Kiki expertly sections off my hair and starts curling it. For as long as I've known her, she's known she's wanted to do hair and makeup. After graduation, she plans to attend the Aveda Institute.

Justin, her boyfriend, is going to UCLA, majoring in accounting.

Tracy feeds into the blonde stereotype—no matter how many times we explain to her that the sun is a star and we orbit around the star, she doesn't believe us because we can't see the sun at night, and stars are visible at night. But even Tracy knows what she's doing after graduation. She's going to USC to study to be a fashion buyer.

I'm the one who graduated early. Everyone assumes it's because I know exactly what I want to do, but they couldn't be more wrong.

I shift uncomfortably in the chair.

"Did I hurt you?" Kiki peers into the mirror with a worried expression.

"No. Sorry."

"Just let me know." She flips another curl over my shoulder. "You have such gorgeous hair. What's Oakley's favorite thing about you?"

That he can treat me like a piece of crap and I don't complain? Of course, I can't say that, but I don't have any other answer. I don't think that guy likes *anything* about me. "What's Justin's favorite thing about you?"

"My boobs. What do you think it is?" She giggles and then drags her fingers through my heated curls.

"Nah, I'm sure it's your killer softball pitch." Kiki's the starting pitcher on Thomas Jefferson High's girls' softball team.

"That, too." One by one she turns my straight locks into bouncy curls. "So does Oakley like your hair or your legs or your eyes? I want to highlight whatever it is that he likes."

I can tell she's not giving up until I reveal something. "He likes that I'm normal."

"Hmmm." She ponders this for a second. "I can see that, what with you wanting to be a teacher. That's pretty normal. Now close your eyes." She waves the bottle of hairspray in front of me.

I do as she commands. If Oakley did like me because I wanted to be a teacher, that would just be one more topping on the metaphorical cake that I'm baking for him.

"Did you know that Justin and me did it for the first time to Oakley's song 'Do Her Right'?" Kiki says casually as she dabs my face with the fat end of a pink sponge shaped like an egg.

"Um, no. I did not know that." Questions such as *What'd it feel like? Was it good?* burn at the tip of my tongue. Because Paisley hated it and I think she wishes she never had sex. Meanwhile, W wants me to give it up to him *right now* and I don't think I can. I don't know if I'll ever be ready.

"Justin can't hear it without getting a chubby."

We stare at each other for a full minute before cracking up. The idea of Justin, her big linebacker boyfriend, getting turned on while listening to Oakley Ford croon that he's going to *do her, do her, do her right*, is so hilarious that I laugh until tears form.

"How many people know this?" I choke out as I try to catch my breath.

"Everyone," she admits. "Apparently it came on in the locker room, I don't know why, and Justin popped a boner. Kirk Graham was teasing him about it at lunch a week ago."

"Maybe we can get Oakley to give you guys an in-person concert," I joke.

Kiki giggles. "I don't think Justin would be able to handle it."

I wonder what Oakley would think of this story? He'd look down at it, I decide. Oakley probably only gets an erection if he's lying on a pool of hundred dollar bills, and Victoria's Secret models are prancing around his bed.

Kiki helps me into the tutu skirt, which is surprisingly soft for all its volume. She also has me stuff cotton balls in the back of the shoes and in the toes until they fit okay. Then we go downstairs and I practice walking from one end of the living room to the other.

"Do you mind if I wait until Oakley comes?" She perches on the recliner situated by the front window.

An invisible hand squeezes my heart as I lay eyes on my dad's favorite chair. If he were around, I wouldn't be dressed up like a strange ballerina waiting for a pretend date to happen. I'd be at USC with W, taking classes in...crap, I don't know. My dad would've figured it out for me. Or Mom. Or both of them.

Instead, I'm lost.

"Sure," I say dully.

Fortunately, Kiki's so distracted by Oakley's impending arrival she doesn't notice my lack of enthusiasm. "So what's he like?"

"Oakley?" I ask.

"No. The mayor of LA." She rolls her eyes. "Of course I mean Oakley."

He's a jerk who can't be bothered to give me his phone number, even though we're supposed to date for an entire year. He demanded I pay attention to him. He kept making fun of W, a guy he's never even met. He's incredibly egotistical. Do I like his guns? Who says that?

He also thinks he's better than the rest of us because no *normal* girl could handle him. Although...when he went through the litany of crazy things his fans do, I felt he might be right.

Then there was that weird, bitter note about his father. And I caught him rubbing my hair last night. I feel like maybe I should report that to W, because Oakley and I were alone and he shouldn't touch me when we're alone—not even my hair, because it does strange things to my stomach.

I don't share any of this with Kiki, because we don't have the kind of relationship where I can tell her all of my ugly inner thoughts without fear of judgment. I don't know if I have that relationship with anyone. So I go with, "I don't know him yet."

She nods sagely as if that makes complete sense to her. "It's different when you don't grow up with them. I sometimes feel like Justin and I know too much about each other. Is that why you broke up with W?"

"I didn't break up with W," I exclaim. "Is that what people are saying?"

She shoots me a glance that says I must be kidding. "You're the one dating Oakley Ford. No way that W broke up with you."

"But I didn't meet Oakley until after we were broken up." I grimace. W won't like that. He doesn't like to look bad in front of his friends. Hence the no cheating accusations. But this is worse. W wouldn't want people thinking that he was thrown over for some famous guy.

"Then why did you break up? Did he cheat on you? Did he end it because you wouldn't enroll at USC?"

Oh, crap. I don't know what to say. When my phone rings, I answer it without even caring that it says "Blocked Caller" because at this point, I'll take salvation via telemarketer.

"Hello?"

"Ty will pick you up at eight thirty."

It takes a moment for Oakley's voice to register.

"Tonight?"

"No, tomorrow morning," he mutters sarcastically. "Yeah, tonight."

"But...what time am I getting home?"

"Are you five?"

Any warm, fuzzy feeling that may have sprung up because he saved me from an awkward situation dies an immediate death. I turn my back to Kiki, who's taken to staring out the window to catch her first glimpse of Oakley. "Are you always this much of a jerk?" I hiss.

"Yeah, pretty much."

I close my eyes and pray for patience. "Where are we going?"

"Private party. Like the outfit?"

I blink in surprise. Oakley picked this out? "Not particularly."

"Of course you don't."

14

HER

"I thought you said we were going to a party." From the back seat of Oakley's Escalade, I anxiously peer out the heavily tinted window. "What is this place?"

Tyrese, who's behind the wheel, just stopped the SUV on an industrial street in south LA. It's not an area I've been to before. I can hear the bass, but there's no sign anywhere on the building, just a black steel door that looks kind of ominous.

Beside me, Oakley wears an annoyed expression. "It's a club."

"So we're not going to a party?"

"It's a party. At a club. What part of this don't you understand, baby?"

I glare at him. "Don't talk to me like I'm stupid. And don't call me baby."

He just smirks.

Ugh! I want to *punch* this guy! I don't care that he's paying me a fortune to date him, or that he looks superhot right now in his faded jeans and forest-green T-shirt that looks like it might have been stitched on his body. None of that takes away from the fact that he's a total jackass sometimes.

"I just want to know what I'm about to walk into," I say tightly. "Who owns this place?"

"Who knows? Promoters put together private events. Parties, record launches, small concerts." He shrugs.

I wrinkle my forehead. "And Claudia wants this to be the venue for our first public date?"

"Yes. This is what she wants," Oakley answers impatiently. "Ty—you ready?"

My pulse speeds up. "Ready for what?" I squeak.

"Just making sure the paps aren't lurking around," Oakley says. "We give 'em the photo op when we're leaving, not arriving."

"Why?"

"Because if they see us now, they might find a way to sneak into the club and get pics we *don't* want to give 'em." He looks at me like I'm dumb for not knowing that.

I am *so* sick of everyone in his fancy-pants world treating me like I've got rocks for brains. But instead of lashing out, I sit there and grit my teeth and remind myself that I'm getting paid twenty grand a month for this.

No, Kiki, there's not one thing that Oakley Ford likes about me. And I'm perfectly fine with that because he's a prick with a capital P.

Oakley and I don't get out of the car until Ty gives us the all-clear. I almost fall five times on the way to the scary black door, and I don't miss the amusement in my "boyfriend's" eyes every time I wobble on the insanely high heels he sent me.

"Could you pick a pair of flats next time?" I mutter.

"Nah. Your legs look wicked hot in those heels."

This time I don't feel any tingles at his use of the word *hot*. I'm starting to think he throws it around like candy on Halloween. Every girl who shows up probably gets a compliment.

Tyrese thumps one meaty fist against the steel door, which opens almost immediately. Another version of Ty appears—a huge, muscly man with trees for arms, only he has dreadlocks instead of a shaved head. He glances at Oakley, nods, and opens the door wider.

I smell the smoke the minute we step into the dimly lit hallway. "Is something on fire?" I sniff.

For some reason, that makes him laugh hysterically. Instead of answering, he surges forward. I chase after him on my death heels and pray I don't twist an ankle.

The corridor opens onto a dark room with a bar on one side, a stage on the other and dozens of tables and couches in between. It's not very crowded, but there's a decent amount of people here, laughing, smoking and shouting to each other over the music. I don't recognize the band that's playing, but the beats are familiar. I've heard this tune or something like it on the radio for the past five years.

The other thing that's familiar is the number of people I recognize, not because I've met them before but because I've seen them in television shows, on magazine covers, in movies. In LA, you can often catch sight of a celebrity if you go to the right places, but the sheer number of them in one place has me feeling superinsecure, even in my expensive designer outfit.

It makes me snappish toward Oakley. "It's illegal to smoke indoors in LA."

One eyebrow flicks up. "You want me to call the cops?"

His disdain ticks me off. "I'm getting cancer just standing here," I grumble. "My lungs have gone from fine to stage four. Maybe the next time we go out, you can take me someplace where I don't have to worry about dying from secondhand smoke."

Ty snickers.

I turn to scowl at him, too. "It's not funny. If I worked for the city, I'd shut this place down in a heartbeat."

"Good thing you don't work for the city, then," Oakley says dismissively. "You work for *me*, remember?"

Jackass.

He hustles me toward the bar area, with Ty trailing behind us like an obedient puppy. I try to keep my eyes in my head as I brush by a gorgeous model who's laughing with a singer. My cheeks are burning. I can only imagine what people are thinking about me—how ordinary I look next to these beautiful girls. How indifferently Oakley's treating me.

I wish I could leave.

At the long counter, we get into our second argument of the night. Or maybe it's the third. I've lost count.

"What's your poison? Beer? Daiquiri? Something harder?"

"None of the above," I reply through clenched teeth. "I'm seventeen."

"So?"

"So that means I'm a minor. I'm not allowed to drink." I've had the occasional beer at a party, but for the most part, Paisley and I try to set a good example for the twins. Kiki's boyfriend once suggested since my parents "weren't around" that I could host all the parties. I didn't speak to him for a week and no one ever brought it up again.

Oakley rolls his eyes. "I can't believe my girlfriend is such a prude."

I can't believe my boyfriend is such a douche!

I swallow the retort and paste on a smile for the approaching bartender. He's got spiky hair, a scruffy goatee and tattoos on his neck. He notices Oakley and grins. "Oak! Long time, man."

"Too long," Oakley answers absently. His green eyes are conducting a sweep of the room. He barely glances at the bartender as he adds, "Lagavulin sixteen on the rocks for me. Virgin anything for my girl."

My cheeks heat, because he put extra emphasis on the word *virgin*. Jerk. "I'll have a Coke, please," I tell Spiky Hair.

"Coming right up."

I should've known by the smoking that being a minor wouldn't prevent Oakley from getting a drink. At least we have Ty to drive us.

We wait for our drinks. Oakley's gaze keeps searching the room as if there's someone specific he's looking for. I try to avoid making eye contact with any famous person, because I know I don't belong here.

"Are you meeting someone?" I demand. Why am I even here if he wants to hook up with another girl? And if he does, do I just stand here like a dummy and pretend not to be bothered by it? That's a lot of pretending to do.

He glances over, blinking, as if he just remembered I'm standing beside him. "What? Of course not."

"You sure? Because I totally wouldn't mind. I can hang out with Ty while you go off and 'cheat'—" I air-quote that "—on me."

His lips twitch. "Aw, baby, I would never, ever cheat on my little love muffin." He tugs playfully on one of my Kiki-created curls and goes back to studying the crowd.

I sigh.

The bartender slaps a Scotch and a glass of Coke on the counter. I take a sip, grateful for the cool soda that slides down my throat. It's hot in here. And Oakley continues to ignore me. This date sucks.

"Oak. Hey." A male voice sounds from our right, and then a guy with messy dark hair and a lean body clad in jeans and a Green Day T-shirt appears in front of us.

I feel Oakley tense up beside me. "S'up, Luke."

The guy—Luke—offers a tentative smile. "Not much. You?"

My date shrugs. He doesn't say another word, not even to introduce me to his friend.

"I'm Luke," the guy finally says, awkwardly sticking out his hand.

I give it a quick shake. "Vaughn."

"Nice to meet you."

"Same." I'm happy to meet him, because he looks…well, *not famous* and that's a huge relief.

Oakley suddenly speaks up. "Luke, keep my girl company for a sec, will ya?" And then he's gone.

He literally takes off and disappears into the crowd, leaving me with a total stranger. Ty's job is to protect Oakley, so he stalks off, too, making things even more uncomfortable.

"So." Luke's finger toys with the label of his beer. The corners are curling over from the condensation. "How do you know Oak?"

"Sorry, what?" I'm not paying attention because I'm too busy trying to figure out where Oakley went. I finally spot his blond head near the DJ station. He's talking to someone, but I can't see who it is.

"How do you know Oak?" Luke repeats.

I force myself to focus on him. "Um, we met online."

"Yeah?" He looks surprised.

I nod and stick to the story Claudia and her minions concocted. "I Tweeted him some fan art and I guess it caught his eye. He Tweeted back, and now we're kinda going out."

Luke pauses. Then his lips quirk up in a wry smile. "Does anyone actually believe that story?"

I narrow my eyes at him, glad that no one from Oakley's management team is standing around. Claudia would give this performance a D. "I hope so, because it's the truth."

"If you say so."

"It is," I insist.

He laughs. "Look, Vaughn—it was Vaughn, right?" When I nod, he keeps going. "I've known Oak a long time. He has assistants doing all his social media, so if you caught anyone's eye, it sure as hell wasn't his."

The accusation brings a jolt of resentment. I can't believe he's calling me a liar.

You are a liar.

Ugh. I totally am.

I decide to nip this dangerous conversation in the bud by asking, "How do *you* know Oakley?"

"I'm with the studio band," he admits. "I played bass on some of the tracks in *Ford*."

"Oh, that's cool. Do you ever go on tour with him?"

"I toured with him for *Ford*, but only for the West Coast leg." His brown eyes focus on someone in the distance.

Oakley's making his way back to us, and he's not alone. The man at his side looks familiar. I can't place him, but I *know* that face. He has dark eyes, close-cropped hair and skin so smooth and flawless that I kinda want to ask him what kind of moisturizer he uses.

As they get closer, something finally clicks in my brain. It's Donovan King, one of the biggest music producers in the world. Normally I wouldn't be able to pick a producer out of a lineup, but I recognize King because he also used to be an R & B artist before he started producing. He sold, like, a gazillion albums before he retired from the limelight.

"That's King," Luke murmurs to me. "Oak's wanted to work with him for years."

They reach us, and I notice that Oakley seems unusually nervous. He's fidgeting with his drink, the ice cubes clinking against the side of his glass, and his normally playful eyes are dead serious. He gives Luke a slight jerk of the head, an unspoken command to get lost. Luke's frown is only noticeable because I was looking for it—it's obvious he and Oakley are on the outs, and I feel bad for him as he excuses himself and saunters off.

"This is Vaughn," Oakley tells King. "Vaughn, Donovan King. I was just telling him what a fan of his work you are and how much you wanted to meet him."

My brow furrows, but Oakley is practically pleading at me with his eyes. *Play along*, he seems to be saying.

So I give King a smile and say, "A really *big* fan. I loved the album you produced for Saturn's Rising." Then I paste on an interested expression and pray that he doesn't ask me about anything else he's done, because I've tapped out my knowledge. The only reason I know he did the SR album is because the twins were obsessed with that band when they debuted last summer.

"Thanks. Good times, cutting that record with the guys." King's voice is as silky smooth as his skin, and deeper than I expected. "They're very serious about their music."

I keep smiling like a dummy, because I don't know what to say to that. I can't play an instrument. Heck, I can't even whistle.

"What do you think of the band playing now?" King asks, slanting his head toward the stage.

I try not to grimace. What do I know about music? When we're watching a singing show on television, I always pick the wrong singer to win.

Oakley's brows are drawn so close together, I'm concerned the lines in his forehead are going to be permanent. That makes me even more nervous.

"I only know what I like," I finally answer.

The side of King's mouth tips up. "You and ninety percent

of America. That's what makes music sell. What is it that you like about Oak's music?"

"What makes you think I like Oakley's music?" I blurt out.

The band stops playing at precisely that moment and I want to crawl under one of the tables. Oakley steps forward as if to say something, but stops when King bursts out laughing.

"I like this girl." He flips his thumb toward me.

"Me, too." Oakley's smile is tight and fake and I have to force myself not to shift away when he wraps an uncomfortable arm around my shoulders. "Even if she does think my music is shit."

Does anyone buy this story? I hear Luke saying. If I was truthful, the answer would be *not likely*.

"That's not true." I wish the floor would open up and swallow me. Where's a stupid earthquake when you need one? My cheeks feel hot and I know it's not from the crush of people in the club. I'm supposed to be convincing everyone that I completely adore Oakley, and I'm failing at it.

I sneak a glance at him for direction, but he's staring toward the stage. If it wasn't for his arm around me, we'd look like we hated each other. Maybe we still look like that.

"I listened to *Ford* on repeat when I was fifteen," I confess. "It was my entire life and it's embarrassing to admit that. I'm trying to be cool about standing here next to him, talking to Donovan King, but it's a little much for me."

King's laughter is replaced with a bemused expression I can't fully decipher. "That's some real talk right there." He raises his glass in my direction. "You don't get much of that in our business. Too many people just want to hear pretty things, but it's the honest stuff that punches you in the gut and sticks with you. So tell me, what do you think of this band?"

"It's…" I struggle for a response. I'm so out of my element

here, it's nuts. It's like surfing on C Street as a first-timer. Might as well call the rescue squad right now.

"Go on. Say whatever you're thinking," King encourages.

"It's not for me. It's too…"

"Common," Oakley interjects. "We've heard it a million times before from a million other bands. Including mine."

And he's right. That's exactly what doesn't sit well with me.

King nods. "All music today sounds the same. That's the problem."

Oakley leans toward King, squishing me in the process. His face is so intent on the record producer that I'm not sure he realizes I'm here anymore. "Except for yours. I'd love to get into the studio with you," he says gruffly.

King stares out into the crowd.

Oh, man, this is awkward. I haven't felt this uncomfortable since freshman year when Leigh Mariner cried at lunch after she saw her ex-boyfriend with his arm around his new girlfriend.

Oakley tries again. "Your work is great, man. We need to do something together."

I can see the wheels turning in King's head. *How do I turn this kid down without making it into a big deal…*

Finally, he tilts his head, twisting his body a bit so Oakley has a harder time seeing his face.

I try to slink farther away from the bar counter.

"Your work skews a little young for me. I don't think we'd mesh. Have you thought about giving Lance Buchanan a call? He's producing sounds a lot like you've done in the past."

Frustration clouds Oakley's eyes. "I'm making new sounds."

King sighs. It's obvious he's tired of this conversation. Me, I just want to disappear. Can I say I need to use the ladies' room?

"Call me in a few years. I'm sure we can do something then."

Oakley's smile is tighter than a drum. "Sure thing."

King turns to me and *his* smile is genuine. "Nice to meet you, Vaughn. Don't let this world change you, 'kay?" He squeezes my hand and then wanders off.

An awkward silence falls over us after he's gone. I feel Oakley's resentful gaze bore into the side of my head, and it's so unbearable that I frantically search for something to say.

"It's loud in here," I offer lamely.

"Then don't talk," he suggests with a glare.

15

HIM

1doodlebug1 @OakleyFord_stanNo1 Is she a model? Wasn't that Gucci?

OakleyFord_stanNo1 @1doodlebug1 Definitely G. And trashy 2 bc hello, club? Dressed like that? Ho.

1doodlebug1 @OakleyFord_stanNo1 ho foshoe

1doodlebug1 @OakleyFord_stanNo1 that dress tho. So gorg

OakleyFord_stanNo1 @1doodlebug1 forget the dress. Can we talk abt how his hand is on her ass. That lucky btch.

1doodlebug1 @OakleyFord_stanNo1 I kno! Last night dreamt it was me.

OakleyFord_stanNo1 @1doodlebug1 same

As usual, everyone is pissed off at me. It's not even nine in the morning, and already I've been yelled at by three different people.

My conversation with Jim went something like this:

"I told you to stay away from King! I've been greasing the wheels behind the scenes! And you show up at his club like a spoiled brat asking for handouts, ruining all the progress I've made! I'm your manager! That means I do the managing! All I ask—no, *demand* in return is that you keep your mouth shut, write your goddamn songs and leave the business to the grown-ups!"

I hung up on him halfway through his tirade, because I don't need to take that abuse. I'm the client. The client is always right. End of story.

Claudia wouldn't let me hang up on her, though. I tried, and she called back immediately, picking up midrant.

"A club, Oak! On your first public date! With your sweet, wholesome girlfriend! No. No, no, no! Your decision-making privileges are revoked! From now on, you do what *I* say! That's why you hired me! I refuse to be sabotaged by my own client! TMI photographed you and Vaughn leaving the club at midnight—this does *not* look good, Oakley! Social media is speculating that Vaughn is a party girl! We need to kill this story! She's supposed to be fixing your reputation, and instead you're destroying *hers*!"

Then she hung up on *me*.

If I'm being honest, that's the only thing I feel bad about. Not about destroying Vaughn's rep, because that's insane. Her image is fine. One night at a club isn't going to change that, and the pap photos that showed up online this morning were harmless. Just a few shots of me opening the Escalade door for Vaughn, the two of us getting in the car. My hand was resting on her lower back, and at one point she touched my arm.

Harmless.

No, what's making me feel like crap is the way I treated her last night. I acted like a jerk. Ignored her. Snapped at her after that disastrous run-in with King even though she tried to play the game. Ignored her some more. Used her to try to impress King.

The only reason I even went to the club was because someone texted me that King would be there. I figured having Vaughn by my side would show him that I'm serious. I mean, if I'm serious about my girl, then I must be serious about my music, right?

Except it backfired. He turned me down again. Squashed me like a bug under his thousand-dollar shoes.

Vaughn hadn't said a single word during the car ride home.

With a loud groan, I stalk down to the basement to my home studio and throw open the door. There are a couple of couches in the corner of the soundproofed room, near the endless row of guitar stands. I swipe my favorite Gibson off its stand and sink onto the sofa cushions.

If I had her phone number, I would text her to apologize. But I don't, and I'm too embarrassed to get Ty or Big D to call her for me. Ty already gave me a long lecture after we dropped Vaughn home. "You can't treat girlfriends like props, brother. Even fake girlfriends."

I spend the next hour fooling around on the guitar. There's been a melody in my head since last night, but I can't seem to make it work. The lyrics don't come, either. I'm still blocked, and the ball of frustration in my gut grows bigger and bigger as I absently strum the guitar.

Maybe it's not the creative block that's getting to me today. Maybe it's something else.

Gritting my teeth, I grab my phone off the side table and dial Big D. "Hey," I say when he picks up. "Get Vaughn on the line for me, will ya?"

"Gotcha."

I end the call then sit there impatiently until Big D's heavy footsteps finally sound on the stairs. He strides into the studio and holds out his cell.

"Thanks," I say.

"No problemo. Shout when you're done."

He ducks out of the room, and I take a breath before speaking into the phone. "Morning," I say lightly.

Vaughn is nowhere near as friendly as I'm trying to be. "Do we have another date today?" she asks without saying hello.

She sounds alert for how early it is. I wonder why she didn't sleep in. She's taking the year off from school and she's not waiting tables anymore. I mean, she's pretty much just on call for me, so there's no reason for her to get up before noon.

On call for you?

Guilt weighs me down. Okay, that's kind of a raw deal for her, being forced to sit around and wait until Claudia decides what she's doing and when.

Then again, she's getting paid a lot of money to be on standby.

"Nah, we don't have a date," I answer. "Claudia wants us to wait a few days before we see each other again."

"So what do you want?"

Yeah, she's not happy with me. But the apology gets stuck in my throat. "Did you see the TMI pics?"

"What do *you* think? I've been answering Tweets about it all morning." Her annoyance ripples over the line. "Not to mention getting yelled at by Claudia."

I swallow another dose of remorse. The guitar is still in my lap, so I try to distract myself from the guilt by strumming the Gibson.

"Oakley? Did you hear me?"

I clear my throat. "Uh. Yeah." I strum again. An idea occurs to me. "I'm putting you on speaker. Hold on."

I click the speaker button then set the phone beside me and readjust my grip on the guitar.

"You still there?" I ask.

"Yes." She sounds confused. "Are you playing guitar?"

"Yeah. Hold on another sec." I do a quick tuning of the high E string. "Sorry, back. Anyway, about last night... I'm, ah, not good at apologizing, so...just listen, okay?"

Before she can question me, I sweep the guitar pick over the strings and strum the intro of the song I'd been playing around with. Then I start to sing, a total freestyle of nonsense that I probably couldn't recreate if I tried. The lyrics aren't great. I apologize for snapping at her at the club. I sing about forgiveness being good for your soul. I even say something about how the word *sorry* is as meaningless as the wind but when there's emotion behind it, it sets your heart free.

The song is mushy and ridiculous and my cheeks are burning with each note that leaves my mouth.

When the last chord fades into nothingness, I'm greeted with total silence.

"Vaughn? You there?"

She gives a slight cough. "Yeah...that was..."

My face is scorching. "I know. It sucked. I sort of wrote it on the fly."

"No," she interjects. "It didn't suck. Not at all. It was really... sweet. And catchy."

Soft laughter floats over the line, and for some reason it makes my heart beat a little faster. "Yeah? So you finally admit you're an Oakley Ford fan?"

"Don't get ahead of yourself. I said I liked your *song*," she jokes. At least I hope she's joking. It's the first time she's ever said a thing about my music.

"It's the same. Love me, love my music."

"How about I accept your apology? No one's ever sung they're sorry to me before."

Not even W? My lips twitch before a smile breaks free.

"So, yesterday," she starts, sounding awkward. "That producer...you really want to work with him, huh?"

My mood immediately sours. "I really do." I put the guitar aside and take Vaughn off speaker then lean back on the cushion and balance Big D's phone on my shoulder. "But he doesn't want to work with me."

"I kind of got that," she says wryly. "He said you have, what was it? Incompatible sounds?"

"Yeah." What he was saying is that he's making unique stuff while I sound like the band on stage and a thousand other voices. "That, and the image thing."

"What image thing?"

"Oh, come on. Why do you think I'm paying a chick to date me, babe? No, why do you think I'm paying a chick like *you* to date me?"

"Like me?"

I can practically taste her annoyance and hurriedly try to explain. "Yeah. Nice. Sweet."

"You picked the wrong girl, then. Because I'm not very sweet."

"You're sweeter than anyone else I've been with," I admit. "Jim and Claudia think you're good for my image. I need everyone else to think that, too, King especially."

"Since when do you care about your image? You didn't seem too concerned about it when you went skinny-dipping with those socialites in Monte Carlo. Or when you were streaking down Bourbon Street during Mardi Gras last year."

I grin to myself. "Someone's been cyber-stalking me."

"No, I just can't turn on the TV without seeing something about your latest screwup."

I bristle. "Screwup? It's called having fun." Then I grimace, because that's the problem. I was having *too* much fun. So much fun that one of the best producers in the world refuses to work with me because he doesn't think I'm serious about my music.

But he couldn't be more wrong. I *am* serious about it. When I was little, everyone assumed I'd get the acting bug like my parents, but I was born with music in my blood. I was writing my own songs by the time I turned seven. Recording them before I hit my preteens. At the beginning of my career, there were all these bullshit accusations that I only got a record deal because of who my parents are, but those whispers died off once the haters realized I could actually sing.

Vaughn's voice jolts me out of my thoughts. "Well, if you're having fun then why change? You're rich, famous, can have all the fun you want. Why not just keep doing that?"

"Because it's affecting where I want to go with my music." Because it ain't fun anymore.

I listen to her breathe while I pluck at the same string, moving up and down the frets wishing I could change King's tune as easily as I can the melody of a song.

The silence lingers and I begin to think about how I've treated her. Not well. And why? I force myself to give an honest answer. I'm sometimes capable of those moments.

The honest answer is because Vaughn's doing something unselfish and that makes me uncomfortable. It's easier to deal with the sycophants, but just because she won't do everything I say doesn't mean I have to be an asshole. I stop plucking and slam my hand against the strings.

"Next Friday I'm playing at a club for a benefit. I'm going to do a couple of songs. Maybe an entire set as a favor to a friend of mine." Although that's not completely true, either. I'm doing it for my own self-promotion. I have to stay in the news, in front of people's eyes, so they don't forget about me while I'm pissing away my life in the studio. Still… "Want to come? You can bring some friends if you want."

"Is this my next date with you?" she asks.

I want to tell her no, that it's just me inviting her to an event where she can watch an actual performance instead of listening to me fumble through a song I'd made up on the fly. I want her to see Oakley Ford, not the douche she thinks is making her life miserable. Again, completely selfish.

But because I don't know if she'll come if I simply invited her, I say, "Yeah, it's our next date."

16

HIM

Is Oakley Ford officially off the market? The singer and his alleged girlfriend were seen at a private event last night. Insiders exclusively told Gossip Central that Ford and his girl were inseparable. Even more exciting are reports that Ford was seen chatting up mega-producer King. Is a new album in the works? We hope so!

The rumored couple left before the party broke up. Click thru to see Ford and his new gal pal display some PDA! It definitely looks like they're more than friends!

"I thought date number four was supposed to be the club," Vaughn remarks. She keeps frowning at me, and she looks as confused as she sounded on the phone earlier when I informed her we were meeting up.

We haven't had any contact in three days, not since I apology-sang to her. Truthfully, I hadn't expected to see her today, either, but my publicist had other ideas.

"Not wholesome enough according to Claudia," I answer

with a sigh. "We need some daylight outings before you're allowed to hold hands with me in the dark."

Which is why we're currently standing in line at a soft-serve ice cream food truck parked at Melrose Trading Post. I guess Claudia wanted to make damn sure every tourist in West Hollywood that possibly wanders off the strip could take a memento photo of Oakley Ford being *normal*.

"Well, this ice cream better be the best thing that milk and sugar ever created. It took me nearly two hours by bus to get here," Vaughn grumbles under her breath.

Ty, Big D and two other hardbodies stand behind us, creating an obvious bubble between us and the crowd. I tug my hat lower.

"Shoulda told Claudia you wanted a car." I shove my hands in my pockets and stare at the selection. It's a retro ice cream truck with three flavors and then your standard California toppings like fried kale crumbles and chocolate-covered quinoa. I hate Claudia.

"I could never ask someone to give me a *car*. That's crazy." Vaughn runs a flustered hand through her messy hair. She's back to wearing her standard uniform of loose-fitting V-neck T-shirt, holey jeans and her colorfully decorated Vans.

One thing you can say about Vaughn—she's not trying to impress me in any way. There's about three feet of space between us. You could park a VW in that space. The pictures the paps are taking right now have captions that are writing themselves.

Oakley Ford's new relationship already on the rocks!

Oakley Ford breaks up before he makes up!

Jim and Claudia won't be happy if that happens. Right now the positive headlines are outnumbering the negative ones. Jim reported last night that we're even seeing a boost in sales for some of my earlier albums. I guess this thing with me and

Vaughn is actually doing what it's supposed to do. But it only works if the public believes we're a real couple.

So I close the distance under the guise of pointing to the display sign. "What's your flavor?"

"God, kale crumbles? Only in LA. I'll take a twist with birthday sprinkles." She pulls out a five-dollar bill.

"Seriously?" I take the money from her fingers. "I got this."

"Oh, right, this is a business expense."

Is she serious? I can't tell. "Two twists. Birthday sprinkles for her and—"

"If you order kale crumbles, I'm leaving right now," she mutters.

"You can leave mine plain." I turn to Ty, who hands me a twenty. I don't carry my own wallet. It's a security thing.

"Hey, man, mind if I get a photo of you for our celeb wall?" the order-taker asks as he makes my change.

I stifle a sigh. "Sure, no problem."

"This your girl? She can be in it." The guy leans out his window and peers directly down Vaughn's shirt. Creep.

I step in front of her. "Nah, just me. Got a phone?"

These days, all anyone wants is a selfie. Autographs are dinosaurs of a different age. Now the proof that you met someone is on your camera roll. Pics or it didn't happen.

The sweaty food truck guy leans over the counter. Two others stick their heads out. I step into the picture, allowing sweaty food truck guy to put his thick arm around my back. I grit my teeth, smile pretty for the camera, endure the billionth unwanted intrusion into my personal space for the sake of my music and wait. Wait for him to figure out that his phone camera needs to be flipped to the front. Wait for another guy in the truck to muscle his way into the frame so now I've got the armpit stew of four guys dripping onto my shoulder. Wait for the whispers to spread from the girl in the cutoff shorts to the dude with the Ray-Bans perched on the top of his bald head to the older lady five-people deep whose handbag is big enough to hold the entire ice cream truck. Wait for someone, *anyone*, to take the goddamn picture.

"Let me help." Vaughn steps in, plucks the phone from the ice cream man's hand and snaps the photo. Before we can get our ice cream, though, Ty and Big D hustle us away from the crowd as the mass closes in on us.

Vaughn looks longingly at the truck but doesn't mouth a word of complaint as we're escorted away.

"Thanks," I tell her. For not pitching a fit. For taking the picture. For not busting my balls...again.

"It looked awkward," she admits.

Awkward is an understatement. I was two seconds from having an epic fit, which would've caused even more problems.

"Is it always like this?" She tips her head back toward the truck.

From the growing crowd size, I guess the ice cream guy has already Tweeted and Facebooked this encounter. People are pointing in our direction. The noise level is increasing. Any minute now, one of them is going to feel brave and start the stampede toward me.

"Pretty much." I scan the crowd for the other two bodyguards, and when their dark jean-clad bodies break through, I give Ty the sign that I'm ready to go. "Where's your favorite beach?" I ask.

She wrinkles her nose. "Why?"

"Because we need to be seen together but I don't want to be trampled by a crowd."

She shrugs a little. "I like the ES. It's not supercrowded. Bathrooms are closed right now, so mostly it's only locals. Plus, it's near the refinery and sometimes it stinks."

"Sounds perfect. The stinkier, the better." I rub my hands together. "Ty, you know where the El Segundo beach is?"

He nods.

"Awesome. Then let's go."

The bald bodyguard with sloping shoulders and no neck appears behind Vaughn, holding up the ice cream. Her face lights up like he just presented her with a Harry Winston necklace.

"Oh, I thought we abandoned these." Vaughn grabs hers. "Thank you so much."

Daniel, I think, grunts a *you're welcome* and then retreats to the second Escalade. Ty holds open the back door, but I can't move.

My feet are stuck to the ground as I watch Vaughn curl her tongue around the tip like a kitten, scooping the soft serve into her mouth. She closes her eyes, savoring the creamy mix of chocolate and vanilla.

And it might be the hottest thing I've ever seen. So hot it melts the ice cream in my own hand.

"You're leaking," she says.

"What?"

"Your ice cream is melting and leaking all over your fingers."

I look down to see that I've crushed the cone in my hand and the ice cream is oozing out, just as Vaughn said. Ty reaches over and takes the cone out of my hand.

"You better get in the car." His words are a warning, but his tone is full of humor. He'll be mocking me over this for a long, long time.

Vaughn dives inside, somehow managing not to smash her cone against the leather seats. I follow behind her, and Ty has us on the road before Vaughn can get upright and buckle her seat belt. So I reach over and do it for her.

Not because I want to touch her. Nothing like that.

Oakley's eyes are on fire. Or maybe that's my skin. The minute his hand touched my hip to grab the seat belt, I swear my entire body lit up—like I'd been dark my whole life and someone just plugged me in.

I hold my breath as he pulls the seat belt across my waist and clips it into place. Did his fingers linger before he pulled away or was that my imagination?

"You're the one who's leaking now," he says in an amused tone. His thumb swipes across one trembling finger to catch a drop of ice cream and then—*and then!*—he sticks his thumb in his mouth and sucks it clean.

A strange sound—a squeak, really—escapes my throat.

He licks his thumb one more time before settling on his side of the SUV. "I didn't realize birthday sprinkles were so tasty. I might have to try that topping next time."

My eyes dart to the back of Ty's head. "Ty, I—I need to go home. I—I just forgot that I have to be there when the twins get home because they need…permission slips signed for…a field trip." I turn to Oakley, who's staring at me from under hooded eyelids. His lower lip looks damp from where his thumb had pressed against it.

Feeling faint, I lean against my window. "I'm sorry about this. I forgot. I'll make it up to you. I can do another daytime date tomorrow. I'll even Google some suggestions. Maybe the skate park at Boyle Heights. No, that's too busy. Um, we could hike somewhere. There's a place near Griffith Observatory where Paisley likes to run when she wants a change of pace." The more I babble, the more relaxed Oakley gets.

"Nah. It's fine, Vaughn. Eat your ice cream before it melts all over your hand."

Too late.

"Why'd you let that guy take a picture of you?" I ask, providing myself a much-needed distraction from the stomach-curling, toe-numbing feeling that should only be stirred in the presence of W.

"Because I owe it to him and to every other fan who wants my picture. Without them, I'd be Dustin Ford's kid."

"You hate it, though." I could see it if no one else did. The strain around the corners of his fake smile. The tension in his shoulders. The way he tried to avoid the grip of the ice cream server only to have three others descend on him. But he stood patiently without complaint.

And then he waited, as the crowd started moving toward us, for the bodyguard to bring our ice cream. I'd given up on that, figuring it would be another aborted attempt at getting food.

Then he'd looked at me in a way I'd never seen anyone look at me. It scared me and drew me at the same time.

"You gotta do stuff you don't like sometimes. The life of a celebrity isn't all glamour and good times."

No, I guess it isn't.

At some point in the forty-five minute drive, I finish the cone, and a wet wipe appears miraculously in front of me. I snatch it away from Oakley before he can offer to do the wiping for me. When Ty pulls up to the curb, I open the door but can't get out. It's not until Oakley reaches over and unbuckles the seat belt that I realize the harness is restraining me. His palm grazes my thigh as he takes his hand back.

I tumble out in a hurry, trying to avoid those long musician's fingers of his from touching me again. I swear I hear him laugh when the door closes.

"Thanks, Ty," I mumble and then run inside the house before he can say a word.

I slam the door shut and lean against it, chest heaving as though I'd just run that Griffith trail Paisley likes so much. I don't understand where those...flutters came from. Up until the other morning, I'd viewed Oakley as a smug, self-absorbed jerk. And then he called me up and sang to me, and suddenly I'm getting all warm and gooey over him like one of his fan-girls.

I want the conceited Oakley back. The one who mocks me about how good he is with his tongue and takes me to a club only to snap at me and ignore me. *That* Oakley I can handle.

But this one? The one who *smolders* at me and writes me apology songs? I'm so out of my element here.

"Hey." Paisley wanders in from the kitchen with a mug in her hands. "How'd the ice cream date go?"

"He touched me," I blurt out.

She stops abruptly and swings toward me. "Like assaulted you?"

"No. No." I wave my hand. "My ice cream was melting and he caught a drip of it on his thumb and then he stuck his thumb in his mouth." I recite the act as if detailing some serious act of pornography. It *was* R-rated, though.

Paisley looks at me with great concern. "Are you okay? Did you get too much sun?"

I don't know how to explain this to her. I can't even explain it to myself. All I know is that Oakley's rough-tipped fingers brushed my hip. Touched my hand. Skimmed my thigh.

And I liked it way too much.

17

HER

Oakley Ford ✅ **Verified** @VeryVaughn Best ice cream ever today. They should make a flavor called Vaughn. I'd order it every day.

Vaughn Bennett @OakleyFord Would you get Kale sprinkles on it? 😛

Oakley Ford ✅ **Verified** @VeryVaughn Nah, I want the pure Vaughn, straight up, not shaken or stirred.

Vaughn Bennett @OakleyFord Sounds boring.

Oakley Ford ✅ **Verified** @VeryVaughn No way. I had a taste of it today. It was delicious. 👍.1

Oakley Ford ✅ **Verified** @VeryVaughn How about you? Favorite flavor?

Vaughn Bennett @OakleyFord Is this where I say Oakley Ford?

"Is dinner ready yet?" Shane yells from the twins' room. "We've got football."

I brush the last two circles of dough with butter and throw them into the cast-iron pan before yelling back, "Five minutes!"

I check the clock again. The lemon and yogurt chicken will be done in two minutes; the boys will scarf down their dinner in under ten. I'll have the table cleared by half past the hour with Paisley's leftovers wrapped and stuck in the fridge. She's working late tonight on some hush-hush project for Diamond.

If all goes according to plan, I should have an entire hour to get ready for the Oakley Ford live performance at the Valor Club, the venue for the charity benefit he invited me and my friends to attend. I flip the naan over and then pull the perfectly baked chicken from the oven.

"What're we having?" Shane asks when the twins bounce into the kitchen.

"Homemade grilled naan with lemon chicken served over a bed of grilled spring onions, pea shoots and a side of yogurt jus."

"So bread, chicken and peas," Spencer says, sniffing the chicken. "Smells good." He gives his brother a thumbs-up.

"This isn't one of your experiments, right?" Shane asks as he pulls out a chair. "Because I'm starved."

"If you don't like what I make, then don't eat it," I inform the two brats. Expertly, I plate the chicken for the boys, drizzle a little of the yogurt sauce over the meat and then set the food in front of them.

The two inhale the dinner in no time, because despite their complaints about my sometimes overzealous culinary attempts in the kitchen, most of the time their meals are pretty darn good, if I do say so myself. It's the one thing I really enjoy doing when I have the time, and now that I'm not waiting tables and we have a little more cushion to buy groceries, I've been enjoying the heck out of whipping up different meals.

Not all of them have been a success, but I think I'm batting above .500. At the rate at which the twins consume the food, it's safe to say they agree—even if they wouldn't admit it.

Soon, the two of them are out the door to go to their practice. One of their teammate's parents is driving them. Then it's time for me to get ready.

Kiki okayed my outfit of skinny jeans, oversize black tank with a new teal-colored lace bra that peeks out the sides of my shirt and a pair of low-heeled boots. I stuff my hair into a high ponytail, brush on a couple of coats of mascara and a bit of gloss. Another black SUV is sent to pick me up, but I don't recognize the driver, and his mirrored sunglasses and frozen expression don't invite any chitchat.

"No limo?" Carrie says when we swing by her place to pick her up, and she's only kidding a little. She's dressed in a tiny black dress with waist cutouts. Her hair is flat-ironed and looks like a shiny, blond curtain.

"I've never seen Oakley in a limo," I admit.

"Too bad. Maybe he saves them for awards shows?"

I raise my hands up in a display of ignorance. "Maybe?"

We both look at the driver, who pretends neither of us is there. He just pulls into traffic, heading for our next destination.

"By the way? Those Tweets you guys were sending each other this week totally turned me on," Carrie announces.

"Ew. TMI."

"*I'm* TMI'ing? Um, you and Oakley were sex-Tweeting about *ice cream*!"

Actually, me and *Amy* were sex-Tweeting about ice cream, but I don't tell Carrie that. Besides, if I'm being honest, a part of me totally forgot about Amy this week. At times it felt like I was talking directly to Oakley, and some of his—Amy's— responses sounded like stuff he'd say in real life.

I guess Claudia's team knows him very well.

"Stop Twitter-stalking me," I tell Carrie, grinning.

She grins back. "Stop Tweeting, then."

"Touché."

Kiki is next on the pickup list, and the first thing out of her mouth when she gets in the car is, "No limo?"

"That's what I said!" Carrie exclaims. "Apparently Oakley doesn't use limos except for awards shows."

"Ah, that makes sense."

My eyebrows shoot up at that declaration, which Kiki takes as gospel.

"God, you look gorgeous," Carrie tells her. "Doesn't she, Vaughn?"

Kiki is beautiful. Her hair is curled and blown out in a perfect beach wave. She's wearing black satin shorts and a sheer black top over a red bra. On her feet are four-inch platform heels.

"Those shoes are badass," I remark.

"I borrowed them from my mom's closet," Kiki informs us.

Tracy's last on our list. I hop out and climb into the passenger seat while she squishes into the back next to Kiki and Carrie.

Tracy bounces up and down a few times. "I can't believe I'm riding in Oakley Ford's SUV!"

"Belt," the driver says.

We don't move.

"Belt," he repeats.

"Oh!" I twist around. "You need to put on your seat belt," I tell Tracy.

She complies quickly and then claps her hands. "Sorry! I was so excited I forgot about that. This is so *sick*! Aren't you excited? I'm going to die tonight! How many celebrities will be there? Do you think Dylan O'Brien will be there? I heart him so much!"

Tracy fills the SUV with her questions—ones I have no answers to, but her enthusiasm is contagious. And she's right to be excited, because the number of famous people at the venue is so astronomical, even Tracy can't keep up with them all. My friends are blown away by the guest list, the fancy digs and the fact that we're so close to the stage I could almost lick Oakley's feet at one point.

As for me, my vision has narrowed to just Oakley, because Oakley Ford on stage is incredible. My whole body is tingling as I watch him own the crowd. His raspy voice belts out note after perfect note. I'm not sure if it's the lights or the energy he's pouring into his performance, but he's worked up a sweat. His T-shirt is soaked through. The strands of blond-brown hair are damp around his forehead. His arms flex with each strummed note.

He looks so good up there. So…hot. And so sexy. And I feel so guilty about standing here and admiring him. I told W that I'd be acting, but I'm no actress. I can't separate fake feelings from real ones, and it's all getting jumbled. Every time I look at Oakley, I think about that moment we shared on our ice cream date. The heat in his eyes. The way he'd made my heart pound.

I almost called W that night to tell him about it. To confess that all the pretend stuff is becoming confusing for me. To get his reassurance that it's okay—normal even—that I had any kind of response to Oakley.

But that's crazy. Of course W wouldn't have reassured me. He would've been furious.

I have to tell him, though. Right? This is the first time in two years that I've felt even a hint of attraction to another guy—that's something W needs to know.

Right?

I swallow a frustrated groan and force myself to focus on Oakley's last song, which is as awesome as everything else he's sung tonight. When he finishes, the crowd is chanting his name, but for some reason he doesn't seem happy with all the adoration he's being showered with. I expected him to shake people's hands, flirt with his female fans, pander to the crowd, maybe. But he doesn't. He simply sets down his guitar, gives the audience a salute and a wry grin and then disappears backstage as if this performance wasn't totally amazing.

A frown creeps onto my lips as I glance around the club, wondering if anyone else finds this odd. Or if anyone noticed how forced his parting smile looked.

But they're all busy raving about Oakley's incredible performance, including my friends, who gush loudly about how gorgeous he looks tonight.

"Sorry," Kiki says hastily, blushing when she notices me eyeing her. "I know he's your man, but...come on. You *know* he's hot."

"Yeah, he is," I say absently. I don't care that my friends are analyzing my fake boyfriend's appearance. I'm more concerned about what put those shadows in said fake boyfriend's eyes.

"I'll be right back," I tell the girls before darting away. "Don't break too many hearts tonight," I yell over my shoulder.

I feel bad about abandoning them, but I get the sense that Oakley needs me. And while that's a stupid thought, I can't shake the feeling, and it drives me to elbow and jostle my way through the throng of people until I reach the small hallway by the far wall. Two muscled bodyguards stand in front of the black velvet rope separating the corridor from the main room, but they lift the rope when I flash my backstage pass.

In the hall, I'm surrounded by more people. Guys lugging huge amps and instruments. Girls in skimpy clothes squealing to each other. People in suits wearing badges like mine. Dozens of cameras everywhere. Some of them point in my direction, and I instantly duck my head so the photographers can't get a clear shot of my face. Uncomfortable with the attention, I keep walking until I see Ty's gleaming shaved head, which is a good five inches above all the other heads in the hall.

"Ty," I call out quietly.

He turns. "Hey, Vaughn. Enjoy the show?"

"Yeah, it was amazing. Where's Oak?" The nickname slips out before I can stop it, surprising me. Since when do I call him *Oak*? He's always bugging me to use it, and I've always ignored him and called him Oakley.

Ty jerks his thumb at the door behind him. A gold plaque says Dressing Room, and on top of it there's a white piece of paper with "Ford" scribbled on it.

I hesitate. "Can I go in there?"

Ty nods. "Go ahead."

He holds the door open for me, and I timidly step through the threshold. The room is smaller than I expected. I figured

Oakley Ford would get a ginormous dressing room with expensive leather couches and a champagne tower and chocolate fountain or something. But this place is about the size of my bedroom, with only one couch—not leather—and a mini fridge under a small vanity table.

Oakley is in the process of pulling a bottle of water from the fridge. He straightens up when he sees me, rolling the plastic bottle over his sweaty forehead.

Once again I'm floored by how attractive he is. He inherited all the best traits from his movie-star parents, though now that I think about it, I'm not sure Katrina and Dustin Ford have any *bad* traits. They're both drop-dead gorgeous, and so is their son.

His sweat-soaked T-shirt is practically glued to his chest, making me realize exactly how unbearably hot those lights out there must have been—and making me notice every single hard, ridged muscle of his chest.

"Hey," I say.

He twists off the bottle cap and takes a swig of water. "Hey." His voice is raspier than usual, probably because he just sang his lungs out for thirty minutes.

"You were good up there."

"Thanks."

There's a beat of awkward silence. I wait for him to make some snarky remark about me finally admitting that I like his music, but he says nothing. Instead, he wanders over to the couch and flops down with a heavy sigh. After a moment I walk up and sit beside him.

"What's wrong?" I ask frankly.

His teeth dig into his lower lip. A drop of sweat slides from his forehead, down his cheek and clings to the five o'clock shadow on his strong jaw. "I didn't sing anything new," he finally confesses.

My forehead creases. "Were you supposed to?"

"No, but..." He caps the bottle and shoves it onto the little table in front of the couch.

"Then what's the issue? You put on an amazing performance. Everyone went crazy for it."

"I know." He sighs again. "You don't get it. Just...singing the same goddamn songs over and over again...it's exhausting sometimes."

My frown only deepens. "Isn't that what you do, though? I mean, it's not like you write new songs every time you do a concert. You have no choice but to sing the same stuff."

"No. I mean, yes. That's the gig—you're right. But you're also wrong, because it's not the same stuff. I mean, it is, but..." A faraway expression passes through his eyes. "Every time I step on that stage, it's a new experience, even if the song is the same. It's a new crowd, a new energy."

"So what's different about tonight?" I ask in confusion.

He makes a frustrated noise under his breath. "It's this stupid block. There's music inside me, Vaughn, and it won't come out. I haven't made a record in two years. Everything I record at the studio sucks. But in my head, it *doesn't* suck. Like, it's right *there*. It's there, and I can't seem to get it out. Know what I mean?"

I nod slowly. "Kind of. This probably isn't the same thing, but that happens to me sometimes with my drawing. I took a lot of art classes in high school, and there were times when I couldn't draw a single line. Especially when it started to feel like work. I'd be rushing to get the assignment done, but drawing is so hard when you're not inspired."

Or when I cook at home. There are times when inspiration hits me and I can whip up the most amazing things out of the meager contents in our refrigerator, like the soup-filled dumplings I made from leftover chicken stock. Other times, I'm stuck making the same thing every week—meat loaf, pasta, hamburgers. And yeah, even though I try to fancy those dishes up, they get tiring. I guess that's what led me to try new things in the first place.

Oakley groans. "The problem is, I *am* inspired."

"Then where do you think the block is coming from?"

"I have no fucking clue."

I mull it over. "My dad used to say that the answer to every problem already exists in our heads. He probably would've recommended you try meditating or something."

"Does it work?"

I grimace. "Not really. He went on this ten-day meditation retreat in India one summer and when he returned, meditation was the answer to everything. Didn't get a good grade on your chem test? Go meditate. Having problems with a friend? Close your eyes and find your Zen place."

I bite the inside of my cheek. After they died, I couldn't find a Zen place. I'd close my eyes and the only thing I'd see was the accident. It took me a year before those nightmares went away. Meditation doesn't work for me.

A sigh slips out. "Actually, you probably shouldn't take any advice my dad gave me. My parents made some terrible decisions."

Oakley looks intrigued. "Yeah? Like what?"

"Like…" I pause, because my parents did so many dumb things it's impossible to pick just one. "Like one time, Dad blew all our vacation savings on a boat, even though he knew nothing about boats. It was *so* expensive, but he swore that it would end up paying for itself with all the countless hours of fun it would bring us. So instead of going to Disneyland, we took our brand-new boat on its maiden voyage—and it capsized ten minutes in."

"Well, that wasn't really his fault," Oakley says carefully, but I can see him fighting a smile.

"And another time, he and Mom decided that we were going to drive across the country, West Coast to East Coast and back. But neither of them thought to get the car checked before we left, and the transmission died somewhere in Nevada, stranding us in the desert for more than a day. I swear, turkey vultures started circling overhead."

Now Oakley laughs for real. I'm happy to see that the deep furrow in his forehead and the tired lines around his eyes have been smoothed away.

"Pretty much, my parents were spontaneous and fun, but utterly irresponsible. They didn't plan ahead. It was 'live for the moment' with them." I hate myself for the pang of resentment I feel. Because Mom and Dad are gone. I loved them and I miss them and I'm not allowed to be angry at them for being impulsive and wanting to live life to the fullest.

But...I am. At least a little bit. Why didn't they put aside money for their children? Why did they refinance our mortgage just to fund that safari in Africa? We didn't need to go on a safari! That money could have gone toward Spencer's and Shane's college funds. *My* college fund. Paisley used every cent of those tiny life insurance policies to keep the house. There was hardly anything left over.

A warm hand latches on to my knee. I jump in surprise, and my pulse quickens when I look down and see Oakley's long fingers lightly stroking me.

"You're allowed to be pissed at them," he says gruffly. "Just because someone dies doesn't mean they automatically become a saint." His fingers rub my knee again, ever so slightly, before he slowly moves his hand away. "With that said, at least your parents were...there."

I see him swallow, and wonder if he's thinking about his own parents, who he barely talks about. "Yeah. They were."

Silence falls between us. I suddenly feel so bad for him. I feel bad about his creative block and his absentee parents and the fact that he's sitting here alone in his dressing room instead of surrounded by friends and family.

I'm tempted to throw my arms around him and hug him tight, but that's superawkward. So I try to make him feel better in another way.

"I'm having so much fun tonight," I say softly. "So are my friends. It was supernice of you to get them all passes. I never would've dreamed of asking you for that, but I'm glad you did. Now they'll love me forever."

He nods. Watching me.

"What?" I mumble, shifting uncomfortably under his intense gaze.

"You actually mean that, don't you?"

"Mean what?"

"You wouldn't have asked for passes for your friends."

"Why would I? It was already ridiculously generous of you to invite *me*. Why would I get greedy?"

Those green eyes never leave my face. He's staring so hard that my heartbeat accelerates to a dangerous rhythm. My breath is caught in my throat. My skin feels hot and tight all of a sudden.

Breaking the eye contact, I stumble to my feet. "Come on," I urge, "let's go back out there. You don't want to miss your friend's performance."

"Set," he corrects, but he gets up, too, and we head for the door.

"Is a set not the same thing as a performance?"

"Well, yeah. It is. But in this business we call it a set."

"Okay, but it's still also a performance," I argue. "They're synonyms. Therefore, both words are acceptable."

"Fine, Miss Know-It-All. Go ahead and ignore the industry professional."

"Ooooh, because your *nineteen*-year-old self is *such* an expert. You've been around the block for *so* long." I'm grinning as I reach for the doorknob.

"Hey, I'm still more of an expert than *you* are. In more ways than one."

Winking, he tugs on my hand. Except he does it at the exact same moment my other hand turns the knob, so the force of him drawing me toward him causes me to let go of the door.

Which means it swings open just as Oakley presses his lips to mine.

18

HIM

The kiss lasts no more than a second. My mouth presses against Vaughn's, catching her midsmile. My tongue sweeps across her lips, but I don't get the chance to slide it past them.

Flashbulbs go off. An explosion of them, like bright bolts of lightning in the cramped hallway.

I catch sight of Tyrese's startled expression, but he doesn't look half as surprised as Vaughn, who stares up at me as cameras continue to click around us.

Shit. She had to choose *this* moment to open the door?

Stifling a sigh, I yank her back into the dressing room and slam the door shut.

"Vaughn," I start to say. *Vaughn, I want to kiss you again. Vaughn—*

She doesn't hear me because she's talking, too. "Wow, talk about perfect timing there." She draws two fingers across her lips. Is she wiping my kiss away? "I didn't expect it, but I guess that's a good thing because this way it looks more natural."

Natural? Did she think— "You think I planned this?"

"Didn't you?" The furrow in her forehead appears.

I run an agitated hand through my hair. I kissed her because she was funny and sweet. She didn't mock me when I confessed I was blocked. She tried to comfort me with silly stories about her family even when it was obvious those same memories caused her pain. She doesn't expect anything from me beyond what we'd agreed upon. She's different and I wanted a taste of that. I wanted to know what it felt like to be *her*, and the only way I knew how to do that was to put my mouth against hers.

But obviously she didn't feel a damn thing, so I have to pretend I didn't, either. "Yeah, totally planned."

She shoots me an uncertain smile. "Well, it worked. You and Claudia know what you're doing. Anyway, I guess we should go? Listen to the next set?"

Now would be a good time for me to come clean, but because this isn't real for her, hell if I'm going to be the one to admit that I'm not on the same page. So I open the door and gesture for her to exit.

Maverick's band is already on stage when we get out there. I endure a few backslaps from acquaintances and do a fist bump with Luke.

"Sorry about that thing with your house and all. I would've said something at the club the other night, but I didn't have the chance," he whisper-shouts in my ear. "I wasn't thinking."

"Yeah, no big deal," I answer even though it is a big deal, but I don't want to get into it here.

"Didn't think so." He grins. "It's just a bed, right? No harm, no foul."

"I burned that bed."

Luke laughs. "You can afford it. Yo, Vaughn, your girls are smoking hot. Any of them single?"

She darts a glance toward me, wanting direction. *What's the plan?* she silently asks. I'd like to tell her that there's no plan now, just as there wasn't one five minutes ago, and that she's flirting with me, Oak Ford, online. Ever since the ice cream date, I've seized control of my social media accounts from my PR team, but I haven't had the balls to tell Vaughn that she's actually interacting with me and not a bunch of assistants.

"Luke's a dog," I warn. "But if your girls are down with that, he plays a mean guitar."

"Hey, I'm not a dog. More like a puppy, really." He spreads his hands apart.

The innocent ploy makes Vaughn laugh, and an unfamiliar feeling that I label annoyance—not jealousy—sweeps over me. Luke is making her laugh? I grab her hand and pull her against me, both grateful and irritated that she doesn't draw away. We're in public now and she's invested in the *act*.

Which is why she shifts her weight and leans into my side. Her small hand finds the back of my shirt and grips it. And I slide my arm around her back, letting my fingers dangle over the curve of her shoulder. Because this is how we're supposed to look. Loved up. Infatuated. Just one washed-up recording artist and his made-for-the-press girlfriend.

From the way the crowd is bobbing their heads, Maverick's killing it on stage. But none of his notes register for me. I can't stop sneaking peeks at Vaughn, who seems more interested in watching one of her friends—a tall blonde with a good rack—flirt with Luke.

But while I'm still sorting out why I kissed her, how good it felt, and that I'd like to do it again right now even in front of all the gossip journos and paps, she looks totally unaffected. Like it was no big deal that I kissed her.

And that pisses me off.

I want to shake the complacency out of her. All the chicks in this room would trample each other to get a chance to lock lips with me. Half of them would let me screw them up against the wall while their boyfriends watched.

But Vaughn's face shows nothing but mild interest—and not in me. Shit, is she crushing on *Luke*?

"That guy sold access to my bedroom." I jerk my thumb toward Luke, who's got his hand on the blonde's shoulder and is pulling her toward him.

Vaughn's head swings around. "Luke?"

"Yeah. And he's twenty-five."

"Eww. That's gross. Why do you even talk to him?"

"He's my bassist. I can't ignore him just because he's a dick-wad sometimes."

"Well, come on. I can't let him slime all over my friend." Vaughn shrugs my arm off, but before she stalks away to rescue her friend, she grabs my hand.

For appearances, I'm sure, but I grip it tight and let her drag me across the bar floor.

"Hey, Carrie."

"Oh, my God, Vaughn! This is so cool!" Carrie throws her arms around Vaughn. The two girls stumble back, Vaughn's body pressing against my already tense one.

I push them both upright. The last thing I need tonight is to show some inappropriate wood in my tight jeans. That'd give Claudia a coronary.

Vaughn slides me another uncertain look, one that I easily read as hurt. I open my mouth to tell her I'm sorry, but I'm tired of saying those words to her because I'm not even sure what I'm supposed to be apologizing for. Kissing her? And then trying to put some distance between us when she'd rather stand here in the middle of a sweat-soaked crowd than make out with me in the green room?

"Thank you for inviting us." Carrie pushes Vaughn to the side to launch herself at me. I catch her because otherwise she'd fall on her face. "You were amazing. So amazing."

"Hey, hands off my merchandise," Vaughn jokes. She slips

between her friend and me, creating space. Her hand reaches for mine again and presses it against her waist.

Again, I have to remind myself that she's just acting. And she's good at it. So good that it makes me think, for a second, that she wants my hand on her. That she likes my body pressed against her back.

It's all getting damn confusing for me.

"I know." Carrie winks. "But I couldn't resist. I mean, God, Oakley Ford. I can't believe I'm standing next to him. Or that I touched him." She prattles on as if I'm not even a real person.

"He's standing right beside you, Carrie," Vaughn chides with sweetness so her friends don't take offense.

I hide my appreciation behind a cocky smile.

"Oakley, this is Carrie, Tracy and Kiki—she did my hair the other night—and her boyfriend, Justin. Justin's favorite song of yours is 'Do Her Right'."

The big dude behind Kiki flushes.

"Hey, man." I hold out my free hand to slap his. "Mine, too." We all know that the first single release from *Ford* is about sex, so it's not like I'm going to bust his chops over it, but his cheeks burn even hotter. He taps my hand and then pulls his chin into his chest.

The girls share a giggle that turns into a roar.

"I'm going to piss," Justin says then stomps off.

"What's that about?" I ask.

This time it's Kiki who blushes, and I finally get it. They must've played the song while doing the dirty.

Vaughn smirks. "Let's just say that you're responsible for a lot of action at Thomas Jefferson High."

"Glad I could be an inspiration."

This sets the girl crew into hysterics.

Luke decides it's time to open his piehole again. "We should hit up Oak's house tonight. How about hosting an after-party, dude?"

If I wasn't standing here in front of Vaughn and her girls, I would've told him no immediately, but now I don't know what to do. I don't want to invite a bunch of strangers into my home. If it was just me and Vaughn? I'd be okay with that. The rest of the crowd? Not so much. But it's Vaughn's friends and I'm kind of weirdly desperate for her to like me.

"No, we need to get home," Vaughn says, and I try not to make my relief too obvious. "My friends have class tomorrow."

"Vaughn," Carrie moans, clearly embarrassed at the implication that they're too young to stay out. "It's fine."

"I'm tired," Vaughn replies. She crosses her arms across her chest and stares mutinously at her friend.

"Me, too," I lie. It's not even midnight.

Luke glares at me.

"In fact, after this set, I'd like to go home," Vaughn says.

"Why?" Carrie presses. "You aren't working. You don't have classes."

There's a slight judgmental tone in her voice, as if Vaughn is a worthless piece of shit. Maybe we can abandon her with Luke.

Vaughn ignores this. "Can Ty take us home?" she asks me.

"Yes."

Carrie relents, realizing that Vaughn's not going to change her mind. And when it becomes obvious that I'm not going to let Luke take any one of these high school girls home with him or host a party at my place, he wanders off in search of easier game. Or at least more available game.

Maverick wails his last note, and the lights dim once and then twice to indicate a break. The crowd makes a beeline to the bathrooms.

"Thanks for inviting us," Kiki tells me.

"Yeah, it was so awesome. We should take a picture!" Carrie shoves her camera into Vaughn's hands.

They mean with me. Vaughn's shrug says exactly what's running through my mind. I can't escape. The two girls insert themselves under each of my arms. Vaughn presses her lips together, trying not to laugh because she knows how much I hate this.

April wouldn't have laughed. She would've been jealous. Vaughn thinks it's *funny* that I'm being felt up by her girl squad. In fact, I think Carrie's hand is halfway down my back pocket.

"Take the picture," I mouth.

Vaughn gives me the thumbs-up and snaps one picture. Her friend Kiki darts out from under my arm and hands her another phone. A bunch of other people are taking pictures now. Inside the club, so dark that I'm certain the only thing that will show up on Carrie's camera is three shapes and three sets of red eyes, there are cameras being pointed at me from all directions.

Somewhere on the internet, this picture's going to be labeled *Oakley Ford's handful at the club. Already stepping out on his girlfriend?*

Thankfully, it's over quickly, and then we're walking out the back toward the waiting Escalades.

"W's going to be so jealous when he hears about tonight," Carrie says.

Next to me, Vaughn tenses. A revolting thought hits me. Had she pretended that W was kissing her? When she leaned against me in the club, was she thinking it was W? When she pressed my hand against her waist, was that W's hand she was holding?

I hadn't planned on kissing Vaughn again tonight. I'm sure Claudia is already in a rage over the first one, but I'm not letting Vaughn get in that truck until she knows exactly who's kissing her. It's not her wannabe, hat-wearing, plaid-loving boyfriend. It's me. Oak Ford.

"Hey." I tug her back before she can climb in behind Kiki.

"Oh, right, our public goodbye." She pushes some of her hair away from her face.

Behind us, I hear the clicks of the cameras. The flashes of bulbs light up her face every half second.

She rolls her eyes, which only stirs up my anger. "Smile for the cameras, baby. That's your job, remember?"

"I'm not your baby," she grumbles.

"You are for a year."

Her eyes flash angrily. All the warm feelings that were stirred up in the green room are getting flushed down the toilet, but I can't seem to stop my stupid mouth. Every time I open it, something assholic comes out.

"Now kiss me like you can't get enough of me." I wind my hand through her hair and tip her head to the side. "A better angle. Tongue this time." With my mouth millimeters from hers, I pause. "What's my name, baby?"

This time her eyes flicker with confusion. "Oakley Ford."

Elation fills me. "That's right."

My lips press hard against hers and I sweep my tongue inside, tasting the sweetness of the cola she sipped on all night and the mint she popped into her mouth as we were walking out.

I kiss her, but she doesn't kiss me back.

19

HER

Oakley Ford engages in serious PDA!

Oh em gee! Oakley and his flavor of the month were seen at the Valor Club for last night's charity concert headlined by Maverick Madsen. The once-a-year benefit raises money for muscular dystrophy. But that's not all that was raising last night...

Stop that! It was eyebrows ;) Oakley Ford was caught giving the lip to his new arm candy, not once but twice last night. Insiders say the two could not keep their hands off each other.

Looks like Oakley's making this good girl go bad...

The Heidi Does Hollywood post makes me cringe. I shut my laptop and remind myself that my love life won't be a circus forever. Once this job is over, I'll be able to make out with

W—who I need to call ASAP—again without seeing the evidence of it pop up on all the celebrity blogs.

And without getting yelled at by Claudia a hundred times a day.

"Tongue!" she screeches in my ear first thing in the morning. "We don't want tongue, Vaughn! We don't want public makeouts! That just makes your relationship look like a dirty sex fest instead of the pure, sweet love we're trying to convey."

"Tell that to Oakley," I mutter. Because it's all *his* fault. I don't know what power trip he was on last night, but I totally didn't like it.

First he sprung a kiss on me in the dressing room, and then he taunted me outside the car and stuck his tongue in my mouth and said "What's my name, baby?" like some kind of gross porn star.

Every time I think he might be a nice guy, he goes and proves me wrong. Thank goodness I don't like him. That tingling I felt after the first kiss was just post-concert adrenaline. Nothing more. Absolutely nothing.

"Amy and I are working on damage control," Claudia says irritably. "You've got a lunch date with Katrina at noon today—"

"Katrina?" I interrupt.

She huffs impatiently. "Katrina Ford. Oak's mother."

My jaw hits the floor. I'm having lunch with Oakley's movie star mother today? Would it kill these people to give me *some* advance notice about these things?

"W-why?" I stammer.

Claudia hisses. "Because it's time to take the relationship to the next level. And a meet-the-family shows that you and Oak are serious about each other."

"Does she know it's a fake relationship?"

"No. So that means you need to sell her on how much you

love her son. We'll leak the lunch location to the paps to make sure they get some shots of you and Katrina. This *might* neutralize the tongue disaster."

"Will Oakley be there?" I swallow hard, because the thought of meeting his mother—alone—makes me very, very nervous.

"No, I'm making sure he's at the studio today. I don't want any pictures of you two for at least a few days. We want the tongue thing to die down first."

"Jeez, it was just a kiss." I'm starting to think everyone in Hollywood is insane. Then again, if Claudia's this worked up about it, what will W say?

I order myself not to worry about it. W will understand. He already knows that this is all for show. At least, I hope he does.

"It was not *just* a kiss. You're supposed to be the good girl. Not the good girl gone bad!"

I wince. Claudia and I must be reading the same websites. I try to turn the conversation back to Oakley's mom. "Does Oakley know I'm meeting his mom?"

Claudia takes the bait. "I'm about to call him and fill him in. It shouldn't be a problem. And I already spoke to Katrina— she's excited to meet you." A slew of commands proceed to fill my ear. "Wear something nice and conservative. Nothing too racy. Some makeup is okay, but not a lot—Katrina doesn't like being upstaged. Oh, and do *not* mention Dusty."

"Dusty?" I ask stupidly.

"Dustin Ford—Oak's dad. Katrina loses it every time someone mentions his name. Amy's emailing you some talking points right now. A car will pick you up in an hour."

She hangs up, and less than a minute later my phone beeps with an email notification. I click to open the message.

Don't mention graduating early from high school. K's touchy about education—dropped out at 16, got her GED at 20.

Do NOT mention Oakley's father.

Don't bring up plastic surgery—K's touchy about it. Swears she's never gone under the knife. They all do.

Don't discuss: politics, the economy, her childhood (K grew up in a trailer park—touchy about it), her last two movies (bombs), the environment, her...

My eyes almost bug out. The list goes on and on, and either I'm dumber than I thought, or there aren't any actual talking points here. It's just bullet points of all the things I *shouldn't* say. And there are so many of them.

I scrub my hands over my eyes and try not to scream in frustration. It seems like Oakley's mom is touchy about *everything*. And why can't I talk about the environment? Does she have traumatic memories associated with climate change?

My phone rings again, and I can't ignore it because it's Tyrese. That means Oakley.

I wonder which Oakley is on the line, though—the one who's funny and sweet, or the jackass who forced his tongue down my throat last night.

"Claudia says you're seeing my mom today."

"Hello to you, too," I mutter. Jackass, then. "It's a beautiful day, don't you think?"

He ignores my sarcasm. "I'm sure she'll have lots to say about what a selfish, awful son I am—"

"Why does she think you're an awful son?"

"Because I had the nerve to file for emancipation when I was fifteen."

Oh, man. I'd forgotten that Oak had divorced his parents. No wonder they never call him. "Why'd you do that?" I ask cautiously then prepare myself to get snapped at.

But he doesn't snap. "Because we had differences over where my career was going. Specifically, Dad wanted me to end it and I didn't." His tone is bored. "Anyway, just wanted to give you a heads-up. I'm sure you'll enjoy hearing her bitch about me, but take it with a grain of salt, okay? Ever since the emancipation she only calls me a few times a year, and that's only when she needs something."

"Okay." I pause. "Are you sure you don't have anything else to say to me?"

"Like what?"

Um, an apology? "I don't know… I thought you might have something more to say. Something to do with last night, maybe?" I prompt not so innocently.

"Nah." His voice takes on an edge. "You got something you want to say to *me*?"

"No. Should I?"

"Well, then I guess we're done here."

He disconnects before I can respond, leaving me equal parts confused and pissed off. Does he really believe what he did last night was cool? I know I'm supposed to put on a show for the cameras, but that doesn't give him the right to stick his tongue in my mouth and mock me about it.

And was he calling to warn me to not believe anything his mom says? Since when does he care what I think about him?

Argh, and why did the hurt, bitter note in his voice make my heart ache? He's got the kind of life people can only dream of. He has zero need for my sympathy, especially after his "What's my name?" bullshit from last night. Which he didn't even apologize for!

Sighing, I walk over to the closet and search for something "nice and conservative" to wear. Eventually I settle on a knee-length yellow sundress with tiny green flowers along the hem and a denim jacket. I stare longingly at my Vans, then pick up a pair of brown ankle boots. Then I drop the boots and put on the Vans. I don't care if it's a faux pas to wear sneakers with a dress. I've always chosen comfort over fashion.

I'm brushing my hair when one of the twins pops into my bedroom. I think it's Shane, but I'm too focused on doing my hair to look at him.

"Are you seeing Oak?" he asks in excitement. "Is he coming over here to get you?"

Ugh. He calls him *Oak* now?

"No, I'm going to lunch with his mom. A car is picking me up."

Disappointment fills his face. Yeah, it's Shane. Spencer is better at hiding his emotions. "Oh. Okay. Did he say when he's coming over again?"

Never, if I can help it. It's one thing to fake-date Oakley in public. It's another to have him in my house. This is my happy place.

"No," I answer.

"But he's still gonna take us to his friend's house, right? The one with the halfpipe in the backyard?"

I frown, because I literally have no idea what he's talking about. So I say, "What are you talking about?"

"He said on the phone the other day—"

"When did you speak to him on the phone?" I demand.

"The other day," Shane repeats. "Keep up, Vaughn. It's not that hard."

Smart-ass. "Oakley called you? Why?"

He nods animatedly. "He wanted to know how the boards were working out, if we got wheels yet. I said yeah, we did, and then I said it was a bummer he can't go to skate parks anymore, 'cause then he coulda showed me and Spence some tricks. So then *he* said that he's friends with a pro skater who has, like, an actual halfpipe and vert ramp at his house and that maybe he'll see if we can go there sometime to skate." Shane finishes in a rush.

I'm confused again. Oakley hadn't mentioned that he'd spoken to my little brother.

"Can you remind him next time you see him?" Shane begs.

"Yeah, sure," I agree, because it's nice to see Shane so animated. The twins shut down after Mom and Dad's deaths, Shane more so than Spencer, so a huge part of me is grateful.

But I'm also wondering what kind of game Oakley is playing now.

Oakley's driver takes me to a small bistro on Rodeo Drive. It's called the Wicker Garden and I Googled it on the way and found out it's *the* place for celebrities to eat lunch. Apparently it's famous for its kale Caesar salad and for being the site where Paul Davenport proposed to Hallie Wolfe. They're famous actors whose marriage lasted about as long as it takes for your food to arrive at the Wicker Garden.

I wipe my damp palms on the front of my dress as I reach the hostess stand. "Ah, hi," I tell the elegantly dressed woman. "I'm Vaughn Bennett. I'm, uh, supposed to meet Katrina Ford?" I never, ever thought those words would be coming out of my mouth.

"Right this way."

She leads me through a white archway that's covered in ivy and I think is made of wicker. The Wicker Garden is really trying to live up to its name. All the tables here give off the illusion of being secluded, thanks to the huge planters of ferns and palm fronds situated all over the patio. But it's not at all private—there are nearly a dozen photographers standing beyond the railing that separates the bistro from the street.

I know they're taking my picture, so I make a conscious effort to keep my shoulders straight and my expression blank. I don't want them getting any shots of me slouching, or catch a weird angle of me scratching my cheek and then reading tomorrow that *Oakley Ford's girlfriend picks her nose!*

Katrina Ford hops out of her chair when I reach her table. She's wearing tight black pants, a loose-fitting black top that somehow accentuates her slenderness, silver hoop earrings and stilettos with the famous red heel. I stare at her for a long second, because she's even more beautiful in person. Her eyes are the same shade of green as Oakley's, but her wavy mane of hair is a few shades lighter.

"Vaughn!" she squeals, and then I'm pulled into an unexpected hug. She smells like expensive perfume. "It's so nice to meet you!"

I offer an uncertain smile. "It's nice to meet you, too, Ms. Ford."

"Call me Kat." She tugs on my hand. "Sit, please. I've been looking forward to this all morning, ever since Claudia phoned on Oak's behalf. She said he was dying for me to meet his new girlfriend."

My brow furrows. Is that what Claudia told her? That Oakley wanted us to meet?

Guilt tickles my belly as I take the seat across from her. A waiter wearing all black rushes up to take my drink order. I ask for a Coke, and Katrina orders a mimosa.

"It would have been nice if he'd phoned himself," she admits, folding her hands on the crisp linen tablecloth. Her fingernails are shiny and perfect, as if she'd just gotten a manicure. "But I get it. Hollywood, right? Everything is done through agents and publicists, even conversations between a mother and son." She smiles carelessly, but it doesn't quite reach her eyes.

That guilty feeling gets worse. It clearly bothers her that Oakley didn't call her. I know why he didn't—he had no clue this lunch date was even happening until after I was informed about it. Claudia set it all up without his approval.

But I can't exactly tell his mother that.

The waiter returns with our drinks and then takes our orders.

"Have the kale Caesar," Katrina urges. "It's divine!"

Gag. Kale is *so* gross. "How about a regular Caesar salad?" I ask tentatively. "Like, with lettuce? Do you have that?"

The waiter arches a brow. "We don't serve lettuce in any of our salads. It's all kale."

Double gag. I give the menu a speedy scan. "I'll have the turkey and avocado sandwich, please."

"Brie or goat cheese?"

"Um. Brie." There aren't any prices listed on the menu, and I'm suddenly terrified I might have ordered a hundred dollar sandwich, but Oakley's mom doesn't seem concerned.

"That sounds fabulous," she tells the waiter. "I'll have the same."

Once he's gone, she beams at me and says, "Tell me about yourself, Vaughn."

I take a hasty sip of my Coke. "Oh. Well, I just graduated from high school last spring—" Crap! I'm already breaking one of the rules. I quickly try to think of a way to change the subject, but Katrina speaks before I can.

"Good for you!" She doesn't seem upset at all. "You must be really smart."

I blush.

"I'm glad for that," she says frankly. "My son needs an intelligent girl. Someone with a good head on her shoulders." Her tone becomes rueful. "Oak is way too impulsive, doesn't always make the best decisions. He gets that from me."

"Does he?"

She nods then swallows the rest of her mimosa in one long

gulp. "I'm nothing if not spontaneous. It's the only way to live life, in my opinion. Did Oak tell you I married Dusty when I was seventeen?"

Great, another no-no topic has been breached. I don't know what to do. Claudia and Amy made it clear I wasn't supposed to talk about Oakley's dad, but *she* brought him up. It would be rude for me not to respond, right?

"No, he didn't tell me that." I pause. "That's superyoung." My age, in fact. I can't envision being married right now. Of course, I can't envision anything about my future, so that's not saying much.

Katrina laughs. "I'm sure it seems young to you, but you have to remember—by that point, I'd already been working full-time for ten years. I started acting when I was seven."

Right, I think I knew that.

"You grow up fast in this business," she goes on. "I was practically middle-aged by the time I met Dusty. It was on the set of the only movie we did together."

Middle-aged at seventeen? Damn, Hollywood is brutal.

She waves the waiter over and orders a second mimosa.

It kind of bothers me that she doesn't thank him, but I'm hoping she makes up for it by leaving him a huge tip.

"Oak was born when I was twenty."

My eyebrows shoot up. Wow. She's only thirty-nine? Except, wow again, because she looks way younger than that. *Do not bring up plastic surgery*, I order myself.

"I'm thirty-two." She winks at me.

I press my lips together to contain a laugh. "And nobody has ever done the math and realized that would mean you gave birth at thirteen?"

"Oh, Vaughn." She's grinning now. "School math and Hollywood math are two very different things."

My laughter spills out, and she joins in. I didn't expect to like her this much, but I do. She's so quick to smile and laugh, and her enthusiasm is contagious. I'm totally aware of the photographers snapping pictures of us from the curb, but Kat pays them no attention. I suppose if you've been acting for three quarters of your life, the sounds of camera lenses whirring is like white noise.

I focus on Katrina and find that it's easy to ignore the outside when I'm this entertained. It's also easy to ignore that I'm having lunch with a woman I'd only ever seen in magazines and movie theaters.

When our food arrives, we munch on our sandwiches while Katrina tells me stories about Oakley when he was young. She explains that when Oak was a baby, she and his dad agreed to alternate their shooting schedules so that one of them was always at home with their son.

"Dusty didn't stick to that, though," she admits, a flash of anger in her eyes. "He's a workaholic, that man. Back-to-back-to-back shoots in his quest for an Oscar. Eventually I had to hire a nanny, because that was the only way I was able to work." She chews slowly, looking sad. "Maybe that's why Oak went through with the emancipation? Maybe he was punishing me for not being at home full-time for him? I struggled with the work balance issue in the *Working Mom* movie I did. Did you see it?"

Before I can respond, she brushes off her sadness again by giving a bubbly laugh.

"But look at me being all serious. Let me tell you about the time I caught Oakley singing Backstreet Boys in front of the mirror when he was seven!"

The rest of lunch flies by. I love Oakley's mom. She isn't the most maternal woman, but it's obvious she's proud of her son, and she doesn't stop talking about his records and awards. She even shows me pictures of him on her phone. Her home screen is a candid shot of Oakley lying on a beach chair. He's not smiling, but he looks happy. He also looks young—sixteen, maybe.

"That was taken at my place in Malibu," she says when she sees me staring at the screen. "A few years ago." She pauses. "He hasn't been there in a while. Not since *Roadside Manners* came out."

Another Katrina Ford movie I haven't seen. I want so badly to give her a big hug, but even if I thought I could do it without embarrassing us both, I don't get the chance. My phone starts vibrating in my purse, buzzing again and again with every incoming text message.

"Oh, sorry. Do you mind?" I awkwardly gesture to my purse.

Katrina waves a careless hand. "Go ahead, sweetie."

I pull out my phone and check the screen, frowning when I find a dozen messages from W. I glance hastily at Katrina, but she's on her own phone, typing away with lacquered nails, so I surreptitiously start reading W's texts.

We need to talk.

Srsly don't ignore this.

Call me.

This is not ok w me. If u care, ur going to call me and explain WTF is going on. Sick of hearing abt u from peeps here. Sick of being the one getting crapped on.

My stomach drops. I meant to call him earlier and explain everything, but I got distracted by Claudia and then Oakley and now Katrina. And while I understand what's driving him—he saw the pictures of me kissing Oakley and he's *pissed*—W knows he's not allowed to be texting me like this.

I say as much, typing a furious response.

We shouldn't be texting.

Hopefully if anyone ever steals my phone and sees what I wrote, they'll think I mean we shouldn't be texting because we broke up, and not because a nondisclosure agreement is forcing us not to.

My message doesn't get the desired response. Instead of backing off, W just calls me.

I press Ignore so forcefully that Katrina looks up in concern. "Everything okay?" she asks.

I take a deep breath. "Yes. No. It's just...my ex—" I trip over the word "—boyfriend keeps texting me. I guess he's still not over the breakup," I say lamely.

She gives a knowing smile. "And I'd bet who you're dating now isn't helping him get any closure."

"No, it's not helping at all." My phone rings six more times before I finally power it off, but the sinking feeling in my heart doesn't go away.

I need to diffuse this W bomb before it explodes in all of our faces.

20

HER

Katrina insists on driving me home. I take her up on it because, yeah, private transportation beats public any day for a hundred different reasons, even though I complained about it to Oakley once. Private cars means no one sitting next to you smelling like day-old gym socks, or having to stop every other second to let off a hundred people before your destination.

"You'll have to help me plan Oakley's birthday this spring," Kat says.

I'm a bit startled that she thinks Oakley and I will be together in the spring. I mean, per my contract, we will, but I wonder what he said to convince his mother that our relationship was going to last that long. "Ah, sure."

"What do you think he'd like to do?"

Record with King. "We should do a retro birthday and do a bunch of little kid games like pin the tail on the donkey and a piñata with lots of candy," I joke. Oakley would probably hate that.

Her eyes widen. "Oh, that's perfect. Let's do that."

"No! I was just kidding," I protest, but Katrina's already

on the phone to someone telling them that they need to look into booking the party room at the Montage. "Really, Katrina. I was totally kidding. I think Oakley would like—" I cast around for something suitably nineteen years old but then realize that Oakley is no ordinary nineteen-year-old, soon to be twenty. He probably wants strippers and girls jumping out of cakes. That thought makes me frown angrily. I hope he's not entertaining other girls when he's supposed to be my boyfriend.

The Escalade pulls to a stop in front of my curb, and Katrina's driver rounds the front to my side. I heave a sigh and climb out. "Skate park. He'd like to go to a skate park," I suggest, because the thought of stripper cakes is gross, but I don't think she hears me.

"Katrina! Vaughn!"

There's a photographer on the street, leaning out of his car window. Did he follow us? Jeez, that's creepy.

Katrina doesn't even react to his shouts. It's like he doesn't exist to her.

"I'll call you, darling." She blows me a couple of kisses that are captured by the photographer, while I jog to the front door.

Great. I'm going to have to warn Oakley about this, although…it might be kinda hilarious to see his face when he walks into his twentieth birthday party and sees a bunch of us wearing party hats and holding paper donkey tails.

Maybe I won't tell him. Maybe I'll keep it a secret and then laugh my butt off. In fact, if I share the idea with Claudia, she'll probably end up dying with glee over the *wholesome* nature of the plan.

A grin spreads across my face as I picture Oakley in a blindfold staggering around with a broomstick while whacking at a papier mâché pony. Katrina would probably fill the piñata with gold coins or hundies, but it'd still be hilarious. And it would serve him right for being such a jerk to me last night.

Speaking of jerks... I power my phone on and call W as I head upstairs to my bedroom. He picks up on the first ring, which tells me he was waiting for me to call him back.

"Why won't you answer any of my texts?" he demands.

"Because we're not supposed to be texting. I could get in trouble if it comes out that we're in contact. I told you that before."

"Is that in your contract?" he mocks. "Do you have specific terms in there like how many times he gets to stick his tongue down your throat or is that a freebie you threw in because you get to hang out with Oakley Ford now?"

My pulse speeds up in panic. "It's not like that."

"Either your thing with Ford is a publicity stunt or you're cheating on me," he says bluntly.

"You know what this is." It's not the greatest answer, but I can't say any more because I'm afraid Jim will appear with his hammer.

"Uh-huh, sure. It's all *fake*, right?" He curses angrily. "Well, it doesn't look fake. You're smiling in those pictures! And in the one where he's licking you like you're an ice cream cone, you're squeezing his arms. And what about those Tweets?" W recites a few of the Tweets Oakley and I exchanged after the ice cream date. "Those don't sound like just friends to me, V!"

"It's nothing," I insist.

"Do you know how this looks at school? Guys look at me like I'm some dumb schmuck. Girls think I'm a big fat loser. Last night I was at some party and my roommates are all getting some. There are dimes everywhere, but me? I'm standing in the corner, holding my dick in my own hand because my girlfriend, who should've been making out with *me*, is kissing some jerk in front of the camera!"

I can practically see him frothing at this point. And what can I say? He's right. If the tables were turned, I'd be super-upset every time I saw a picture of W with his fake girlfriend. I'd have a very hard time believing it wasn't real. When I look at those pictures, they don't look like I'm hating life or hating Oakley. I look...happy and excited.

"I'm sorry," I whisper.

There's a pause. "I'm sorry, too."

"About what?" But I know even before he says the words. I know because of the guilty note in his voice that's mixed with a sort of triumph.

Rather than respond, he goes quiet again. Then he swears. "Look, I'm coming over tonight. We'll talk about it then, okay?"

I don't want to talk about it. I... Oh, God, I don't want to know. And yet I still find myself saying, "Talk to me now."

W remains stubborn. "No. I want to see you. My last class ends at six. I'll head over right after and be at your place around eight."

It's only three! He's going to make me wait five hours to hear whatever terrifying thing he has to say? Who does that?

"Please just tell me now," I plead.

"I'll be over later," is all he says.

Then he hangs up.

I spend the rest of the afternoon and most of the evening worrying about W's visit. Paisley gets home from work to find me curled up on my bed watching a slideshow on my laptop. Pictures of me and W from high school flash across the screen. The ones that used to make me smile don't inspire the same response tonight, no matter how hard I focus on all those good memories.

"You okay?" my sister asks with a frown.

"I'm fine," I lie.

"Is W mad about the kiss?" she guesses.

I nod miserably. Paisley comes over and sits down on the bed. Her hand smooths over my hair. "This is harder than you thought it was going to be, isn't it?"

An image of W and me at the beach pops up. His arm is wrapped around my waist and he's looking so happy. I don't think I'm ever going to see that smile directed toward me again.

"I think he hooked up with someone else at a party last night." I slap the laptop shut. "He's coming over to tell me something because he's 'sorry, too.'"

Paisley's mouth thins out. I'm not sure if she's upset at me inviting W over or him hurting me. Probably a mixture of both. "Unless he's involved in some make-believe relationship, too, that is so not cool."

"But is it fair of me to be angry with him?" I counter, torn between my own guilt and my anger. "Because I did kiss Oakley last night."

Or rather, he kissed me.

"This is your job. It's like you're an actress and you're playing a part."

"But W doesn't know that."

Paisley's hand stops on the top of my head. "I know you. I know you tried to explain as much as you could without breaking the NDA, and W's smart enough to put two and two together. If he cheated on you, it's not your fault." She sighs. "Now, I'm not going to call Claudia and tell her you're breaking the rules, because I love you and this is difficult, but you can't invite him over again without Claudia's permission. There aren't cameras camped outside—yet."

I clench my hands together. I hate this, even though I know Paisley is right. The other times W has come over, Claudia made sure to arrange some PR event for Oakley so that the cameras would be drawn to him and not to me.

"You going to be okay?" Paisley asks.

"Sure." I climb off the bed, because sitting in my room moping isn't going to accomplish anything. "I'm going to make a cake. Have a preference? Red Velvet? Molten Lava?"

A smile appears on my sister's face as she considers the options. "How about your milk cake?"

"Tres leches? I can do that."

Baking the cake gives my brain something to think about other than W, Oakley and the complicated mess my life has become. On the bright side, at least I'm not worrying about how I have no vision for the future. On the not-bright side, the anxiety in my stomach might give me ulcers before the age of twenty.

When my boyfriend finally shows up, it's eight thirty and my nerves are high. Neither of us speaks as we walk into my bedroom and shut the door. We just stand there for a moment, eyeing each other.

W looks the way he always looks. Jeans, a rugby shirt, sneakers and a backward baseball cap. But his crooked grin is missing, and his eyes contain a bit of a chill.

After a few seconds he throws himself on my bed, which he knows I hate. I like things tidy and he's messing them up, but I feel guilty about so many things that I don't have the nerve to tell him to get off my bed and sit in the chair like a normal human.

Irritably, I pull out my desk chair. "Will you please get your shoes off my comforter?"

"Oh, so Oakley Ford can French you, but I can't have my tennis shoes on your bed?"

I guess we're getting right into it. Awesome.

I sigh softly. "Look," I begin, "I know how hard this has been on you. It's been hard on me, too."

He snorts.

My eyes darken. "W."

"Sorry." He sounds sheepish, albeit grudgingly.

"It's been hard on me, too," I repeat. "I don't particularly enjoy doing what I'm doing even if I'm with Oakley Ford." Just the sound of Oakley's name makes W frown. "And I know it looks like we're having so much fun together. I know it looks real. But it's *not*."

"What about the pictures at the club?" he mutters. "His mouth on yours looked pretty real, Vaughn."

"I know. But I told you there would be some harmless kissing."

"Harmless?" he echoes, raking both hands though his hair. "Do you know how much it sucks seeing my girlfriend kissing some other dude? Some other *famous* dude? Do you even care how it affects me?"

"Of course I care."

He doesn't seem to hear me, because he just keeps going. "I don't know how much longer I can do this. It's only been a month and I can't imagine having to deal with it for eleven more."

"I know," I say miserably. "But this is *us*, W. We're stronger together than apart, remember?"

The hardness in his features slowly loosens. "Do you really not like him?"

I draw my legs up and sit cross-legged on the chair. "I do like him." When W's eyes narrow, I hold up my hand. "As a friend."

A friend? When did that happen?

"He's not what I thought he was. I mean, yeah, he's spoiled

sometimes and kind of a jackass other times. But he's talented and hardworking and...lonely."

W scoffs. "Lonely? Yeah, right."

"It's true, or at least I think it is. His life is tough. Just spending time with him and being in his world, you'd be amazed how little privacy he has. He doesn't even know if his friends are friends with him because they like him or because they want something from him. It's very isolating." I let out a tired breath. "I feel sorry for him sometimes."

Sorry for him? Is that all you feel?

Argh. I really wish I could shut out that voice.

W falls silent. For a long time. As in, almost a full minute goes by.

"W?" I say hesitantly.

He slowly meets my eyes. "I didn't want to do it, but it happened."

My heart stops. "W..." It's almost a warning, because... because I can't hear this. If he says it out loud, I don't know if we'll ever be able to come back from this.

"At the party last night..." He trails off.

"You don't have to tell me," I blurt out.

"No, I do. There was this girl there. I had a little too much to drink."

My palms are so damp I have to wipe them on my knees. "I don't need to hear this," I mumble.

He barrels forward. "All night, guys were giving me these side glances. And she was there. She had barely anything on. I swear, I wouldn't have done it if it wasn't for those pictures. I could see his *tongue*. It was in your *mouth*." He makes a disgusted sound in the back of his throat.

My eyes start to sting. "I'm sorry."

"Do you think of me at all when you're posing for that trash and putting it out there for all our friends to see? Because last night, when this girl was all over me, I kept thinking about you and how I wished you were the one dancing with me. I wanted you to be the one I was kissing, not this chick."

"Oh, W, no." The tears slip out and slide down my cheeks. It was one thing to suspect W hooking up on me, but hearing it confirmed is more painful than I imagined. "Why?"

He reaches forward to squeeze my cold, clammy hands. "I didn't want to. I swear, I wouldn't have kissed her at all if it hadn't been for those pictures. He had his hands in your hair. The two of you were making out and I looked like a chump. It made me angry." I try to pull away, but his grip is too strong. "And I realized something the other night."

I clench my teeth. "A moment of epiphany when you were kissing some stranger?"

"Exactly." He doesn't register my sarcasm. "If we're going to make this work for us, we need to have a stronger connection than the one we already have."

"But I love you." Those words have never sounded more pathetic.

"You say that, but there's still something you're holding back." He reaches out and wipes away a few of my tears with his thumb. "We need to take it to the next level. I've been real patient. Some guys would've pressured you, but I never did. Prom night, remember? I stopped when you asked me to stop."

After a lot of bitching and moaning and telling me that we were the only ones stopping, but yes, you stopped. I pull my bruised fingers from his and rub my forehead. He wants me to be grateful that he stopped and that...that pisses me off.

And that he's using my kissing Oakley as an excuse to cheat on me; that makes me even angrier. But I have my own issues. I can't deny that when I was in the car with Oakley after the ice cream date, I felt things I'd only ever felt when I was with W.

"Why is everyone we know having sex but us?" He shoots to his feet to loom over my chair. "My roommates all got laid the other night. With girls they didn't even know. These chicks at college aren't uptight like you are. And they definitely aren't making out with other guys and telling me no at the same time. I could've slept with that girl last night but I didn't."

I grind my teeth. "Gee, thanks for the restraint, W. I should give you cookies for not sleeping with her? Just kissing her?"

"Yes. If you're kissing Oakley Ford—with tongue—then I need something more from you."

"It's not a competition."

"So you're saying you won't sleep with me?" He sounds utterly disgusted with me, like I'm refusing the most reasonable request ever.

The pressure makes my stomach churn. I search for a way out, and, as if a higher power decided to take pity on me, the doorbell suddenly rings.

I bolt off my chair. "I need to answer that."

"Paisley can do it," W says coldly.

"She's in the shower." I toss out the lie over my shoulder on my way to the door. Truthfully, I have no clue what Paisley is doing, but I need a moment to regroup.

Unfortunately, W decides to follow me, which brings a silent scream to my throat. I need...distance, damn it. I need to collect my thoughts and figure out how I feel about everything we just talked about.

He kissed someone else.

So did you...

Yeah, but my kiss was staged! It wasn't real.

Wasn't it?

I'm two seconds away from releasing the scream. I've never

been more confused in my life, and feeling W's breath on my neck on the way downstairs makes me tense and anxious.

We reach the front hall, where he finally quits crowding me. He leans against the wall with his arms crossed and his surly expression fixed on me.

I open the door to find Oakley standing on my porch.

"Oh," I squeak. "What are you doing here?"

Before he can speak, W's enraged voice sounds from behind me.

"Oh, *hell*, no!"

21
HIM

1doodlebug1 @OakleyFord_stanNo1 She looks like trash in those pics!

OakleyFord_stanNo1 @1doodlebug1 she IS trash. Don't know what Oak sees in her.

1doodlebug1 @Oaksgirl69 Think he's a good kisser? @OakleyFord_stanNo1

OakleyFord_stanNo1 @1doodlebug1 um, DUH!!! Best kisser ever!!!!!!

1doodlebug1 @OakleyFord_stanNo1 How do u kno??

OakleyFord_stanNo1 @1doodlebug1 b/c he looks like it. Sooooooo much tongue in those pix!

1doodlebug1 @OakleyFord_stanNo1 She doesn't deserve him.

OakleyFord_stanNo1 @1doodlebug1 nope.

"What the hell is *he* doing here?" the asshole behind Vaughn growls. "Did you invite him over?"

I look from Vaughn to the asshole, wondering the same damn thing. What's *he* doing here, and did she invite *him* over?

"No, I didn't invite him," she says.

Her words are like a knife to the gut. To think I came over tonight to apologize to her.

"And this isn't a good time," Vaughn adds, turning back to me. "I'm kind of in the middle of something."

I bet she is. I swallow a dose of anger, but I'm not sure why I'm so pissed. I knew going into this that she had a boyfriend. I've made fun of the douche bag on more than one occasion. But knowing and seeing are two very different things.

This frat boy loser is in her *house*. They were probably having a romantic evening before I showed up. Maybe I even interrupted them having sex.

Another rush of bitterness coats my throat. Fuck this. I shouldn't have come in the first place. I should've just ignored the guilt that was gnawing at me all day, ever since I hung up on Vaughn. But it had been impossible to ignore. My mom called a few hours after her lunch with Vaughn, and I've never heard her rave about someone so much. Listening to Mom gush about how smart and sweet and wonderful Vaughn is only twisted the guilt knife deeper, made me feel even worse about the way I taunted her outside the club yesterday.

I came here armed with an apology, but now, as Vaughn's boyfriend and I stare each other down, I feel like *I'm* the one who deserves a fucking apology.

"Do you have a hearing problem?" W asks frostily. "She said we're in the middle of something."

For some reason, I stay rooted in place. "Maybe I'll wait until you're done." Jesus. What am I saying? I don't want to do that at all. But something about this jerk brings out my hostile side.

"No, you're gonna turn around and get back in your limo or whatever the hell you drove here. She's off the clock, asshole."

"W!" Vaughn chides.

"Wait, are you paying her salary now?" I give him a cool smile despite the fact that his arrow actually stung.

"I don't have to. Vaughn doesn't need to be paid to be with me."

"W!" Vaughn nearly shouts. She takes a breath and addresses me again. "You need to go," she says in a trembly voice that cuts right through me.

"Yeah. Whatever. I'm gone." I jerk open the door but try to get one last dig in. "Enjoy the rest of your night. Looks like you've got a real keeper there, babe."

Then I stomp out, ignoring Vaughn's protests and W's sputtered threats, and march back to the Escalade.

Ty's face is a picture of concern, and even that makes me snarl. "Everything okay?"

"She's busy," I mutter. "Let's go."

"Where we going?"

I'm already reaching for my phone. I scroll down until I find the perfect companion for tonight. "Feel like getting wasted?" I ask Luke.

"Always." If he's surprised to hear from me, it doesn't show in his voice.

"How about The Head and we'll go back to my place after."

"Solid plan, my brother. I'll be there in twenty."

Ty shakes his head in disapproval but changes directions immediately because he's paid to protect me, not to argue. I don't know why that makes me feel worse, but it does. Is there anyone in my life who *isn't* on my payroll?

"Women are complicated," he says.

"You're single, Ty," I remind him.

"Because women are complicated."

And the ones you like are employed by your boss, I nearly retort, but after shooting off my mouth to Vaughn, I don't feel real talkative anymore. I slink down in my seat, replaying the disaster that just happened.

I don't know what I'm angrier about—that Vaughn was on a date with that douche or that she didn't correct him when he said I was only her job. What the hell is the matter with her? Does she realize how many chicks would kill to be with me? If I wanted to, I could give out the address of The Head and a few thousand girls would raze the club to the ground trying to gain access to me.

I work myself into a self-righteous rage by the time we reach The Head. Ty pulls up and puts the SUV in Neutral.

"I'll go in and tell the manager you're here."

"No. I'm walking the line," I insist. I need…something. A hit off the adulation stick.

Ty frowns. "That's way too dangerous."

But like a good employee, he knows his limits. He doesn't tell me no because that's not his place. I hop out and slam the door. The tail end of a string of curses is cut off before Ty joins me on the street. At first no one notices me as I walk toward the entrance.

But as I pass more people, the whispering swells until it's a wave of noise. *Is that Oakley Ford? Holy crap, I think that's Oakley Ford. Ask him for a picture! A picture. Oakley! Oakley! Oakley!*

Hands reach for me. The bouncer at the door is on his feet, holding the line back. Girls are jumping over the rope-bound barricades.

What the hell was I thinking?

I quicken my stride and then realize I'm not going to make it unless I do *something*. I halt, turn toward the crowd and raise my hand. "I'm going inside and hope to see you there."

The crowd pushes forward. Ty grabs my arm and drags me inside.

"Okay, not my best moment," I admit, brushing a hand through my hair.

Ty avoids my gaze, likely trying to hide his irritation at having to babysit my punk-ass self.

I wonder if I should warn him that his babysitting duties are only getting started, because I plan on fucking shit up tonight.

But nah. I'll let him find that out on his own.

HER

"So he's just showing up at your house for booty calls now?"

W is livid as we face off in the living room two minutes after Oakley's angry departure. His cheeks are a scary shade of purple, and the vein in his forehead looks like it's going to burst any second.

I want to tell him to keep his voice down because my sister and brothers are right upstairs, but I can't get any words out. I'm still in a stunned stupor over what just happened. Why was Oakley here? Why did I let him and W get into it like that?

"Answer me!"

I jolt at the violent command. Taking a breath, I meet my boyfriend's eyes. "It wasn't a booty call."

"Then why did he come here? How often do you have him over?" W asks bitterly.

"Never. He's never been here—no, once. He's been here once, but that was a PR meeting. All his publicists were here, too. Other than that, I've *never* had him over." I exhale in a rush. "Look, I don't know why Oak showed up, but—"

"Oh, you're calling him Oak now? Is that in your contract?"

I hadn't even realized I'd done it. "No, it's just..." God, what do I even say? "Everyone calls him that."

"Is this is a game to you?" W snaps.

"No, of course not—"

"What are you telling him about me?"

The question confuses me. "Nothing. We don't talk about you."

W's eyes blaze. "So you pretend you don't have a boyfriend? That I don't exist? Is that what you do when no cameras are around? What, are you embarrassed of me?"

Argh! I just want to scream until my lungs are sore. Everything I say is being twisted. If I don't talk about him, I'm forgetting him; if I do, I'm betraying him.

"What do you talk about, then?" W demands.

I swallow. "Stuff. Stupid stuff."

"Like what?" he insists.

"I don't know. Music. My parents. His parents."

"So stuff we used to talk about. Couple stuff." He snarls. "And you're telling me that it's all fake and you still love me, right?"

I rub my forehead. Every word that comes out of W's mouth is an accusation of wrongdoing. Angry words fill my mouth. Things like *at least Oakley doesn't pressure me for sex. At least he doesn't view this as a competition. At least he doesn't kiss other girls.* But I don't say those things, because unlike W, I don't say the first spiteful thing that comes into my mind.

"This is a bunch of BS," W fumes. "You're ruining my first year of college, you realize that? I'm a frickin' laughingstock. I get up in the morning and people can't shut up about how Oakley Ford is screwing my girl. Do you have any idea what that's doing to me? How do you think it feels being the guy whose girl dumped him for a rock star?"

"What does it matter what other people think?" I ask desperately. "Remember after Mom and Dad died, and I had that awful, embarrassing moment in morning advisory where I just started crying and had to run out of the room? Everyone started calling me a head case, and you told me it didn't matter what they thought. That it's only the people you love whose opinions matter."

My attempt at reasoning with him fails. "Well, I love my friends," W snaps back. "And their opinion is that I'm a total loser. And I can't even tell them the truth because of some stupid thing I signed."

I choke down my frustration. "We both signed it, and there's nothing we can do to change that. Jim Tolson will murder us if we—"

"Oh, we're talking about Tolson now?" W interrupts snidely. "Great, let's talk about Tolson. Why the hell is he taking so long to get back to me about the show?"

I freeze.

Oh, crap.

I might look convincing when I'm kissing Oakley for the paparazzi, but my poker face doesn't stand a chance in front of the guy I've been dating for two years.

W immediately steps closer, his dark eyes narrowed in suspicion. "What aren't you telling me? Did Tolson hate the show?"

"No," I say quickly. "He didn't hate it. He…" *Didn't see it.* I swallow the awful confession.

"He what?" W pushes.

Crap. *Crap.*

Maybe W is right. Maybe I am the worst girlfriend on the planet. How else do you explain the fact that I totally, *completely* forgot to send W's clip reel to Diamond?

"He hasn't had the chance to look at it yet," I lie weakly.

Very weakly, because W sees right through me. I know the exact moment that the truth dawns on him. His features sharpen. His lips twist into an ugly line that matches the ugly cloud in his eyes.

"You didn't give it to him." He speaks softly at first, almost thoughtfully, but it doesn't take long before his rage boils to the surface and then spills over. "You didn't fucking give it to him?"

I stumble backward from the force of his fury.

"Vaughn," a tentative voice calls from the stairs. It's Paisley, and she sounds more worried than I've ever heard her.

"Leave us the *fuck* alone, Paisley!" W shouts at the doorway.

I gasp in horror. "Don't talk to my sister like that!"

"I'll talk to her any way I want!" He's swaying on his feet now, as if his anger has infected his motor functions. His incensed gaze burns so hot that I'm scared it'll turn me to ashes. "I can't believe you did this to me, Vaughn."

I struggle for air. "I…forgot. I'm so sorry, W. It slipped my mind—"

"It *slipped your mind*?" he explodes. "My career, my future, slipped your mind? You're a tease, you know that? You make a lot of promises about everything. About how much you love me. About how you're going to help me get on TV. But it's all a bunch of bullshit words. And you know what? I'm done."

He marches to the doorway then stops, turns to glower at me, and repeats himself for good measure. "I'm *done* with you."

I'll never know how I manage it, but I'm able to keep the tears at bay. I stare at him, unblinking, unmoving, until finally, he stalks out of the living room.

That's when the tears pour out, accompanied by a sickening mental recap of every horrible thing that happened tonight.

W sniping at Oakley.

Oakley storming off.

W's fury over me kissing Oakley.

His confession that the pictures drove him to kiss someone else.

And it's not until I hear W's car engine start that I realize he couldn't have seen the photos last night.

They weren't online until this morning.

22

HIM

1doodlebug1 @OakleyFord_stanNo1 He's at The Head!!! You're in socal, rite??? GO!!

OakleyFord_stanNo1 @1doodlebug1 I don't have a driver's license!!!

Ty leads me toward the VIP stairs of the club, not so gently shoving people out of our way. The bouncer at the door recognizes us immediately and swings open the panel behind him.

The Head's VIP lounge is a lot more private than some. A one-way glass mirror that can be turned into a see-through panel with a flick of a switch spans the wall between the so-called important people and the rest of the crowd. We get to watch the normals like they're animals in a zoo.

In reality, we're the main attraction and everyone's paid to see us perform—like monkeys. I throw myself into a velvet lounge chair while Ty takes up position behind me. Despite my not-quite-legal status, a highball appears at my right hand before I even think to ask for one.

"Hey, Oakley," an eager voice says. "Mind if I sit down?"

I look the newcomer over in her tight black dress, high heels and perfectly done hair. There's a light sheen on her forehead, maybe sweat worked up while dancing or maybe it's nerves from talking to me. I've seen girls faint before from merely laying eyes on me.

"I'm waiting for someone." I try to keep my tone friendly, but fail.

She winces and tries again. "I can wait with you."

I debate what to say to her when my phone buzzes. I whip it out thinking that maybe it's Vaughn apologizing. I'll graciously accept it and send a car to pick her up. We can— Oh, hell, it's Luke.

Need your help man. Assholes won't let me in.

Ty probably told the bouncer to be extra careful, which the bouncer likely took to mean: hot chicks only.

"Sorry. Gotta go get my friend," I tell the girl.

She stands there like a statue as I walk toward the door, apparently paralyzed by the fact I even spoke to her.

See, Vaughn, lots of chicks out there would love to be in your shoes. This girl is so starstruck she can't even move.

"He's with me," I inform the bouncer, holding up my phone to show him a picture of Luke.

"Just being careful," the no-neck tells me.

"Hey, Oak, getting the party started without me?" Luke says as he bursts through the door. Behind him about ten more people stream through, guys and girls.

The bouncer raises his eyebrows as if to ask if I meant for all these people to come. I shrug. It's Luke. I knew what I was getting into when I called him.

"Thought this girlfriend of yours had taken your balls and

put them in her backpack." Luke pulls me in for the standard clenched fist, backslap bro hug.

Anger stirs up at the insult toward Vaughn, but then I remember what she's doing, no, *who* she's doing right now.

"Nah. Just wasn't feeling it before." I'm not feeling it now, either. The music, the action, the girls don't interest me at all, and I know, even before Luke calls for the first thousand-dollar bottle of Cristal, that this is a mistake.

The waitstaff busily rearranges a seating area for my new entourage. There are other celebrities here. I recognize a television actress and a couple of guys well-known for their comic action films, but the others combined don't have the star power that I do. Which is why the staff of Head is bowing and scraping for me.

I opt for a chair on the end and leave the middle for Luke, because even though I thought I wanted company, I now realize it's the last thing I'm in the mood for.

A girl—I don't know her name because I paid zero attention when Luke was introducing everyone—touches my arm for about the hundredth time in the last ten minutes.

"I'm not interested," I respond, sharper than I should be. Across from me I see Ty frown, and I soften my tone at her stricken expression. "Sorry. Just...not a good night, okay? And I've got a girlfriend."

A girlfriend who's currently having a romantic evening with her boyfriend.

I raise a hand, calling out, "I need another round. Stat."

Ty's frown lines grow deeper. Fuck, he's not in charge of me. The booze comes in a steady, unceasing stream. I can feel myself loosening up.

What do I have to be uptight about anyway? There are girls here of every variety. It's like a candy store. I'll take a red-head, a brunette and two blondes. Package them all up and send them over to the Marmont. One of the Garden Cottages would do nicely. Private entrance. We don't want my image to be tarnished.

I laugh sourly.

"What's so funny?" someone near my feet asks.

Since when did it get so crowded in here? There are people everywhere. I swear there are more people inside this VIP lounge than there are out in the main club. Having run out of chairs, the girls have settled for sitting on the dingy floor that people have likely spit on, puked on, pissed on. But they'd sit in a pit of snakes if it meant touching my leg.

"Nothing's funny." That's the honest truth. One of the boys passes me a joint. I take a hit and exhale a cloud of smoke. I wait for it to lighten my mood, take the weight off my chest, but nothing happens. I take another hit and then drag on the herb until it's a stub.

"Dude, that was some quality hash there."

"He's good for it," Luke assures them.

I'm good for it? Oh, yeah, I'm good for the money, the status, the girls. What I'm not good for is actually dating a real person. Not good enough for her to pine over.

Suddenly this whole scene looks gross and if I stay here another minute, my head's going to explode.

"I'm bailing."

Luke protests. "I thought we were going back to your place."

He has one arm slung around a chick with a low-cut top and even lower-cut jeans. I can see the straps of her thong poking out. And if she's legal, I'll eat my frickin' hat.

"Another time."

Luke protests until Ty pulls out a wallet and throws some cash on the table. That shuts up Luke real fast. He'll start up the moment I'm gone. Telling everyone there about how I can't function without him and that he's the glue that holds the band together.

Ty hustles me out the back door of the club, but several photogs are there. I feel like he moves slower than normal, as punishment for coming here. *Passive-aggressive, are ya, Ty?*

The paps shout questions at me. "Where's your girlfriend?"

"Is it over?"

"Is she tired of you?"

The questions tumble over each other, mixing up in my head, pounding at the edges, pushing words out before I can think twice.

I'm not completely sure of how I answer, but it must be satisfactory since everyone stops for a moment, a blessed sliver of silence. Then I dive into the SUV and Ty speeds away.

I wake up the next morning to find seven missed calls from Claudia. Shit. That's never a good sign.

When I sit up, the pain that shoots through my temples is so strong that I collapse onto the mattress again. I groan loudly, but that just makes my head hurt worse. Man, what's with this migraine? I didn't drink that much at the club last night, so I'm not sure why my head is so foggy—

The hash. I forgot about the hash.

My stomach churns as I stare at Claudia's name on my phone. I must have done something last night. Something bad.

But what? Did I whip off my clothes? Mack on some random chick? Oh, crap, did I real-cheat on my fake girlfriend?— no, that couldn't have happened. Ty was with me. There's no way he would've let me touch another girl.

Instead of calling Claudia back, I open the web browser on my phone, wondering what I'm going to find. Maybe I threw up on some fan's shoes? That wouldn't be too damaging to my image.

I wait for the home page to load and then click on the entertainment news tab.

My stomach drops. The headline on the page reads:

Oakley Ford disses new girlfriend's ex!

Damn it.

I quickly scan the article, but I don't remember saying any of that shit. I must have, though. Nope, not must have—I definitely did. There's a video link to the TMI site. I click on it, press Play and promptly see my high, drunken self stumbling out of The Head. Flashbulbs go off, highlighting my bloodshot eyes. Paps shout out at me, but I keep walking with my head ducked down and my hand shielding my face.

Except then one of them asks, "Is she tired of you?" and I do the most boneheaded thing on the planet.

I stop, turn toward the microphone and I say:

"Tired? You kidding me? Her ex is a total waste. She's got a real man now—you think she'd tire of that?"

Cringing, I shut off the video and whip my phone across the room. It slams against the wall, but luckily I've got a heavy-duty case for occasions such as this. This isn't the first time I've thrown my phone over something stupid I did, which then became national news.

There's a sharp knock on the door, followed by, "Everything okay in there?"

I guess Ty heard my phone greeting the wall. "It's fine," I bark.

He opens the door anyway. Nosy bastard. He scans the room, spots my phone on the floor and says, "I guess Claudia called."

"Yup." I glower at him. "Why the hell did you let me speak to them last night, Ty? You know I wasn't in the right state of mind."

"Let you?" he echoes. In a rare occurrence, Tyrese actually looks pissed off at me. "Brother, you were out of control last night. Snapping at peeps, smoking all that shit you shouldn't have been smoking. I tried to haul you away from the vultures. Watch the video again. Closer, this time. I'm sure you'll see your punk-ass arm shoving me away when I tried to step in. Spoiled brat."

My eyebrows shoot up. "This spoiled brat pays your bills," I say tightly.

He looks wounded, and I immediately feel guilty.

"I'm sorry," I mumble. "I shouldn't have said that. I'm just… hungover and mad. But I'm not mad at you, okay? You did what you could."

I don't know if he fully accepts my apology. He simply nods and then ducks out without another word.

Look at me, alienating another person in my life. Awesome.

I call Claudia back. After she yells at me for five minutes, we discuss the statement I need to make. The public apology to Vaughn's douche bag boyfriend. I can't believe he was over at her place last night. Why is she still with him?

And why is he still with *her*? The whole world thinks she's my girlfriend—how can he stand that?

Bitterness lodges in my throat. I guess it doesn't matter what the world thinks. It only matters what Vaughn thinks. What Vaughn wants.

And it's not me.

But I still need to make things right with her, and when Claudia mentions the charity benefit I supposedly agreed to attend tonight and had forgotten all about, I realize it's the perfect place to apologize to Vaughn—a public event where she can't slap me. She can wear a pretty dress, listen to some good music, eat some good food. The CF Society always puts on a great spread.

Claudia packs as many of these fund-raisers into my schedule as possible, as if giving money away offsets my asshole behavior. Wonder if Vaughn will see it that way.

Except when I bring it up to Claudia, asking what time I should send a car for Vaughn, she's quick to say, "No, Vaughn's not coming with you tonight."

I clench my jaw. "Why not?"

"Why do you think, Oak? Because she's furious with you."

My stomach sinks. "You spoke to her already?"

"No. She's not answering her phone. Neither is Paisley." Claudia's voice tightens. "So, yes, I'm taking that to mean that she's not happy about you belittling her boyfriend's masculinity."

"Well, goodie for her. She still *works* for me. She can't bail on an important event just because I insulted her stupid boyfriend."

"Normally I would agree with you, but Vaughn can be unpredictable. I'm not sending a pissed-off fake girlfriend to this event with you. Who knows what she'll do."

Claudia has a point. "Fine. So when can I see her again?"

"Give her a couple days to cool down. By then you'll have given your public apology to W, so I'm sure that will help."

"Okay," I say, feeling disheartened. "Just send me the statement you want me to make—"

"Oh, you won't be making it," Claudia says firmly. "We're writing a statement, I'll send it for your approval and then we'll release it to the media. You will *not* be speaking with them directly. Not after last night."

Since I hate speaking to the media in the first place, I'm okay with this.

HER

I've never been dumped before.

I guess that makes sense seeing as how W was my first

real boyfriend. But it still feels terrible. It's awful and soul-crushing and has the power to turn a normal, solid-head-on-her-shoulders girl into a blubbering mess.

Like a total loser, I cried myself to sleep last night. I was midsob when I finally drifted off. And then the dreams came. Terrible, terrible dreams that involved W throwing bricks at my head while Oakley kept jumping in front of me to deflect them. At one point he started singing and the bricks stopped midair.

A therapist would probably have a field day with that. Me, I'm just exhausted from dodging dream bricks all frickin' night.

To make matters worse, Claudia has been calling all morning. I finally had to shut off my phone, because I am *not* in the mood to deal with her or Oakley or any other living human today. All I want to do is curl up on this patio swing and pretend that last night didn't happen.

The back door hinges squeak, and I jerk in surprise when my sister lowers herself next to me, a plate of the tres leches cake I made last night in her hand.

"Here," she says.

"It's ten thirty in the morning. Way too early for cake," I say weakly. My throat is raw from crying. I rub it, but the pain doesn't go away, because it's inside me.

"It's never too early for cake." She smiles gently. "I know you're more of an ice cream moper, but we ran out. I ate it all last week."

"Seriously?"

Paisley shoves a forkful of cake into her mouth before answering. "Yes. I think I'm in love with Oakley's cute body-guard and so I ate the entire carton to cheer myself up. But cake does the trick, too. Try a bite. You'll see." She extends the fork to me, but I don't want it.

"You're in love with Ty?" I squawk in surprise. I mean, I suspected she had a crush on him, but the *L*-word? Seriously?

"Okay, well, maybe not *love*. But I really like him."

"You've only met him once," I point out.

She shakes her head. "Not true. He's around Diamond sometimes," Paisley admits. "But he'd never date me because I work for Jim's brother and that's too close for Ty's comfort. Besides, I'm concentrating on my career, so it wouldn't matter if he liked me back."

"Wow. I had no idea."

She shrugs. "It's just a crush, and I usually forget about it until I run into him." She takes another bite. "And like I said, something sweet usually fills my cravings."

"Cake has never made me feel better." I think of all the sweets that were delivered to the house after Mom and Dad died. Not one of them had filled the ache. The only thing that did was being with W.

"Not true. W is your cake. Was your cake," she corrects.

"You mean, fatty and bad for me?" I mutter, because we both know she never liked him.

Paisley eats two huge bites before setting the plate on the step. "I love you, Vaughn, you know that, right?"

I make some noise of acknowledgment, but I don't want to talk to Paisley about this right now. She's never had a serious boyfriend because she's always been focused on moving forward. I don't like moving forward. I want things to stay like they were forever. Mom and Dad around the table. The twins little. W holding my hand.

"The twins' school barbecue is this Friday," she says when it becomes clear I'm not going to contribute to the conversation. "You're still coming, right?"

I respond with a noncommittal grunt.

"Claudia wants you to bring Oakley."

Now I grit my teeth.

"She won't stop calling, by the way." Paisley pauses. "Oakley gave a hell of a sound bite last night."

That gets my attention. "What did he say?"

"Not the nicest stuff," she admits. "He spoke to the press about W."

I look over sharply. "Are you serious?"

She nods. "He called W a waste of space. And, uh, insinuated that W isn't a real man."

Oh, God. No wonder Claudia is freaking out. "Let me guess—you totally agree with those observations," I say sarcastically.

My sister releases a heavy sigh. "Vaughn."

"What? We both know you hate W."

"I don't hate him."

"Yeah, you do," I say irritably.

"No, I don't. *Hate* is a strong word. I don't hate people." She speaks in a firm tone. "But you're right—I wasn't fond of him. I didn't like W because he wasn't good to you. You were convenient for him."

"That's not true," I protest.

"Yes, it is. When he canceled at the last minute, you didn't care. When you won those Dodgers tickets at the school raffle and he wanted to go with *his* friends, you coughed them up without an argument. You wear those shoes around constantly—" She points accusingly at my Vans "—but where are his? I know you drew on his, too."

I fight the urge to cover one foot with the other. "You're forgetting all the times he held me after Mom and Dad died. Or all the times he let me hang out at his dorm while he was busy doing his YouTube show. He was there for me."

"He was there," she agrees. "W was there, physically, but

he wasn't ever *there* for you—emotionally. And frankly, you knew that. It's why you didn't have sex with him."

"I wasn't ready!" I yell at her.

She leans back against the swing, unfazed by my shouting. "And you weren't ever going to be ready with W."

"Because I'm too immature?" I shoot back.

"Nope. Because you never loved W like you thought you did." She reaches out for my hand. "It's not like I don't think you're capable of that kind of love. Just that whatever feelings you had for W weren't as strong as you thought they were."

I jerk away. "Because I didn't gorge myself with cake?"

"Because W's a selfish jerk and you're more upset about the fact that you lost an anchor in your life than you are that you lost W."

I turn away and fold my arms around my waist. I hate her matter-of-fact tone.

But mostly I hate that she's probably right.

23

HIM

The benefit is at the Wilshire. It's a fancy dinner, followed by a silent auction—all proceeds go to medical research—and then a performance by Deadhead Bloom. I hadn't realized they were the headliner. King produced their last album, which means there's a chance that he…crap, he *is* here tonight.

I feel sick when I spot him at a nearby table. I had no idea he was going to be here. I'm about to avert my eyes, but it's too late. He's already noticed me.

He tips his head in a nod, and there's a smile on his lips that doesn't quiet reach his eyes. Then he turns to talk to his companion, a gorgeous woman in a white cocktail gown.

The people at my table are all industry people, none of

whom I know well. Three are members of a hot new boy band. The rest of the table is filled out with a couple of music execs and a brunette in a silky red dress. Her chair inches closer and closer to mine throughout dinner until she's practically in my lap. I ignore her and talk to the exec to my left, but I can feel her staring at me, and every now and then she tries to cut in.

"Oakley, how's the new album coming along?"

"When's your next tour?"

"Are you still with the same label?"

Every time, I answer with one-word grunts before turning to the label exec and pretending to care about what he's saying. Something about marketing strategies and utilizing Facebook groups to build an online fan base. Even though I hate social media, I know what's current, and this exec doesn't have the first clue. I want to tell him that Facebook is practically a dinosaur now and everyone's on Instagram and Snapchat, but he's so into his speech and I let him drone on because he provides a good buffer between me and the overeager brunette.

The silent auction goes by fast. The only item I bid on is a trip to Paris, because it seems like something Vaughn might enjoy. I don't win, but I don't care. She probably wouldn't have gone with me anyway.

Then there's a brief intermission as the band sets up. I quickly excuse myself from the table, but even trying to leave the ballroom is an ordeal. People keep intercepting me while I smile and nod and constantly repeat the same thing, "Sounds great, but I got to hit the little boys' room."

I keep walking until I reach the French doors that lead to a small terrace. I'm not sure anyone's supposed to be out here. The smoking area is on the main patio, but I don't care if I'm in an off-limits zone. I'm Oakley Ford. And I need a break from all these people and their nonstop chatter. It's choking me.

I don't smoke, but I kind of wish I had a cigarette right now. Knowing my luck, someone with a telescopic lens across the street would snap a picture of me sucking on a cancer stick at a cancer benefit, and the next thing I know I'm the poster boy for antismoking campaigns and the dangers of fame.

When I hear footsteps behind me, I stifle a sigh and reluctantly turn around. I expect to see the brunette, or maybe some other chick who saw me sneak out, but it's King. He steps out holding what looks like a joint, but I think it's a hand-rolled cigarette because the sweet scent of tobacco wafts over to me.

"I didn't know you smoked," I remark.

"Every now and then." He shrugs. "I mostly use it as an excuse to get out of talking to a bunch of strangers."

I half smile. "You should take my lead." I hold up my bare hands. "Don't even make an excuse. Just walk out."

"Yeah, I suppose you don't make excuses. You do what you want and say what you want, doncha, kid?"

I'm hit with a pang of shame. I have a feeling he's referring to the sound bite of me bashing W that's all over the internet.

Sure enough, he says, "You already got the girl, Oakley. No need to twist the knife deeper in the one who had her before."

My shame deepens, mingling with guilt and regret, and forming a ball in my throat. "I screwed up," I admit.

"Yup."

"It's just…and this isn't an excuse," I say hastily. "It's not me trying to say that what I did was right. But…they have history, man. Two years of it."

"Yeah, most people do. Have history."

"Not me." My voice cracks slightly, and embarrassment shoots through me. I'm like a prepubescent boy all of a sudden. I don't know what it is about this man that makes me feel so insecure and exposed. Vaughn makes me feel that way, too.

"I've never dated anyone for more than a few weeks," I find myself confessing. "I've never had a long relationship, the kind where you have time to build inside jokes and learn to finish each other's sentences, when you reach that point where you're so comfortable that you can read the other person's mind." I hesitate. "She had that with the ex."

He nods again.

"I was jealous," I mumble.

That gets me a response—a soft chuckle. "Yeah, you were. You have a lot of growing up to do, Oak. We're all jealous."

My eyes flare in surprise.

"Yeah, even me. I've been without a Grammy nomination for three years. There are singers I'd like to work with who don't want to work with me. Everyone's got the green bug inside them. It's how you process that jealousy. Acknowledging it and fueling your creative energy is one way. Another is standing outside a club, drunk and high, spouting off against a defenseless kid. Which one makes you look like an entitled prick?"

I know he's right. And the more he talks, the lower my spirits sink. I can see my chances of working with him slipping away.

But then he surprises me. "You screwed up. But you know what? You owned up to it." He gives a rueful look. "I'm sure the press will forget all about it once your publicity team releases your *heartfelt* apology to Miss Bennett's ex-boyfriend."

My cheeks heat up. He knows I'm not writing my own apology, and that makes me feel even worse.

"You want my advice?" he asks lightly.

God, so badly. "Please," I almost beg.

"All those volatile emotions of yours? The jealousy and the anger and the self-consciousness? Keep owning them. More than that, channel them into your music. You feel me?"

I nod slowly. "Yeah, I think I do."

He walks over and pats me on the shoulder. "I'll see you around."

I watch him walk away, and when I hear the first strains of an acoustic guitar, I hurry inside, too, dutifully returning to my table and settling in my chair to listen to Deadhead Bloom's set. It's not exactly my kind of music, but it's not bad, either.

I stay for three songs before ducking out. Claudia said I didn't have to stay for the whole thing, and nobody expects me to anyway. Besides, I already donated half a million bucks to this thing.

Ty and I leave the hotel through the front entrance. There's a lot of press waiting outside, but the area's been sectioned off to accommodate the high-profile guests. All we have to do is stay on our side of the gate and we have a clear path right to the car.

"Oakley!'"

"Oakley, over here!"

"Do you have any comment about what you said last night?"

I find myself hesitating.

"Jesus, brother, don't you ever learn?" Ty murmurs under his breath.

But I have learned. I'm not high, I'm not drunk, and I'm not overcome with jealousy. I'm humbled after that talk with King.

I slowly take my hands out of my pockets and approach the screaming crowd. My gaze sweeps over the sea of microphones until I find the most well-known media outlet. I stop in front of Samantha Wright from Channel 9.

The blonde looks stunned, probably because I'm notorious for sneaking out of events to avoid talking to the media. Of course, that doesn't stop them from snapping shots of me doing stupid things and reporting on me anyway.

"How was the concert?" Samantha asks me.

I smile. "It's still going, actually. I have a bit of a headache, so I left early. I hope the CF Society forgives me."

"I'm sure they're happy you showed up to support such a good cause."

"A great cause," I correct. "Though I wish I hadn't shown up with a hangover. I made some bad decisions last night, partied harder than I should have."

She looks startled by the revelation. I don't think she expected me to be so candid about my partying, particularly given my age.

"Yes, it did look like you had a busy night yesterday," she says tactfully, before pausing.

I can see her brain working overtime trying to figure out her next question. She doesn't know if she should ask about my jackass remarks regarding W, but I opened the door with the hangover comment and she can't *not* walk through it.

I take pity on her by saying, "Yeah, I had quite a night, Samantha. Almost lost my girlfriend because of it."

Her perfectly shaped eyebrows soar to her forehead. The other paps swarm toward us, shoving microphones at me. Several glare at Samantha for getting this scoop. Their sound bites will be muffled, while hers will be as clear as a bell.

"I suppose you're referring to the comments you made?"

"Yup, I am." I give a sheepish look. "Believe me, I was in the doghouse for that, and I deserved to be. What I said about Vaughn's ex-boyfriend was uncalled for. Not only that, but it was juvenile and completely inappropriate. I sincerely regret my behavior, and I'm not making any excuses for it. I disrespected my girlfriend and her ex, and my hurtful words are more of a reflection about me and how I still have a lot of growing up to do. If anyone isn't a man, it's me."

She's nodding fervently. "Have you apologized to them in person?"

"I've apologized to Vaughn," I lie, though I do plan on doing that when I get home. But I can't act like there's any strife in our relationship, not in front of these vultures. "She forgave me. She understood I was just being a jealous caveman but made me promise not to do it again. As for…" I trail off, because I have no idea what W is even short for.

"Mr. Wilkerson?" she fills in.

His name is W. Wilkerson? For fuck's sake.

"As for Vaughn's ex," I continue, "I do intend to call him and apologize. What I said about him was untrue. He's a great guy." *Gag.* "He and Vaughn have history. He's still a good friend of hers, and the jealous dude in me needs to understand and accept that. Anyway—" I flash a million-dollar smile "—thanks for taking the time to chat with me."

Then I give a little salute and stride off to where Tyrese is waiting for me.

His dark eyes flicker with humor. "Claudia is going to…" He drifts off.

"What?" I ask warily. "Kill me?"

"For once? I don't think so." He shakes his head in amazement. "I think she might send you a fruit basket, dude."

I snort as we get into the Escalade. Truthfully, I don't care what Claudia thinks about this. All that matters to me is that Vaughn forgives me. And I'm confident she will, especially after she hears the mature statement I just gave.

Sure, I still think her boyfriend is a jackass who doesn't deserve her, but so what? I'm not going to win her over by pointing out W's weaknesses.

I'm going to do it by pointing out my strengths.

I feel totally rejuvenated as Ty drives us away from the hotel. I find myself tapping my foot, drumming my fingers against my thighs. I'm energized, like there's a live wire running through my body, making it crackle with electricity.

"We're not going home," I tell Ty.

He glances over. "Where we going, then?"

"The studio." My fingers drum harder. "I'm feeling in-spired."

24

HIM

1doodlebug1 @OakleyFord_stanNo1 Oakley is so amazing. I've watched the apology a hundred times. I cldn't love him more.

OakleyFord_stanNo1 @1doodlebug1 same. so much. Proves why he's worthy of our stanning.

OakleyFord_stanNo1 @1doodlebug1 see screenshot @OakleyFord you're forgiven

Oakley Ford ✅ **Verified** @VeryVaughn I am sorry

@OakleyFord I kno. 4 the rec, I think you're a real man. ☺

@OakleyFord_stanNo1 thank you!!!!!!!!!!!!! They're so cute. I wish I cld see their tweets all the time!

Vaughn is acting strange. She's quiet and withdrawn and she's made only one sarcastic remark all evening, which tells me that my public apology didn't make up for dissing her boy-friend in the first place.

"You having a good time?" I ask as we move away from the barbecue line and walk farther down the sand to a quieter area. Our paper plates are piled with hot dogs and macaroni salad.

"Sure," she says noncommittally. "You?"

"This barbecue's sick. I'm having a blast."

I'm not lying, either. I was dreading this thing all day, ever since Claudia called this morning to inform me I was hanging out with Vaughn's family tonight. First, because Vaughn and I haven't talked since the whole W thing, and second, because attending a charity barbecue for Cardell Hills Middle School, where Vaughn's little brothers go to school, seemed like a recipe for disaster.

I was expecting to be under a microscope all evening, but to my surprise, nobody even cares that I'm here. The barbecue is on El Segundo beach, but the school hired security guards to keep interlopers from sneaking into the party and eating all the food. Not that anyone is going to sneak into a boring middle school event. The guest list is a mixture of sixth to eighth graders, teachers and parents. Everyone here is either under thirteen or over forty.

This is about as anonymous as I've ever been, and it's the best feeling in the world. The only thing that would make it better is if my date wasn't sulking, but that's my own fault.

I really need to stop being such an ass to Vaughn.

And I really need to stop thinking about kissing her again.

"Pass it 'ere! I'm open!" one of the twins shouts to a class-mate.

I jerk out of my thoughts and turn toward the soccer game that's in progress a hundred yards away. Spencer and Shane are playing on the same team, but I can't tell them apart because they're both wearing blue T-shirts and khaki cargo shorts.

But Vaughn knows which one is which, because she yells, "Way to go, Spence!" and cheers loudly when one of the blue-shirted boys scores a goal.

I cheer, too, and so does Paisley, who's standing a few feet away from us chatting with Ty. Vaughn's sister is so obviously into Ty that it makes me smirk. She's blushing, and her eyes widen as he touches her arm to shift her out of the way when a group of kids comes whizzing past them.

Ty has a weirdly gentle look in his dark eyes as he moves her to safety. Oh, man. I don't think it's one-sided.

"I think your sister and my bodyguard are making a love connection," I tell Vaughn, hoping the bit of gossip might snap her out of her Downer Debbie mood.

It does, sort of. She looks over at them and smiles faintly. "Maybe."

"It sucks that nothing can happen between them."

"Why not?"

"Ty'll never date anyone who works for Jim," I explain. "It'd be too messy if they broke up."

"Paisley works for Jim's brother."

"It's pretty much the same thing."

"Maybe they won't break up. Maybe they'll fall in love and get married and have ten kids and grow blissfully old together."

There's a note of desperation in her tone that makes me uneasy. "You okay?"

She sighs. "I'm fine. Everything's fine. Just eat your hot dog."

I take a bite and she turns back to watch the twins' soccer game. I keep watching *her*. I don't like quiet Vaughn. I'd rather she make smartass comments to me.

"What's wrong?" I push.

"Nothing's wrong."

"Is this about the shit I said about W?"

Her features instantly tighten at the mention of W's name. "No. I accepted your apology." There's a sharp bite to her tone. "I even Tweeted about how mature and awesome you are, remember?"

"We both know your Tweets are just orders from Claudia." I search her shuttered expression. "Do you really forgive me for trashing him?"

"Yes. God. I forgive you, okay? Can we please not talk about W?"

A crease digs into my forehead. "Why not?"

Before she can respond, two girls shyly approach us. One has pigtails and the other has an adorable pixie cut. They don't look older than eleven or twelve, and they're practically trembling with apprehension as one of them holds out her phone.

"Hi. Um… Oakley, w-w-w-would you…c-c-c-c-could we get a picture with you?" Pigtails stutters.

I swallow a laugh. "'Course."

The two turn bright red and stare at me for a long, uncomfortable moment.

"I'll take it," Vaughn finally intervenes, reaching for the cell phone.

I'm about two feet taller than these girls, so I have to crouch on the sand between them. I tense up as I wait for them to paw at me, but they don't. They're so painfully timid and fearful standing on either side of me, and for the first time in, well, *ever*, I gesture for them to come closer. "C'mere, otherwise we won't all fit in the picture."

They come closer. I sling an arm around each of their shoulders, and they look like they're about to faint.

After Vaughn snaps the pic, the girls sprint off like they're competing for Olympic gold. Seconds later a dozen other girls congregate around them, whispering wildly and squealing as they all bend over the phone.

Nobody else comes over to ask for a picture. Weird. I guess Pixie and Pigtails were the only ones with the nerve to ask.

That's…refreshing.

"They were so sweet," Vaughn says, giving me the first genuine smile of the evening.

"Adorbs," I agree.

She raises a brow. "You initiated the physical contact."

I nod.

"Why?"

I think for a second. "Because they didn't try to touch me. They viewed it as a treat, not a right." I shrug. "Besides, sometimes physical contact is nice."

I take her hand, and she freezes.

Frustration rises inside me. I almost remind her that this is what she's being paid to do, but damn it, I don't want her to hold my hand because of the money. I want her to do it because she *wants* to.

So I wait.

And wait some more.

And then…she laces her fingers through mine, and something inside me thaws.

"Come on, let's walk for a bit," I suggest.

We toss our empty plates in a nearby trash can and then head down the sand. As we walk, I can't help sneaking peeks at her. She's wearing flip-flops instead of her usual ratty sneakers. Tight blue jeans hug her thighs and ass. A striped top falls off one shoulder and reveals her tanned, smooth skin. I can totally see why Jim and my PR team think of her as "the girl next door." There's something genuine and sweet about Vaughn.

Her dark hair is tied in a long braid that swings behind her back with every step she takes. I can't stop myself from tugging on it with my free hand.

She glances over uneasily.

We walk in silence, not venturing too far from the party. I look over my shoulder and see that Ty's hawk-like gaze is fixed on us, even while he listens to whatever Paisley is saying.

Vaughn and I stop at the edge of where the water meets the sand, both of us staring out at the ocean.

"My mom really liked you," I find myself confessing.

"I liked her, too. She's awesome."

I'm instantly skeptical. Then I feel like an ass for being skeptical, because it's not like my mom is some evil shrew. Almost all of my memories of her are good ones, full of joy and laughter and lots and lots of fun. But the fun died a few years ago. Pretty much since she stopped calling me.

"She's so proud of you," Vaughn adds.

I shift in discomfort. "Yeah... I doubt that."

"She is. I swear, she wouldn't stop talking about all your accomplishments. And she showed me a ton of pictures of you."

I narrow my eyes. "What pictures?"

Vaughn smiles. "Nothing too embarrassing. Unless you consider dressing up as Iron Man for Halloween embarrassing."

"I was going through a superhero phase," I say defensively. "And I was *eight*." A frown mars my lips. "She has all those pictures on her phone?"

"Her phone has nothing but pictures of you as far as I could tell. She even has baby pics on there. I told you, she's proud of you..." She trails off in hesitation.

"What?" I say warily.

"I think she thinks you hate her."

I swallow the huge lump that fills my throat. Then I cough. "Nah, there's no way she thinks that."

Vaughn shrugs. "I'm just telling you what it seemed like."

I'm sure it did. My mother is a phenomenal actress. She was probably trying to paint me as the villain just to make herself look good.

I answer in a bitter voice. "She called me after you guys had lunch. Before that, I hadn't heard from her in a month. Before that, it was six months. If anyone's in the wrong here, it ain't me."

"How often do you call *her*?"

She has me there. I grit my teeth. "I don't call because I know she doesn't care to hear from me."

Vaughn shakes her head in disapproval. "Sure, Oakley, keep telling yourself that."

I frown. "You're not in any position to judge. You spent all of two hours with her. That doesn't exactly make you an expert on Katrina Ford."

"Okay. Whatever. Forget I said anything." She sounds grumpy again.

Great. Now we're both cranky.

I take a breath and regroup. "Why are you in such a bad mood tonight?"

Since I don't expect her to tell me, I'm not surprised when she stays quiet.

Her silence rubs me the wrong way, though, stirring up my inner shit-disturber. "What, did you and the frat boy get in a lover's quarrel?"

Vaughn flinches.

"Did I hit a nerve?" I raise one eyebrow.

Her lips flatten in a thin line.

"Must have been a doozy of a fight, huh? Let me guess, he—"

"Dumped me," she interrupts.

I blink. "What?"

"He dumped me." Her eyes take on a defiant glint. "That's

what you want to hear, right? How W dumped my ass? Well, he did. He broke it off the night you showed up at my house unannounced."

It's hard to suppress the happy smile that's begging to spring free. "Oh. That sucks. I'm sorry."

"Don't pretend to care," she mutters. "Since we've met, all you've done is say nasty things about W. You think he's pretentious and douchey."

Yeah. I do. "Aw, you know I was just joking around," I lie.

"Bullshit." Her expression becomes pained. "I guess you can say whatever you want about him now. Because we're done. And I don't want to talk about this anymore, okay?"

She looks on the verge of tears, and I feel like a total ass for needling her about it. I need to lighten the situation, distract her before she runs into the ocean and tries to drown herself or something. Luckily, I know just how to distract chicks—by turning up the Oakley Ford charm. That unique blend of annoying jerk and irresistible rogue.

"Does that mean you're going to stop sulking and enjoy this barbecue?" I ask cheerfully.

She glares at me. "I'm not sulking."

"Babe, you're totally sulking. It's incredibly unattractive, if I'm being honest." I'm grinning as I say it.

A reluctant smile tugs on her lips. "You know what else is unattractive? Watching you stuff your face with hot dogs all night. How do you not weigh five hundred pounds?"

Operation Distraction is a success. "I work out." I flex both biceps at her. "Guns like these don't grow on trees."

"What is it with you and your *guns*? You're obsessed with yourself, dude."

"Why shouldn't I be? I'm a hottie."

She snorts.

"You laugh, but we both know you agree. Come on, say it—*you're a hottie, Oak*."

"Never," she declares.

"I really think you should say it…"

"Or what?" she challenges. "Whatcha gonna do, Oak? Pull my hair?"

"No, but I will do *this*." Before she can blink, I yank her forward and haul her over my shoulder.

A shriek fills the air. "Put me down right this second, Oakley Ford!"

"Maybe later." I secure her in a fireman's carry and race toward the water. "I think you need to cool off with a nice swim," I taunt as she pounds at my back with her small fists. "My fault, really. Most girls get overheated when faced with my manly good looks."

"Don't you dare!" Vaughn sputters, but she's laughing.

I keep running. She bats at my shoulders.

"It's *February*!" she shrieks. "I swear, if you throw me in that ice-cold water, I will murder you!" Then she manages to get a solid kick to my gut, which causes me to stumble slightly. That's all she needs to get out of my hold and scramble to her feet.

She takes off running back toward the sand, and I hurry after her. "Come back here!" I shout between laughs.

"Never!"

I manage to grab the bottom of her shirt, but before I can tug her into my arms, she trips on something and goes flying forward, taking me with her. We land on the sand with a thud, Vaughn on her back and me nearly on top of her.

We're both still laughing as we try to catch our breath. I rise up on one elbow and peer down at her, and almost immediately, the humor is replaced with something serious. Something hotter.

Her cheeks are flushed pink.

My breathing goes shallow.

Her lips part.

My head dips, just slightly.

I've never wanted to kiss anyone more than—

Sand sprays into our faces, and we break apart abruptly. I look over in confusion and notice the soccer ball lying on the beach. Great. Perfect timing.

"Hey! Kick it back!" one of the soccer players calls from the playing area.

I hop to my feet, walk over and boot the soccer ball across the beach to the waiting children. Then I turn to Vaughn and reach out my hand.

After a beat, she takes it and lets me pull her to her feet.

"We should go back," she says without meeting my eyes.

"Yeah." My voice sounds hoarser than usual.

We return to the party to find that a music circle has formed. A dark-haired woman is playing the guitar, while a group of kids and parents gather around. She's singing Katy Perry's "Firework." Some people are singing along, but most of them are just listening.

"That's the twins' music teacher," Vaughn whispers to me. "Mrs. Greenspoon. She had the school band play that song."

I try to envision a bunch of French horns, flutes and clarinets tooting out the melody and move a bit closer. Mrs. G is a decent guitar player, and although her voice doesn't hit all the right notes, she's having fun and it shows.

Vaughn and I sit on a nearby beach chair and listen to the "show." I absently thread my fingers through Vaughn's hair, but I don't even realize I'm doing it until she turns with a sharp look.

"Sorry," I murmur.

"No. It's okay. It's…nice." Her tone is grudging and confused and a tad upset.

Eventually the music stops. Mrs. Greenspoon sets the acoustic guitar on a chair and goes to talk to a few parents. Everyone else just wanders off, none of them even glancing in my direction. They all saw me sitting there…and nobody asked me to sing something.

For once in my life, I feel…normal. It's nice, hanging out with people who don't want a damn thing from me.

"We can leave after the game," Vaughn says, gesturing to the soccer match still in process.

"I'm in no rush." My gaze strays to the abandoned guitar. "Do you think they'll care if I mess around on the guitar?"

Vaughn looks at the chair, then at the deserted area around us. Most of the crowd has moved toward the soccer game. "I don't think they'll even notice."

I'm pretty sure that's the first time I've ever heard that.

With an odd jolt of excitement, I get up to grab the instrument then return to our chair. Vaughn moves to the opposite chair, sitting cross-legged, her braid hanging over one shoulder, as she watches me play a few random chords.

"Any requests?" I joke.

She considers it seriously, though. "Do you know any Lumineers?"

I lift my eyebrows. "Seriously? You don't want an Oakley Ford song?" I can't believe she wants me to do a *cover*.

Her lips twitch. "I thought you were tired of your own songs."

"Fair enough." I grin at her then rack my brain for the chords to "Ho Hey," the folk band's most popular single.

I mess up the intro, but once I start singing, the melody takes over and the chords just play themselves. Vaughn is totally engrossed, her eyes never leaving mine. When I get to the chorus, I switch it up a bit—gotta give the song *some* sort of original spin—and her eyes widen in delight. The faster, slightly more rock version of this ballad is sounding kind of awesome. I'm enjoying the hell out of myself.

When I finish singing, a huge burst of applause breaks out. Startled, I almost fall out of my chair. I was so into the music that I didn't realize anyone but Vaughn was listening. A few cameras go off, and...so much for feeling normal. *This* is normal, me being unable to sing a song to a girl without someone documenting it.

Vaughn's still staring at me, the confusion back in her eyes. I want to ask her what's wrong, but people are suddenly coming up to me to say how much they enjoyed the song. Several ask for an encore, but I politely decline. Instead, I take Vaughn's hand and the two of us quickly move away from the crowd.

The game has wrapped up, and the twins, sweaty and disheveled, run over to us. We join Paisley and Ty, and all of us make a unanimous decision that it's time to take off.

"That was really beautiful," Vaughn whispers as we trudge down the sand.

"Ah. Thanks."

She stops when we reach the stairs that lead to the parking lot, letting the others go on ahead.

"What is it?" I ask.

"Half the time when you open your mouth, you say something that makes me want to punch you." Vaughn gives a rueful smile. "But when you sing...you make it really hard to hate you."

I take that praise with me all the way up to the parking lot. The twins pile into the back seat of Paisley's Nissan, while Paisley slides behind the wheel.

Before Vaughn can get in the passenger seat, I tug on her hand. "Hey. Wait. Can I see your phone?"

Her forehead furrows. "Ah, sure. Why?"

I don't answer. I just take the phone from her outstretched hand and pull up her contact list. I key in ten digits then hand it back.

"My number's in there now," I say gruffly. "Call me if you ever need to talk, okay?"

Vaughn looks stunned.

Before she can question me, I lean in, plant a kiss on her cheek and then stride off toward my Escalade.

Ty and I get in, and he glances over as he starts the engine. "Fun time, huh?" he says.

"The best." And I actually mean it.

A short clip of me singing "Ho Hey" pops up on Instagram before I even open my eyes the next morning. I only know about it because Jim wakes me up to tell me. He doesn't sound mad, but pleased.

"The video has more than a million views already!" he crows. "And the comments. Go read the comments. I just sent you the link."

Groggy, I sit up and put the phone on speaker so I can click on the link he texted. It takes me to the Instagram video, but I don't press Play. I just scroll down to the comments.

OMG So beautiful!

He's back, bitches! SEE! Told you he's not washed up!

SO GOOD TO HEAR OAKLEY SINGING AGAIN!

Is that his girlfriend there? The Vaughn girl? Ugh. I want someone, anyone to look at me like he looks at her.

*ShiversSHIVERS

Oh. Em. Gee. I have shivers right now.

I find myself smiling. *Shivers* is a musician's favorite word. I stop scrolling, because there are more than five thousand comments and it'll take me the rest of my life and then most of the afterlife to get through all of them.

"Your fans miss you," Jim says frankly. "This just proves it. You need to put out a new album, Oak."

"I'm trying." As usual, my joy is short-lived. He just *has* to remind me how much I'm sucking, doesn't he?

"Try harder."

I clench my teeth.

"You're at the studio today, right?"

"Yeah, I'm leaving in an hour." I pause. "I was thinking of asking Vaughn to come along."

"That's a good idea. You were with her last night and ended up recording something genius—maybe she's your muse."

"I sang a cover," I mutter.

"Doesn't matter that it wasn't an original," Jim argues. "You changed up that song and made it your own. Better yet, you sang it with *emotion*. People respond to all that emotion bullshit."

I laugh. "Emotions are bullshit? I feel bad for your wife, dude."

He ignores that. "Go record some music, kid. I'll check in with you later and—I'm getting another call. Hold on."

"Why? We were already hanging up—"

"Stay on the line," he commands, and then the extension goes silent.

I swallow my irritation, because, seriously, I'm just supposed to sit here twiddling my thumbs while he talks to another client? I have better things to do with my time than—

"King is calling you in about one minute," Jim suddenly barks in my ear.

My breath stalls in my throat. Holy *hell*. "Are you serious?"

"Yup. Be cool. Do not push him. Let him talk."

I slowly release a puff of air. "Got it."

"Be cool," Jim presses.

"I got it." When the phone beeps, I pull the screen away from my face to see a blocked caller. "He's calling right now. I'll call you back." I switch over before Jim can give me the order to be cool one more time.

I rub my hands on my bedspread, trying to control my nerves. "Yo, King," I greet him.

"Hey, Oakley."

"Oak," I tell him. "All my friends call me Oak." *And you and I are going to be closer than brothers by the time we're done.*

"Yeah, all right. I've been watching your Insta likes pile up. You're getting a righteous response."

"It's sweet." And then because I hate the uncertainty and I don't want to hang back and wait, I do exactly the opposite of what Jim ordered. "You gotta know that I'm a fangirl of yours. The only reason I'm not stalking you is because Jim would kill me."

King laughs.

"We both know I'm dying to work with you. And since this is the first call you've returned of mine, I'm guessing it's for something more than congratulating me on a viral hit."

"You're right. I'm seeing maturity in your music. The sounds you had before could have been produced by anyone."

He's not wrong. I could try to bluff my way out here, tell him I've been working on new things since the drop of my last album, but he'd be able to hear the lie the moment he walked into the studio. I opt for brutal honesty. "If I don't create something new, my career could be over. We both know single artists have a very short shelf life."

"You want to make a new sound so you stay relevant? Because teen girls are the only fans that matter in this business and they still love you. If staying famous is what you want, then you don't need me."

"No, I want to make a new sound because I don't relate to my old one. I'm not trying to reinvent myself so much as..." It's going to take some leap of faith, some shedding of my protective layer, some introspection to get King to come on board. "As trying to find myself," I admit. "I'm lost and have been for a while." Then I shut up and for once in my life, I wait.

"Ahhhh." It's a satisfied sound. "I can work with that, Oak. How about I come over, say, Thursday?"

"Sounds good, man, real good."

We chat for a few more minutes, arranging a time and place. When I hang up, my hands are shaking and my palms are damp and I'm close to throwing up.

And yet I've never felt better.

25

HER

@OakleyFord @OakleyFord_No1Stan @sabaataani @vogue
@VeryVaughn please follow me

@OakleyFord I wanna bite you

@OakleyFord be my VALENTINE!

"So," Oakley says in a conversational tone, "is this the best Valentine's Day you've ever had, or the worst?"

Those two measly words—*Valentine's Day*—bring a sharp ache to my heart. I know Oakley is simply trying to lighten the mood, but the reminder just hurts. I never in a million years thought I'd be spending Valentine's Day this year without my boyfriend.

But I am. Because I don't *have* a boyfriend. Not anymore.

It's still surreal every time I think about the breakup. It's been two weeks since W stormed out of my house. Two weeks with no contact, no text messages or make-out sessions, no... tears. Not a single tear, and that's what bothers me the most.

W and I were together for so long, and yet after that first sob-fest the night he ended it, I haven't cried over him at all.

Sure, I get a pang in my chest when he crosses my thoughts, and I might have been swallowing repeatedly when I forced myself to delete some of the pictures on my laptop. But for the most part, I'm just...numb.

And...

Relieved.

God. I feel awful every time that sensation of relief washes over me, but I can't seem to stop it. And every time I experience it, I think back to my conversation with Paisley when she told me I hadn't truly loved W.

"Purse your lips together."

The command jolts me from my troubling thoughts. It comes from Belinda, a five-foot tall, blue-haired terror who gives me a stern look and makes a circle in front of her lips.

I roll my eyes but do as I'm told. According to Claudia, Belinda's in charge of me this morning.

"No. That's too much like a fish," she chides. "We want you pouty, not like you belong in a koi pond."

Next to me, Oakley laughs so hard the entire sofa shakes.

"This is insane," I mutter. "And to answer your question, this V-Day is neither good nor bad. It's just weird."

"What? Your Instagrams aren't all staged and posed?"

There's a note in his voice, a warm, affectionate one that causes my breath to hitch, and once again I'm struck by the inappropriate response I'm having toward Oakley. I've spent the past two weeks reminding myself that he's not my real boyfriend, but he's making it hard to remember that.

Like, with his texts. The ones that come directly to my phone and not by way of Twitter or an Instagram message. Ones that sound suspiciously like his flirty Tweets.

I'm too chicken to ask if it was him on the other end of our public exchanges, but surely he doesn't have Claudia's team text me things like:

I woke up at nine this morning. I didn't realize the sun was up this early.

And:

I'm at the music store, fondling guitars. I need another one like I need another tat. This is why I shouldn't get up early. Come and entertain me.

That was the first of his offhanded requests to spend time with him. And I wanted to. Boy, did I ever. But the idea of spending nonwork time with Oakley freaks me out a little. My breakup with W isn't even a month old. I'm scared Oak's magnetism might suck me in, lure me into some kind of rebound thing I'm not sure I'm ready for. So I've been making up excuses.

Can't. Cooking dinner right now.

Can't. Trying to find a good recipe for tiramisu.

Can't. Picking up twins from lessons.

With the new influx of cash, Paisley was able to pay for the twins to attend a basketball camp—something they've always wanted but we've never been able to afford before.

The day after my last excuse, I got a video from Oak.

Whaddaya think?

He was playing music again, toying with the arrangements of his old songs. Nothing new lyrically, but the sound was definitely different. It had an older, more rock sound than his previous three albums.

It's good.

Good is a devil's word. It's lukewarm, like day-old coffee. No one wants that.

I'm not a singer. I can't play an instrument. I can only tell u if I like it or don't like it. I like it.

Am I giving u shivers?

Every time I read a text, I wanted to type back. Every time I hear my phone buzz.

But he was asking about my response to his music, not to him, so I said

Not yet.

Making me work for it?

Being honest? I like it.

I want u to love it.

I didn't love it, though. It sounded good. It sounded different. But there were no shivers and I wasn't going to lie to him.

Then, yeah, making u work for it.

He didn't text me until several hours later and I wondered if I'd offended him.

Thanks for being straight with me. Someday I'll rock your world.

I hoped not. I don't know if there are defenses strong enough to resist an Oakley Ford determined to *rock a girl's world*. I wanted to text back, *Please don't. I can't handle that.*

Instead, I texted

We'll see.

Which, in hindsight, might've been worse. It sounded su-perflirty, especially when Oak's reply was

Challenge accepted.

And it was worse the following day when the only text I received was an ice cream cone pic along with the message

Went back. Ice cream didn't taste as good this time. Just FYI.

I wanted to Tweet out to the world of fangirls who message me on Twitter daily that FYI, Oakley Ford is too charming for his own good and I need someone to save me from myself.

Keeping an emotional distance from a guy you have to pretend to be dating is the realest struggle ever. And it's not helped by the fact that I'm currently lying next to his muscled frame on a cozy sofa, his arm cushioning my head and his fa-mous green eyes sweeping my face.

"You don't like having our first Valentine's Day as a couple being recorded by—" he squints at the group hovering at the end of his giant sectional "—five individuals?"

"I think that's five too many."

The muscle under my head bunches. "I agree."

I gulp, and a knowing smile tips up the corners of his lips. His head dips lower and his body shifts so that he's all but shielding me from the others in the room. I know what's coming and I remind myself it's all for show, but the gleam in his eyes tells a different story,

"Don't touch her!"

Oak closes his eyes in frustration and then slumps against the cushion. Suddenly, I'm in love with Belinda. She saved me from what I know would've been a toe-curling, butterfly-rousing kiss that I would be thinking about for far too long.

When Claudia called me this morning to inform me we would be taking a romantic Valentine's Day photo for social media, I had no idea it was going to be one so...personal. She declared it was time for Oakley to make a public declaration. It wasn't enough that I'd been photographed eating lunch with his mom or that there were numerous grainy photos of Oakley at the beach with my family.

Oakley needs to make a statement. And that statement requires us to be together, legs tangled up, faces close.

"The lighting is too bright," Claudia complains. "We want this picture to say 'late night watching a movie together' and not 'just woke up in bed.'"

"You can get all that with lighting?"

Oakley props his head up on his hand and peers down. "You'd be amazed at what people read into one photograph. I remember when I was on a break from the Ford tour. I went to a club in Germany with my friend, Trevor David, you know, the drummer from Twenty Four Seven?"

I nod. Twenty Four Seven is an older rock band that's been around for probably a decade. I've never loved their stuff.

"Anyway, he was dating this Vic's Secret model from London. She had some weird name. Biblical name. Ezrah? Hezbollah—"

"Bathsheba?"

"Yeah, that's it. So we were all at this club and someone bumps into her. I put my arm around her to make sure she doesn't fall. In the process, a schmuck takes about five shots and sells them to a German tabloid. Those five shots made it seem like I'd been hugging her all night, and the next morning the headlines were that she was cheating on her man with one of his best friends. Trevor's standing right next to her. In one of the photos, you can even see the edge of his arm." He shakes his head. "They cropped him out."

"That really sucks."

"It does."

"What about…" I trail off.

"What about what?" he prompts.

Oh, heck, I might as well ask. "What about the Brazilian supermodel?"

He grins. "Which one?"

I reach up and pinch his side.

He yelps and catches my hand. And doesn't let it go. And for once, I don't pull away. He pulls me closer.

"You mean Izabella Duarte? You do stalk me."

I look down at our clasped hands, more than a little embarrassed. "I may, at one time, have been tremendously interested in all celebrity things," I hedge. The Izzy/April scandal was what put me off Oakley, and then my parents died. I think my emotions were frozen at that point.

"This is why publicists drum up fake relationships. You wouldn't have been half as interested in me if I was single. Relationships make the world go 'round."

"Maybe, but I'm no April Showers."

"No, you're Vaughn Bennett. I like Vaughn Bennett."

My heart flutters wildly. To cover up my feelings, I bring up April again. "Don't you ever get jealous when you see her on the cover of a magazine?" April is on a cover every other month.

"You do realize she doesn't look like that in real life, right?

Those pictures are airbrushed and Photoshopped so much that I think it's hard for her own mother to recognize her."

"So is that a yes?"

"If you're asking me if I'm pining over her, then no. April and I were two teenagers whose handlers thought a relationship like ours would spur more publicity, and they were right. It did help, but it wasn't anything more on my part than a media thing. So, yeah, I might've had some fun with Izzy, but she never got my phone number." His voice drops low. "I'm not a cheater, if that's what you're asking. If April and I had a real relationship, I wouldn't have looked twice at another girl. I'm a one-woman man, babe."

I swallow hard. He has no idea what it does to me when he calls me *babe*.

"Come to the studio with me today," he says.

And because I can't talk, I nod. He smiles brilliantly at me, and I almost miss Belinda ordering me to move.

"Let's switch it up. Let's put Oak's head in her lap," Belinda suggests.

I heave a sigh of relief and sit up immediately. Oakley takes a bit longer to uncurl his body from mine. We move into position, but having his head in my lap doesn't make it easier on me. My fingers itch to brush the hair away from his forehead. I shudder a tiny bit, but Oak catches it.

His eyes sparkle as he asks, "Cold?"

Belinda hears him and snaps her fingers. "A blanket. That would be perfect."

Someone runs to find a blanket.

"Relax," he murmurs.

How can I? I don't think anyone could relax in this position.

"Darla, smudge the eyeliner under her eyes. It looks too precise," Belinda orders. The makeup artist leans over with a brush and dabs under my eyes.

"A lot of work for these pictures."

"One. Singular," Oak says.

"Who knows. We might do a collage," Claudia suggests. Beside her, Belinda's blue hair bobs in agreement. "Oak, reach up and touch her neck."

His long fingers curve around my neck, lightly pressing against my skin, reminding me of the way he pressed the frets of his guitar. He has beautiful, talented fingers that are capable of pulling so much emotion from six little metal strings.

"I'm never going to believe another thing I see on the internet," I whisper.

His thumb brushes my cheek. "This isn't the internet."

Once the photos are finally taken, Oak whisks me into his SUV before Belinda can suggest another pose. Claudia and her assistants are arguing about the caption as we're leaving. I have no idea what they settle on, although it seemed they'd narrowed it down to either just a heart emoji or the hashtag "feels."

In the backseat, Oakley reaches into his pocket. His hand emerges with something, but I can't tell what. The look on his face is weirdly awkward, though.

"Are you okay?" I ask, raising a brow.

"Yeah. Uh. I got you something."

My other eyebrow shoots up to join its pair. "Like, a present?"

He gives an adorable little shrug. "It's Valentine's Day. Figured I should get you something. But I didn't want to give it to you in front of the PR peeps, otherwise they would've tried to incorporate it into the pictures, and, ah, I didn't want that."

I can't hide my surprise. Or my guilt, because it sounds like he bought me something without Claudia ordering him to, while I didn't get him a single thing. Not even a Valentine's Day card. Should I have?

"Anyway..." Another shrug. "Here."

He hands me a square of paper. I stare at it, because, well, I wasn't expecting a folded-up piece of paper. Did he write me a letter? My heart speeds up. Or maybe a song?

My confusion returns once I unfold the sheet and see what's written on it. It's a list of ingredients, followed by instructions like *stir* and *mix* and *dust with cocoa*. It takes me a second to realize it's a recipe for tiramisu.

"Oh," is all I can think to say.

"You said you were looking for a good tiramisu recipe, so..." Oakley shifts in his seat, looking slightly uncomfortable. "So I called Francisco Bello—you've heard of him, right? He's on—"

"*Cast-Iron Cookoff!*" I finish, naming one of the most popular cooking competition shows currently on TV. Excitement builds in my tummy. "Are you saying he gave you his recipe? His *secret* recipe?"

"Yup." He offers a half smile. "It pays to know Oakley Ford, huh?"

I can't even believe this. Francisco Bello is notoriously tight-lipped about his dishes. Outsiders aren't allowed into the kitchens of any of his restaurants, and on the show they blur out some of the things he does so that the audience can't guess the recipe.

"Oh, my God. This is..." I shake my head in astonishment. "*So* cool. I can't wait to make this!"

That gets me another smile. "Thought you'd like it."

Like it? I *love* it. Except, it's just another gesture on Oakley's part that fills me with pure and utter confusion. Why is he giving me gifts? And why won't my heart stop racing every time he's around?

I swallow hard, wishing I had answers, but it seems like lately all I have is more questions.

"Thank you," I tell him.

"You're welcome."

Our gazes lock for a beat. I think Oak wants to say something more, but the car comes to a stop, and we abruptly break eye contact.

"We're here," Big D announces.

"You been to a studio before?" Oak asks as we wait for a gate to open. The moment between us has passed, but my chest still feels warm and gooey as I tuck the prized recipe into my canvas purse.

"No, never," I admit.

"It's not very fancy. Soundproof rooms, a lot of equipment. Want a tour?"

Outside the gate, a few photographers who must camp out at the studio waiting for artists to show up yell for Oak to turn his head. Some of them even yell my name. Big D positions himself between Oak and the street, and Oak ignores them as he pulls the door open.

"Sure."

The studio is two stories. "Offices are up top, three sound studios down here and one upstairs."

"How does it work?"

"Depends on if your band is getting along."

"Really?"

"Yup." He throws one door open and gestures for me to go in. "If you're all getting along then you record together. Otherwise, you have a session band record the melody and then each band member comes in and lays down their individual tracks. The sound engineers put them all together and then everyone comes back to do their vocals."

"That sounds complicated."

"No question it's a lot easier when the band is a big happy family."

In the room, there are black leather sofas sitting at an L, a couple of stools, guitar stands and a synthesizer. "No drums?" I ask.

"Nah, drummers are the worst. Each guy has his own kit. The best ones refuse to work on anything but their own."

Oak lets me poke at a few of the instruments before opening the door to another room—this one with a ton of machines with dials and levers, three huge computer screens and more sofas. It's littered with empty beer bottles and reeks of cigarette smoke.

"Stinks, doesn't it? This is Ren Jacobs's mixing room. He's a genius with the computer, but smokes like a chimney. If he wasn't so talented, they'd have kicked his ass out a long time ago."

"You don't record here?"

"Nope. Thankfully, these pipes don't need Auto-Tuning." He taps his throat.

"What is that exactly?"

"It's a computer software program that allows a sound guy to nudge a note up or down the scale, making sure everything's in tune. I prefer to sing until it's perfect and my engineer splices the recordings together. More time-consuming, but at least I know it's all me. Okay, so here we have the different mixers—analog and digital for the multitracks—"

I watch his arm as he points, his muscles flexing. I guess I'd be proud of my arms, too, if I had "guns" like his. They really are impressive.

Oak catches me looking and gives me a knowing wink. "Every piece of equipment in here is state-of-the-art."

So I was staring. Sue me. "Why are you so..."

"What? Good-looking?"

"No, built. Like, why do you have muscles? Is it because you like looking that way or for the image or what?"

He tucks his hands into the tops of his pockets. "Playing tours is hard work. You gotta be fit. And yeah, looking like this sells records. Not gonna lie. Plus, the ladies love it."

It's a good thing he doesn't wink again, because I would've hit him, but he's not wrong. He is lovely to look at.

"Why are you so eager to work with Donovan King?" I ask when we reach the hall again.

"You're full of questions today, aren't you?"

I shrug. "You seem full of answers."

He stops and leans against the wall. I take up a position opposite him. "King's a genius. He can pull music out of you that you didn't even know existed. I've been trying to make a new record for two years. I've been through four different producers. I've collaborated with a dozen different songwriters. I've invited in all kinds of artists to jam with me. Pop stars, rock bands, reggae, rap. I even did a session with an acapella group. Every time I've cued up one of the recordings, they've all sounded exactly like my previous three albums. I don't need to record a new album. I'll just mix up the previous three and shit that out." He drags a frustrated hand through his hair. "But I don't want that. I don't think my fans want that. At the very least, I can't go on tour and sing this same crap over and over. The idea of going on a multicity tour all over the world in a replay makes me want to drown myself in the ocean." He gives his hair one last scrub, tips his head and looks at me.

"When you were at the club singing, every person in there thought you sang to them. It doesn't matter what your sound is. People are always going to want to hear you."

"That's nice of you."

"I'm never nice to you." We both snicker. "It's the truth.

I wish I was half as passionate about something in my life as you are about your music."

He cocks his head to the side. "What about your art?"

I wave a dismissive hand. "That's just a hobby. I'm not interested in being an artist." I pause. "I'm going to get my teaching degree."

"But if you're not passionate about that, why do it?"

"My parents were teachers," I explain, trying to articulate something out loud that's not entirely clear in my head. "My father was a middle school science teacher and my mom taught fourth grade."

"So before the kids become little shits."

"Basically. They were— We were happy."

"Hmmm." He slowly nods. His face shows that he understands without me having to say another word. How my dreams of the future are tied with my loss of the past.

But teaching makes sense to me, or at least it used to make sense. I mean, I have to pick *something*. I can't exactly go my entire life without any direction. I'll need a career, and following in my parents' footsteps seems like the logical thing to do.

Right?

Troubled by my uncertain thoughts, I hastily change the subject. "Were you a little shit?" I ask him.

"Absolutely, but I've been privately tutored since I cut my first album. No high school hijinks for me." He sounds wistful. "If teaching is what you want to do, then that's awesome. You'd make a great teacher."

"I would?"

"Of course. But…"

"But what?" I ask warily.

Oak goes thoughtful for a moment. "You said your dad was spontaneous, right?"

"Right." I'm not sure where he's going with this.

"I'd bet you my entire music catalog that he'd want you to do something you loved."

I hesitate. "I...don't know what that is."

Oak doesn't even blink at my uncertainty. "Then you look until you find it. You don't settle until you find it." He pushes away from the wall. "You'd be good doing anything." As he ambles down the hall, he says over his shoulder, "But you should do something you love."

Easy for him to say.

Inside this last studio are a number of musicians. Oak introduces me around. There's Luke, who I met before, along with Rocco, Oak's drummer, and Mallik, his keyboardist. There are two other guitarists who look faintly familiar. I try to hold my shock in when they're introduced as Con and Dalton from Saints and Sinners, one of the hottest bands of the moment. I watched them on MTV last year.

"My girl, Vaughn."

I can't keep the smile from my face. "Nice to meet you."

There are a number of smirks around, but I don't care. Much.

"Can I get you something to drink? Eat?"

"I wouldn't mind a Coke."

"On it." He drags an upholstered chair next to a stool. "Sit here. I'll be back in a second."

I settle into the chair, feeling like I don't belong. That sensation is intensified when Luke leans over.

"So you're still around." He smiles, and it isn't a nice one. "They paying you a lot?"

I beat back a blush. "I don't think anyone needs to be paid to date Oakley."

"Yeah? Because I'm pretty sure no chick would choose to celebrate Valentine's Day at the studio unless she was banking some green for it."

"We're going out for dinner later," I lie.

"Uh-huh. Where?"

"I don't know yet. Oak said it's a surprise." The lies flow out smoothly, but there's anger welling up in my stomach. What's this guy's problem? I almost shout out that Oakley got me a Valentine's Day present, so *ha*! But I swallow the words at the last second because it was an awesome, private moment and I don't want Luke to ruin it.

"You gonna put out after dinner?" Luke asks with a smirk. "'Cause I notice you're not real handsy with him, are you now?"

"Luke," Rocco growls. "Shut up."

"What? I'm just asking questions." He waves his hands. "I'm curious. Curious George."

He's a monkey, all right. Trying to stir up trouble. I stare at my shoes.

"All I'm saying is that we've seen fangirls. Slept with them. We know what they're like. And they can't get enough, particularly of Oak."

I don't like being touched. The idea of all those random girls running their hands over him turns my stomach.

"Maybe that's the whole reason Oak is with her," Rocco says. "You," he corrects, "because she's not all over him."

"Maybe." Luke's tone is heavy with skepticism. The other three remain completely silent.

Oakley returns, which shuts Luke up. When Oak hands me the soda, I ignore it and grip his wrist to pull him down low enough to give him a kiss on the cheek. His eyes widen in surprise, probably because it's the first time I've ever reached out to him.

He sits on the armchair, his leg rubbing against mine, his arm draped across the back of the chair. Then he leans close and whispers in my ear, "There aren't any cameras here."

It looks like he's giving me a kiss or murmuring something naughty to me. Everyone but Luke pretends not to watch us.

Annoyed with Luke's visible skepticism, I turn to Oakley and kiss him straight on the mouth. At first, he's too surprised to kiss me back. But he recovers in short order, digging his hand into my hair and angling his head just right. His tongue slides through my parted lips, flicking over mine in the hottest, wettest caress I've ever experienced. I clench the cold can of Coke between my fingers to keep from grabbing him in return. And I forget about the audience, the contract, the very pretend nature of this whole thing. I forget it all until someone bangs a cymbal, bringing me back to earth.

When I pull back, Oak's lips look red and swollen. His eyes are twin flames of brilliant green. I could get lost in them.

There's a long, drawn-out silence before Luke releases a low chuckle. "Well, okay then," he drawls. "Maybe y'all aren't faking."

26

HER

@VeryVaughn Best day I had in a long time. Thx for sharing it
w me

@OakleyFord It was amazing

@VeryVaughn Good thing I can have V-day whenever I want

@OakleyFord ☺

@1doodlebug1 Did u see the insta messages???

@OakleyFord_stanNo1 I'm shipping this so hard.

Was in the studio until four a.m. Gotta be back here at nine. Kill
me. But I wrote this song and need your opinion.

I stare at my phone, alternating between reluctance and curi-
osity. My finger hovers over the audio attachment that Oakley
included in his text. I want so badly to click on it, but I'm kind

of scared to hear his voice. In the week since Valentine's Day, he's sent me half a dozen songs, and every time I listened to one, his raspy voice had me melting into a puddle on the floor.

I'm having trouble with the whole pretend thing again. Even though Oak and I haven't kissed since the day at the studio, I think about it all the time. No, I *obsess* about it. When we went on a public date to the aquarium a few days ago, I spent the entire time staring at his mouth, wondering what it would be like to kiss him without anyone watching us. No cameras, no smirks from his bandmates. Kissing him just for me.

And last night I tossed and turned for hours, because he sent me some pictures from the magazine shoot he did earlier that day and he looked so gorgeous in them that my eyes nearly popped out of the sockets.

I think I might be crushing on Oakley Ford...and it freaks me out.

My phone pings again.

That bad? Or so good you're listening to it on repeat? Pro tip—another word musicians like is "mesmerizing."

I give in and play the song, because whatever my confused feelings are, he doesn't deserve to be left hanging. Then I find myself gaping at my phone, because everything Oak is saying in this song is exactly how I feel. Confused, disoriented, wondering why I even got up from bed this morning. He's the voice of my head.

I prefer the night
The dark, the shadows
The corners and the shallows
Where no one knows you

Where we all pretend
The mask is all we see
All we see
Until the end.
I play the song again.

Vaughn, you're killing me. I'm literally dying here. There's blood on the floor. The crime scene techs aren't gonna be able to figure this one out.

It's good, I text back.

Good? Is that the only word in your vocabulary? I already suggested two alternatives. Shiver-inducing or mesmerizing. U could also use awesome, bodacious, crackalicious, devastating, entertaining, fantastic, great...

I'm impressed by your vocab. Do you have a thesaurus?

I'm a songwriter. Words are my weapon. Give me something here.

Oak is something else. At his most vulnerable, he's the strongest. When I was fifteen, his music made me happy, but I don't think he spoke to me in the way that his lyrics do in this song. He's opening up, showing people what he really feels.

And all he's asking from me is whether I like the song. I can't hold that back from him.

The song was amazing.

Yeah?

Yeah.

Shivers?

I smile at the screen.

I'll need an in-person performance first before I can confirm any shivering.

Done. Done. Done. And...oh crap. King is here. I gotta run. But we're meeting later today and I'm singing this to u.

Now *that* sends shivers down my spine that have little to do with Oak's music and everything to do with Oak. I play the song again and listen to him tell me that he's lived a short time but it feels too long, how nobody can see through the mask he shows to the world. And how, despite everything he's seen and done, he's still lonely. The vision of his future is a cold, shapeless fog.

And isn't that how I feel? In my family, lost without my parents, wondering what my next step in life is?

But unlike him, I've never laid myself out there like that—confessing my wrongs, pleading for forgiveness, admitting my ignorance. I've never taken off my mask and made myself this vulnerable in front of someone else. Not even W. Or maybe especially not W.

Paisley bursts into my room, jolting me from my thoughts. She's dressed for work, and I'm surprised she's still home. The twins already left for school.

"Have you seen this?" she asks grimly, holding out her phone.

"Seen what?"

Her cheeks are bright red, and I can see that she's struggling to...to what? Keep her anger in check?

"Just read it."

I catch the phone she tosses me. When I look at the screen, I instantly feel all the color drain from my face.

The ex's response to Oakley Ford's apology: "Enjoy my sloppy seconds!"

"Oh, my God," I whisper, sick to my stomach. "This... can't be real."

It can't be. W would never say something like that, and especially not to a reporter. He signed an NDA that forbids him from...crap, from saying anything about my fake relationship with Oak. As far as I can recall, the agreement didn't say he couldn't talk about Oak in general.

But this awful comment... It's not even about Oak. It's about *me*. *I'm* the sloppy seconds. How could he do this?

"Paisley."

She eyes me in concern. "What is it?"

"Can you give me a minute? I need to call W." I'm amazed by how calm I sound.

"Sure. I'll be downstairs if you need me."

She closes the door quietly but I'm not paying any attention. This is a mistake, I decide. Something a blogger made up to gather hits. W and I might be over, but he'd never call me a slut to the national media.

"What part of 'I'm done with you' didn't you understand?" he snaps into the phone without even a hello.

I gasp into the phone. Did he really just say that?

"Don't worry," I snap back, fighting to contain my anger. "This won't take long."

"You've got five seconds before I hang up."

Sickness swirls in my belly. How on earth did it come to this? W used to love me. How could he speak to me so cruelly and viciously? Did our relationship mean nothing to him?

"Did you talk to the press this morning?" I demand, and a part of me prays he'll deny it. Or, in the very least, that whatever he said was taken out of context.

W is silent for a beat. Then he bursts out with, "Yeah, I did! What the hell else was I supposed to do? I've had reporters hanging around the dorm for a week now. Today a guy showed up outside my psych lecture hall asking me to comment on that jackass's apology. I'm supposed to say nothing?"

I stand up and clench the phone tight in my fist. "That's exactly what you're supposed to do!"

"Tough shit. He can say stuff about me and I can't say anything back? That apology was a joke—he didn't mean it. He was just trying to look good to the reporters. You said so yourself. It's all about his image. What about mine?"

"What about *mine*?" I screech. "You called me sloppy seconds! You pretty much told the entire country I was a slut! How could you do that?"

There's another pause. W clears his throat. "I didn't call you a slut. But...I'm sorry I said what I did, okay? I didn't mean to hurt you."

I swallow a lump of pain. This is the difference between W and Oak. When he publicly apologized for trash-talking W, Oak *meant* it. He was open and honest about his mistake, even if it meant making himself vulnerable.

Whereas W won't even tell me the truth when we're alone. He *did* mean to hurt me. He meant to hurt me more than he meant to hurt Oakley, otherwise his comment wouldn't have been about what a whore I am. It would have been something like Oakley Ford's music sucks and he doesn't know how anyone would want to date a washed-up pop star.

"Whatever, W," I mumble. "I guess the two years we were together didn't mean anything to you."

"Are you kidding me right now?" he shouts in my ear. "*I'm*

not the one who threw our relationship away. *You* did that. You're the one who took a job that hurt us. You're the one who made out with that asshole. You're the one who lied to me about giving the agency my tape. You, Vaughn!"

A wave of exhaustion crashes over me. I can't do this anymore. Not again.

But W isn't done twisting the knife deeper. "We're not going out anymore. I don't owe you shit, and I can talk to whoever I want and say whatever I want about you." Heavy breathing echoes on the line. "Stop calling me. I don't want to see your name on my phone anymore. Actually, I'm deleting your number, how about that?"

My bottom lip starts trembling. No. I refuse to cry over him again.

"By the way, I saw those Instagram pictures of you and your has-been boyfriend—sweet and cozy and boring, huh, V? Made me even happier that I dumped your boring ass." He laughs harshly. "Oh, and in case you were wondering, yes, I *did* get laid on Valentine's Day. And I enjoyed every goddamn second of it."

With that final stab of the knife, my ex-boyfriend hangs up on me.

27

HIM

1doodlebug1 @OakleyFord_stanNo1 her ex is a loser

OakleyFord_stanNo1 @1doodlebug1 yeah but did it sound like she was cheating on him? He's cute.

1doodlebug1 @OakleyFord_stanNo1 maybe? But who wouldn't throw over a normal for Oakley Ford?

Vaughn's a mess, and it's killing me to see her torn up over some asshole who never loved her more than he loved himself. She showed up at the studio about twenty minutes ago with swollen eyes and a red nose. When I brought her into the sound room, the guys scattered immediately, Luke muttering something about crying girls being bad juju.

"I can't believe he said all those horrible things to me. And he made it sound like the two years we went out were some kind of torture for him!" She peers up at me with big, sad eyes. "I always tried to be his perfect girlfriend. I never argued with him. When he wanted to go to prom in the limo and

I couldn't afford it, I didn't make a fuss that he chose to ride around with his friends for an hour *pre-gaming*. When Paisley got premiere tickets for *Last Superhero II* and W couldn't go, I stayed home. When she wanted to treat us all to Disneyland and W thought it was childish, I stayed home with him. I always chose him because he was there when I needed him."

Oh, Christ. So that's why she wasted so much time with the douche bag. Her parents' deaths left her with a big gaping hole in her heart and she filled that hole with W. And she stayed with him so she could keep telling herself all those missed times with her family were worth it because she loved W. Even when she probably stopped loving him a long time ago.

I put my arm around her, drawing her close to my body, not sure of what to say. I don't have a lot of experience with comforting people. Not only have I not had a real girlfriend in forever, but I don't remember the last time a friend came to me with a problem.

Her hands curl into the cotton of my T-shirt and she practically climbs onto my lap as she cries. Part of me wishes I could take back my public apology to W. He clearly didn't deserve it, but mostly I wish I could soak Vaughn's pain up like my T-shirt is soaking up her tears.

I rub her arms. Kiss the top of her head. Remind myself that this is about her and that I'm a terrible human being for enjoying the closeness between us. This is the only time she's willingly allowed me to hold her. There aren't any cameras here. This isn't for show.

This is as real and as awful and as wonderful as it gets. I'd hold her forever if she'd let me.

After too short of a time passes, Vaughn pushes away and sits up, swiping her face with the backs of her hands. "I look terrible."

She always looks beautiful. I drag my thumbs across her

cheekbones, wishing I could kiss her tears away. "I can get my makeup artist here," I offer.

"You have a makeup artist? I thought that was just for the photo shoot."

"You think I apply that concert eyeliner myself?"

She lets out a watery laugh.

"That's my girl." I wrap my arm around her shoulders. She snuggles into my side and I swear, my damn heart flips over because I want her to be my girl. For real. "Can I sing to you?"

"Yes, please."

"Do you have a request?"

She thinks about it. "You pick."

I start humming, and she tucks her head into the hollow of my shoulder while I sing Jason Mraz's "A Beautiful Mess" and the words that turn to knives and wound so deep.

I sing until her raspy breaths even out and she falls asleep, exhausted from her storm of tears and emotion. Gently, I ease away from her and throw a discarded sweatshirt over her bare legs.

Out in the hall I find the guys quietly shooting the shit. "We're done for the day," I inform them.

"You should take her out tonight," Rocco suggests.

Even Luke nods. "Yeah, night on the town. Get her mind off things."

If it had been Luke's recommendation, I'd have ignored it, but Rocco's been married for nearly a decade, which, in LA terms, is like three lifetimes. So I nod back and say, "I guess we're going out tonight."

"You having a good time?" I ask Vaughn later that night.

She nods and shoots me a foggy smile. My girl's been downing glasses of champagne like they're water. I wonder if I should cut her off, but the past three hours have been the first sustained period of time that she hasn't been crying so... I'll take it.

It took a bit of persuasion to get her out to the club, but I guess I don't blame her for hesitating. Our track record with clubs isn't all that great. The first time, I ignored her the whole night. The second time, I bullied her into kissing me.

I'm not about to repeat those mistakes tonight. I've been glued to her side since we got here, and I won't kiss her unless she asks me to.

Man, I hope she asks me to.

"You can ease up on the champagne. There'll still be bottles available tomorrow," I joke.

"Not if I have anything to say about it!" She throws back her head and drains another glass.

Crap. If she's determined to get completely wasted, maybe we should take off so she can do it somewhere private. I feel a little like I'm corrupting an innocent. But...Vaughn is having fun. I *like* Fun Vaughn.

At the same time, I find that I also kind of miss the straight-laced, I-don't-drink Vaughn.

Figure that out.

"Want to go home?" I suggest. When her pretty face creases with dismay, I hasten to add, "For an after-party. Want to take the party home?"

"Yes! That sounds awesome."

So I signal for Ty to get the car. He looks relieved.

I draw Vaughn's hand in mine and go find Luke. If we're going to have a party, he's the go-to guy.

"After-party at my place," I shout at him over the heads of about three chicks. Clearly he's enjoying himself tonight.

"Party at Ford's!" he yells, and half the people in the VIP room raise their hands in the air.

Good Christ. *The things I do for you, Vaughn.*

She looks a little dazed by the response. "You sure you want all these people at your house?"

Her head bobbles shakily. She's so drunk. Poor girl.

Guilt swirls in my stomach. Maybe we should have gone to the beach instead of a club.

"Yeah, party at Ford's. Woo." It's the weakest woo in the history of woos. I pull her into my arms and press her head against my shoulder. "Stay close to me. These after-parties can get wild."

She pulls back far enough to pin me with her first clear stare of the night. "I want wild."

"Then you'll get it."

If that's what she needs tonight, I want to give it to her. And somehow Luke knows that the reins are loose, because thirty minutes later clothes come off before I can even get my front door closed.

"Everyone needs to be legal," I remind him as he arrows straight for the pool. I should've turned off the heat to that thing so it would shrivel his balls when he jumps in.

"Have Ty card people." Luke shrugs off my hand. "I'm not the fuzz."

No, you're an asshole.

I drag Vaughn into the kitchen and lift her up onto the counter so she can lean against one of the cabinets. In the fridge, I find a bottle of Perrier. I twist the cap off and curl her fingers around it. "Drink this. I need to talk to with Ty about something, 'kay?"

"'Kay!" She swings her legs. She's still on the upward trajectory of drunkenness, which is good. At some point, though, I fear that all the feelings she's been keeping at bay with the boatload of booze are going to come crashing down. I've tried drinking my sorrows away, and it never works. She's going to learn that the hard way.

For now, I'm hoping she can sit tight for five minutes until I can see how Ty's doing and whether he's going to need help.

"I'll be right back."

She toes me in the thigh with one gold-sandaled foot. "I'll be fine. Go. Do your business."

I don't want to leave her. I place my hands on either side of her hips and lean in. "I'm going to take care of you."

"Tonight?" She quirks an eyebrow.

"For starters." I give in to the temptation I've been fighting all night and press a kiss against her temple. "For starters," I repeat against her sweat-damp skin.

I hustle out to find Ty in the front room on the phone. "You calling in reinforcements?" I ask.

"Yup."

"Sorry."

His eyes widen. I'm not known to apologize for the extra workload I place on him. "It's my job," he says easily.

"Yeah, but I'm still sorry. Your job sucks sometimes."

He laughs. "It pays well, and the guy I work for is generally pretty decent."

That faint praise makes me want to bust out in song, but since I have a little pride left, I allow myself only a big-ass smile.

"I'll be with Vaughn if you need me."

"You take care of her. I got the rest of this mess."

"Thanks, man."

"Anytime."

Back in the kitchen, I find Vaughn chatting merrily with Paxton Hayes, an actor from a very popular vampire television show. Uh-uh. Paxton has to find his own girl. Vaughn's mine. I don't know when that happened, but somewhere along the line Vaughn went from the girl I was forced to have on my arm to the girl I want to have in my life.

"Pax, when'd you get here?" I put a foot of space between him and Vaughn under the pretext of slapping his fist in greeting.

"I was coming into the bar when your party was leaving. Thought I'd tag along."

"Absolutely." I pat him heartily on the back. "What're you drinking? You look thirsty." I lead him away from Vaughn and toward the living room where the bar is stocked.

He gives me an amused look. "I could use a Jack and Coke."

"One Jack and Coke coming right up." Some stranger is manning the bar. "Hey, man, Paxton needs a drink. Can you fix him up?"

The stranger nods and I head back to the kitchen, only to find that Vaughn is gone. I wander around the house for fifteen minutes until finally asking Ty for help.

"She needed to use the bathroom," he informs me, and then frowns. "But that was ten minutes ago."

"Aw, shit. Maybe she's passed out."

I take the steps two at a time and check the guest rooms. Two of them are occupied, but not by Vaughn. I ignore the couples rolling around on the guest beds and duck back into the hall.

As I make my way toward my bedroom, I pass by Luke. He's making out with a brunette in a blue tank top and gold sandals—

I back up two steps. No. I'm totally hallucinating, right? Because there's no way he's making out with…

"Vaughn?" I demand.

28

HIM

As my heart beats triple time against my rib cage, I watch the
girl's dark head pull away from Luke and peer around his arm.

"Oak?" Vaughn slurs.

The sight of her swollen lips makes me want to slam my
fist into the wall. Or into Luke's jaw. Or maybe into my own
jaw, for being such a stupid, pathetic tool who actually thought
that...that what? That she was into me? That she would ever
see me as something more than a job?

I nearly choke on the pain. "What the hell is going on?"

Luke grins drunkenly at me. "Dude, I was just coming up to piss and your girl threw herself at me."

Vaughn's unfocused eyes flick from me to Luke and then back at me. Something registers, although I have no clue what. Then her hand flies to her face and she whirls around, fumbling with the bathroom door. She lunges inside.

Luke and I stare at each other as the sounds of retching fill the air.

He waves a hand toward the bathroom. "She's all yours, man."

My anger turns to rage. Pure, white-hot rage as I grab him by the collar and shove him up against the wall.

"That's my girlfriend!" I growl at him. "You were kissing my goddamn girlfriend!"

Panic fills his eyes, eclipsing the haze of inebriation. "I...I..."

"You what?" I snap, but then he makes a choked noise and I realize he can't answer because my forearm is digging into his windpipe. I loosen my grip, just barely.

"I thought..."

"You thought what?"

"Thought it was a media thing," he mumbles. "Like it was with April."

"Well, it's not," I snap.

"C'mon, Oak, be real with me. No way are you into some normal. You go for supermodels, tall blondes with big tits and—" He moans when my arm presses into his throat again.

"You don't know a damn thing about me." I'm so pissed off I'm starting to feel dizzy, but I let the anger continue to flow. I have to, otherwise the pain will come back. And the jealousy. I refuse to think about the way her lips had been fused to his. I refuse to.

"I'm sorry, okay?" he wheezes. "She told me she felt sad and needed some cheering up. I thought—"

Every word disgusts me even more. So he thought he'd take advantage of some girl who was too drunk and too distraught to know what she was doing? Luke's always been an asshole, but I didn't realize he was this bad. "You thought wrong."

"I didn't know it was like that. But now I know and it won't happen again, okay?"

"Damn straight it won't! You're not gonna get within five feet of her ever again, you hear me? If you so much as *look* at her, I'm gonna beat you so hard that—"

"Oak," a stern voice booms, and then a pair of beefy arms yanks me away from Luke.

My former friend staggers to the side, clutching his throat with one hand. He looks at me as if I've gone insane. Maybe I have. I can't stop thinking about how this creep's mouth was on Vaughn's mouth. His hands on her waist. His body pressed up against her.

"You all right, brother?" Tyrese asks in a low voice.

I manage a nod. "Get him out of my house," I mutter.

He doesn't need to be asked twice. Luke protests as my bodyguard drags him toward the staircase. He shouts out that he didn't know it was real, he's sorry, he'll make it up to me, but I don't even spare him a glance.

I'm done with him. First thing tomorrow I'm calling Jim and requesting a different bassist at the studio. I don't give a crap how he makes it happen, but it is *absolutely* going to happen.

Vaughn's retching has stopped, I realize. I knock softly on the door, but a part of me almost doesn't want her to answer. Doesn't want her to open it.

"Oak." Her weak voice sounds from behind the door, which

swings open to reveal her ashen face and bloodshot eyes. "I don't feel so good."

The pained, embarrassed note softens something inside me. She's so drunk that she's swaying on her feet, and I can't help but reach out to steady her. Damn it. I want to rage at her for kissing Luke. I want to ask her what the hell she was thinking. But it's obvious she's in no shape to talk.

"Everything is spinning," she whispers.

My heart stutters. "I know," I say gruffly. "Come on. Let's get you to bed."

She takes a step forward and almost falls over.

Sighing, I lift her into my arms and carry her to my bedroom. She buries her face in the crook of my neck and lets out a little whimper. "Head hurts, Oak."

"I know, baby. It's okay. I'll get you something for the pain."

I gently deposit her on the bed, then pop into the master bath to grab some ibuprofen and a glass of water. I force her to swallow two pills and then chug the whole glass. She does it without protest then crawls up the bed and hugs one of my pillows.

"Spinning," she moans.

"Just close your eyes and go to sleep." Hard as I try, I can't move her to urge her under the covers, so eventually I grab the other end of the blanket and pull it over her. She's passed out before she's even fully covered.

I stand at the edge of the bed and watch her for a minute. Curled up on her side, eyes squeezed shut. I want to lie down beside her and spoon her against me and stroke her hair and tell her it's okay that she kissed Luke.

But it's not okay, dammit. It's not.

Letting out a tired breath, I turn toward the door and flick off the light. Darkness bathes the bedroom. I take one last look at the sleeping girl on my bed and then go downstairs to help my bodyguards kick all the strangers out of my house.

The last stragglers don't leave until four. I stumble into the bedroom and find Vaughn wrapped up in the blanket like a burrito. I drag a tiny bit of the sheet across my tired ass and fall asleep before my eyes close completely. When I wake up, the blanket's spread across me and the afternoon light is filtering in.

The other side of the bed is empty.

I bolt upright and jog downstairs. Hands on my hips, I survey the empty, spotless living room. Big D must've called in the cleaners. And I slept through the whole thing, including Vaughn's sneaking away.

"Big D," I call.

"Kitchen."

I find him sitting at the kitchen table drinking a bottle of Perrier and doing a crossword puzzle. "Where's Vaughn?"

"Home, I suppose."

"When did she leave?"

He checks his watch. "About four hours ago. Had Daniel from ice cream day drive her home." He pushes one of my business phones toward me. "You've got a bunch of messages starting with Jim. Call him the minute you get up."

Four hours. That's a while. Wonder what she's doing now? "Any bad press I should know about?"

"Nope. It's all quiet in Oakville." Big D smiles to himself over that witticism.

"Good," I grunt. As I pull out a bottle of Powerade, I pause and turn back to Big D. "Hey, good morning. Thanks for coming."

He sets down his paper and subjects me to a long appraisal.

"Ty said something about how you were changing. I wouldn't have believed it if I hadn't seen it with my own eyes."

I force myself not to shuffle my feet like a five-year-old caught with his hand in the cookie jar. "Is that your way of telling me I was an asshole before today?"

"Nah. Just that you've had so much sun shining in your life that sometimes it blinded you."

"So I was an asshole before today?" I nudge the refrigerator door shut with my shoulder.

Big D laughs. "We're all assholes, Oak. Call Jim before his head explodes."

I take the phone, my drink and a banana out to the deck and call Jim.

"How's the recording going? When can I hear some music?" he asks.

"I thought I sent—" I pause midbite when I remember that no, I hadn't sent Jim a thing. I sent the first recording to Vaughn. Vaughn, who made me wait ten minutes before spitting out the word *good*. I swear she only has one adjective in her whole damn vocabulary. I'm going to work on that.

She needs to learn things like *hot* and *ripped* and *awesome*. All of which she should apply to me. When I see her again, we're going to start those lessons. Right after she explains why in the hell she kissed Luke. In the process of kicking everyone out, I came to the conclusion that she was so drunk she probably thought Luke was me. We're about the same height. Same color hair. In her drunken state, she got us confused.

Once she realized she'd had her mouth pressed against the dickface, she'd thrown up. The only correct response after recognizing that you've kissed a loser.

"You sent me nothing. Or if you did, it didn't come through. Resend it."

"No."

"No, what?"

"No, I'm not sending you anything. Not until King and I are done with the album. Or at least half of it." I don't want anyone listening to the songs right now. Criticism might derail me at this point. There are only two people I care about hearing my music and it's King and Vaughn. In fact, she should come to the studio today and listen to me live. I'd like to see her tell me that song is *good* to my face.

"You always send me your music," Jim reminds me. "I'm your manager. You send me your music. I tell you if it works and then both of us make enough money that the Saudis are calling us for loans."

"All of that is going to happen," I assure him, mostly because I want to hang up and call Vaughn. "But it'll happen in my own time. Gotta run, Jim. Text me if you need anything."

Meaning, don't call because I'm not answering.

I dial Claudia next because I don't want any distractions when I go into the studio. I'm going to lay down some righteous tracks between now and whenever King is tired of me, and the last thing I want to do is deal with Claudia and her little plots. Besides, Vaughn and I have this figured out.

"Claud, hey, it's Oak."

"I'm so glad you called! I've got interview opportunities for you from *GQ*, *People*, *USA TODAY* and *ET*. The rumors about you working with King, along with your new relationship, are generating real, positive interest. Which one do you want? I think you should bring Vaughn, not to have her answer any questions, mind you, but her presence should be noted. Maybe we'll even have a picture of you with her. She can sit on the piano bench. You'll be on the floor with your arm raised around her bottom. That's tender, yet not too provocative."

I eat the rest of my banana as she chirps in my ear. While

Claudia talks about the clothes we'll wear in this fantasy photo shoot she's cooked up, I return inside to hunt down my personal phone so I can call Vaughn. I locate it on my nightstand.

I need to shower before meeting King in the studio. Wait, do I even know what time we're meeting? I check my messages and see that he texted this morning that he'd be available around two. I text back the thumbs-up emoji and then pull up Vaughn's contact.

"I can't do any of those, Claud. I'm recording. Maybe after."

"But what about Vaughn?"

"I got that covered."

And I hang up before she can tell me all the ways that I'm screwing up. I've heard that stars like me are supposed to have a bunch of yes-people. Where did I go wrong?

I throw my business phone on the bed and call Vaughn.

"Hey," she says, her voice all tentative and wary. No doubt she's feeling embarrassed about last night, mistaking Luke for me and all.

"How're you feeling?"

"Like death."

I muffle a laugh. "You should've stuck around. Big D knows all the best hangover cures."

"He mentioned something about a hairy dog, but that made me want to barf again."

"You still in bed?"

"No. I've managed to haul myself downstairs to the living room sofa so I can pretend like I actually got up like a normal person."

"Normalcy is overrated, baby. If I send a car around will you come to the studio today?"

I hear a deep sigh. "Is that what Claudia wants?" she asks.

The banana in my stomach curdles. Haven't we gotten beyond that? It ticks me off that she's still making decisions based on what she thinks Claudia wants or what's good for my image.

I open my mouth to tell her that, no, that's what *I* want, when a wave of insecurity swamps me. If I say no and she turns me down, that'll feel like shit. And I want to see her today. I want her to hear me play. I want her to kiss me, Oakley Ford, without the cameras, without the booze, without anything. Just her and me.

"Yeah. Claudia."

It isn't a full-on lie. Just a small one. Infinitesimal, really.

"Is an hour okay? I haven't showered and I smell like someone spilled a case of beer over my head."

"No problem. I'm sending a car over now since it's going to be an hour in this traffic."

"Okay, see you then, Oak."

At least she's calling me Oak. I'll take it.

When you're inspired, stuff happens in a nanosecond. While I'm waiting for Vaughn to show up, I jot down a bunch of lyrics. After nixing about a dozen of them, I shuffle the rest into something resembling a song and hand it off to King. I drum a few different beats on the desk while he considers the words.

"Yeah, I like this." He hums a few chords. "Maybe faster over the bridge. Like—" He drops the notepad on the console and demonstrates.

I sing the first verse to his beat and it's perfect. We grin at each other. Something is cooking here and it's delicious. Working with King is everything I thought it would be. He makes me feel comfortable, even when he's asking probing questions like when was the last time I was moved by a song, any song? He shares personal stories, ones about his own failures, and that courage prompts my own. King's like a producer and therapist wrapped up in one genius mind.

My phone beeps and I lift a finger for King to hold on for a minute.

I'm here.

A jumble of words fight for dominance: *yes*, *finally* and *thank God*.

"Vaughn's here," I tell King. "Mind if we take five?"

"Nope. I'll go out back and pretend I'm trying to stop smoking."

We slap each other's hands and I go to let Vaughn into the studio.

"You came," I say.

Her face is a bit pale, but she still looks beautiful. I'm starting to love the fact that she doesn't wear makeup. Everything about her is natural and honest and so frickin' awesome. As I pull her inside, I'm fighting the urge to kiss her.

Inside the studio, a water bottle is waiting for her on a side table, and I bribed a blanket off one of the studio assistants upstairs. It's kept cool in the studio because of the instruments and the equipment. She might get cold since she lives in tank tops.

"I didn't see any cameras outside," she says as we reach the studio door.

I push it open for her and then lead her over to the chair I set up for her. "Yeah, about that. I might have lied." I gesture for her to sit, and she collapses into the chair. "Claudia didn't say you needed to come."

A furrow creases her forehead. "Then why am I here?"

I pull up a stool and pick up my Les Paul guitar, settling the body across my thighs. "I thought you might want to hear the music I'm doing with King."

"Huh."

There it is again. The big sigh.

I set down the guitar and stand up, irritation crawling across my neck. This is a big deal and not only doesn't she appreciate the gesture, I don't think she has a clue what it means. I rub a finger across my forehead. How do I explain this to her without coming across like a giant douche?

"So generally when artists are making music, it's just them and other musicians and the producers."

She winces. "So this is a big thing?"

Pride makes me shrug carelessly. "Not so big."

"I'm screwing up everything, aren't I?" Her gaze darts toward the door, as if she'd like to be anywhere but here.

"Am I keeping you from something?" I can't keep the chilliness out of my tone.

"No. I'm just…hungover. I drank too much last night." She gives me a wan, unhappy smile.

Her lack of enthusiasm, her obvious desire to flee, is like a punch to the gut. "That all you regret from last night?" I say harshly.

"I guess. I mean, I'm sorry I drank so much and passed out in your bed." She's studiously avoiding my eyes.

"You're sorry for passing out in my bed," I repeat. "That's what you regret? Drinking too much and passing out in my bed? What about fucking Luke?"

"I *slept with* Luke?" She leaps to her feet, horrified. "How—"

"No, I meant Luke. You kissed Luke."

Guilt flashes across her face. "Oh. That. I was hoping you wouldn't mention that." She visibly swallows. "It wasn't the best idea I've ever had."

Not the best idea? I nearly shout. Talk about an understatement.

"Then why'd you do it?" I ask tersely.

"Because I was drunk. And because I felt crappy and awful after all that stuff W said to me. And because Luke was there."

Pain arrows through me. I'd convinced myself that she'd mistaken Luke for me, but apparently that's not what happened at all. She'd *known* she was kissing someone who wasn't me… and that realization is crushing in a way I hadn't expected.

I stare at her in disbelief. "So you would've made out with anyone? Is that what you're saying? Didn't matter who it was as long as they had lips and a tongue?"

Vaughn cringes. "No, that's not it. I was…drunk," she says again, sounding defeated. "I was drunk and upset and I wanted you and couldn't find you, and Luke was suddenly there and he was flirting with me and…" She trails off.

One of her jumbled sentences sticks out to me. "You wanted me?"

She bites her lip.

"You were looking for me?" I study her embarrassed face. "Because you…wanted me. What does that mean?"

"Nothing," she mumbles. "It means nothing, okay?"

"Dammit, we both know that's not true." I jam my hand through my hair in frustration. "It does mean something. You were upset and you went looking for *me*. Because you want *me*, Vaughn. Just admit it."

"You want me to admit it? Fine! I admit it! I like you, Oak. I like you and I'm tired of pretending and I can't stop thinking about kissing you and—"

I don't give her time to finish that thought. I grab her, instinct overriding rational thought. I grab her and kiss her like I wanted to last night. Like I've wanted to since…since she stared at me with stars in her eyes at the beach. No, before then. When ice cream dripped on her fingers and I had my first taste of her sweetness. Maybe even earlier, when she was tart and sassy.

I've wanted this kiss for so long that I drink from her lips as if she's the only pool of water in the biggest desert on earth. And under my mouth, she melts. Her own lips part and she kisses me back.

And it's everything I'd imagined. Better than fifty thousand people shouting your name. Better than a sold-out Madison Square Garden crowd singing your lyrics back at you. Better than the greatest song ever sung. Her arms twine around my neck and I lift her up, face level so I can kiss her longer, harder, deeper.

Her tongue slides into my mouth and someone moans. I think it might be me. But then it's both of us, because my lower body starts grinding against her, and I know it feels as good to her as it does to me.

I want to kiss her forever. We should stay like this forever. Generations from now, they'll find us in the rubble, two lovers who died kissing.

All too soon she pulls away and stares at me. Confusion mars her pretty face.

"Just wanted to remind you that I'm still here." King's voice filters through the million-dollar sound system.

"Oh, my *God*." Vaughn turns redder than my mom's famous lipstick. Confusion switches to mortification. She slaps her hand over her mouth and runs out of the room.

I stand there like a stupid dumbass because I'm too stunned by my response to move. Is *that* what kissing is supposed to feel like? Holy *hell*. And if so, why did she run off?

I jerk myself into action and follow her, but she's already darted into a bathroom and locked the door.

"Vaughn, baby. Come out." I hear the faucet turn on. I jiggle the knob a little. "Are you sick?"

"Go away. Go away and make your music. That's what this is all about anyway."

I turn to see if there's anyone around who can help me interpret what just happened, but I'm alone and my girl has locked herself in the bathroom. Probably for the best. I'd rather no one else witness this humiliating exchange.

I make my way back to the control room, shaking my head the whole way.

King doesn't say a word as I collapse into a chair.

"What?" I ask after a prolonged silence.

"Nothing, man." King grins. "I should've come here sooner. Had no idea I'd be getting a show and an album in one deal."

I scowl. "Maybe I'll find a different producer."

If possible, his smile grows bigger. "Nope. I'm not leaving now. There's fire and magic in the air. Perfect music-making conditions."

I merely grunt as I pull out my Bic to scratch out the first line of how my head's so messed up that I'm starting to think the sky is green.

King peers over my shoulder. "She's changing you." I don't acknowledge him and write the next line about how I'm feeling like my heart's a junkyard, filled with spare, discarded parts. "The best ones do."

He slides over to fiddle with a panel, but I feel the heat of his eyes.

"Got something to add?" I mutter.

Over his outstretched arm, he says, "The good ones put your character to the flame and burn away all the rest of the shit until you come out a better you. She's one of the good ones."

"How do you know?" I challenge, chin out, glower on my face.

King gives me a mysterious smile. "You just do."

29

HER

Top 5 reasons why fans should expect a new Ford album ASAP! Click now!

5. It's been two years since the last tour and album. Fans are dying for something new. Oakley Ford has always treated his fans right.

4. Oakley Ford and King have been spotted together at several public benefits, and yesterday the two were seen ducking into the famed Hollow Oak recording studio. Sharp-eyed Ford fans posted this picture on the FordNews insta feed.

3. It's also been two years since ShOak was a thing. New girl definitely means new music, right?

2. He's growing up. Oakley will be twenty soon and that means he's leaving his teen years behind. He will want to show us all how his grown-up music sounds.

1. Surprise albums are all the rage. Beyoncé! Kanye! Frank

Ocean! Releasing an album with no lead up is a huge power
move and one that would fit the new, grown-up Oakley.

I'm acting like a six-year-old. I mean, who locks themselves
in a bathroom to avoid talking to someone? Me, that's who.
Vaughn Bennett, a mess of a girl, the kind of screwed-up person who kisses two boys in the span of one day.

Jeez. When did my love life get so exciting?

Except…only one of those kisses had actually excited me.
Only one of those kisses made my heart soar and my toes curl.

Oakley's kiss.

The other kiss was a mistake before it even happened. I
thought Luke was kind of sleazy from the moment I met him,
but the stupid alcohol made me forget that last night. And
then he was flirting with me and saying how cool I was, and
when he kissed me I didn't stop it because I thought it would
make me feel good.

It didn't. Kissing only feels good for me when I like someone. I felt nothing when Luke's lips were on mine. But *Oak's*
lips? My whole body vibrated in response, and that totally
freaks me out.

I bury my head in both hands and groan into my palms,
hoping the running water muffles the frazzled sound. I've
never been more confused in my life. I can't seem to focus
on any one thought—my brain is a huge jumble of them.
Thoughts about Oakley. About that amazing kiss. About the
fact that I took the year off to work but instead accepted a job
that gives me way too much time to think about stuff I don't
want to think about.

It's like everyone is making decisions for me these days. W
decided to dump me. Claudia decides what I'm going to do
every day. Oak decided to kiss the living daylights out of me
and make me feel things I've been trying not to feel.

I lift my head, and my gaze falls to my Vans. Seeing all the doodles scribbled on the sneakers just ticks me off. I used to love these shoes, but I look at them now and they seem…silly. The dumb squiggles of a foolish girl who thought her boyfriend would love her forever.

Slowly, I lean forward and slip the shoes off my feet. I pick them up and walk over to the trash can by the door. I hesitate, only for a moment, and then toss the shoes in the trash.

Oakley isn't waiting in the hall like I expect him to be. Through the glass windows spanning the corridor, I see that he's gone back into the studio. He and King are talking animatedly, while Oak tosses a pen in the air and then catches it in his hand.

My cheeks get warmer and warmer as I approach the door wearing nothing but black footie socks. I hope King doesn't bring up the kiss he witnessed. I hope Oak doesn't bring it up, either, at least not in front of King.

"Hey," Oakley says when I enter the room. His tone is light, but there's a note of wariness there, as if he's unsure of what I'm going to do.

"How's the writing going?" I ask, trying to sound casual. I flop down onto the sofa along the wall of the studio and wrap my arms around my knees.

"Awesome."

Our eyes lock. I see the questions in his, but he doesn't voice them.

King voices one, though. "What happened to your shoes?"

"I lost them," I mumble.

The two males exchange a look. Oak arches a brow at me.

"All right, then," King drawls. "Ah, how 'bout you lend us your ears, Miss Bennett? Our boy keeps trying to slow down this bridge and I keep telling him that's not fresh, but he won't listen. Maybe you can back me up."

Oak rolls his eyes. "She's not gonna back you up, 'cause you're wrong." He picks up his guitar and strums a chord. "Check this out, Vaughn, and tell me I'm right."

As his raspy voice fills the studio, all the distress I felt in the bathroom starts to fade away. His music is that powerful. Every time this guy sings, it's like time stops and you're sucked into his world.

The lyrics are angrier than I expect, until the bridge, when they become kind of melancholy. I can see why he wants to slow that part down. It's so different in tone from the rest of the song.

"So?" King prompts when Oak is done.

They both eye me expectantly.

I give a sheepish smile. "Um. I disagree with you both, actually. I don't think it works either fast *or* slow. The lyrics in that part sound like they're from a totally different song. I mean, sometimes that's a good thing, but in this case, it's kind of...jarring." I stare at my hands so that neither one of them can glare at me.

"Yeah... I can see your point." King sounds thoughtful. He grabs the pen from Oakley and starts jotting something down on a notepad. "What if we tweak these lines to this?"

Oak instantly leans over to look, and the two of them start brainstorming again.

I curl up on the sofa and listen to their soft murmurs. I don't remember falling asleep, but I must have, because my eyes suddenly pop open to the feel of a warm hand on my cheek. I blink, realizing that King is gone and it's just me and Oak.

He's perched on the edge of the couch, his fingertips stroking my cheek as he looks down at me with those gorgeous green eyes.

"You fell asleep," he tells me.

I sit up with a yawn. "Oh. I'm sorry. It's the hangover, not your music. I swear."

He laughs before his expression goes serious. "What happened to your shoes?"

"I threw them away," I confess.

"Any particular reason why?"

"They're part of my past."

Oak nods slowly. "All right. Can I buy you a pair of new Vans?"

"No." I shake my head. "I'm going to get my own. Color a new story for myself."

He settles into his chair and picks up his pen. "Hope you have room on there for a tree or two."

"A tree?" I ask, puzzled.

"You know...maybe an *oak* tree?"

I feel a smile tug on the sides of my lips. "Yeah... I probably do."

Later, we go to Oak's house. Not because Claudia says we should, but because by mutual, silent agreement, that's where we want to be. We order pizza and eat it outside on a pair of lounge chairs in front of Oakley's gigantic pool. By the time we finish eating, the sun has already dipped below the horizon line, but that doesn't stop him from popping into the pool house to change into swim trunks.

My breath catches when he reappears. This is the first time I've seen him with his shirt off. Well, in person, anyway. I've seen his chest in pictures, but the real thing is so much...yummier. And his tattoos are hotter than hell. He's got a cross on his arm with his mom's name underneath it. A swirl of music notes and what I think is a guitar fret on his other arm. Black rows of dates and coordinates between his shoulder blades—I gave in and Googled him again the other day to figure out what the back tattoo meant, and it turns out it's the dates and coordinates of some of his favorite tour stops.

Sometimes I forget that he's nineteen. He's so tall and muscular and masculine that he looks older. Actually, he's looking more and more like his movie-star father, but I keep the comparison to myself because I don't think Oak would appreciate it. He hardly ever mentions his dad, and it's obvious they've got some kind of beef.

"Always checking me out, huh?" he teases. "Careful, babe, or you're gonna give me a complex."

"You already have a complex. It's called egomania."

"Ha." He marches over and tugs on the braid hanging over my shoulder. "Maybe if you quit staring at me all the time, my ego would be normal-size."

"Nothing about you is normal-size," I shoot back, and then blush because that sounded like a double entendre, and I totally wasn't trying to make one.

He waggles his eyebrows. "You saw the *Vogue* spread, huh?"

I blush harder. "Just shut up and do a cannonball or something."

"You're really not going to join me?" Oak looks disappointed. He told me there were spare bathing suits in the pool house, but swimwear isn't my issue. I'm just not in the mood to swim.

"I'm so lazy today," I say ruefully. "Seriously. This hangover kicked my butt."

"Note to self—lock up the liquor cabinets next time Vaughn comes over for a party."

"Please do," I beg.

Chuckling, he drops a towel on his chair and walks to the edge of the deck. Rather than dip a toe in to test the temperature, he dives cleanly into the water and swims all the way to the other side of the pool. His blond head pops up near the shallow end, and then he does a slow backstroke while I admire the strong lines of his body.

I lie back and look up at the dusky sky, marveling about the drastic upheaval of my life. Two months ago I never would've dreamed I'd be lying on a chaise longue in Oakley Ford's luxurious backyard, while the pop star I'd once crushed on swims laps in his pool.

Oak's life isn't normal, though. The bodyguards, the money, the fans, this house on the beach with its blue tiled pool, his friends—although for someone so famous he doesn't seem to have very many friends. Or, at least, not good ones.

"You're thinking so hard I can hear your gears grinding. What's bothering you?"

I contemplate him for a minute. There are tiny drops of water on his long eyelashes and they sparkle like jewels in the late-afternoon sun. "I don't know. I just…" I trail off.

He levers himself out of the pool and throws his wet self down next to me.

I toss him a towel so he can cover up his perfect body. It's way too distracting.

He rubs the towel over his head and swipes it haphazardly down his torso before tossing it behind him. "Come on," he coaxes. "Tell me what's twisting you up inside."

"Are you going to turn this into a song?" I'm beginning to suspect that the music he's making is all about himself— a confessional of sorts. That kind of bravery is stunning and powerful.

"Maybe." He tilts his head toward me. "It's kind of a hazard of dating a songwriter."

Hmmm. I hadn't considered that, but weirdly I trust him. As in, I don't believe he'd write a song that would hurt or humiliate me.

I fix my gaze on the fading light in the sky.

"My parents died two summers ago," I say softly. "Dad had taken Mom out for date night. They were coming home from the Cheesecake Factory—my mom's all-time favorite place. She loved the meat loaf there, of all things." I shake my head over that memory. "Anyway, something happened and Dad lost control of the car. It crashed into the concrete barricade and they both died on impact." The sharp pain of loss forces me to stop and catch my breath. "I hadn't planned on taking summer classes. Dad wanted me to. He said if I graduated early, I could take a year off before going to college. He thought I could spend the year backpacking across Europe, getting educated in the school of life."

"Did you go last summer?"

"No. I ended up graduating early just like he wanted, but that was so I could help out my sister. And after they died, I didn't want to go to Europe anyway. I was..." I trail off.

"You were what?"

I swallow. "Too scared to go. I think I'm scared of life. That's why I was dating W for so long even though I think we both ran out of feelings for each other a long time ago. That's why this fake dating thing I had with you was okay. I'm good at pretending, but not so great at living. Everyone knows what they want out of life. Carrie is going to Berkeley because she wants to be a lawyer like her mom. Justin is going to UCLA to be an accountant. Kiki is going to be a cosmetologist. So I told everyone I wanted to be a teacher like my parents and I figured that if W was going to USC, I might as well, too."

"None of that sounds like it's making you happy."

"My parents lived for the moment. But I want to have a plan, a future. You told me not to settle. You said to find my passion, but I don't know what that is. I only know what I don't want."

"That's as good a place to start as any."

"Is it?" I turn my eyes to his. He reaches across the span between our loungers and rubs a thumb along my wet cheek.

"Yes." His broad palm cups my cheek. "Yes," he repeats.

The tears slip out of my eyes and pool in his hand. I watch as the salty water runs against the side of his wrist and down his forearm. My messy emotional state isn't scaring him away. He scoots closer, the metal legs of his lounger scraping against the deck.

"When did you know you wanted to be a singer?"

"Four? Five? I felt like I was born knowing. I think my parents were afraid that I'd want to go into the acting business, like them, but I've always loved music and telling stories through songs. I loved hearing my voice form and hold notes. It was all I ever wanted."

"LA is filled with people with purpose." I reach up to touch his hand. It's warm and solid in my grasp. "All these people come here with huge dreams. I don't want their dreams, but I'd like *a* dream."

"Maybe you have one but are afraid of it."

"Maybe." I look down at our clasped hands and think about the things that stir me. My family, cooking for them, drawing pictures. Can I make a living out of that? Is that my future?

He reaches over and lifts me off my chair and onto his. "If you had all the money in the world, what would you do?"

"Travel and see the world," I answer immediately.

"Then you should do that."

"W thought that was stupid."

Next to me, Oak's chest vibrates when he grunts. "We both know what I think of W. You're better off without him. Good thing you broke up with him." Oak sounds disgruntled and jealous, which is adorable in so many ways I can't even count them.

"Um, he broke up with me, remember?"

"He only did that because he knew what was coming."

"And what was that?" I bend my neck to check if Oak is about to make some smart-ass remark about how *he* was coming.

"That you were just marking time with him, and eventually you would've realized you could do better." Oakley shrugs. "Besides, he's probably got a tiny dick and was overcompensating."

I roll my eyes. It's all about size with guys. "I wouldn't know."

His eyebrows draw together. "You never—" He makes a short punching motion with his fist.

"What is that?" I laugh. "Is that sex? No. I never had sex with W."

His eyes get comically big. "You never even touched him downstairs?"

"Oakley Ford, do you really want to know all the gory details of what I did with W?"

He actually thinks it over. I slug him in the shoulder.

"So wait, if he never got any downstairs action from you, does that mean you never got any downstairs action from *him*?" Oak looks horrified now.

"Can we please just drop this?" The pool might be only sixty degrees, but it's looking more appealing by the minute. If I jump in, maybe this mortifying conversation will end.

"No, no, we can't." He sits up and drags me with him. "Did he ever—"

I slap my hand across his mouth. "Oh, my God. Stop talking. Please."

He hesitates and then nods, but the moment I drop my hand, he's back with the commentary.

"Damn, what a selfish asshole. Bet he had no problem asking you for attention."

"I can't believe you really want to discuss this." I cover my face.

"Have you ever done it to yourself?"

Where's a good ol' California earthquake when you need it?

"Yes, okay, I touch myself. It feels…fine. Good, even."

"Shivers?"

I sigh. Clearly, if I don't give him something, he's going to keep pressing me. "No, not shivers, but it's good."

"Come on." He stands abruptly and holds out his hand.

"Where we going?"

"Inside. I don't think you're ready for the outdoor messing around yet."

I arch an eyebrow. "You think you're getting some?"

"No. Not me." His eyes darken. "Come on."

I push to my feet and slide my hand into his. I'm not entirely certain where this is going, but Oak's never been one to pressure me. He's never even brought up sex until now. I allow him to lead me through the living room and down the hall to his media room. He dims the lights, flicks on a movie and then pulls me down on the sofa.

He sticks his finger under my chin and tips my head up so we're eye to eye. "Do you trust me?"

"Yeah…why?" I say uneasily.

Rather than answer, he clasps my face in his hands, the calluses that he's built over years of playing guitar scraping against my skin. His lips catch on mine—tender, sweet, undemanding. We kiss for a brief moment, my raging case of humiliation fading under his caress. Then he draws back.

"You're beautiful. Every day I'm with you is brighter and more exciting than the last. And if we ever have sex, it'll be because you want it, not because I want it or because you think it's necessary to keep me." He brushes his thumb against my lips and a bolt of energy tightens my entire frame. "But until you're ready, there's a ton of other stuff we can do to make you feel good."

Goose bumps rise on my skin. "Wh-what about you?"

"I've got two hands—" he winks at me "—and a damn good imagination. So yeah, I can put on a movie and pretend I'm paying attention, but all I really want to do is kiss the hell out of you."

"You want to kiss me again even though I kissed Luke?" Guilt pokes at my belly. I avoid his eyes, but he tips my chin to the side so I have no choice but to look at him. "You're not still mad?"

"Are you ever gonna kiss him again?"

"No. God, no."

"Then I'm not mad." He grins wickedly. "And yeah, I want nothing more than to kiss you again."

"That's it?" I'm down for kissing, but the look in his eyes tells me he wants to do a lot more.

Sure enough, he answers bluntly. "I'm not limiting my kisses to just your mouth."

I blush…all over.

"And you're not going to want anything in return?" I always knew that if I let W touch me, he'd expect the same thing in return and…I just didn't want to go there. But yeah, I've ached in places. My breasts have tingled. My clothes have felt too tight. But something has always held me back.

Oak closes his eyes briefly. "You sure I can't go to USC and beat the hell out of W?" Apparently he understands my dilemma without me giving voice to it.

"Can we not talk about W anymore?" I say softly.

"Yeah, no more W." He lies down on the sofa and pats his chest. "Come here. You're in charge."

I lean over him. "Maybe I want you to watch the movie. Do the whole 'pretend you're yawning and slide your arm around my shoulders' thing."

He yanks me on top of him. "Oops, you tripped and fell."

"Not the same thing," I retort.

"Pretty much." He leans forward and kisses me before I can say another word.

His tongue sweeps in and rubs along mine. One hand tangles in my hair, while the other glides up under my loose T-shirt.

Between my legs, he feels muscular and hard. I move against him, and his hands grip me harder in response. Against my lips, he groans, and the deep, manly sound takes my breath away.

I, Vaughn Bennett, turn Oakley Ford on. He's pressing against me. He's groaning when I move. I try it again and his lips curve against mine.

"You're so hot, Vaughn. So fucking hot."

The coarse words send shivers down my spine. Oak's fingers dance lower, down the back of my jeans. Suddenly, I want to know more. What can he do? How will it feel?

Carrie and Kiki have talked about this. They both enjoy sex, and now here's Oakley, willing, more than willing, to show me what I'm missing. Without any expectation of anything in return.

I reach between us, the back of my hand bumping against his hard-on. He gasps but doesn't move an inch. I'm in charge. I push away from him, just enough to flip open the button on my jeans. His hand reaches for the zipper.

"May I?" His voice sounds hoarse.

"Yeah." Mine isn't much better.

He drags the zipper down and then his long, talented fingers cup me, over my underwear, under my jeans. He moves his hand slowly in a wide circle and there's so much sensation it's as if I have a thousand nerve endings between my legs.

I brace a shaky hand by his head. His mouth finds my neck, his lips brushing against the outer edge of my ear.

My toes curl and my breath comes in shorter and shorter pants.

"I've got you, baby," Oak whispers against the base of my throat. "I've got you."

He rubs and rubs and rubs for what seems like hours and only a few seconds at the same time, until sparks fly in front of my eyes and my whole body becomes tense as a wire as an electrical charge spirals through me. I gasp and moan and then collapse against him, my heart beating wildly. His heart is galloping, too.

"Oh, Jesus, that was so beautiful." His palm is still cupping me, and I can feel my body vibrating against his as the aftershocks cause me to tremble like a newly formed leaf.

I try to formulate words, but I have none. Luckily, Oak doesn't need them. He just holds me until I drift off into slumber.

And either I imagined it, or that was actually his raspy voice singing me to sleep.

30

HIM

1doodlebug1 @OakleyFord_stanNo1 I think they're a real couple

OakleyFord_stanNo1 @1doodlebug1 yeah he's into her

1doodlebug1 @OakleyFord_stanNo1 ☹

SIX WEEKS LATER

I'm having the time of my life. And that's saying a lot, because I've done some pretty awesome things in my life. Lazing around on private islands. Playing sold-out shows in some of the most gorgeous cities in the world. Not to mention spending time with gorgeous women, from models to actresses to fellow singers.

But none of them were half as gorgeous as Vaughn, and none of those concerts or vacays come close to all the fun Vaughn and I are having. This last week alone, we've made enough memories to last me a lifetime.

On Monday we wasted the whole day away on El Segundo beach. It was completely deserted because everyone was at school or work, so we had some actual privacy as we horsed around in the water and then stretched out on an oversize towel, talking about random shit as we shared a huge plate of nachos from one of the boardwalk food trucks.

And on Monday night we fooled around on her bed.

On Tuesday she came to the studio again.

And on Tuesday night we fooled around by my pool.

On Wednesday I kept my promise to her brothers and we took them to my buddy's house to make use of his halfpipe.

And on Wednesday night we fooled around on my bed.

On Thursday we went to King's club, where I did an impromptu performance that Vaughn actually called "amazing." Her vocab is getting better.

And on Thursday night we fooled around in my kitchen. Ty wasn't thrilled about walking in on us, but we were fully clothed so I don't know what all his bitching was about.

I ain't gonna lie—we still keep our clothes on every time we hook up. Is it frustrating as all get-out? Hell, yes. Am I pressuring Vaughn to show me the goods? Nope. Because I promised her I'd be patient with her, and that's a promise I intend to keep…no matter how much my body hates me for it.

Now it's Friday and I'm in Vaughn's backyard for a barbecue on this gorgeous late-March afternoon. The twins are trying to build a house of cards on the patio table, but their flimsy structure keeps toppling over every other second. Paisley's cooking steaks on the grill, while Ty stands beside her telling her everything she's doing wrong. Big D is a few feet away, chuckling as Vaughn's sister and my bodyguard bicker like an old married couple.

Ty's technically not even on duty tonight. It's Big D's shift, but when Ty texted to check up on me and found out I was at the Bennett house for a barbecue, he invited himself along and then showed up before I could even check if it was okay.

He's crushing on Paisley. Hard.

"He totally likes her," Vaughn whispers to me. She's watching Ty and Paisley, as well, a faint smile on her lips.

"And he thinks he's being stealthy about it," I whisper back. "Men are idiots."

That makes her laugh, and the sweet, melodic sound gets the usual reaction out of me—my heart flips and my palms get sweaty. Ty's not the only one who has it bad.

I'm so into this girl it's not even funny. And I know she's into me, too. I see it in the way she giggles at my jokes, and how she laces her fingers through mine every time I take her hand. How she stares at me when she thinks I'm not looking. And bites her lip whenever our eyes meet.

"Vaughn! Your stupid phone won't stop buzzing," Shane calls from the deck. "It keeps knocking down our cards!"

"Ha!" she calls back. "Your cards keep collapsing because your foundation sucks!"

She's right. I've never seen a more pathetic pair of card-house builders. Vaughn and I drift over to the deck, where she swipes her phone off the table. She checks the screen then walks several not-so-discreet steps away and starts typing furiously.

I come up to her. "Who you texting?"

"Uh…no one," she says absently, angling the phone to shield it from my view.

"No one?" My hackles are instantly raised. Is she still in touch with W? She told me yesterday that she hasn't heard from him since the sloppy seconds comment, but what if that was a lie? What if she's still talking to the jerk?

Vaughn lifts her head. When she notices my dark expression, she puts on a reassuring tone. "It's not W."

"Then who is it?"

"No one," she repeats.

I swallow my rising irritation. "You just shot off five text messages. You're saying they were addressed to nobody and just disappeared into some weird cyber dead zone?"

Vaughn tucks her phone in her pocket. "I promise you, it's nothing shady, okay? Can we just drop this?"

"Have you met me?"

An exasperated laugh pops out of her mouth. "Just this once, can we pretend you're not a nosy busybody?"

"I'm not a busybody," I object.

"Then drop it."

"No." I stubbornly cross my arms. "Who are you texting?"

She hesitates.

"Come on, tell me. If it's nothing shady, then what's the big deal?"

After another long beat, Vaughn lets out a heavy sigh. "It's your mom, okay?"

I blink in surprise. "You're texting with my mom?"

"Yes."

"Why? And since when?"

"She's messaged me a couple of times since we had lunch," Vaughn confesses. "Just to say hi and see how I'm doing."

Something twists in my stomach. I think it might be jealousy, but that's crazy, right? Why should I care if Mom is texting Vaughn? I know they both liked each other when they met, so I guess it makes sense that they've kept in touch.

Must be nice.

I choke down a rush of resentment. Well. Lucky Vaughn. Katrina Ford likes her enough to say hi and ask her how she's doing. You'd think she'd like her only son enough to do the same for him, but apparently that's hoping for too much.

"I was telling her about the barbecue and I think she was fishing for an invite."

I stiffen.

"But I didn't invite her," Vaughn adds quickly. "I wouldn't do that without asking you first."

"Are you asking me?" I ask in a tight voice.

"No… Yes? I don't know. Do you want her to come? We've got plenty of food."

Which Mom probably won't even touch. She's been off red meat since I was in diapers. And why the hell does she want to come anyway? A backyard barbecue is way too pedestrian for Katrina Ford. She prefers black-tie events with shiny lights and swarms of admirers.

"I don't care either way," I answer, hoping my tone sounds as indifferent as I'm trying for it to be. "But I don't get why she's even interested. Barbecues aren't her style."

Vaughn jerks suddenly then fishes the phone out of her pocket again to check the incoming text. Her teeth sink into her bottom lip. "Oh, Oak. I think she really wants to come. Look at this."

I peer at the screen that Vaughn flips toward me.

I haven't had a steak in years! Now I'm craving one, thanks to you. Might need to ask my asst to run out and get me one.

Yup, she's fishing for an invitation, because the woman doesn't eat meat.

"Just invite her already," I mutter.

Vaughn brightens. "Yeah?" She immediately starts typing a response.

I leave her to it, wandering over to the grill to have a word with Ty. "My mother's on her way."

His shaved head swivels toward me. "For real?"

I nod.

"She bringing her entourage? Should I call in for more bodies?"

"I don't think so. Besides, Mom knows how to move under the radar. If she doesn't want the paps to track her here, then they won't."

"I hope she wears the red Annie wig," Big D pipes up. "And those big seventies-style shades? Remember that combo?"

"And the pink leather pants," Ty reminds him. "Don't forget the pants."

I can't help but laugh as I remember the disguise Mom wore to my last concert in order to sneak backstage unseen. Not that she wasn't seen. *Everyone* had been gawking at her. Except the outfit was so ridiculous that not one person suspected it was Katrina Ford, because Katrina Ford wouldn't be caught dead in something so awful. It was brilliant.

Right now, though, I'm less concerned about the outfit Mom's going to be wearing, and more concerned about how awkward shit is about to get.

31
HER

Kat Ford joins Weisenberg's all-star lineup!

Another A-lister has come on board for Oscar-winning direc-
tor Mick Weisenberg's upcoming thriller, set to begin production this summer. Katrina Ford, star of such rom-coms
as *Mr. Right Now* and *Hopeful Romantic*, has just signed on
to join the cast of Weisenberg's newest nail-biter. Ford will
be putting her comedic chops on the shelf and bringing her
former scream queen experience (*Machete Head 2*, *Dead
Night 1-3*) to this much-anticipated film.

Also attached to the untitled project are Julie Drake, Oscar
winner Freddie Herrera, and up-and-comer Natalie Gale.

"Is your mom wearing an embroidered sweat suit?" I gawk as
Oak's mom steps gingerly into our backyard.

Katrina has brought a few people with her—two big muscly
guys who I peg as bodyguards and a black-clad assistant carry-

ing two phones, a huge bag under her arm and a giant white box. Kat is clad, head to toe, in a Kelly-green sweat suit with flowers all over it. It's one of those things you'd see in a store window and know that you're supposed to like it, but don't. Somehow, Oak's mom pulls it off.

"Who knows," he mutters.

Clearly he's still not superhappy his mother is here, as if her arrival signals the end of his fun. I'm a little astonished at how much he's enjoyed himself these past couple of months, just hanging out with me and the family.

If he's not in the studio, he wants to be here. And the boys can't get enough of him. They've missed having Dad around more than I ever realized, and Oak is the big brother they've always wanted. It helps that his toys are out of this world, but they'd be following him like little ducks even if he showed up with empty arms.

Oakley is a kid at heart, and I suspect he's never had a lot of playtime. Oh, he has tons of people who want to be with him, but his guard is up. And that has to be stressful.

"Hopefully Ty comes back with more food. I didn't buy enough meat for all these people," Paisley frets.

"My mom doesn't eat meat," Oak assures her. "Whatever you have is fine."

"Do you think you should say hello?" I ask him.

"You invited her here."

Yup, still grumpy. I grab his hand and drag him toward Katrina. I've been doing that more and more lately—holding his hand. It feels…right.

W was never into public displays of affection. Holding my hand in public was a pretentious form of love, he'd said. Real couples don't need to brag about their relationship. I agreed, of course, because I never felt like rocking the boat with W. I needed him more than I needed to have my hand held.

But gosh, it always sends tingles up my spine when Oak's hand immediately closes around mine. He holds me tight in his clasp, like he never wants to let me go.

He does that when we're making out, too. And when we're doing…other things. Just thinking about all the naughty things we've done sets my cheeks on fire. Oak hasn't pushed me to go further than I'm comfortable with, but the kissing…and the touching…it's…incredible.

I force away my inappropriate thoughts as I greet Oak's mother. "Hi, Katrina. Thanks for coming."

"Oh, no, thank you for allowing me to come." Katrina leans down to give me a hug. She's four inches taller than me without shoes. In heels, she's nearly as tall as Oak. "I brought something for our meal." She waves her hand toward her assistant, who offers me the white box. "When I was in *Small Wonders*, my character always brought food and flowers whenever she was invited to a person's house. Flowers were her signature item. It's why, at the end of the movie, it's so meaningful when Sassy—that's the stepdaughter—gives her flowers from Sassy's mother's garden. It's such a beautiful scene. Did you see it?"

I shake my head and then regret it immediately when her face falls.

"Vaughn's more of an action girl," Oak interjects. "Let me take that. Vaughn, this is Amanda, Mom's assistant. And the guys behind her are Gary and Tobias."

He lets go of my hand to take the box and carry it over to the table that is already full of food. Paisley went kind of crazy at the grocery store, wanting to make sure that Oak wouldn't be unhappy with the food at our house. I shouldn't judge, though, because I made three desserts last night.

I shake hands with everyone, even Gary and Tobias, who look at my hand like it's a snake's head. "Come and meet my family." I lead Katrina over to my sister. "This is my sister, Paisley. She keeps us all together."

"God, I can't believe I look like a sweaty line cook in front of Katrina Ford," Paisley laments. She wipes her hand on her apron before holding it out.

Katrina bats the hand away and hauls Paisley into her arms, meat-stained apron and all. "Goodness, aren't you beautiful. Why are you working behind the scenes instead of in front of a camera?" Kat exclaims as she draws away.

Paisley blushes. "I like working at Diamond," she mumbles.

Katrina's attention is a little intimidating, but fortunately, I'm able to distract her from my sister by directing her toward the twins, who are now tossing the ball with Big D.

"These are my brothers, Spencer and Shane."

"Oh, oh, my heart." Kat pats her chest. "Your family is so adorable. I want to gather you all up and take you to Malibu with me to live full-time."

"Do you live on the beach?" Spencer asks. "Because we'd be down with that."

Shane nods his head eagerly.

"Of course! It's a public access beach, but you can certainly walk right from my deck to the sand."

"Radical." He and Shane exchange fist bumps. "When're we moving in?"

"You two aren't moving anywhere," I inform them. "Go inside and wash up. Paisley's almost done cooking."

The twins grumble a bit but know from past experience that they won't get to eat if they don't wash their hands. As they take off, Katrina's smile turns to me. "And your parents?"

I shoot an awkward look at Oak, who grimaces in return. He doesn't talk to his parents, so why would Katrina know about my past?

"They passed away a couple of years ago. Car accident," I explain.

Her face falls. "I'm so sorry. I didn't realize."

"It's okay." I mean, it's not okay. It'll never be *okay*, but it's getting easier to tell that story, easier to pass it off as one of those incidental facts about my life. Seventeen, went to Thomas Jefferson High and my parents died when I was fifteen.

"Mom, is that cashmere?" Oak interjects.

I sag with relief that we're moving on from the sad and uncomfortable topic of my parents' deaths.

"Isn't it wonderfully obnoxious? Carlo sent it over from Gucci today."

"It's seventy."

"It gets chilly at night," she protests.

"You look great," I tell her and then grab Oak's hand again, this time to pinch the tender skin between his fingers. He shuts up and I almost regret that more.

Fortunately, Paisley calls for us to come over because dinner is done. The kitchen table has been carried out the patio doors so we have enough seating for everyone. My sister refuses to eat until everyone is seated, even the bodyguards and the assistant.

Katrina sits between the twins, who take turns staring at her in confused adoration and shoveling steak into their mouths.

"Be nice," I mutter under my breath to Oak, who's decided he needs to sit so close to me that we're practically on top of each other. I'm not going to examine why I don't move away even though there's enough space for another family between me and Paisley.

"My mom makes me crazy."

"You'll miss her when she's gone."

Oak's face grows somber. His hand skates up my back to

rub lightly along my neck. "I know you're right. I'll try harder for you."

"Do it for yourself."

I have to give Oak credit. He tries. During dinner, he asks how her renovation is going and the two laugh about the number of times she's redone her Malibu home, although there's an underlying thread of sadness there, as if they both know she's trying to rebuild something in her life but never achieves any satisfaction in it.

"Maybe I should put a slide in it? I saw the other day where someone had put in a slide for their kids."

"We like slides," Spencer says.

Both Paisley's and my mouth drop open, because our twelve-year-old brothers would rather be dropped in acid than be caught on a playset.

"You do not," Paisley accuses.

"Do, too." Spencer glares. Shane nods in fierce agreement.

"Since when do you like slides? I asked if you wanted to go the park last weekend and you said it was for babies."

"We do like them," Spencer insists. "We just didn't want to go to that shi—stupid one over on Fifth Street. It smells like a Dumpster."

"That's the nicest park in El Segundo," she protests.

"Then El Segundo smells like a Dumpster."

"Oh, well, I don't need to put a slide in," Katrina interjects. Her head bobs back and forth between Paisley and the twins.

"No. Slides are awesome. Paise doesn't know what she's talking about."

Shane chimes in. "She's getting old. She might need a hearing aid soon."

"Shane Bennett, what are you talking about? I'm not even twenty-three!" Paisley cries. She looks to me for help, but I'm too busy giggling into my napkin.

Oak buries his face in my neck, trying to muffle his gales of laughter. "I love your family," he says between gasps.

Me, too. Me, too.

After dinner, we all clear the table with Oak muttering something under his breath about how he hasn't seen his mother lift a plate outside a movie since he was five. But Katrina helps as much as anyone else. Maybe one of her roles has helped her interact, but she comes off as sincere and sweet.

In the garage, Big D finds the ladder game, which he drags out into the backyard.

"What's your point system?" Big D asks Paisley as he swings the tethered golf ball in his hand.

She shrugs. "One point for the bottom pipe, two for the middle and three for the top."

Ty frowns. "No. You count how many bolas are left on the steps. Each one is a point."

"What's a bola?" Katrina asks nervously beside me. "I've never done this before."

"The bola is the string with the two golf balls on either end," I explain. "The goal is to get as many of the strings as possible to wrap around the three posts."

"If we were at your house, you could set the rules, but you're at mine so we're keeping score the Bennett way." Paisley juts out her chin.

"I recognize that look," Oak says on the opposite side of me. "It's the look that says we're doing it this way and no other." He cups his hands around his mouth. "Give in now, Ty. I can tell you from experience that there's no point in arguing."

I turn and punch Oak in the shoulder.

"Ow!" he fake cries. "Don't damage the goods."

"Your dad make this?" Big D asks, interrupting before I can punch Oak again.

"Yeah. It's just PVC pipe." The simple structure is about

five feet high and consists of three rows of pipe on a stand. The goal is to get your two golf balls glued to the ends of a piece of rope, or bolas, wrapped around the pipes.

"And a lot of glue!" Spence adds. The twins exchange high fives.

I grin happily, glad that the memory of them putting the game together is a good one instead of a sad one.

"They were silly on a glue high for a day," I explain to Oak and his mom.

Ty and Paisley are still arguing about the rules when Big D separates us into teams. We decide it's going to be the Bennetts against the Fords. Ty plays with us while Big D and Katrina's bodyguards stand over on the Ford side.

Amanda offers to keep score, the Bennett way.

Halfway into the game, the Bennetts are kicking ass. Ty mutters it's because we're cheating.

"You're on our team, Ty," Paisley points out.

"It's no fun winning when you're cheating," he grumbles.

"Throw the damn—darn bola," Oak yells. "You're holding the game up. You should get penalized for that."

"See, you're going to make us lose," Paisley says, then pulls the bola from Ty's hand and whips it across the lawn with perfect aim.

The bola knocks off one of Oak's balls, which means we win again. The twins run around, high-fiving everyone while Paisley and I slap hands. We grew up playing this with our parents. There's no way the Fords are going to beat us, no matter which way the game is scored.

"Come on, Mom, you got this," Oak encourages when Kat steps up and swings her bola.

Oak's behind her, so he doesn't see her face tighten with emotion and her eyes flutter closed. She shuts her eyes as if to make a perfect mental imprint of this moment. When her son called her Mom, when he cheered for her, when they were in perfect harmony.

"Go, Katrina," I yell.

"She's on the other team." Paisley scowls at me. "Between you and Ty, it's like you want us to lose."

I merely grin. I'm too happy to care about the outcome of this game because, as corny as it sounds, the day is a win.

After we defeat Team Ford three times in a row, the twins drag Katrina's bodyguards inside to show off their gaming rig. Paisley and Ty bicker as they stow away the game. Big D trails behind them. Amanda has disappeared, leaving Oak, his mom and me out on the lawn.

Katrina and I settle into a couple of deck chairs, but Oak decides he'd rather sit on the ground, leaning against my leg.

"How's everything going?" Katrina asks. The friendliness of the game has burned off a little, showing that the underlying tension between mother and son isn't going to be erased with one game of ladder golf.

"Good," Oak replies. He leans his head against the side of my leg, his soft hair rubbing against my bare leg. I reach down and smooth some of the hair out of his eyes. "You?"

She shrugs. "You know how it is. I'm old now so I'm only getting scraps, but there are a few things that interest me."

"That sucks," I say.

"What projects?" Oak wants to know.

"A couple small side roles in a few upcoming films. I just signed on for Weisenberg's latest thriller. The others are mostly dramas and I'd be playing someone much older than myself." She glances at her hands, almost in embarrassment. "I'm vain, dear. You know that."

"They'd be lucky to have you," Oak replies gruffly. The two speak to the ground, afraid to look at each other.

"Thank you. But enough about me. What are you working on?"

Silently, Oak makes circles with his finger on the stone pavers. When Katrina looks disappointed by his lack of response, I blurt out, "He's working on new music."

His mother's eyes widen. "You are? That's fantastic."

He clears his throat. "Yeah, I'm trying out a new sound. Don't know if it's going to go anywhere. It will probably suck."

"It does not suck. It's awesome. I had *shivers*," I proclaim.

He twists around to peer up at me. "This is the first I've heard of it."

"You don't need to get a bigger head. Your ego is threatening to take over the entire southern coast." I squeeze his shoulder to let him know I'm joking before turning back to Katrina. "It's wonderful. More of Oakley and less of everything else."

"That does sound wonderful. I can't believe Oak is letting you hear it as he creates it. He never does that. What does Jim think?" Katrina asks.

"I haven't shared any of it with Jim," Oak admits, rubbing his cheek against my hand.

Katrina's eyes, so like Oak's, miss nothing. "Whatever it is, I'm sure it's marvelous."

"I know you and Dad never wanted me to sign that contract," he mutters.

"Oh, Oak. Your father was just concerned that you'd be taken advantage of and you were so young. There are so many people who wanted to exploit you."

"We both know that's not why Dad was against it." There's bitterness in his tone.

She bites her lip. "We just wanted what was best for you."

"Really? Because both of you basically stopped talking to

me after I signed it." This time he does raise accusing eyes to Katrina.

"You filed those emancipation papers!" she cried. "What were we supposed to think? You didn't want us as parents anymore."

"No, I wanted to make my own decisions about my music and my career."

At first, Katrina opens her mouth to protest, but then she wilts, her desire to reconnect with her son overcoming any feelings of self-righteousness. "Then we didn't do right by you. I don't think either of us quite realized what happened until our little boy had become Oakley Ford—a man in his own right at the tender age of sixteen. We didn't handle it well, and I'm sorry for that. We love you and I miss you, Oak. I want to spend more time with you. Can we do that? Maybe a little?"

Her plea is so heartfelt that my throat thickens. I'd give anything to have another day with my parents. Oak tilts his head to look at me and I know he sees my envy and grief because he reaches out to clasp my hand in comfort. It's not Katrina he gives his answer to. "Okay, because I know it's important to you."

32

HER

Wanna come to a party? Justin's parents are gone.

I show the phone screen to Oakley. He's leaning against the counter, eating a piece of chocolate cake, which was what was in the big white box that Katrina brought. She left about thirty minutes ago, and Oak has been hanging around ever since. He doesn't seem in any hurry to leave.

"Yeah, can we?"

"I don't know. Do you need to check with Ty or Big D?" This earns me a frown, but I don't back down. "What if they go all nuts on you?"

"These are the people who came to Maverick's show with you?"

"Yeah."

"They seemed cool."

He clearly wants to go, so I text Kiki back.

I'm w/ Oak. How bad do u think everyone will freak?

OMG. Seriously? I'm freaking right now. Does he have any friends w him?

Yeah, dummy, me.

Ha ha.

If we come, everyone has to act normal. No asking him to sing. No trying to get in his pants. Do not make a big deal out of this.

Treat him like a normal guy from TJ?

Exactly.

He's Oakley Ford, V. U R asking the impossible!

Then we're not coming.

"I still want to go," Oak says, peering over my shoulder.

"Does the word *private* mean anything to you?"

He rinses his plate off in the sink. "Yeah, it means that the stuff you and I do isn't anyone else's business."

I roll my eyes. "That's not what I meant."

"I know." He kisses me on my temple. "But that's my definition. Let's go."

"She hasn't agreed to my terms," I balk.

"We're going to a party, not negotiating a hostage release."

"Fine." I call out to my sister, who's at the dining table across the room. "Paisley, we're going to Justin's tonight. His parents are gone and he's having a party."

Ty starts to get up, but Oak waves him off. "No, not tonight, Ty. We're just going to a friend's house."

Ty looks worried. "I dunno, man. I don't think Jim would like it."

"It's fine. Vaughn's friends are good people. They'll drink but no one will drive and it won't be superbig. Maybe twenty kids, tops," Paisley reassures him. Weirdly, Paisley's completely cool about Oak and me dating for real.

Ty settles back in his chair. He doesn't want to leave Paisley. Oak and I exchange another smirk before I find my keys to the car.

"No singing?" he asks as he climbs into the passenger seat.

"Justin's friend Matt likes to pretend he's a musician. Kiki and Carrie are going to have to sit on him so he doesn't attack you with his uploaded YouTube videos."

"Hey, plenty of stars got discovered that way. Don't knock the internet hit-making machine." Oak moves the seat all the way to the back before buckling in. It reminds me a little of Dad and his long legs.

"I'm not. I'm knocking Matt. He doesn't do it because he loves music but because he thinks it makes girls want to drop their panties." Something that probably does happen far too often for Oak.

"What if I want to sing?"

I roll my eyes. "Knock yourself out, champ."

He smirks and falls silent, tapping his fingers against his knees. Justin doesn't live far away, only about a mile. When we arrive, there are a few people outside the house. Oak flips his hood up and tugs his baseball cap low, but no one even glances twice at us.

Before I can get my hand up to knock, the door flies open.

"Oh, God, it's you. You're in my boyfriend's house!" Kiki exclaims. Then she slaps a hand over her mouth. "I'm trying to be cool. As cool as I can be. Can I touch your cross tat?"

"No," I say rudely and push by her. "No touching. No saying 'Oh, God.' No staring."

"I can't stop staring. He's so gorgeous." She trails behind us as I drag Oak inside.

"Oak, you remember Carrie, Justin and Kiki. This is Colin, Matt, Tracy." I reel off a bunch of names.

Oak takes the initiative and shakes everyone's hands or slaps their palms. It takes a moment for everyone to settle down, but someone, probably Carrie, cranks up the music and shoves a beer into Oakley's hand.

"Red Solo cup," Oak murmurs with delight.

"This is as normal as it gets," I tell him as I accept the bottle of water Carrie hands me. I'm not drinking tonight, not after what happened at Oakley's house.

We rest our butts against the side of the dining room table, just off the kitchen. He takes a cautious sip and then another. After drinking half the cup, he leans over. "This is terrible."

I take the cup from him and indulge in a tiny sip of the keg beer. "Oh, man. It really is."

"I love it."

"So Oak, you a Rams fan now?" Justin asks.

"Christ, I guess so? I haven't been to a game yet. You?"

"I went to a preseason game with my dad and brother but we haven't pulled the trigger on the game tickets. Damn expensive."

Oak nods as if he understands. His hand slips around my waist. "My dad was a huge LA Rams fan but they moved before I was born. Dad was so pissed they left that he refused to cheer for them again."

"Same with my dad," Matt interjects. "When they got the okay to move back, I thought he'd be happy. Instead he told me that he'd cheer for the Rams when hell froze over."

A few more people drift over to join the football talk. Since sports bore me more than anything, I drift away to find Kiki and Carrie out on the deck.

"Straight up, is it weird dating Oakley Ford?" Carrie offers me her cigarette.

I shake my head in refusal and boost myself onto the top of the deck railing.

"At first, it was weird, but now, he's just… Oak."

"Oak, huh?" Kiki wiggles her eyebrows. "Aren't you worried about when he goes on tour and there're all these girls throwing themselves at him?"

I hadn't given it a lot of thought, but something in my bones tells me that I don't need to worry. "Oak's not the type to cheat. He'd tell me if he fell for another girl."

This is a guy who doesn't like being touched, and in all the time I've been with him, there's never been another girl on his radar.

"Really? I don't think I could deal with that." Carrie taps the cigarette over the side of the deck. "I'd be too stressed out and superjealous all the time."

"Vaughn's always been chill," Kiki says.

"It's not me." I laugh. "It's Oak. He's not that kind of guy." Unlike with W, I've never found a group of strange girls hanging out at Oak's house or the studio. And he has access to hundreds of them if he wanted to. Plus, he doesn't even make offhand comments about how different celebs are hot or how he'd like to tap that—W used to do that all the time.

"What about April Showers?" Carrie protests. "He was with, like, a dozen girls while he was dating April."

I catch my lower lip between my teeth. How do I explain this to them without giving everything away?

"It's not always what you see in the press," Oak says from the doorway.

The two girls turn bright red as he approaches. When he

reaches me, he slides his arm around my waist again, either anchoring himself or me. Maybe both.

"April and I were friends. We did some stuff together but it didn't work out. Sometimes the magazines and websites like to stir up controversy for hits and views. Touring isn't all that it's cracked up to be. It's a lot of work and the down days are often spent traveling from one location to another. You miss your family, your friends, even your own bed."

"That actually sounds amazing," I tell him.

We lock eyes. "You should come with me next time."

"Maybe I will." I grin, but when he doesn't grin back, I realize he's serious. Going on tour with him as he travels all over the world? That would be amazing.

"And on that note, I think I'm going inside," Carrie announces. "You, too, Kiki." She pulls Kiki off the railing.

"But I wanna see what happens next," Kiki wails.

Oak's lips curve up.

"They're not a television show," Carrie scolds as she drags Kiki inside the house.

"No, they're better."

I can't help but laugh. "We should go inside, too."

Oak's hand tightens on my hip. "Do we have to?"

My skin is too tight for my frame. Every sense I have is heightened. His fingers feel heavy against my jeans. The cool night air is tickling all my nerves.

"How'd you do it? You and April?" I ask quietly.

He answers without hesitation, knowing exactly what I mean. "We weren't ever friends, despite what I just told your girls. We were two bratty kids who thought we deserved more than we got even though the world was pretty much on a platter. I thought she should do whatever I wanted and she thought the same, only in reverse. I wasn't very nice to her." He makes a face. "Are you going to hold this against me?"

"No. I just wondered how you kept it all separate. Did you put April in the friend compartment and then take her out and slot her somewhere else when you needed to be… affectionate with her?"

He places a thumb at my chin, gently pulling me around so that I have nowhere to look but at his face. "So I need you to look at me while I tell you this. April and I were never a thing. What you saw in public wasn't anything more than the two of us acting in order to get more mentions in the press, more coverage. I was on tour and Claudia wanted me on the cover of something every day. April and her family live for that shit. There were feelings that got hurt at the end, and I didn't see it coming because I thought she was a great actress. I'm sorry she got hurt. If there's anyone who's in trouble here—" he waves a finger between us "—it's me. I think you know that."

"I'm confused right now." I rub my sweaty palms on my knees.

Oak drags his index finger along my lower lip. "I know, baby. And scared?" I give a small nod. "I'm scared, too. But let's work this out together. Let's see where it goes. We don't need labels or words. We just need to be together."

I let my anxiety go in a huge rush of breath and reply, "Okay."

He squeezes my hip and then lifts me down off the deck. "So Matt sings, huh?"

"You're going to play?"

"Why not?" He slides a grin toward me. "I heard it's real popular with the chicks." He slips inside before my punch can land. "Anyone got a guitar?" he asks loudly.

Matt jumps up so fast that he nearly tips the table over. Miraculously, four guitars are produced, including one from Justin, who, in the fifth grade, slammed his recorder onto the concrete in his driveway and then proceeded to ride his bike over it again and again. The recorder was plastic and suffered no damage whereas Justin got his butt whipped by his dad.

"You don't even play an instrument," I accuse.

"I know. It's for Ford. Just in case," he says sheepishly. "I borrowed it from my uncle."

"This is a righteous instrument." Oak swings the body of the guitar up and strums a couple of chords.

"What do you want to play?" Matt asks eagerly. "I know your whole catalog. Even the new stuff."

The girls and I hide a smirk behind our hands.

"I'm up for anything but my tunes. Know any Smashing Pumpkins?"

Matt nods. "Yeah, I can play 'The Everlasting Gaze' or 'Today.'"

"'Today' it is. Where we doing this thing?"

Matt leads the way into the living room. "You can sit here." He points to the middle of the sofa. Oak takes a seat and Matt then positions himself on the ottoman right in front of Oak.

"I'd be worried that Matt is going to try to steal your man," Kiki murmurs in my ear.

"He does look infatuated."

"Infatuated," Carrie scoffs from my other side. "If Oak batted his eyes at Matt, Matt would be down on his knees so fast, the house would shake."

"Mmm. Nice visual."

"Come sit by me, baby," Oak calls and pats the cushion to his right.

"Baby?" Carrie and Kiki mouth to me.

I ignore them, try to keep from turning beet-red and climb over a dozen people to slide next to Oak. He cants his body slightly so that his back is pressed against my side and the neck of the guitar is slanted away from us. The closeness of our position means I feel his arm move as he slides his fingers up and down the fret.

The guys sing one song and then Matt leads them into the next. Pretty soon, they've moved on to 1D songs. Oak even sings a lower rendition of "I Knew You Were Trouble" by Taylor Swift, sending me sneaky glances the entire time that no one in the room misses.

Oak singing to me in public is different than him singing in the studio. At the studio, he's working. The songs are often cut off at the halfway point and then he and King will try something totally different. You almost never hear the whole song.

But here, it's as if every word that comes out of his mouth is some message about how he likes me, thinks I'm the best thing that has happened to him, that I'm saving him in some way.

By having me sit by him, by him looking at me almost the entire time, he's making a public declaration of his feelings. Something that W hardly ever did. The boy wouldn't even wear his Vans that we decorated. He said he wanted to save them, but I knew then, as I do now, that he was embarrassed of them.

But Oak has no problem singing about how happy he is to be in love with me.

"Play one of your new songs," I urge him. I know he's insecure about his music, but it's more amazing than he realizes. An appreciative audience like this one would be the perfect place for him to test out a song or two.

Oak must agree, because he starts strumming the one with the bridge that neither he nor King have been happy with. "Yeah?" he says.

There's a chorus of yeses. Oak ends up playing half his album before he stops and admits he's thirsty. A herd of feet trample into the kitchen to be the first to get him a drink.

Oak's neck is sweaty. Playing the guitar is a lot of work.

I draw my finger down the middle of his neck. He shivers and then leans all the way back, resting his head against my shoulder.

"What's it really like, being you?" Justin asks. The jam session has broken down the barriers, and whatever rules Carrie and Kiki tried to impose have been strummed and sung away.

Oak reaches up and brings my hand down over his shoulder. He laces his fingers through mine, settling our entwined fingers against his chest. "I can't complain."

Meaning he won't. He has so much it would be gross for him to say his life is terrible even if it can be at times.

"What's the best thing?" Justin presses.

"Is it the girls? The girls must be awesome," Matt says. He ducks when a bunch of Solo cups are thrown at his head. "What? It's true, right?" he protests.

Oak's lips twitch. "Even if it was true, and I'm not saying it is, I wouldn't disrespect Vaughn by talking about someone else. She's my girl and the only one I care to talk about these days."

The words are so sincere that they make the heart of every girl here flip over, including mine. I grip his hand tighter. He thinks he's the one in trouble? No way. I'm in it up to my eyeballs.

He taps the top of the body of the guitar with his palm a few beats before continuing. "The best thing is walking out on stage and hearing thousands of people sing your lyrics back to you. You can stop, anywhere in the middle of a track, and they keep going. That's incredible. I can't even describe how it makes you feel. But in those moments, you literally feel invincible. Like you could fly based on their raised voices."

Matt looks disappointed at the answer, but he's the only one.

"What's the hardest thing?" Carrie asks, handing Oak a glass of water. I throw her a grateful look.

"Thanks." He takes it with his free hand, refusing to let go of my fingers. "I don't get to do stuff like this very often." He waves his hand around the room. "Everything is a production. If I want to go to the Rams game, I can't sit on the fifty with Vaughn. My people have to call the Rams' front office. We will need sideline passes for me and probably four bodyguards. On the sidelines, there are reporters, other people, and maybe in the first quarter, no one is asking me about anything but by halftime, someone knows someone else who has a sister's cousin who wants into the music industry and would I care to hear the stuff. And those that aren't asking about music connections are taking snaps and selfies to be the first to say that they saw Oakley Ford.

"And as I say this stuff, I know I sound like a self-righteous pig. Oh, poor Oak, can't do anything ordinary people can but tonight, hanging out with you guys, jamming with you, playing Frisbee in the back? It's been awesome. No one's bragging about tonight. No one's treating me different."

Matt glances a little shamefacedly at the guitars.

"Nah, I don't mind playing. This has been great. But so much of the time when you leave the house, your guard's got to be up and that isn't great. It sucks. On the other hand, fans pay the bills and if it wasn't for fans, I wouldn't be where I am. So I'm grateful for all of it and try not to complain." He slaps the guitar. "Now that I've bummed you out, how about we play a couple more songs before I take my girl back home?"

Matt readily takes up his guitar again and Oak reluctantly releases my hand and sits up.

I know he's doing this because he wants to, but this year that I'm with him? I'm going to watch out for him. I'm going to try to give him things that he can't get because he's Oakley Ford. Whether it's space to hang with kids his age, whether it's a reconnection with his mother, whatever it is, I want him to have it.

33

HIM

lilbabyblue @Gracie33Dawson OAKLEY FORD WAS AT A HOUSE PARTY IN ES 2NITE!!!!

Gracie33Dawson @lilbabyblue WHAT????? how do u kno?

lilbabyblue @Gracie33Dawson my couzin goes 2 TJH. She got 2 meet him!!!

Gracie33Dawson @lilbabyblue omg. *dying of jealousy

I kick my shoes off and then collapse on Vaughn's bed fully dressed. She stands in the doorway, laughing at first, but then her expression becomes serious.

"What is it?" I ask as I make myself comfortable.

"Are you…um…sleeping over?"

The blush on her cheeks is so frickin' cute I have to fight the urge to lunge off the mattress and kiss her. Instead, I prop my hands behind my head and say, "Do you mind? It's almost three and I'm exhausted."

"What about Ty?"

"He's fine crashing on your couch." Vaughn was surprised to find him at her house when we got home, but I wasn't. Ty followed us to the party and sat in the Escalade until we were done, but I didn't tell Vaughn because she would've wanted him to come inside, which I didn't want. The dynamic would've been messed up.

Vaughn bites her lip. "That couch is way too small for him. He's going to be so uncomfortable."

I love that she's worrying about my bodyguard. The girls I dated in the past didn't give a hoot about the comforts of the "staff."

"He'll be fine," I assure her. "Trust me, he's slept in worse places."

"Still. I'm going to get him some blankets." Vaughn hurries out of the room.

I hear her footsteps in the hall then the creak of a door opening. I'm too lazy to go downstairs and help her, so I just lie back and think about everything we did today. The barbecue. Seeing my mom. No, *hanging out* with my mom. That was surprisingly...fun. And that party tonight was awesome. I've been to hundreds of parties, but I can honestly say that this one tops them all. Vaughn's friends were so laid-back, and that jam sesh was righteous. I'm feeling so inspired right now that I almost wish I was in the studio, laying down some tracks.

But if I was in the studio, then that means I wouldn't be in Vaughn's bedroom. On Vaughn's bed. I wouldn't be smelling the sweet scent of her shampoo on her pillows, or running my fingers over the soft bedspread that she sleeps under every night.

She returns a few minutes later, grumbling under her breath. "Is he always this difficult?"

I grin. "Ty? Yeah. Why? What'd he say?"

"He said he's fine sleeping without a pillow. Who doesn't need a pillow?" She sounds horrified. "I gave him one anyway, and a blanket, and I put sheets on the couch, so hopefully he's comfy. I offered to leave the night-light on in case he gets up in the middle of the night, and he laughed at me for a whole minute."

I laugh, too, because the thought of Ty needing a night-light is hysterical.

Vaughn hesitates at the foot of the bed. "Um." She visibly gulps as she sweeps her golden-brown eyes over me. "I need to get ready for bed."

"Who's stopping you?" I drawl.

"I'm not changing in front of you. What kind of girl do you think I am?"

My girl, I want to say, but I don't want to make her more nervous than she already is. I know what she's thinking—that I'm staying over so the two of us can…you know. But that was never my intention, and I'm quick to tell her that.

"I can sleep on the floor if you want," I offer.

"What? No, that's ridiculous. You won't be comfy!"

I fight a smile. "You have a weird obsession with other people being comfortable," I inform her.

"Gee, Oak, I apologize for being a *considerate* person. Fine, sleep on the floor like a dog if you want."

"Nah, I'd rather snuggle up with you. But if you want to think of me as a dog, I wouldn't mind it at all if you rubbed my belly and petted my hair."

Her cheeks turn crimson again. She walks over to her desk chair and snatches a couple items of clothing off the back. "I'm going to brush my teeth and change into my pj's. If you want to wash up, there are extra toothbrushes in the bathroom, but I'm using it first so you wait your turn." She darts out of the room again.

I sit up, peel my shirt over my head and toss it onto the floor. Then I shove my jeans down my hips, leaving me in a pair of black boxer-briefs. I realize that this is my first sleepover with a girl. I've never let anyone spend the night at my place or any of my hotel suites. I suddenly wonder if W ever slept in this bed and my hands curl into fists. I hate the idea of that loser sleeping with Vaughn, even if he wasn't *sleeping* with Vaughn.

"Oh." A squeak sounds from the doorway. Vaughn's gaze darts from my face to my underwear and then back up.

"I made myself comfy," I say, hoping the magic word—*comfy*—will make her stop fidgeting like that.

It does. Kind of. She's still blushing as she climbs onto the bed, but she doesn't ask me to put my clothes on. She's wearing enough clothes for the both of us anyway. Flannel pajama pants and an oversize pink T-shirt with the words... I squint...

"I'm sorry, but does your shirt say Bennett Family Fun-Time Weekend?"

She sighs. "Don't judge me. It's not my fault that my parents were dorks."

"Nuh-uh, babe. You're the one who's choosing to sleep in that monstrosity. Take responsibility for it."

"But it's so soft," she protests. "It feels nice against my skin."

I tug her toward me. "You feel nice against *my* skin," I say thickly, and then I slide one bare leg between her flannel-clad legs and nuzzle her neck with my chin.

She makes a breathy sound. "What are you doing?"

"Holding you. Got a problem with that?"

"I thought you were tired..."

"I'm never too tired for this."

Her laughter vibrates between us. I love the sound of it. I love that *I'm* the one who summons it out of her.

I groan in displeasure when she sits up. Oh, good, she's only leaning over to turn off the light. Darkness bathes the room, but her curtains are sheer so there's plenty of moonlight shining through them, illuminating Vaughn's pretty face.

"Do you want to get under the covers?" she whispers.

My mouth runs dry. I cough. "Uh, sure." I know that's not an invitation to…do stuff, but it still succeeds in confusing my body. I angle my hips away to spare us both any embarrassment. She'll probably freak out if she realizes I'm turned on.

The bedsheets rustle as Vaughn and I slide under them. This time I don't even have to reach for her—she nestles against me willingly, one warm hand resting on the center of my chest.

"Your heart's beating superfast."

Shit, I was hoping she wouldn't notice that. But she's so close to me, and she smells so good, feels so soft and warm, that I can't help but be affected. My lips go as dry as my mouth. They even start tingling.

"Are you okay?" she asks.

I run my fingers through her hair. "I'm great."

There's a long pause. "You are. Great, that is." Her soft breath tickles my shoulder. "Are you too tired to kiss me?"

Her teasing voice makes me chuckle. "I was trying to be a gentleman."

"I don't want you to be."

Her whispered response sends my heart soaring.

I roll over so we're both on our sides. Her eyes gleam in the darkness, and she licks her lips. It's so hot that I shudder. My heart hammers so fast and so hard that I'm afraid she might be able to hear it. But if she does, she doesn't say anything. She leans closer until our lips are an inch apart.

I touch her cheek then bridge the rest of the distance and press my mouth to hers. Oh, man. It's always like this when I kiss her—that incredible sense of belonging, a fierce jolt of pleasure as her lips melt into mine. She tastes like toothpaste and something sweeter, something uniquely Vaughn. We're breathless by the time we break apart, but our mouths don't stay idle for long. Before I can speak, she kisses me again, and those amazing sensations rise up all over again.

"Oak," she whispers.

"Mmmm?" My hand moves up and down her slender hip before resting on her ass.

"This feels nice."

I laugh hoarsely. "Yeah, it does." We kiss again, long and deep, our tongues dancing. "I…"

I'm falling in love with you.

In a miraculous feat, I manage to hold back those words. They'd only scare her off, and I don't want anything to ruin this perfect moment.

Vaughn gasps when I cup one of her soft breasts. "Oh," she says, and there's wonder in her voice.

I'm so gone for her. So. Gone. I'm not sure how I end up on top of her, or when my body starts slowly grinding against hers. I'm mindless, overcome with need for her. She loops her arms around my neck and kisses me hungrily.

It takes all my willpower to wrench my mouth away. "Are we—" I suck in some air "—moving too fast?"

Her beat of hesitation is all the answer I need. As painful as it is—*physically* painful—I roll onto my back and gulp in another burst of much-needed oxygen.

"We definitely are," I say, answering my own question.

Vaughn sits up. Her hair is a tousled mess, and even in the darkness I can see that she's biting her bottom lip, which is swollen from our kisses. "Actually, I think…" She nibbles on her lip some more. "I think…I'm ready for more."

I try not to grab her. "Yeah? You had a beer tonight."

"A sip of yours," she corrects. "All I drank was water." She exhales slowly. "I'm in charge, right?"

"Of course." I spread my arms out wide. "I'm yours. Do what you want."

She licks her lips and I about die. I curl my fingers into the sheets so I don't attack her, even though I want to. Carefully, she swings one leg over my hip and settles onto my lap. This is the most exquisite torture ever.

Her finger traces the outline of the cross tat on my shoulder—the one I got after my first gold record. "This tattoo is hot. Is it bad that I think that since your mom's name is on it?"

"Don't talk about my mom right now," I beg.

She nods seriously. "Good idea." Her caress moves down my shoulder and squeezes my biceps. "You really do have nice guns."

She acts like she wants to spend a dozen weeks exploring my body, which is great and terrible at the same time. I'm throbbing between my legs.

"Why are you breathing so heavily? Is it painful?"

Yes. Very. "No," I lie. "It's all good." Just a small lie. I'd rather have her touching me than doing nothing, even if each light touch stokes my desire as surely as a soft breeze turns an ember into a raging fire.

"What should I do?" she whispers.

Her hands have moved back to my chest and I'm discovering there are areas of my body that are more sensitive than I ever imagined. Most of the time, I just want a girl's hand on me. Or her mouth. But I'm so excited to be with Vaughn, to be near her, that every square inch of me is trembling from her featherlight caresses.

"Whatever you want," I say hoarsely.

"But I don't know exactly what I want." She bites her lip again. "Can I put you in charge?"

No person in the history of Earth has moved faster. I bolt

up, flip her over and cover her with my body in less time than an ant breathes. "What do you want?"

Her eyes gleam in the darkened room. "Everything."

"You sure?"

"A hundred percent."

"Because we can wait." Now that I have her under me, I'm reminded of my promise to be patient. I do want to wait for her.

"I'm tired of waiting."

Oh, thank God. I bend down and kiss her, taking the time to learn her responses. How she likes to be kissed. How a light nip at the side of her throat makes her breath catch. How a hot breath at her ear sends shivers down her spine.

I kiss her everywhere. Along her collarbone, the delicate slope above her breasts, the shallow of her flat belly. And down farther.

"I thought we were having sex," she chokes out. Her fingers tangle in my hair as if she's not sure if she wants to press me against her or pull me away.

"We will. But I need this first."

"Are you sure?"

"I'm dying for this."

She lets me go and I take her, kissing her softly and then more roughly until she's squirming and trembling and gasping. This time it's her hands curling into the sheets.

When I can't wait a second longer, I reach for my discarded jeans and pull out a condom, slipping it on. "It might hurt," I whisper.

She gives me a nod to let me know that she's with me. I press forward slowly, and a startled cry flies from her throat. I wait for her body to adjust to mine and when her legs fall open and her fingers dig into my shoulders, I move.

We both move, slowly, carefully, until sensation blurs my

vision. We hold each other as the storm of emotion crashes over us. I cradle her body in my arms afterward. Her face is buried in my neck. Our hearts thunder against each other, her beats answered by mine, and on and on in a perfect, synchronized rhythm. I love this girl. So much.

"Vaughn?" I murmur before I drift off.

"Mmm?" she says drowsily.

"Today was the best day of my life." The moment I say those words, I feel a pang of embarrassment. Did that sound pathetic? I hold my breath as I await her response.

"Good. I'm glad." Her lips brush my chest in a tender kiss, and then we fall asleep tangled up together.

34

HER

@OakleyFord hi

@OakleyFord We love you. We love you. We love you.

@OakleyFord follow me

@OakleyFord I drew this for you

@OakleyFord Just bought tix for the 1st tour stop! Can we please meet?

@OakleyFord When r u coming back to Dallas?

@OakleyFord It's my birthday! Can you message me back. Pls! it's all I want.

@OakleyFord I love you

@OakleyFord Can't wait for the tour!

@OakleyFord how do I get VIP passes 4 ur tour?

@OakleyFord xxxxoooo

@OakleyFord dump that girl she's not good enuf f u

@OakleyFord @mrsoakleyford such a gold digger

@OakleyFord @weirdmagicalone she dumped her boyfriend to get with oak #slutacular #gohomethot

I close Twitter and wonder if I'd be allowed to delete the account altogether. Nothing positive is on there these days. I'd gotten into the habit of not reading it, but for some reason, after checking my texts, I opened the app and checked not just my feed, but Oakley's, too. Big mistake.

"You're up to something," Oak says.

I shove all thoughts of Twitter aside and smile at him. "Something awesome." Oak has been bugging me for weeks, wanting to know what all my text messages with his mom have been about. I've only managed to hold him off by telling him that he'll know…soon.

Sometimes Oak's spoiled upbringing shines through. He doesn't like to share and he doesn't have much patience. He's used to getting whatever he wants, whenever he wants it.

Other than my V-card. He waited for me, but I was happy to give that up. It was indescribable. No matter how many adjectives Oak teaches me, there aren't any that I can use that would articulate how he made me feel.

It hurt at first, but he waited, again, taking his time, whispering to me about how wonderful I felt and how it was like heaven for him. For me, too. I shiver thinking about it. I'm falling so hard for him. I know that I didn't love W, because what I felt for him is like the teeny flame of a candle compared to the inferno Oak evokes in me.

But while he's patient as it relates to *those* things, everything else in his life he wants immediately.

Oh, there's a pair of sneakers that had a limited run of, like, ten? No problem, Oak, we'll send a pair out for you. Do you want someone to come and have a custom insole made, as well?

I've had to be careful about showing any interest in anything. I was cruising Instagram and stumbled onto a travel photographer's account. I probably spent two hours flipping through her pictures. The next day someone arrived at my doorstep with a camera and a note that said, "Vaughn, your friend Oakley asked what camera I used. I told him that as a starter, you might like this one instead. You have a real gem there."

When I complained to Oak about it, he replied, "You'll need something to do when you're on tour with me."

And there's no point arguing with him. There are times when he simply refuses to listen and the camera is one of those times. As are the pristine set of white Vans, a cross-body bag I mentioned casually one time and a pair of gold sandals I admired in a store window.

I'm not the only one who's gotten goodies. Shane and Spencer both got new sneakers and passes to an exclusive skate park, along with one-on-one lessons with some guy I didn't recognize, but the twins did because for once in his life, it was Spencer who couldn't speak when they met. Paisley got a beautiful Prada bag in scarlet-red.

I protested, but she said that he could easily afford all this stuff with the money that fell into his sofa cushions. I guess that's true. Still, I watch myself around him. I don't need more surprise gifts. Hopefully once the tour starts, he'll be too busy with sound checks and rehearsals to remember to buy me things.

I still can't believe he wants me to go with him. I made a huge fuss about it at first, but like I said, it's pointless to argue with Oakley Ford. He's leaving tomorrow morning for New York City, the first stop of the international tour. I'm flying out to meet him a few days later, because Paisley is away for work and I need to be at home for the twins.

Truthfully, I'm a bit nervous. I've never traveled without my family before, and I'm not sure what I'm even going to do on this tour. I'm not a groupie or a roadie or anyone connected with the music industry. For now the only item on my agenda is to take pictures of Oak with my new camera. After that, who knows?

Since Oak will turn twenty during the first week of his tour, we're throwing him an early birthday party tonight, which is what his mom and I have been so hush-hush about the past few weeks.

"I don't like surprises." He tugs on the black eye mask I borrowed from Paisley.

"You don't like the ones you've had in the past. You'll like this one."

"How do you know?"

I lean over and kiss him on his cheek. "Because it's from me."

"Ty, help a brother out. What's going on?"

Ty snorts from the driver's seat. "You've got to be kidding. I'm not crossing the Bennett sisters."

He slides to a stop in front of the restaurant we booked for this event. Katrina's funding most of it, but Paisley and I did all the decorations. Even the twins helped assemble the gift bags full of mix tapes and cassette players that Paisley and I found at garage sales and thrift stores. I'm following through on my threat to throw him a kid's party—a normal one since most of his past parties involved lavish things like ice sculptures and famous singers.

Ty and I lead Oak to the back door.

"Five steps," Ty instructs.

"I have a bad feeling about this," Oak says. "My gut says to run away."

"Are you sure it's not saying your girlfriend is going to punch you in the gut if you don't stop complaining?" I warn.

"No, but I'm hungry so I could be getting mixed messages." He reaches out and grabs my hand to pull me beside him. "I'm going to buy you something outrageously expensive to punish you."

I flick his ear. "Maybe that's my whole goal. To get you to shower me with gifts and goodies."

"Nah, you're after my body. Which is very superficial of you, by the way, but I'm learning to deal."

"Deal with this first," I announce and then pull off his eye mask. "Surprise!"

"Surprise!" yell the forty-some people gathered in the private room. It's a mix of my friends, his people and a few of his friends—or at least the ones that he's indicated he's somewhat close with.

Oak arrows straight for Kinney Banks, a solo artist he once opened for. "Dude, when did you get in?"

The two give each other hefty backslaps.

"Last night. Your girl reached out to me and I figured I couldn't miss Oak's twentieth birthday party." Kinney lifts up a tack with a donkey's tail on the end. "Because where else am I going to get to play pin the tail on the donkey?"

Oak turns to me with a huge smile. "My gut was wrong." He lifts me up and spins me around. "You're the best, baby."

"I know."

He sets me down but doesn't let go. Together we make the rounds. King and his gorgeous wife came. The band members—sans Luke, who disappeared after the drunken kiss and hasn't come back. Oak said that any guy who would take advantage of a drunk girl wasn't one he wanted in the band. I'd protested, but he was adamant. Ty spoke up and said it was a liability because Oak had so many young fans around.

When we get to Katrina, she clutches her son for a long, emotional moment. Before he breaks away, she holds him briefly by the shoulders. "Look at you. Twenty. I can't believe it."

"You look great, Mom."

She flushes with joy at his compliment.

"Carrie, Kiki, thanks for coming." He gives them each a kiss on the cheek.

"We wouldn't have missed it for the world," Carrie says. She shoves a small wrapped box into his hand. "We didn't know what to get and Vaughn isn't much help." She casts a dirty glance in my direction.

I merely shrug. It's not easy to shop for someone like Oak.

"I'm sure it's awesome." He tears into it and pulls out a key. "What's this?"

"We're having an after-prom party. The same group as before and we'd like you to come," Kiki explains. "We have entry rules. No cameras. No slobbering over the guests. Just a good time for all of us."

Oak tucks the key in his back pocket. "I'm there. Time and place and I'm there."

"Vaughn will let you know."

I squeeze his hand as we move to the food table. "Still thinking it's a bad surprise?"

"No, you did good." He dips his head to kiss me. "Real good."

"Where's the birthday boy?" a hearty voice booms from the door.

Oak's head jerks up and the pleasure and warmth drains away. "Did you invite my dad?"

"Yeah, all of your family." I'm a bit uneasy at his expression. When I brought up the idea of inviting Oak's father to the party, Katrina had been hesitant, but eventually she came around and reached out to Dustin personally. And her reservations had been wiped away when he responded nearly immediately that he would come.

I figured, stupidly, that Oak's strain with his parents had to do with a big misunderstanding, but now I think it's something else.

"Oh, babe. I knew I should've trusted my gut." He drops my hand and stalks toward the door.

I hesitate and then scamper after him. Crap. Dustin Ford has brought an entourage with a capital *E*. There must be fifteen people that stream in behind him.

I detour to Paisley. "Um, can we order more food?"

She eyes the new group with dismay. "No. The restaurant said they couldn't provide more food than what I ordered. I said the party was fifty, and I honestly didn't believe everyone would show up. When has that ever happened before?"

But we've never hosted a thing for famous people before. Everyone came. King. Paxton Hayes. Even Kinney Banks, who flew a private plane from Chicago to LA to make this event.

Mr. Ford has stopped by the food table and is now surveying the crowd. Near the wall, I can see Carrie and Kiki and the rest of my friends staring at him with stars in their eyes. I guess I don't blame them for being starstruck. Dustin Ford is megafamous. He was named *People*'s Sexiest Man Alive three years in a row. He has an Oscar. And two private jets.

Oh, and he's ridiculously attractive. It feels weird noticing that, considering he's my boyfriend's dad, but it's true. Everything about him is chiseled and expensive and magazine-cover worthy.

"I can't believe my boy is twenty!" Dustin crows as Oak approaches him. He pulls Oak in for a warm hug and then gives him a manly backslap. "Where does the time go?"

"Hey, Dad." Even from five feet away, I can hear the suspicion in Oak's tone. "Nice of you to make it."

"Where else would I be?" Dustin flashes a million-dollar smile, but I notice it's aimed toward the crowd and not at his son. "This is a nice turnout. Small, but intimate. Where's your mother?"

"In the kitchen," Oak answers. "She's talking to the chef."

I cautiously join them. "Hi," I say awkwardly.

"Dad, this is Vaughn." Oak grabs my hand and drags me forward.

Dustin nods. "Ah, the girlfriend everyone is talking about." He gives his son a pointed look. "I was wondering when you would get around to introducing us."

One of Mr. Ford's assistants walks over and whispers something in his ear. I make out the words *cameras* and *outside* and *photo op*.

Clearly, Oak picks up on the same words I do. "There's paps outside?" he demands.

I swallow a frustrated groan. Crap. Katrina and I purposely arranged everything under pseudonyms so the press wouldn't catch wind of this. We figured it would leak at some point during the night, but not right from the get-go.

Dustin heaves a big, what-can-you-do sigh. "I'm afraid so. We tried to lose them on the way here, but they tailed us from the mansion." He turns to me. "Did Oakley tell you about the Brentwood mansion? I'd love to show it to you sometime. We've got three tennis courts, an indoor and outdoor pool, a bowling alley in the basement."

"Oh." I stare at him, dumbfounded. A bowling alley? In his *house*? Why? "That sounds...cool."

Luckily, we're interrupted before he can try to hammer down an exact time for me to visit his bowling alley mansion.

"Mr. Ford," a tentative voice murmurs.

I'm startled to discover that it belongs to my friend Tracy. Since when does she *murmur?* The girl is all about ear-piercing *squeeees!* and *omigods!*

"Do you… Could you… Could I get a picture with you?" she finally manages to get out, thrusting her phone at him.

His straight white teeth gleam under the overhead lighting as he once again flashes his famous smile. "Of course, sweetheart." He chuckles, and Tracy looks ready to faint. "Should we take a selfie?"

Tracy's courage spurs a few of my other friends into action, and soon Oak's dad is swarmed by admirers who are eager to tell him how much they love his movies and how he's the best actor *ever* and will he please, please take a selfie with them, too?

Oak slinks away without a word, but before I can go after him, Jim Tolson sidles up to me.

"I'm guessing it was your idea to invite Dustin?" he mutters.

I nod.

"Well, I hope you have a good plan on how to reel Oak back from the edge of the cliff. He hates his father. His father hates him. There's no way this ends well."

And then he departs, leaving me to stand there alone like a fool.

The evening doesn't get much better. Although it's supposed to be Oak's big night, Dustin Ford sucks up all the attention in the room. He regales the partygoers with anecdotes about his experiences on different film sets. He talks about what it felt like when he won the Oscar. He even plugs his upcoming movie by showing everyone a sneak peek of the trailer on his phone.

Not once does he talk about *Oakley's* accomplishments or congratulate his son for finishing another album. To an on-looker, it would seem like this was Dustin Ford's party. Oakley is all but invisible, and it breaks my heart every time I look at him. He tries to shutter his expression, but flashes of pain peek through. It kills me.

We don't do any of the silly childhood games I had planned. They all seem ridiculous in the face of Dustin's elegance and overpowering presence. Oak barely says more than a hand-ful of words to anyone, and when the party breaks up three hours later, I'm grateful.

"Go home or to Oakley's," Paisley urges. "I'll take care of the cleanup."

"I don't think he wants to talk to me." He's been staring at the back door ever since his dad got here.

"His father's an attention hog," my sister says with a sigh. "He's probably embarrassed, and you need to be there for him. Tell him it's okay and that you love him regardless."

I swallow hard but force myself to Oak's table. "Want to take off?"

"Sure," he answers dully.

I signal Ty, who nods briskly and ducks out to get the car. Taking Oak's hand, I lead him to the back door, where I pause for a beat.

"I'm sorry," I say quietly.

"Yeah" is his sullen response.

It's obvious he doesn't feel like talking—or listening—so I just hold his hand tighter and push the door open.

The second we step into the back alley, there's an explosion of light and noise. The incessant strobe of flashbulbs and the eager voices of the vultures that are always circling Oakley.

"Oakley! Are you and your father speaking again?"

"How was the family reunion?"

"What does Dusty think of your new girlfriend?"

"I love her," a male voice booms, and suddenly Dustin himself appears behind us.

I almost jump three feet in the air when his muscular arm wraps around my shoulder. Oak's dad squeezes me tight and then plants a loud kiss on my cheek. More flashbulbs go off. More shouts pierce the night air.

"Dusty! How was the party?"

"Are you giving Vaughn the Ford stamp of approval?"

"Will you be appearing at any of Oakley's tour stops, Dusty?"

It's chaos. The questions keep coming and coming and coming, and Oakley's face gets darker and darker and darker. Dustin, however, is reveling in it all. He eats up the attention, smiling for the cameras and answering questions, all the while keeping his arm around me like we're father and daughter and he couldn't be happier that I'm dating his son.

"Vaughn! Is this the first time you've met Dusty?"

"Vaughn! How does it feel to be welcomed into such a distinguished family?"

"Bitch! Get your hands off my man!"

The last shout doesn't just catch *me* off guard—it also brings a stunned silence to the paparazzi. I don't know who the screamer is, but she's not just content with screaming. Before I can blink, something smashes into the side of my head. Moisture drips down my face and splashes into my mouth. It's bitter and gross and—an *egg*. Someone threw an egg at me!

I'm too stunned to move. Fortunately, Oak takes control, dragging me away from the back door and elbowing his way through the crowd until we clear the alley.

Ty and the Escalade wait at the curb, and we throw ourselves into the backseat. Oak slams the door and the SUV speeds off, while I sit there in horror, egg yolk sliding down my neck and into my shirt.

"Are you okay?" Oak finally asks. His voice sounds like gravel.

I manage a weak nod. "I'm…fine."

Out of nowhere, he produces a pack of tissues. Neither of us says a word as he gently wipes the egg off my face. Or at least he tries to, but he can't get it all off. My skin is sticky and there's a gooey trail running between my breasts.

I don't even know why she egged me. "Did April ever get treated like this?"

"No eggs that I can remember," he says softly.

"So I'm special, huh?" I can't keep the bitterness out of my voice. This night was a disaster. A total disaster. I wanted so desperately to do something nice for Oak, and it backfired in a way I never, ever expected.

"I'm so sorry," I whisper.

"For getting egged?" he says tightly. "That's not your fault. Some fans can be insane. Don't take it personally."

"No." I take a breath. "I'm sorry I invited your dad. I thought…I thought it would be nice if your whole family was there for your party."

His face tense, Oak tosses the wet napkins on the floor. "So you could see what a shit show my childhood was?"

"No. Because I thought you could reconnect." I struggle to explain. "I did this for you."

His head swings toward the window as if he needs to hide his expression from me, and his voice is brutal and harsh when he answers. "No. You did it for yourself. You weren't thinking of me. You were thinking about how you'd like your parents back, but my parents aren't like yours, Vaughn. My dad's a self-righteous prick. And my mom might be okay half the time, but I was raised by nannies."

"Your mom thought—"

"Oh, my mom? Of course she did. She probably wants to

get screwed by Ol' Dusty again. She's feeling her age because I'm getting older so she needs to be reminded she's still young and beautiful."

"I'm sorry," I whisper again. "When your mom called to invite him, he agreed to come right away. He seemed excited about it, so I thought..." I bite my lip. It doesn't matter what I thought, because I thought wrong.

Dustin Ford clearly doesn't give a crap about his son. He burst into the party like a thundercloud, darkened the room, poured rain all over the celebration and then left.

"My dad came because he had an agenda," Oakley says flatly. "He always has one. Everyone in my life does." Bitterness washes over his handsome face. "He doesn't give a damn about me. He couldn't take it when my first album went platinum. When I made my first million. When I won a Grammy. And then the label offered me the kind of deal every musician dreams of, and the old man ordered me *not* to sign it. He kept saying it didn't make sense business-wise and how I would be indebted to the label forever. But Jim went over that contract with a fine-tooth comb. If anything, I was coming out ahead. The deal was *that* good. And Dad didn't want me to sign. Not because he was looking out for me, but because he was jealous."

I bite the inside of my cheek. Gosh, that's so sad. I don't even know how to respond to it.

I swallow hard, remembering the hesitation on Katrina's face when I mentioned inviting Dusty. But I'd ignored the warning signs. The distance between Oak and his mother had been the result of a stupid misunderstanding, and I was hoping it was the same for him and his father.

"I didn't know it was that bad between you two," I say weakly.

"I told you I don't get along with him. Did you think it was for no reason? Just me being a spoiled, stubborn brat?"

I stare at my hands. I don't like being on the receiving end of that thunderous expression.

"God." Oak runs both hands through his hair. "I'm so sick of everyone's agendas. And I'm so tired of everyone wanting a piece of me. You know, if I was stranded in the middle of the desert about to take my dying breath, and a bunch of fans came up and found me? I honestly don't think they'd save me. They'd just be scrambling to get scraps of my clothing, locks of my hair, something to show their friends later—*look, I got Oakley Ford's shirt right before he died!*"

My worried gaze meets Ty's in the rearview mirror. The deep furrow in his forehead tells me he's concerned, too, but he doesn't say a word. Neither do I. I simply reach for Oak's hand and squeeze it.

"It's all about what I can give people," he's mumbling. "A shot at getting record deal, a chance in the spotlight, money. Everyone here is fake. It's a plastic, made-up world full of people who only want one thing…"

He keeps talking, but my mind halts at his words *money* and *fake*, and suddenly I'm so guilty I can barely breathe. That's why I started this, wasn't it? For the money he was giving me? I have a hundred thousand dollars in the bank, courtesy of Oakley Ford, and thinking about it makes me want to throw up. It's that same gut-churning sensation I got when Paisley showed me the last check she deposited.

It doesn't feel right accepting money to date Oakley when I *want* to be dating him. It's not fair to him. I want him to know that I'm here in this car, holding his hand, because it's something I desperately want to do and not because I'm getting paid to do it.

Suddenly dried egg is the least problematic thing in my

life. Oak has gone silent. His troubled green eyes peer out the window, and I wonder if he's thinking the same thoughts that I am, that his girlfriend is just another person who "wants" something from him.

I can't do this anymore. I can't take money for fake-dating Oak, because there's nothing fake about it. It's *real*. But as long as I keep cashing those checks, there will always be that shred of doubt in Oak's mind about us. A part of him will always wonder if I'm with him because I want to be, or because I have to be. I almost regret having sex with him, at least before I told him I loved him. I hope he doesn't feel like I did it because I had to. That would be terrible. Worse than terrible. It would be devastating.

I'm a basket case by the time we reach my house. Ty stops the car. Oak and I get out, but it's not until I'm halfway up the front path that I realize he's not following me.

"Vaughn," he calls softly.

I walk back to him. "What is it?"

"I…" He meets my eyes. "I don't think you should come on the tour."

My heart stops. "Wh-what?"

He wrings his hands together before sliding them into his pockets. "That girl back there, the one who threw the egg…" He shakes his head. "That's the kind of shit you're gonna be dealing with on a daily basis if you tour with me. My fans will eat you alive."

I can't help but frown. "You didn't seem worried about that when you asked me to go with you."

"Because I wasn't thinking," he mutters back. "I let myself forget about…about my *life*. My fucking life, Vaughn, the one where I can't even have a fucking birthday party without it turning into a media storm. The one where my own father cares about his image more than his son. The one where my girlfriend is called a bitch and is attacked by some stranger because how *dare* I go out with someone who isn't her."

"Her?" I echo.

"Her, them, the world," he snaps. "They think I belong to them."

You don't. You belong to me.

But I don't say the words out loud. His expression is too bleak, his voice ravaged.

"It'll be better if you stay behind," he says roughly. "You shouldn't have to deal with my shit show of a life. You don't deserve the backlash you'll get if you come with me."

I want to argue, but the look in his eyes tells me now is not the time. He needs to calm down first. He doesn't leave for New York until tomorrow morning. Hopefully by then he'll have forgotten about this disastrous night, had a chance to regroup and will realize that he still wants me to go with him.

Oak thinks I can't handle his life, but he's wrong. I don't care if a hundred eggs are thrown at me. I can deal. Because he *needs* me. He shouldn't have to go through this stuff alone, and as long as we're together, he won't have to.

"Let's talk about it tomorrow," I finally say. "Okay?"

He nods. "Okay. But…I don't think I'm going to change my mind."

"We'll talk about it tomorrow," I repeat, firmer this time.

A ghost of a smile tugs on his mouth. Then he leans closer and bends his head, but the kiss he gives me lacks its usual warmth.

"Night, Vaughn," he whispers.

"Good night, Oak."

With a knot of misery in my stomach, I watch him walk away.

35

HER

1doodlebug1 @OakleyFord_stanNo1 She cheated on Oakley?

OakleyFord_stanNo1 @1doodlebug1 She's trash. Like he should literally throw her in the garbage

OakleyFord_stanNo1 @1doodlebug1 I feel sooooo bad for him. He tries dating a normal and she ends up cheating on him with one of his band members.

1doodlebug1 @OakleyFord_stanNo1 I heard that Luke isn't even on the tour. This is why. So it must be true.

OakleyFord_stanNo1 @1doodlebug1 She's a disgrace to our gender. Hey @VeryVaughn u suck ur terrible go away

1doodlebug1 @OakleyFord_stanNo1 He deserves so much better. He's never going to date another fan again. @VeryVaughn's ruined it for fans everywhere.

The phone rings at six in the morning. Groaning, I roll over to check the display. Then I groan again, because the caller is Claudia. I can't believe I have to suffer through a lecture about the disastrous end to the birthday party before I have any food or caffeine in me. I decide that Claudia can yell at me later, but as soon as the voice mail kicks in, the phone starts ringing again.

With a huff, I throw off the covers and answer the phone. "It's six in the morning, Claudia, and no one in California but surfers and fishermen get up this early."

"And publicists who are forced to clean up client messes left over from the night before," she replies. Her voice is decidedly cool.

I grab my laptop. Did something happen last night with Oakley? He'd been upset, but I figured he just needed time to cool off. "What's wrong? What happened?"

"You tell me," Claudia snaps. "If you were tired of dating Oakley, why didn't you simply come to me or Jim? We would've found a way to wind this down without dragging Oakley through the mud."

"What are you talking about?" My stupid computer won't boot up fast enough.

"I'm talking about the fact that you decided to publicly cheat on my client. Not only have you destroyed our narrative, you took advantage of Oakley."

"What? I never..." Oh, hell, there was that one kiss the night W broke up with me. Is that what she's talking about? "Is this about Luke? Because I told Oak—"

"We're not interested in your excuses. A courier will be delivering your severance check today. Feel free to change your passwords to your social media accounts. They're all yours."

"But Claudia—"

"You're done," she says and then hangs up.

My mouth is still open as I do a search for Oakley Ford. The first couple of headlines tell me everything I need to know.

The Ford's Been Breached.
Out with the Ford, In With the New.

Sick to my stomach, I click on the first link.

Oakley Ford's latest fling has found love—in the arms of his best friend. Luke Sellin has been Oakley's bassist for five years, but Luke isn't satisfied with playing backup. He wants to be the front man. Last night at the Sweetheart Lounge, Luke admitted to hooking up with Oakley's new gal pal, Vaughn Bennett. Oakley had no comment when we reached out to him, but Vaughn's old boyfriend did. You'll remember that Vaughn was dating a USC student when she tried to upgrade to Oakley.

William Wilkerson told our cameras that once a cheater, always a cheater.

You can do so much better, Oakley! Call us now that you're single.

I don't need to read the comments. I already know everything they're going to say. Quickly, I dial Oakley's number, but it rings once and transfers me to voice mail. I leave a message.

"Hey, it's me. I read the gossip this morning. How do you want me to respond? Is this going to hurt your tour? Call me!"

I text him the same thing.

There's no response, but I tell myself the silence is because he's sleeping. Oakley is allergic to early mornings. Six a.m. is an ungodly hour for him.

I try to go back to sleep, but my mind is racing, so I get up and make oatmeal cookies. And then snickerdoodles. And then lemon bars.

By the time Paisley comes downstairs, every surface in the kitchen has a baked good on it.

"Claudia called you already," Paisley guesses.

I nod miserably. "And Oakley hasn't called, but he's probably up by now. I think I should go over there. Can I use the car or do you need it?"

Her eyes grow soft. She slides an arm around my shoulders. "Honey, Oakley left for New York an hour ago."

My stomach drops. "What?"

She bites her lip. "Ty texted me when they were at the airport."

"But…" I fumble with the phone I've been checking every spare second. "But he hasn't said anything! I've left him messages. Called him." I search her face for any sign that she knows what's going on.

"Claudia says he's blocked you," Paisley admits. "Your calls will go to voice mail. Your text messages will disappear into the ether." She avoids my panicky gaze. "He doesn't want to hear from you."

I feel sick. Like, about-to-throw-up sick. I shrug out of her grasp and sag against the counter. "But…why?" I choke out. "This thing with Luke happened before. When it was all fake. Right after W broke up with me, I was stupid and drank too much and kissed Luke, but that was it. I haven't said more than five words to him since then." I charge forward and grab her shoulder. "Call them and tell them!"

She gives me a sad look. "I can't. It's done."

I scan my brain, trying to figure out what I could've done to make Oakley react like this. He already knew about the

Luke thing, so it can't be that. Was it the party? Because I invited his dad?

You did it for yourself. You weren't thinking of me. You were thinking about how you'd like your parents back, but my parents aren't like yours, Vaughn.

Oakley's words buzz through my mind, making me light-headed. Is that the reason? Does he think I was acting out of selfishness when I tried to bridge the distance between him and his dad?

Or maybe he's purposely pushing me away. Maybe he was so freaked out by the angry fan incident that he decided the only way to make me stay away from the tour was to end it?

None of those options make sense to me, though. Nothing makes sense right now.

Before I can argue with Paisley some more, the doorbell rings. Shoving past my sister, I fly to the front door, hoping that Paisley's wrong and it's Oakley at the door. He changed his mind about me not going with him to New York. He's here to pick me up. I know it.

I wrench open the door, but instead of Oak's gorgeous face, a thick-jowled man in brown hands me an envelope.

"You Vaughn Bennett?" Is that disgust in his voice? Am I currently the most hated individual in LA? If I got egged before when Oakley loved me, what happens when he hates me? I shudder.

Deliveryman takes that as a sign of assent and shoves an electronic pad into my hands.

"Sign, please."

Numbly, I sign. He jerks the pad out of my hand and slaps the envelope into my slack palm.

"Shouldn't have screwed him over," the guy says unhelpfully.

Yup, that was disgust all right. I slam the door in his face.

In the hall, I rip the envelope open and a sheaf of papers falls out. I'm even more panicked when I realize it's the contract I signed after I agreed to work for Oakley—and on the front page is a big red stamp that says "Canceled." Also enclosed is a letter that thanks me for services rendered, advises me to abide by the terms of my NDA or my entire life will be destroyed, and, finally, that I'm not to have any contact with the subject of the NDA for any reason whatsoever or the entire proceeds will be forfeited. A check slides out of the envelope and floats to the floor.

My phone buzzes. This time, when I pull it out of my back pocket, I'm a lot less eager than I was before. I'm numb. And shocked. And so close to tears that my eyes are burning.

I'm blinking back the tears as I read the text from Carrie.

Babe. Saw the IG post. So sorry. W is an ass. Oak's an ass.

Trying valiantly not to cry, I open the Instagram app. It doesn't take long to scroll to Oak's feed and see the picture of him standing on the stage at Madison Square Garden. His back is to the camera, but you can see that he has a guitar strapped around his neck. The arena is empty.

On my own and loving life. Can't wait to perform in front of NYC tonight, reads the caption.

I crumple the papers in my fist and walk away, leaving the five-figure payoff lying in the entryway.

36

HER

"What do you think about me egging Oakley's house?" I ask Paisley three nights and a raft of tears later. We're side by side at the sink, washing dishes after dinner. "Would that get you fired?"

"I'm going with yes, but only if we get caught." She smiles gamely. "I'm in."

"Nah, forget it. He's not worth the risk." I shove a wet plate into Paisley's hands so she can dry it. "Honestly? I think this is the lowest point in my life," I admit. "I had an egg thrown at me by an angry fangirl. My fake boyfriend broke up with me through his publicist, and I still don't know what the hell I'm supposed to do with my life."

"It's very Hollywood, though," she points out.

"What's my redemptive arc then? When does that start? Or do I need to be humiliated some more?"

She places the dry plate in the cupboard before asking, "Have you really not talked to him at all?"

"Of course not." I shoot her a bitter look. "You said he blocked me."

Paisley pauses for a beat. "Ty says he's miserable."

I frown. "Ty's miserable?"

She wipes her hands on a towel and hands it to me. "No. Oakley's miserable."

"So? He should be." I snap the towel in irritation.

"If you're both miserable, you should do something about it."

"Like what? Beg him to take me back? Forget it." I toss the towel on the counter. "You know, this was stupid right from the start. I should've just gone to USC this year. Actually, I should sign up for summer courses. Get a head start."

She slants her head. "And what will you study?"

"I don't know. I'll figure it out when I get there."

Paisley doesn't answer, but she gives me the *look*. The one that says she's so much wiser than I am.

"What?" I say irritably. "Do you have a problem with that?"

"Nope." Her tone is light, but her eyes are serious. "But... Vaughn. Look. It's perfectly okay for you to not want to go to college right away. It's okay for you to not know exactly what you want to do with the rest of your life. You shouldn't be a teacher just because you feel like that's going to keep Mom and Dad alive in your heart, because they're always going to be there, no matter what you do. And no matter how broken your heart is, you got something valuable out of it."

"Money?" Seriously? Is that what she's talking about? Because money doesn't seem like such an important thing right now.

"No. You got to see what it looks like when someone's pursuing something they love. You're not doing that, and you should."

"But I don't know what I love." I throw my hands up in the air. "That's the whole problem. Everyone else knows what they want out of life. You love your job. Oak has his music.

Kiki's wanted to be a hairdresser since fourth grade. When Carrie started in mock trial as a junior, it was like her whole path became rock solid. And here I am, a ton of AP classes later, and all I know is what I don't want to do."

"Okay."

"Okay what?" I ask in frustration.

"Okay, start there."

Oak's exact words. I lower my hands to my sides, an odd sense of defeat washing over me. "That's what Oakley said," I confess.

She raises her eyebrows. "Wow. You, the person who pretends all the time that she's happy and confident, admitted to some celluloid pop star about your insecurities? You must've really liked him."

I nod miserably. "I did. No, I *do*." The tears that I've been trying to swallow form a big, huge ball in my throat. "Oh, Paise, why'd he stop talking to me?"

"I don't know." She takes my hand. "Easy way to find out, though."

"How?"

"You fly to the next stop on his tour. I think it's Miami next?"

"He doesn't want me there," I whisper.

"Well, too bad for him. At the very least, you'll get the closure you need." Paisley shrugs. "I've always been a big believer in breaking up with someone in person. Oakley took the coward's way out, and that's not doing a lick of good for you. You need to find out *why* he did what he did, otherwise you'll never truly get over him." She offers another shrug. "And maybe when you see him and hear his reasoning, you two might be able to work through it. Either way, you won't know unless you go."

"And have him kick me out? No, thanks."

"So stay here and pretend to be happy. Or for once, lay yourself out there. Take a chance."

"Like you're doing with Ty," I say sarcastically.

"Exactly like I do with Ty." She whips out her phone and shows me her last text.

I'll find a new job if that's what's keeping us apart.

I rock back on my heels. I'd been so wrapped up in my own personal drama I hadn't realized that Paisley and Ty's romance was going somewhere. "Wow."

"Yeah, wow. For the right guy, Vaughn, it's worth getting hurt. Would you trade all those years with Mom and Dad so you wouldn't have to have the pain of their loss?"

No, but the emotions are so thick in my throat I can't answer out loud, so I settle for shaking my head.

"Stop being afraid of life. Go out and let love take you on a journey. Would you rather go to Miami and have Oak kick you out, or wonder *what if* for the rest of your life?"

"Go to Miami," I manage to croak.

"Good." She reaches behind her and presents me with a printout. "Because Ty and I got you a seat on a private plane that leaves in three hours for Miami. You may not know what you want to do with your future, but you know who you want to do it with. Better get packing."

37

HIM

1doodlebug1 @OakleyFord_stanNo1 this concert is so lit

OakleyFord_stanNo1 @1doodlebug1 I'm dying

@OakleyFord I love you

@OakleyFord your so beautiful

@OakleyFord please like me back. It's my birthday! Pls!!!!!

@OakleyFord you slay king

There are fifty thousand screaming fans waiting for me, and the last thing I want to do is face them. I just want to lock myself in this green room and never come out. Or maybe take a page out of my mom's book, throw on a crazy wig and sunglasses and sneak out altogether.

And go where?

The internal question makes me wince. Because really,

where *would* I go? Back to LA? Back to Vaughn, the girl who doesn't want to be with me?

Nah, I'm better off staying in New York. At least the fans here want to be around me. Hell, they'd sell their firstborns, cut off an arm, maybe both, just to breathe the same air as me.

Funny enough, I'd do all that, too, if it meant breathing the same air as Vaughn.

I miss her.

I miss her sarcastic remarks and her beach bum clothes and her rare but unbelievably contagious laughter. I can barely think about her without feeling like I've been sucker punched. Then again, it's only been four days. Maybe in a week or two the pain won't be as raw. Maybe the wound will start to heal and then I'll be able to remember her without falling apart.

A part of me still can't believe it's over, though. Or that she broke up with me through *Jim.*

I couldn't even understand what I was seeing when my manager slapped the terminated contract in my hand as I sat in the waiting room at the Van Nuys airport. At first I thought it was a joke. I'd just been about to call Vaughn to apologize for our argument, and to give her a head's up about the "cheating scandal." Claudia had sent me the links, which I'd laughed off. The Luke thing was old news to me. I didn't give a shit if he wanted to run his mouth to the press. I figured Vaughn wouldn't care about it, either.

But I figured wrong. Jim said she'd called him that morning and told him she wanted out. That she was humiliated. That my life was too much for her.

I texted her immediately. She didn't respond. I called her. She didn't pick up. And then, after hours of radio silence and about a hundred unanswered messages, she finally texted me back. Every word of that message is still branded in my mind.

I'm sorry, Oak, but I'm done. It's too much for me.

I told her when we first met that not many women could handle my life. And I told her again after the paps ambushed us at my birthday party. I asked her not to tour with me, because I knew what she would encounter if she came along. The rabid fangirls who want to claw her eyes out. The constant questions from reporters. The bogus rumors and accusations in the tabloids. I didn't want that for her.

I guess she decided she didn't want that for herself.

She was egged, for crying out loud. I can't blame her for bailing.

Yet I do.

Ty asks me what's wrong, and I tell him to mind his own fucking business. Then, because I was a dickhead, I avoid him. Hell, I avoid everyone as much as possible.

The only person I want to be around is Vaughn.

The upside to my fucked-up heart is some good music. My misery has already given me inspiration for a new song, which I've been playing all week in my hotel suite. I'm playing it now, too, as a knock thuds on the door and King walks in without waiting for an invitation.

He wasn't able to make it for the tour's kick-off shows in New York, but luckily he managed to swing these Miami gigs. The tour has been a massive success so far. Not only that, but my new record is still topping the charts since its release. My fans love my new sound. I've gotten thousands of Tweets and emails from people saying it was one hundred percent worth the wait. I forwarded a few of those messages to Jim as an *I told you so* for his whole "two years with no album, everyone's going to forget you!" spiel. This new album has already surpassed the sales of *Ford*, my highest-selling record to date.

"Damn shame you wrote this after we finalized the album," King says when he notices what I'm playing.

He took me out for a drink after the show last night because I didn't feel like going to any of the parties, and afterward, the two of us hung out in his suite, where I played him the new song. He loved it.

Still does, apparently, because he whistles softly. "I think it's the most brilliant thing you've ever done."

"We can put it on the next record." I slowly meet his eyes. "*Will* there be a next one or are you moving on?"

I hold my breath, anticipating the latter. Nobody stays in my life for longer than a heartbeat. Just ask Vaughn.

"You're never getting rid of me now. But you will have to wait. I've got albums with three other artists to produce first."

"But you'll always make time for me, right?"

"Damn right." He smiles.

I smile back, but it's halfhearted and puts a strain on my facial muscles. But I do appreciate everything he's done for me, and I make sure to tell him that. "Thanks for having patience with me, man," I say awkwardly. "For believing that I was ready to…grow up, I guess."

"No problem." He raises a brow. "Except it seems like you're relapsing, kid. Sitting here sulking when you've got thousands of fans waiting for you ain't exactly a sign of growing up."

He's right. I set down the guitar and hop to my feet. I'm already decked out in my concert gear—ripped jeans, tight T-shirt, hair perfectly gelled and a little smudge of eyeliner under the eyes because the girls dig it. Speaking of girls, I know there are about fifty of them with backstage passes gathering outside the door. One tried to sneak in earlier, but Ty was quick to stop her.

Last night there were just as many chicks swarming the backstage area. To my surprise, April was one of them, but luckily she wasn't there for me. Turns out she recently started dating the front man for the band that's opening for me. They're an up-and-coming group from Cali, and they play a mixture of surf/pop/punk/emo...actually, I'm not quite sure how to describe them, but their music isn't bad.

I don't know if April and the guy are dating for real or if it's another made-for-media arrangement, but if it's fake, then they're awesome actors. They were all over each other last night.

I guess it's nice to see her happy. God knows I made her miserable, though I refuse to take all the blame for that. April knew the deal. She never should've fallen for me.

Just like I never should've fallen for Vaughn.

It's ironic. I'm April in this situation. I knew going into it that Vaughn was doing it for the money, and yet I still allowed myself to get lost in the illusion.

But...*some* of it had to be real, didn't it? The way she looked at me, the way she kissed me. Was I imagining that?

Call her and find out.

I silence the voice. Nope, I'm not *that* pathetic. I refuse to chase after a girl who dumped me.

"You need to get out there. The promoter is starting to get antsy." King gives a wry smile. "And I'm pretty certain the stage manager's losing his mind."

I nod and follow him to the door, where I pause to take a breath. I can hear the commotion out there and all I want to do is cloak myself in solitude. But I can't. This is my life. This is what I've always dreamed of doing. Which means I can't be a little bitch and complain about it. All I can do is go out there and sing my heart out.

Or rather, pretend to sing my heart out.

Because I'm pretty sure my heart is back in California with Vaughn Bennett.

HER

My pulse is racing as I'm ushered into the concert venue. My flight was delayed for thirty minutes because of some mechanical issue that I didn't dare to ask about. The last thing I needed to know was that there might be something wrong with the plane I was boarding. But the pilot didn't seem concerned about it, and eventually we took off.

I've got to admit, it was pretty sweet flying in a private jet. I was sharing it with another Diamond client, a songwriter who spent the five-hour flight raving about Oakley's new album. Hearing him gush about the "purity" of the lyrics just made me sad. It reminded me of all the time I spent at the studio with Oak, watching him and King work together. Watching him write and rewrite and labor over every word. The whole process was...beautiful. I still don't know what I want to do with my life, but I do know I want what Oak has. Something that completely captivates me. Something I love so much that I forget myself when I'm doing it. He's so lucky. I wonder if he realizes that.

Since my flight landed a half hour late, the concert's already started when I reach the venue. Ty arranged for some poor assistant to take me to Oakley's dressing room, but Oak is already onstage and I've accepted that I'm going to have to talk to him after the show.

We're halfway down the crowded hallway when I spot Ty. His eyebrows shoot up and then he breaks out in a huge grin. "Vaughn!" he calls out. "Paisley said you were coming but I didn't believe it till just now."

He surprises me by pulling me in for a big hug and swinging me around. I notice the curious stares around us, mostly coming from scantily clad girls with VIP lanyards around their necks. I gulp, wondering if any of them had been in Oakley's dressing room. If they'd gone to the after-parties yesterday and spent time with him. I scan the crowd for April, but don't see her.

I suddenly feel nervous. Maybe I shouldn't have come. Maybe Paisley's wrong about the closure stuff. What if Oakley takes one look at me and orders me to get lost?

"Want to go out on the floor?" Ty offers. "I can get you out in the front row or the VIP area in front of the stage."

I shake my head. I don't think I want to be surrounded by Oak's adoring fans. It'll just be a reminder that I'm not the only one who's in love with him. That millions of fangirls think he belongs to them.

But I don't want to miss the show, either. "Is there a way for me to stand in the wings? Is that what you call it? The wings?"

He chuckles. "Yeah, you're getting the lingo down. Come on."

Ty takes my arm and leads me down the hall. It's blistering hot in here, making me sweat under my tank top. And there are people everywhere. Carrying equipment, scribbling on clipboards, barking orders, talking into radios or cell phones. It's a madhouse.

"Is Jim here?" I ask warily. I haven't spoken to the man since he couriered the terminated contract to my house.

"Naw, he's still in LA. He's flying out for the rest of the East Coast dates. We should probably see him in Chicago."

We. I don't know if I should correct him or not. Ty just assumes I'll be coming to Chicago, too, but it all depends on how Oak reacts when he sees me. Or how I'll react when I see *him.* As much as I want him to throw himself at my feet, apologize for ending it and beg me to take him back, I'm not sure I can do that. He broke up with me through managers and paperwork and social media, for Pete's sake. That's unforgivable, right?

As we near the end of the hall, I begin to hear the music. My heart beats faster when I recognize that trademark Oakley Ford voice, deep and raspy and beautiful. He's singing one of the up-tempo songs he and King were superenthusiastic about during the recording. It's not my favorite track on the album, but it's the one the label chose as the first single, and the crowd is loving it.

Ty opens a door and I'm nearly knocked over by a wave of sound. We climb up some metal steps. It's dark and I have no idea where we're going, but I know we're close to the stage because the music gets louder and louder. I hear the band. The drums. The guitar. Oak's voice. I love his voice.

We walk a few more steps and all of a sudden I can see the stage. There are two sets of huge stairs leading up to a second-floor balcony. The railing is made of lights that flash in sync with Oak's beats. Behind the balcony is a screen so big I think the astronauts in space can see it.

And then I spot him at the tip of the stage that bisects one half of the stadium from the other.

My heart lodges in my throat. He's so gorgeous that it almost hurts to look at him. Sweat from the lights and the heat dots his forehead. I can't see the crowd, but I can hear them—it's a never-ending wave of sound. No, of *love*. All the love these people, most of them strangers, feel for Oakley, rolling in his direction as he sings.

"Vaughn?" someone says shrilly.

I recognize that high pitch. It belongs to Claudia, who's standing a few feet away next to a man holding a clipboard.

I turn toward her, not missing the way her entire face pales at the sight of me.

"What are you *doing* here?" she demands. Her voice is so shrieky I can hear her over the music.

"Hey, Claudia," I answer, a bit tersely.

Her eyes are a tad wild as she glances at the stage then back at me. She hurries over and snaps, "You shouldn't be here."

I shrug. "Why? Because he doesn't want to see me? Well, too bad. I have some things I want to say to him."

"But—"

I push past her and step closer to the stage. I don't care if Claudia's mad that I'm here. Paisley was right. I need to talk to Oak. I need him to look me in the eye and tell me why it's over.

I peer out again in time to hear Oak play the last chord of the song. When he's done, he grins at the crowd. "You guys enjoyed that one, huh?" he jokes.

A deafening roar goes through the stadium.

He turns slightly, and I groan in disappointment because all I can see is the back of his head now. So I creep even farther out then sigh happily when my gaze makes out his profile. He's still joking with the crowd, telling them a story about his time in the studio.

"My producer—Donovan King—you know him, right? He threw a pencil at my head during this jam session. Almost took an eye out."

There's a huge burst of laughter. I feel it vibrating under my feet.

Something tugs on my arm. No, someone. It's Claudia, trying to yank me away from the stage. I shoot her a death glare and she promptly lets go of me. With a resigned look, she edges backward and begins typing rapidly on her phone.

"But it was worth it, all the fighting, 'cause we came up with something even better. This is one of the lesser-known tracks on the album, but I want you guys to give it a chance, 'kay? I almost sacrificed an eye for this sucker."

Still grinning, Oak sets down his guitar then turns toward the stagehand who jumps forward to pass him another guitar.

And that's when he spots me.

His jaw falls open, and he stands there for a moment, frozen in place.

He stares at me.

I stare back. I want to smile or wave or do something, *anything*, but what the heck am I supposed to do? He's in the middle of a show. It's not like he can—oh, my God, what is he *doing*? Is he actually walking toward me?

I watch, stunned, as he pauses to utter a hasty remark into the mic. "Gimme a sec, guys."

And then—*and then!*—Oakley Ford, in the middle of the concert he's headlining, rushes across the stage and runs in my direction.

"What are you doing here?" he demands when he reaches me. Rivulets of sweat trace down his neck, dampen his forehead. The aura of the stage surrounds him and he's bigger, brighter, and more compelling than I've ever seen him.

"I don't know," I stammer. What kind of fool was I to believe that this guy, who not only has purpose in his life but inspires others, too, would want to be with me? He's Oakley Ford. I'm Vaughn Bennett. *Of course* he broke up with me.

"Let me guess. You came for the gun show." The line is delivered caustically, an accusation almost.

I lick my lips, stalling for time because I don't know how to respond to this.

"Or wait—maybe you came to dump me in person." Bitterness flashes in his eyes. "Well, you coulda saved yourself a trip. I got the message, Vaughn. Loud and clear."

Confusion has me blurting out, "What the heck are you talking about?"

He frowns at me. "Are you kidding me?"

I just stare at him, anger rising inside me. "You're the one who needs to dump *me* in person. And I got *your* message. Loud and clear," I mimic.

Oak blinks. "What's happening right now?"

"I don't know!" I shout.

We stand there for a second, and I see my own bewilderment mirrored in his eyes. My mind is one jumbled ball of confusion, so I take a breath and force myself to slow down my thought process.

"You blocked my number," is all I can think to say.

He looks startled. "No, I didn't."

We stare at each other some more.

"You broke up with me over text," he says.

"No, I didn't."

More staring.

Then, as if we're both struck by the same terrible thought at the same time, we spin toward Claudia.

"What did you do?" Oakley growls at his publicist.

Her flushed cheeks and guilty look say it all.

"Goddammit!" Oakley yells. Then he takes a breath as if trying to calm himself, but his voice is colder than ice when he addresses Claudia again. "The text from Vaughn...how did you do that?"

Claudia looks down at her expensive high heels. "We swapped out her number on your phone. Amy sent it."

I gape at her. "Why?" I burst out. "Why would you make us think we broke up with each other?"

"Why else?" she shoots back, her voice dangerously high again. "You torpedoed his image, Vaughn! All the work we put into this, all the time we spent to make your relationship seem sweet and wholesome—you destroyed it with one stupid mistake! You cheated on him with his bassist!" Her breathing grows heavy. "Jim and I were doing damage control—"

"Jim?" Oak interrupts. His eyes are on fire. "He was in on this, too?"

Claudia huffs. "We were trying to protect you, Oak. We needed your fans to focus on your tour, not on your girlfriend scandal. We made a PR decision."

"Screw your PR!" Oak glares at her. "You crossed the line, Claud. Both of you. You're lucky I'm not firing you on the spot."

Frankly, I don't know why he isn't. I can't believe Jim and Claudia orchestrated a breakup behind our backs. I can't believe I've spent four days cursing Oak and imagining sticking pins in his eyes when this whole time he thought *I* was the one who broke up with *him*.

"Go downstairs," Oak barks at Claudia. "I can't deal with you right now."

Her face goes stricken. "Oakley," she says softly.

"I mean it. We'll talk about this later. And you better call Jim and prepare him, too." He rakes both hands through his gelled hair, messing it up a little. "You crossed a line," he repeats.

After a long, awkward moment, Claudia spins on her fancy heels and disappears down the staircase.

With another breath, Oak slowly turns back to me. "You didn't break up with me," he says, and there's a note of awe in his voice.

"You didn't break up with me," I say, equally amazed.

Our eyes lock. I'm acutely aware of the crowd beyond the wings. From the wave of grumbles and screams, it sounds like they're getting impatient. But Oakley makes no move to return to the stage.

"I'm sorry I was such an ass to you after the birthday party," he says softly. "I know you were just trying to do something nice for me."

"I'm sorry I invited your dad, Oak. I honestly didn't think he'd act like that."

"I know." He pauses, still eyeing me, and then his expression blazes with emotion. "I missed you. So freaking much."

And suddenly I know that I was right to come here. To see this moment of exhilaration on his face directed toward me? It doesn't matter what the tabloids write about tomorrow. The thousands of mean Tweets telling me that I'm not pretty enough, smart enough, talented enough, for Oakley Ford... it all burns to ash under his smile.

I might not be able to play the guitar or sing a note. My future is cloudy for me. I don't know what lies ahead. But what I do know is that I want to face the future with Oakley's hand in mine.

I let my palm slide down his arm to grasp his hand. And then, in front of a dozen people I don't know—including one who I think must be a journalist by the way she's typing furiously into her phone—I tell him all the things I've been afraid to give voice to.

"I missed you, too. I was miserable without you. And I..." I swallow. "I..." Argh, why can't I get the words out?

"You what?" he teases.

He's not making this easy on me. But isn't anything worth having worth an effort? Oakley is worth the effort. He's worth everything and he doesn't always know it.

"I'm glad we terminated the—" I lower my voice, because there are people all around us "—contract. You said that everything in your life was fake, but we're not fake, Oak. We're real. We're *so* real."

A smile lifts his lips.

Beyond him, the crowd is restless. I hear his name chanted in a discordant rhythm as if the crowd's confused and can't get it together. Sort of like me in this moment, searching for the right words to explain to him how I feel.

"I don't know when it happened, but I'm not pretending anymore," I say fiercely. "I can't pretend that I don't love you. That you don't make my heart sing. That I don't look forward to seeing you every day or reading a text from you or hearing your amazing voice say *baby*." He grins and I feel my own smile stretch across my face. Maybe it isn't so hard to be open, after all. "I know I'd be fine without you. I'd live a perfectly good life. But I don't want a perfectly good life. I want a messy, exciting, happy, sad, emotion-filled, loud life with you."

The screaming fans are starting to shout together, as one body. Everyone seems to hear it but him. In the near pitch-black of the side of the stage, his eyes burn into mine.

"Then that's what you're going to have, *baby*."

"Oak, your fans…you need to get out there," a brave lady murmurs in his ear.

"Go on. Sing for me," I urge.

He hesitates as if he's afraid I'm going to disappear.

"I'll be right here," I reassure him.

"Promise?"

"Forever."

With a beaming smile, he runs back toward the front of the stage, grabbing his guitar from one of the roadies.

Ty comes up behind me and places a hand on my shoulder. "Damn, girl. You're inspiring me."

"I hope so," I say without taking my eyes off Oak. "Because if you aren't as brave as my sister, you don't deserve her."

"I hear you. But that means I can't body for Oak anymore. Conflict of interest."

"You're his friend, though, right? That's all he wants." I watch as Oak settles onto a stool and adjusts the microphone.

Ty squeezes my shoulder. "I'm always going to be his friend."

"Think of it this way—you and Oak can play on the winning side of Ladder Golf now, as one of the Bennetts."

"Why do you think I'm giving in? I hate losing."

My laughter dies out as Oak starts talking over lightly strummed notes.

"As you all know, I haven't put out a record in nearly three years, and it's not because I wasn't making music. It was because I was finding my voice again. Our world is full of filters, Photoshop, and, well—" he shrugs "—fakes." He strums a few more chords. "And it's because we want everyone to think we're perfect. Problem is that no one's perfect and the nonstop drive to appear that way crushes our voices. Or, at least, it crushed mine. It wasn't until I stopped being afraid of facing my flaws that I found the music inside me. The music I wanted to make. And the only reason I'm here, sitting in front of you on this stage today, is because I met someone who gave me the courage to break out of that make-believe cage and just be real."

The random chords morph into a melody and he starts singing. It's not a song I've heard him sing before—not in any of the studio sessions, not in the impromptu jam sessions with my friends—but I recognize the lyrics.

They were the first ones he sang that ever gave me shivers. The ones about preferring to hide until he found the one person who made the masks unnecessary. The one who turned pretend into real.

He's singing from his heart…and mine.

38

HIM

OakleyFord_stanNo1 @1doodlebug1 That song. I swear I cried abt a bucket of tears

1doodlebug1 @OakleyFord_stanNo1 me too did he sing it for her u think

OakleyFord_stanNo1 @1doodlebug1 he sang it for all of us

I don't remember much of the concert after I sing "When It's Real." I know the audience lifted up their phones. I can tell by the thunderous applause that goes on and on that they loved the show.

The waves of adulation that normally carry me off the stage fly over my head because the only person whose opinion matters is standing right where I left her.

Larson, one of the roadies who worked the *Ford* tour, hands me a towel. I rip off my sweat-soaked shirt and start wiping myself down. Vaughn's eyes widen and then follow my hand around. I take a lot of silly pleasure in knowing I affect her this way, but I'm dying to know what she thought.

"Well?" I demand.

"It was incredible." She looks at me with a light so bright, she illuminates the entire soundstage. "But now I'm spoiled. I'm going to want to only stand on the side during concerts."

"Nah, you've got to see the show from the floor. The energy there's amazing. Thanks, Lars." I toss him the towel and he hands me a clean T-shirt. I don't particularly want to wear it, because it feels like a hundred and twenty degrees back here, even out of the lights, but I've got to walk by about a hundred fans on the way to the green room.

"Good show, Oak," Darsh Sethi, one of the tour's money men, calls out, patting me on the arm as we pass.

I don't flinch at the unwanted touch, but mostly because I'm too focused on Vaughn. She snuggles close to me, tucking a finger around the belt loop of my jeans. I can't believe she's here. And as happy as I am to see her, I'm also furious. Not at her, but at the people who were supposed to have my back. Jim and Claudia are going to face my wrath for this. What they did was wrong. It was unacceptable. This is my *life* they tried to mess with. Not to mention Vaughn's.

A dozen other people stop to congratulate me, shake my hand, pat my shoulder. I'm greeted by VIPs who paid a shit-ton of money so their daughters can get a pic with me later.

Through it all, Vaughn never leaves my side. I wonder if she knows that she's what's holding me upright. Probably not, but I'll tell her later.

It takes forty-five minutes to cross about fifty feet from the side of the stage to my dressing room.

"What's next after this?" Vaughn asks.

I drag her to a couch and collapse. A roadie brings me a

bottle of water and asks Vaughn what she wants. A Coke, hold the Jack.

I chug half the bottle before answering. "First, I'm going to kiss you and then I'm going to shower. After showering, I'm going to kiss you some more. Once I've taken the edge off, I've got to do a meet-and-greet with some fans. When that's done, we're going back to the hotel and kissing some more."

She blushes and laughs and then blushes again. She's so fucking adorable, I can barely stand it. So I lean over and kiss her right then. Her lips soften beneath mine and her hands come up to grip my shoulders. I'd like to do this all night— her holding me, our lips together.

Someone who I'm going to fire later clears his throat and interrupts us. "Sorry to do this to you, man, but if you want to get out of here before dawn, you should get a move on."

I press my lips against Vaughn harder until she pushes me away.

"I'm not going anywhere." She brushes my sweaty hair away from my forehead. "There's plenty of time for everything—" she flushes at that innocent word "—later. After all, we have two months on tour together. I get to do that traveling thing I wanted."

"It's nearly three months and that's barely any time at all. We'll be missing entire countries."

"Well, then we'll be back in LA and you can walk me to class at USC." She purses her lips. "If I even choose to go."

"Fine." I let her push me to my feet. "Ty, it's a good thing I love you, man, or you'd be fired."

He laughs and slaps me hard on the back. "Too late. I'm quitting when this tour is over."

"What? I was joking."

"I'm not. Paisley and I are gonna start seeing each other *for real*—" he waggles his eyebrows "—which means I can't work for you anymore. Conflicts, you know? I'm still going to be around all the time. Vaughn says that we get to be on Team Bennett for all our competitions."

"We're winners," Vaughn says merrily. "And you always want to be on the winning side."

I grin. "I know. Why do you think I've been trying to keep you?"

"Because you love me," she says without a hint of self-consciousness.

Emotion clogs my throat. "I do, you know."

"Duh. That's why I just said it."

A laugh pops out. "Wait—aren't I supposed to be the conceited one in the relationship?"

"I'm not conceited," she argues. "Just confident that you love me. And I'm still pissed at Jim and Claudia for making me think otherwise."

"Me, too." I glower. "But don't worry. They're going to get an earful from me about that."

"Good." She arches a brow. "By the way, it would be nice to hear you say the actual words."

"Oh, you want words, huh?"

I walk back to the couch and lean down, caging her between my arms. I duck my head so my mouth touches her lips. Everyone in the room probably thinks I'm kissing her. I'm not. I'm doing something way more important.

"You're the one person in my life who wants nothing but me and it's terrifying and awesome at the same time. Don't ever leave me. I love you. You're my heart."

Vaughn's breath hitches. "Wow. Okay. Those were some amazing words." Her lips brush mine in a sweet kiss. "You're mine, Oakley Ford."

"Yes. I'm yours." I smile against her lips. "And you, Vaughn Bennett, are mine."

EPILOGUE

Starstalkerz.com.
Holy canoli! Lots of Ford sightings this week! Scroll down for pics.

Spotted: Katrina Ford taking time out of filming the new Weisenberg thriller to support her son in Chicago. The proud mama sat in the front row with Oakley's GF and the two were photographed screaming their lungs out.

Spotted: Oakley and his girl at an ice cream truck in Portland, accompanied by Vaughn's twin brothers. Aren't they adorbs?

Spotted: Dustin Ford talks to the press at the premiere of War Hero, gushing about Oakley's new album. "Transcendent!" he raves.

Spotted: Bah-ston, folks. Grabbing pizza near Beacon Hill: Oak, Vaughn, Paisley Bennett—and is that Oak's former bodyguard holding hands with Sister Bennett? Double dates, anyone?

★ ★ ★ ★ ★

Thank you for reading WHEN IT'S REAL!

*Keep reading for a sneak peek
at the next sensational story from Erin Watt,*
ONE SMALL THING,
*a heart-wrenching new novel about a girl falling
for the one boy she should never have met.*

1

"Hey there, pupster." I laugh as Morgan, the Rennicks' dog, races across the lawn and jumps up on my khaki pants.

"Morgan, come here," yells an exasperated Mrs. Rennick. "Sorry, Lizzie," she says, rushing over to pull the big black mutt off me, without much success. She's small and he's so big that they're about the same size.

"It's no big deal, Mrs. R. I love Morgan." I crouch down and scratch the big boy behind his ears. He yaps happily and slobbers all over my cheek. "Oh, and it's Beth now," I remind my neighbor. I'm seventeen and Lizzie is a name I wish would go far, far away. Unfortunately, no one seems to remember.

"That's right. Beth, then, don't encourage him," she scolds, tugging on his collar.

I give him a few more rubs behind his ears before releasing him.

"Your mom's going to have a fit," Mrs. R frets.

I look down at the dog hairs that are now dotting my white button-down shirt, which was already spattered with food stains from work. "I need to wash up anyway."

"Still. Tell her I'm sorry." She drags Morgan away by the collar. "I promise to watch him better."

"Don't," I say. "I love all the time I get with Morgan. It's worth the punishment. Besides, it's not like there's any reason for us to not have a pet now." I stick out my chin. The reason for our pet-free house has been gone for three years, even if my parents don't like acknowledging that fact.

Mrs. R falls silent for a moment. I don't know if she's holding back curt words toward me for being callous, or toward my mom for being too strict. And since I don't know, I'm too cowardly to press.

"I'm sure she has her reasons," Mrs. R says finally and gives me a small wave goodbye. She doesn't want to get involved. Good choice. I wish I wasn't involved, either.

Morgan and Mrs. R. disappear inside their garage. I turn and squint at my house, wishing I was anywhere but home.

I check my phone. There aren't any messages from my best friend, Scarlett. We talked this morning about going out tonight after my shift at the Ice Cream Shoppe. School starts on Monday. For Scarlett, the summer of fun is over. For me, it means I'm one day closer to true freedom.

I roll my head around my shoulders, trying to loosen the tension that always appears the minute I see my house. I exhale heavily and order my feet to move forward.

Inside, Taylor Swift's "Bad Blood" trickles into the mudroom. Mom's playlist is set in an eternal 2015 loop of Sam Smith, Pharrell, and One Direction, back when One D was still a group with five members. I toe off my ugly black work shoes and drop my purse onto the bench.

"Is that you, Lizzie?"

Would it kill her to call me Beth? Just once?

I grit my teeth. "Yes, Mom."

"Please tidy up your locker space. It's getting messy."

I glance down at my section of the mudroom bench. It isn't *that* messy. I've got a couple of jackets on the hooks, a stack of Sarah J. Maas books that I'm rereading for the eightieth time, a box of mints, a bottle of body spray that Scarlett bought me at the last Victoria's Secret sale and some random school supplies.

Stifling a sigh, I pile everything on the Maas books and walk into the kitchen.

"Did you pick up in there?" Mom asks, not bothering to look from the carrots she's chopping.

"Yeah." The food looks unappetizing, but then all food does after I'm done with work.

"Are you sure?"

I pour myself a glass of water. "Yes, Mom. I cleaned up."

I guess I'm not believable, because she sets down her knife and goes into the mudroom. Two seconds later, I hear, "Lizzie, I thought you said you tidied up."

Urgh. I slam down the glass of water and join her. "I did," I exclaim, pointing to the neat pile of supplies and books.

"What about this?"

I follow the line of her finger to the messenger bag hanging on the hook in the section next to mine. "What about it?"

"Your bag is in Rachel's section," she says. "You know how she didn't like that."

"So?"

"So? Take it off of there."

"Why?"

"Why?" Her face grows tight and her eyes bulge. "Why? You know why. Take it off now!"

"I—you know what, fine." I reach past her in a huff and drop the bag in my section. "There. Are you happy?"

Mom's lips press together. She's holding back some scathing comment, but I can read the anger in her eyes clear enough.

"You should know better," is what she says before spinning

on her heel. "And clean off that dog hair. We don't allow pets in this house."

The furious retorts build in my mouth, clog up my throat, fill up my head. I have to clench my teeth so hard that I can feel it in my entire jaw. If I don't, the words will come out. The bad ones. The ones that make me look uncaring, selfish and jealous.

And maybe I am all those things. Maybe I am. But I'm the one still alive and shouldn't that matter for something?

God, I can't wait until I graduate. I can't wait until I leave this house. I can't wait until I'm free of this stupid, awful, *fucking* prison.

I tear at my shirt. A button pops off and pings onto the tile floor. I curse silently. I'll have to beg Mom to sew this on tonight because I have only one work shirt. But screw it. Who cares? Who cares if I have a clean shirt? The customers at the Ice Cream Shoppe will just have to avert their eyes if a few strands of dog hair and chocolate sauce are sooooo offensive.

I shove the dirty shirt into the mudroom sink and strip off my pants for good measure. I saunter into the kitchen in my undies.

Mom makes a disgusted sound at the back of her throat.

As I'm about to climb the stairs, a stack of white envelopes on the counter catches my eye. The writing is familiar.

"What are those?" I ask uneasily.

"Your college applications," she replies, her voice devoid of emotion.

Horror spirals through me. My stomach turns to knots as I stare at the envelopes, at the handwriting, the sender addresses. What are they doing there? I rush over and start rifling through them. *USC, University of Miami, San Diego State, Bethune-Cookman University.*

The dam of emotions I was barely holding in check before bursts.

I slap a hand over the pile of envelopes. "Why do you have
these?" I demand. "I put them in the mailbox."

"And I took them out," Mom says, her eyes still focused on
the carrots in front of her.

"Why? Why would you do that?" I can feel myself tearing
up, which always happens when I'm angry or upset.

"Why would you apply? You're not going to any of them."
She reaches for an onion.

I place my hand on her wrist. "What do you mean I'm not
going to any of these colleges?"

She plucks my hand off and meets my glare with a haughty,
cold stare of her own. "We're paying for you to go to school,
which means you'll go where we tell you—Darling College.
And you don't need to keep asking for applications. We've
already filled yours out for Darling. You should be accepted
in October or so."

Darling is one of those internet colleges where you pay for
your degree. It's not a real school. No one takes a degree from
Darling seriously. When they told me over the summer that
they wanted me to go there, I thought it was a joke.

My mouth drops. "Darling? That's not even a real college.
That's—"

She waves the knife in the air. "End of discussion, Elizabeth."

"But—"

"End of discussion, Elizabeth," she repeats. "We're doing
this for your own good."

I gape at her. "Keeping me here for college is for my own
good? Darling's degrees aren't worth the paper they're printed
on!"

"You don't need a degree," Mom says. "You'll work at

your father's hardware store, and when he retires you'll take that over."

Chills run down my spine. Oh, my God. They're going to keep me here forever. They're never, ever going to let me go.

My dream of freedom has been snuffed like a hand over a candle flame.

The words tumble out. I don't mean for them to come out, but the seal breaks.

"She's dead, Mom. She's been dead for three years. My bag hanging from her hook isn't stopping her from coming home. Me getting a dog won't stop her from rising from her grave. She's dead. She's *dead*!" I scream.

Whack.

I don't see her hand coming. It strikes me across the cheek. The band of her wedding ring catches on my lip. I'm so surprised that I shut up, which is what she wanted, of course.

Her eyes widen. We stare at each other, chests heaving.

I break first, tearing out of the kitchen. Rachel might be dead, but her spirit is more alive in this house than I am.